WHAT
REMAINS
of ## HEROES

DAVID BENEM

WHAT REMAINS of HEROES

A REQUIEM FOR HEROES
BOOK ONE

What Remains of Heroes
A Requiem for Heroes, Book One
© 2015 David Benem. All rights reserved.
ISBN: 978-0-9961939-0-0

Cover and formatting by Damonza.com

ACKNOWLEDGEMENTS

Though writing is a personal endeavor, it can't be done in seclusion. This book would never have grown to its present form without the welcome encouragement and thoughtful critiques of others. For that, I am deeply indebted to my loving wife, my dear family, and my excellent friends. Many thanks to those who took the time to dig through this project even when it was an ugly, half-formed thing. Thanks to those who read it and offered inspiring words, meaningful changes, or just spent time at the pub listening to me blather on about it. You know who you are, you mean much to me, and I thank you.

A special thanks also to my son Ben. Your unending enthusiasm made your dad feel "cool" about writing. Your books are next, Best.

1
MISTAKES

THE RAFTERS RATTLED and the floorboards hummed at *The Wanton Vicar*. Sword-wearing scoundrels of every sort crowded the tables, howling for ale and baiting the serving girls with bawdy talk. A fiddle squealed from the tavern's far end, and folk either stomped with heavy boots to the melody or hurled insults and worse at the minstrel.

Any respectable person would have avoided the place, but then Lannick was anything but respectable.

Not anymore, anyway, he thought with a crooked grimace. *Not after what happened to my family.*

He hunkered against the bar in his usual spot, the place where he reckoned he'd spent much of the past nine years. It was the barstool farthest from the door and deepest in the shadows. The place where he could spend time with his last friends in all the great city of Ironmoor: the barkeep and the drinks the man served.

He raised his cup of wine to his family's memory,

then tipped the chewed wood to his lips. After a hearty gulp he slammed the cup against the bar and signaled the barkeep for a refill with a belch and a nod. Soon, perhaps with another cup or two, his melancholy would fade and he'd feel right once more.

"You are going to *pay* for this one, right?" grumbled the burly barkeep standing guard before a wall of sweating casks and stoppered bottles. His round face looked much like a bowl of lumpy porridge, and his apron was spattered with greasy stains. His mouth tilted with a weary smile, then he splashed a bottle's dregs into Lannick's cup.

"Don't you remember who I am, Brugan?" Lannick said, puffing his chest. He snatched the cup from the bar before the barkeep could protest and took a pull.

The big barkeep's smile wavered as he scratched his close-cropped hair with thick fingers. That hair had retreated much from his face in recent years, like it feared the face's nubby ugliness. "Lannick," he grunted, "I'm only this kind to you because I remember who you *were*. But my charity has its limits, even for an old friend. You do have means of paying, don't you?"

"Isn't my charming wit worth at least its weight in coin?" Lannick said, flashing a grin before realizing the comment made no sense. Of course he had no means of paying, but he swore to himself he'd make things right with his old friend. He'd make things right with a lot of folk, someday.

Brugan muttered some kind of curse and lumbered toward another customer. Lannick's gaze followed the man, and came to rest upon a woman. But not just any woman, and certainly not one of the tired, painted harlots stalking the tavern. This was a breathtaking beauty, with a delicate face framed by a cascade of auburn curls. Her silk dress was purple, like she was noble or at least wealthy or important, and about that dress swelled soft curves that whispered of treasures beneath.

Lannick winked and saluted her with his cup. She didn't notice him, but then hardly anyone did, anymore.

He turned back to his drink, shoulders slumped. *If only I were younger, handsome, rich, and a bit less of a drunken wretch.* He plucked a hair from his head and studied it in the tavern's orange flicker. Gray, like most of the others in the salt-and-pepper mop on his head and the stubble on his scarred face. His blue shirt was faded and threadbare, the coarse fabric of his trousers was the sort for beggars and barnyards, and the short sword tucked in his cheap scabbard was beginning to rust. He sighed. *If only I were something closer to my old self.*

He looked longingly again at the young woman. Even though he hadn't a faint chance at winning her company, he couldn't help staring. Her features and mannerisms seemed familiar, somehow. Something about her told him he should know her, but after a moment he shook his head. Such a desperate lout would never have known a woman of such refinement. He looked back to the bar and assumed his usual pose, elbows on the sticky planks and shoulders hunched high.

"My friend has caught your eye?" came a voice. A hand rubbed his arm.

Lannick nearly jumped from his stool. "Who—" he spat, sloshing a few sips of wine upon the bar as he turned to see another woman. She was older than the other, with hair cut short and her earthy-colored clothing practical. Though not as striking as the woman in purple, she was far more attractive than the old slatterns usually willing to endure his company. "What?"

"My friend," she said, nodding toward the other woman. "She *is* fetching, yes?"

Me? She's asking these questions of me? He felt blood color his cheeks, but whether from the wine or the women he could not be sure. "Uh, why yes," he said, draining his cup in a single swallow. He grinned awkwardly, and chanced his wink again. "I suppose most fellows would think so."

"You're not with anyone, are you? You're alone?"

His spirits rose. His life was such a lonely hell, and here was a terribly rare offer of companionship. "Well," he ventured, "you happen to have caught me on an uncommon evening alone."

"Really," she said flatly. But then a playful smirk danced across her full lips. "Why don't you join us?"

Can this be happening? Lannick sat with mouth agape while the woman stared back expectantly. He rose to stand on long, unsteady legs, and as he teetered over the woman he realized he'd had too much wine to be graceful. He forced his mouth shut and braced himself against the bar. "Brugan?" he announced, emboldened. "A bottle of your finest for me and my new friends."

The barkeep rushed over and pulled Lannick close. "Not a wise decision, my friend. Tread carefully. You have no idea who—"

"Bah," Lannick said, prying the barkeep's hand from his shoulder. "I said your finest."

"Not unless you have the coin," Brugan said, folding beefy arms across a broad chest.

"You needn't worry about that," the short-haired woman said, digging into her green jerkin and producing a handful of silver crowns. She shoved them toward the barkeep and looked to Lannick with mischievous eyes. "Come. Join us."

Brugan huffed and barged through the swinging door into the tavern's kitchen. Lannick ambled toward a stool between the two ladies, a dumb grin splattered across his face. The young lass in purple appeared even more elegant as he approached. His head buzzed giddily. It had been so very long since he'd been in the company of a beautiful woman, and he wondered what he'd done to have the dead gods bless him so.

He tried easing himself atop the stool but stumbled off when his rump missed half its surface. "Damned thing," he cursed, pointing to the sword slung against his thigh. "Tangles me up all the time." After a couple of attempts, he managed to balance himself upon the seat. He smiled at the ladies before snapping shut his mouth and licking his teeth, certain they were dyed from the wine.

The younger woman turned to him, her garnet-green eyes wide. She blinked slowly, as though entranced. "Hello," she breathed, her tongue sounding as clumsy from drink as Lannick's own.

He felt a hand upon his thigh. His heart raced. *Could there be some of that old glimmer within me?* "Well, then!" He knew he'd said it too loudly, but they didn't seem to care. The hand on his thigh moved upward, closer to his…

Brugan slammed a dusty bottle on the bar before them, his face curdling to a scowl. He seized Lannick by the collar and pulled him close. "You're making an awful mistake, my friend," he hissed. "You have no idea who that is. I'm begging you, Lannick, don't do this!"

"We'll take this outside," the short-haired woman said sharply as she grabbed the bottle from the bar. She wrapped a hand under Lannick's arm and yanked him from the stool. "Let's go. Your friend here doesn't seem to want us to have our fun."

Lannick staggered, mouth hanging open as he studied the girl in purple, the undulation of her hips and buttocks as she walked toward the door. He followed along in a daze.

"Lannick!" cried Brugan over the din of the crowd. "This is a mistake!"

Lannick allowed the short-haired woman to lead him through the crowd. He then ducked his tall form through the doorframe and into the cool spring night.

"Lannick!" shouted Brugan again from the bar. "That's—"

The woman slammed shut the door behind them, cutting off the words.

No matter, Lannick thought. He looked upon the ladies. The soft shape and ravishing beauty of the younger one, the playful eyes and devious smirk of the other. Things like this didn't happen to the likes of what he'd become. *I don't care who they are.*

"To my m-manor," the girl stammered. "Father's off in the country playing with his little soldiers."

Lannick thought again he should know the girl, but

his head swam and his body tingled. Thinking about anything other than what he hoped was before him was futile. "Lead the way, my ladies," he said with a bow and stumble. "I am at your humble service."

Ironmoor's many belfries tolled midnight, their echoes dull against a thick blanket of fog. The city's rain-slicked cobblestones were all but empty at this late hour, and the full moon above seemed no more than a milky smear in the sky.

The three of them walked arm-in-arm, passing the wine between them and taking long draws from the bottle. They laughed, but Lannick hardly heard their words anymore to know whether there was anything worth laughing about. Yet, like anything else at this moment, it mattered not at all. His body was warm with wine and expectation, and he felt happy for the first time in years.

They walked along streets crowded by ramshackle homes shouldered against seedy taverns, then through the old city's merchant district with its storefronts shuttered for the night. Down another street, beneath the gilded shingles of artisans' shops. They tottered through the shadows of walls surrounding the Nearer Ward and the High King's castle, and saluted the pacing guardsmen with a tip of their bottle.

They moved through respectable places Lannick had avoided for nearly a decade, places he used to wander with pride but could no longer. He took another deep draw of wine, hoping to press such thoughts from his head.

After a time they turned again, and climbed a street

lined by palatial homes and gated gardens. They'd walked quite far and the bottle was nearly drained, but the ladies seemed to grow more excited with every step.

"Are we close?" Lannick asked hopefully.

"There," the younger woman said, sipping from the bottle and then handing it to Lannick.

After staring at the girl's breasts for far too long for even less-than-polite company, Lannick brought the bottle to his lips and found it almost empty. He sucked down what he could, tossed it into a nearby garden, and heard it shatter. He shrugged and the ladies snickered, and together they blundered across the street.

Lannick rolled his head as he was pulled along, and saw before him the blurred image of an imposing estate. A massive home of charcoal-gray stone crouched behind stout pillars, all of it surrounded by a fence of twisted iron. It seemed the girl was quite wealthy, indeed. Lannick chuckled at his sudden turn of fortune.

The girl produced a key and opened the gate leading to the manor's grounds. They tumbled through, trampling over flowerbeds and toward the side of the home. Soon they reached a narrow door, which the girl in purple said would be untended by the servants. Lannick wondered for an instant whether there was cause to worry, but dismissed such notions after another glance at her buttocks.

She produced another key and they entered the home. They staggered down a hallway and into a kitchen lit by low-burning candles and a dwindling fire in its brick oven. The short-haired woman rummaged through a pantry and found another bottle of wine. She watched as Lannick and the girl drank deeply from it.

Lannick's head was a mess, but he was determined to see this through. "So," he blurted, trying to present his most dashing smile, "I'm Lannick."

"Alisa," said the short-haired woman. "And that's Nara. But enough talk. You'd like to head upstairs with us? To the bedchamber?"

Lannick blinked, dumbfounded. *How can this be? This must be some kind of mistake!* He took another drink and handed the bottle to Nara.

Nara stared at him glassy-eyed and noisily slurped the wine. She dropped the bottle and it rang against the floor but did not break. They all laughed.

"Go to him, Nara," Alisa said, her tone kind but commanding.

Nara stumbled into Lannick's arms. "Now," she said softly.

Lannick held her close and gazed upon her. Her soft cheeks, pink lips, and green eyes. He breathed sharply as desire flared within him. She was gorgeous.

"Upstairs," Alisa said. She snatched another bottle of wine then directed them up a staircase near the kitchen.

Lannick squeezed Nara's hand. His breath quickened and his heart raced. Together they followed Alisa through candlelit corridors, past a study filled with maps drooping from a table, past several well-appointed bedrooms, and at last to an opulent bedchamber set aglow by a fire crackling in its hearth.

"Well, then," said Lannick. He had no idea what to say. The only women he'd spoken with over the past decade had been those he'd paid for. Yet, it seemed with these ladies his charm—or lack thereof—mattered not at all. He scratched his tangled hair and greasy stubble. *Perhaps it's my looks?* He smirked. "To the bed?"

Alisa waggled a scolding finger before pulling Nara away from him and toward the bed. "Why, Lannick, you're every bit as naughty as I'd hoped." She stood beside Nara and began helping her out of her dress.

Lannick stood wide-eyed, staring as the girl's flawless skin and firm breasts were revealed. She was the most stunning woman he could remember setting eyes upon, save for perhaps his dead wife. He winced at the sudden recollection of his family, and tried to focus only upon the girl.

Alisa led the girl to the bed and through the heavy curtains hanging about it. She positioned her on the bed, in the middle of a brown bearskin. Nara's body shimmered in the firelight, shadows dancing about her flesh. Alisa whispered something in her ear and the girl parted her legs. She lay there, her bosom rising with deep breaths, and looked to Lannick with lusty eyes.

"Lannick?" Alisa called. "Bring the wine."

His jaw dropped and he fumbled with his belt and scabbard. His sword fell to the floor with a loud clunk, and he grabbed the bottle from a table. He stumbled toward the bed and took a long, disbelieving drink. The room spun and his balance was failing. His vision blurred, and for an instant there seemed to be six women on the bed, not two. He grinned shamelessly. *It seems my newfound fortune knows no end.*

He steadied himself against a bedpost and passed the wine to Alisa. For a moment he stood at the bedside, agog at the sight of Nara. Her hair spilled across the pale skin of her shoulders and parted to curl about her breasts. Her belly was trim but not overly so, and farther down was the flower of her womanhood, a jewel Lannick never would have imagined would be his to enjoy.

He could resist no longer. He kicked off his boots and nearly ripped his pants as he removed them. He dove headlong into the bed.

Lannick kissed Nara deeply, finding her lips soft and sweet. He could taste the wine upon them, which only added to his passion. He moved his lips to her breasts and kissed them hungrily. He was awkward and rough, he knew, and hadn't bathed in a good number of days. Nevertheless, the girl embraced him with desire, as though she truly wanted this. It was something he'd not felt in years.

How?

There was a hand twisting in his hair, pulling his head upward. "She wants you," Alisa said.

Lannick panted, his blood hot. "And you?"

"I'll watch," said Alisa, her brown eyes teasing. "Take her. She is ready."

Lannick rose to his knees and tore his shirt from his torso. Nara squirmed beneath him, inviting. He needed no further encouragement, and in an instant was inside her. Inside the sort of woman he'd only dreamed of these last nine, awful years. The sensation was warm and wondrous, and his entire body felt as though it were aflame.

Nara moaned beneath him—painfully at first—but in time her sounds seemed those of pleasure. Her breathing quickened and her eyelids drooped. She looked at Lannick with seeming longing, the sort of look Lannick had only rarely seen. A look of satisfaction, of wanting...

"Whaaat!"

It was a chilling shriek, a rattling scream that seemed to shake the bed and stir the hearth's fire. Lannick pulled away from the girl and his lust vanished immediately.

Not him.

Even in his drunken state, Lannick knew that voice. He slunk away from the bed, into the shadows between it and a shuttered window.

Anyone but him.

The scarred, stunted man in the crimson surcoat charged toward Nara. He reared back, struck her with the back of a black-gloved fist, then seized her by the throat. "My daughter is nothing but a filthy whore!" he screamed.

Dead gods. Not him.

Lannick's guts ran cold. He looked to the sword he'd discarded at the opposite end of the room and knew it was too far away. What was more, the man was armed and Lannick had consumed more than a little wine. There would be no chance for vengeance.

He had to run.

Now.

He grabbed what he could, threw open the window, and tumbled into the gardens below. He smashed painfully against prickly shrubs, but struggled and recovered. He tugged on his clothes and his boots and then ran. Ran as quickly as his clumsy feet would carry him. Over a fence and into the dark.

"I will find you!" came a cry after him. "And I will kill you!"

Mistakes are the bedrock of wisdom. If the proverb were true, Lannick reckoned he'd be the wisest man in all of Ironmoor, perhaps in all the vast kingdom of Rune. He chuckled at the thought, then retched as he pulled himself from the gutter.

He braced himself against a wall of flaking plaster, stumbling as the alley listed before him. His vision blurred, sharpened, then blurred again as he caught wind of his odor. There was the stink of vomit, along with other scents he was loath to identify. He brushed the more substantial chunks from his clothing, remembering his brown shirt had been blue the night before.

The wine still muddled his thoughts and his head pounded in the light of morning, but he knew trouble would be coming for him. The very worst kind, and soon.

Yet, he couldn't help but revel in the wine-numbed memories of the prior evening. There was the wine, of course, fruity and bold and so much tastier than his usual swill. And then there'd been the flesh. Lannick's smile widened as he remembered just *who* she was. None other than the daughter of the distinctively hideous General Thalius Fane, commander of all the High King's armies and the very man Lannick hated more than any in all the world.

Not exactly the vengeance I'd imagined, but it will have to do for now.

He felt his wits returning with the daylight and knew he had no time to reminisce. He knew all too well the general was a monster of a man. He would beat from his daughter the details of their encounter, then track

Lannick to one of the taverns where he was too often a customer. Someone was bound to betray him.

A few blocks away was Temple Street, known as much for its seedy taverns as for the ruined cathedrals shading its cobbles. Lannick knew the taverns quite well, particularly *The Wanton Vicar*. Considering it was still early morning, he decided to chance a return. Perhaps his good luck would continue, and his old friend could help him into a new set of clothes before he was hunted down and killed.

"Lannick, you miserable rascal!" said Brugan, polishing the bar with a rag. He laughed heartily. He always did. "Did you bed your lovers in the sewers?"

"No," Lannick said with a smirk, "but it seems I slept there. Those ladies wanted me just for my body, such as it is."

Brugan laughed again, a big, belly-shaking chuckle that seemed to move the entire tavern.

Lannick slumped into his usual stool and his smile withered. "You know who she was, don't you?"

"Of course I do. I know practically every citizen of Ironmoor, and many of their darkest secrets," he said with a wink. "Which is why *that* girl was a particularly poor object of your… affections. But you're alive, at least."

Lannick pressed his hands to his face. "I had no idea she was Fane's daughter until it was too late. You should have warned me, Brugan."

"I did. Not once but four times," Brugan said, rapping his heavy knuckles against the bar. "But, as usual, you were drunk, and thinking with something other than your head. I'd have had an easier time convincing shit not to stink." He eyed Lannick up and down. "Or you for that matter."

"It seems I have a knack for bad choices. This may be the one mess I don't survive."

"With any luck that girl will have the good sense to be ashamed of her choices last night, and will keep the entire matter from her dear father."

Lannick pressed closer to the bar, his voice sinking to a whisper. "But Fane found us. In his own bedchambers, even. I'm in real trouble, Brugan."

"Dead gods! Did he get a good look at you?"

"Perhaps not my face." Lannick grinned in spite of himself.

"Did he recognize you?"

"I doubt it—it's been many years, and I haven't exactly kept up my appearance." He pointed to the scar that ran down his cheek, then patted the swell of a belly that'd known too much drink.

Brugan shook his head and chuckled. "You awful bastard. We're on the verge of war! Word is the High King's entire council has convened to discuss how the 'skirmish' with the Arranese has brought us to the brink of all-out war. They say those savages are massing to cross the Southwall Mountains and invade the kingdom of Rune itself! The council's even asked for oath-bound soldiers from all eight thanes of Rune, in case things take a bad turn. And here General Fane arrives home to find you—*you*—despoiling his daughter!"

"I know. Perhaps someday I'll laugh at this, but right now I'm scared, Brugan. Scared to death. Fane will not suffer this. Not from anyone, and least of all me. Even if he didn't recognize me, he'll have me hunted down and killed. I need a place to hide. I reckon if I hide out for a few days, he'll have left for the war and this whole thing will be forgotten. Eventually, anyway." He looked to Brugan sheepishly. "Can I count on you? Can I stay here for a couple of days?"

The plea was met with a hard look. "No, Lannick. Absolutely not. You and I are friends—old friends—but I can't keep saving you from your mistakes. Fane's no friend of mine, either, remember? I'm not about to cross him and his brutish Scarlet Swords. Besides, he's sure to head this way. Don't you reckon he'll think to ask this barkeep a question or two? Like whether I know a certain patron who was here just last night?" He pounded the bar with his fist. "Damn it, Lannick! Fane and his Scarlet Swords will shake the timbers of every alehouse and whorehouse in Ironmoor until you're found. Someone's certain to betray you, if they haven't already."

"Fair enough," said Lannick, knowing the barkeep was right. He wasn't much for honor these days, but he couldn't ask Brugan to place himself in harm's way. Not again, and not for this. "Any chance I could trouble you for a hot bath, at least? Perhaps some clean clothes?"

Brugan laughed, the sound of it grating. "And how about a purse full of gold crowns? And perhaps a stout horse and all the wine you can carry? After all, it seems you think there should be no end to my charity!"

Lannick's shoulders sagged. He hadn't paid his bills at the place in weeks, maybe months, and even Brugan's goodwill had its limits. "Work's been slow, Brugan. You know I'll make it up to you."

"Work?" The mirth left the barkeep's face. "Is that what you call acting as a strongman for that bastard Silas? The man's a crook. Shaking down debtors for coin at the point of your sword is hardly something I'd call work."

"It's a living, Brugan. Not something I'm proud of."

Brugan leaned across the bar, drawing uncomfortably close to Lannick. "Nor should you be. It's filthy work, Lannick. The sort suited for criminals and cutthroats. Not the likes of you." He pulled back and again set about polishing the bar. "Lannick, I've helped you only because I know who you once were, not because of who you are now. The man before me now is a ghost of the one who earned my friendship. I wonder at times how you can stomach the sight of your own reflection, knowing how far you've allowed yourself to fall. If you and I had any less of a history, I'd tolerate you not at all."

Lannick found himself unable to meet the barkeep's gaze. "I don't have a lot of options here, Brugan. A shirt, at least? Even your most ragged will do. Certainly you can do that for an old friend?"

Brugan placed a hand on Lannick's shoulder. "You were a better man, once. A hero, even. Has so much changed?" His expression grew wistful for a moment, but then hardened again. "I can't watch you live like this any longer, Lannick. I can no longer stand here with a smile and a full tankard for you as you piss away what little honor you have left." He fixed Lannick with a serious look. "I have a couple of spare shirts in the kitchen. Grab the burlap one. Not one of my good linens or aprons, mind you. And then get out."

Lannick searched the kitchen, only finding the shirt after a close inspection of the piglet roasting in the fireplace. His mouth watered at the scent of it, but he couldn't wrong his friend any further by stealing a morsel. Instead, he peeled off his shirt, taking care to avoid contact with its moist stains. He cursed his bad judgment, knowing he deserved no better than this.

As he reached to retrieve Brugan's shirt his eyes rested momentarily on the small symbol tattooed upon the inside of his forearm. A watchtower under which was a word: "*Variden.*" It meant "Vigilant Ones" in the elder tongue. A sadness came upon him as it often did when he encountered remnants of his old life. Brugan was right— Lannick had fallen far. He sighed and tugged Brugan's shirt overhead.

He turned toward the kitchen door and was about to declare his gratitude when he heard a crash. The hard crash of the tavern's front door being thrown open. A din of shouting followed and boots thundered upon the tavern's planked floor. Glass shattered. Wood splintered. Lannick froze.

"Barkeep!" sounded a high-pitched voice, like a sword scraping free of a scabbard. Lannick knew the voice well. It was General Fane, and likely several members of his Scarlet Swords.

Lannick smacked at his head and tried to focus, frantically searching his surroundings. The cramped kitchen had no openings to the outside beyond a couple of narrow flues over the fireplaces. There was the swinging door into the common room and the bolted door to the cellar. The swinging door was sure to be thrown open in scant moments, at which point he'd be skewered just like piglet in the fireplace.

I'm forgetting something!

There came another crash from the common room and the crack of wood breaking. He picked out Fane's voice. "There was a man last night, here at your tavern..."

The Wanton Vicar, Lannick thought. Brugan had told him the story behind the tavern's name, once. Something about finding shackled skeletons and instruments of torture in the catacombs below the adjacent church. He cursed his wine-softened head, knowing there was something relevant, something important about the story he was forgetting.

A thud resounded from the bar, followed by a muted cry. Lannick winced, imagining Brugan's face smashed against the bar top by one of Fane's bloodthirsty henchmen. He thought of rushing in to save his friend from the beating, but quickly dismissed the notion. Both of them would end up dead if he tried, especially in such tight quarters and without a proper weapon. Instead Lannick uttered a quick prayer for his friend's safety. As vicious as Fane was, he wasn't likely to gut Brugan if he didn't think the barkeep had been complicit in his daughter's deflowering. At least Lannick hoped it was so.

Another crash sounded, forcing Lannick's thoughts back to a means of escape. There was something about the place that Brugan had mentioned...

"I do not enjoy repeating myself," said Fane in

his screeching tone. "Don't tempt me to bury you in your cellar!"

The cellar.

Brugan had once told him he'd found an entrance to the catacombs in his cellar. That's why he kept it bolted shut, just in case anything or anyone ever tried wandering into the tavern from below. It was said the catacombs wound under the entire city of Ironmoor, a relic of an older time. It stood to reason there'd be another portal to the outside world, somewhere nearby.

With a silent apology to Brugan and a silent prayer the barkeep could hold out just a little longer, Lannick grabbed his old, vomit-stained shirt. He looped it about his hand and used it to grab an ember from the fireplace. The bolt to the cellar yielded with only minor protest and Lannick dashed down the stairwell and into whatever lurked below.

The cellar was a series of cramped chambers serving as storage for all manner of necessities for *The Wanton Vicar*. In the gloom Lannick discerned wheels of cheese, casks of ale, and seemingly endless bottles of wine. He managed to find a hand lamp amidst the stockpile, and judged there was some oil in it from the sloshing sound it made. He lit the wick with the burning ember from the fireplace and light spilled across the chamber.

Hard footfalls sounded on the planks overhead. Fane's men were either leaving or tossing the place. Lannick scanned every dark corner of the cellar and at last spotted a low, bolted door. This bolt did not give easily, scraping and squealing as he pulled. Eventually, though, it gave way, and a rush of stale air from the catacombs beyond threatened to extinguish his lamp. Lannick could see nothing in the narrow corridor before him, but the thudding sounds from above permitted no other choice.

Just before plunging through the doorway, he turned back to the racks of wine. There were many bottles, so he reckoned Brugan could spare just one for an old friend. He grabbed it and departed.

Take care, Brugan, and may we both survive long enough for me to repay you.

The catacombs were said to be haunted, and the utter dark yielded little to the light of Lannick's lantern. Strange winds whipped at him from every direction, and the air carried the sickly-sweet reek of decay. Occasionally a howl or scream from something, somewhere, pierced the wind's moan. If the Scarlet Swords behind him weren't enough, the thought of undead beasts stalking the darkness was sure to spur his pace.

Lannick was a tall man, which didn't match well with such low ceilings. He winced as he scraped his head again and again upon the roughly hewn rock. What was more, the tight passages twisted and turned, and he slammed into the walls more than once. But he figured the haphazard design provided him some small advantage. He guessed there was some chance his lantern's light would be concealed from the Scarlet Swords, and they'd have no clue as to his path. The henchmen were certain to find the tavern's entrance to the catacombs, and he needed to reach his quarters before General Fane.

The passage straightened and ran on for a distance.

Lannick dimmed his lantern, growing worried of being found.

Dread settled upon him in the dark. This was no ballroom fop or petty noble he'd wronged, but the kingdom's most ambitious and dangerous man. Lannick had gotten crossways with him once before, and the price Fane had exacted had been nearly too much to bear. The fleeting joys of the previous evening disappeared entirely. It seemed that after all he'd been forced to suffer over these years, he'd die at the hands of his tormentor, General Fane.

I am a dead man.

After a time the cramped corridor began sloping upward. Lannick was certain the air was freshening and there was a faint murmur of what sounded like voices, likely the Scarlet Swords behind him. He shuttered his lamp closed and tried to quiet his breathing to better focus on the sound.

There *were* voices. But these weren't gruff exchanges of soldiers. Rather, it sounded like the hum of many conversations occurring at once. He tiptoed forward a few more paces, his head fixed at a tilt in hopes of hearing better. He guessed he was beneath some kind of meeting place, a market or square. What was more, there was the thinnest ribbon of light penetrating the gloom ahead. Lannick moved on, caring little for the resonating scrapes of his leather boots upon the limestone floor.

The rough-hewn ceiling gave way to blocks of carved stone, and between two blocks was a tiny hole. Lannick pressed his eye as close to the hole as his nose would allow, but he could make out nothing but the gleam of light.

But light it was, and he was certain there were people milling about the space above.

"Help!" he hissed, hoping someone above would hear him. "Help me!"

He waited there a moment, awaiting some sort of reply. But there was no response, and seemingly very little chance he could be heard. He cursed and pulled away from the light, and looked again into the gloom of the passageway.

Just then an angry shout resounded from the darkness behind him. "Stop, you bastard!" came a gruff voice.

Damn my wine-muddled head! Lannick charged forward as quickly as the strangled passage would allow. He could no longer afford caution, so he opened wide the shutters of his lamp. He ran, and the path ahead continued its upward slope. There had to be an exit somewhere.

Another shout boomed from the darkness. Lannick swung his lamp around and saw a glint of steel not more than thirty feet behind him. He nearly stumbled as he turned about, trying to move faster than his legs would carry him. He ran with a frightened pace, a hare from the hound.

He did not see the rubble strewn across the floor where a wall had crumbled and he lost his footing. He spilled across the stone, barely managing to keep hold of his lamp. He twisted about but fell back again, his boots sliding on the rubble.

"Stay down, bastard!" The voice was close, almost upon him.

At last Lannick scrambled to his feet and grabbed from a pocket the wine he'd stolen from Brugan's cellar.

The Scarlet Swordsman was no more than ten feet away, blade brandished and eyes agleam with fury. But he was alone.

Lannick directed the lamp's glare at the soldier, hoping the bright light in the utter dark would disorient him. With his other hand he threw the bottle. It struck the Swordsman square in the face, not hard enough to break the bottle but enough to make the man misstep and lose his footing on the same rubble which had toppled Lannick. He skidded to a stop at Lannick's feet, and Lannick dashed his lamp across the Swordsman's skull. Flames engulfed his head and shot across his red cloak. His screams told of horrific pain.

Lannick looked frantically about for the man's sword, and finally spotted its point protruding from beneath a flailing arm. He couldn't chance trying to pry the thing away, nor could he wait for the flames to sputter and die. If there were other Swordsmen in the catacombs, they were certain to hear the cries of their comrade. Lannick turned his back to the burning body and tried to outrun the light of the blaze. The screams followed him for a long while, but that was well enough. His heart held a special hatred for Fane's Scarlet Swords, those awful thugs retained by the general to do his darkest work.

Like what they did to my family.

After a time, the cries fell silent. Lannick fumbled through many turns and twists in the dark, and then the corridor came to an abrupt end at a door of moldy wood. Lannick grimaced as he neared it, for the air carried a gut-turning stench. He pulled an arm to his face, burying his nose in the crease of his elbow, then tugged at the door.

The door opened to a sewer bathed in light from iron grates above, a brown and yellow stream of waste. Putrid lumps floated amidst eddies of oily liquids, and Lannick swallowed hard to keep his stomach from emptying. *Perhaps one thing smells worse than I do today.*

He cursed and forged ahead in knee-high muck, thinking this to be a suitable place for him after his actions. His boots would be more difficult to replace than his shirt had been, but such was his fate. He thought of Brugan, and knew he owed his friend far more than coin.

He located a grate he was able to shake loose, although its weight was not easily moved. With some effort he worked it far enough to a side, and pulled himself from the sewer.

He found himself in the middle of a livestock tent, surrounded by more than a dozen lowing cows. Lannick looked at their wide, confused eyes and felt a strange kinship. They were all destined for slaughter.

"I know the feeling," he said, patting them gently as he passed.

He emerged from the tent and into the midst of Ironmoor's Old Market. It was a vast square crowded with tents of every color and patrons from every corner of the world. Bejeweled Khaldisian merchants jabbered with thick-faced highlanders from near the Waters of World's End over the proper price of wool, while tall, dark-skinned warmasters from Harkane tested swords and bows with skeptical frowns. All mentioned the coming war as either a reason to inflate or decrease the price, and Lannick guessed both merchants and patrons saw their game approaching an end.

He walked slowly as he moved among them, figuring the crowd would swallow him and that running would only draw attention. He was close to his quarters, where he kept another sword and a few other possessions. From there he could make the docks. Perhaps he could manage a long journey as a stowaway or even a stint as a deckhand if there was work to be had. By the time he returned, maybe his indiscretions would be forgotten or he'd be presumed long dead.

The colorful tents of the Old Market gave way to storehouses and then to rough industry, with filth-covered roads separating slaughterhouses from rendering mills. Lannick's already-sullied boots squelched through what seemed a mix of entrails and mud, and his nose burned from the hot stink.

Beyond lay the Hollows, the roughest, bleakest corner of Ironmoor. A maze of alleyways weaved amidst dilapidated shanties and unsavory establishments, all crowded against Ironmoor's outer wall like garbage swept into a corner. The city guard had long ago abandoned any notion of enforcing the High King's Law in the Hollows, so it provided a welcome home for every manner of burglar, prostitute, and panhandler in the city.

Lannick slowed as he entered the Hollows, looking for any suspicious eyes. A couple of ruffians sat fingering their blades on a bench outside a tavern. Lannick guessed they were looking for someone with coin, such as a wealthy merchant seeking a discrete dalliance in one of the local establishments. They merely glanced at Lannick, and for the first time this day he was glad to be covered in shit. He had nothing to give them, of course, but it would have been a painful explanation.

Many of the other denizens appeared far less ambitious, shuffling tiredly through the tight streets. Historians instructed that the Hollows were used as a quarantine during a plague long ago, and the name derived from the gaunt look of its residents. Lannick felt the place still reeked of sickness, and that its residents still wore the haggard masks of the nearly dead.

At last, a reason to flee this place.

He pressed ahead through the narrow streets, shouldering between prostitutes and their patrons and ignoring their complaints. He hoped against hope that General Fane's men were still blundering through the catacombs. He rounded a corner, passed a brothel, then bounded up a set of rickety steps lining the side of a pawnshop. He fumbled frantically through his pockets, searching for the key.

"Ho there, Lannick!" called a scratchy voice from the bottom of the stairs.

Lannick froze for an instant but breathed a bit easier when he saw it was Silas, the pawnbroker who served as his landlord and occasional employer. Silas was a measly man with a patch for one eye, and was owed money by virtually every resident of the Hollows.

"You're well past due on your rent, lad," Silas said slowly, his face as eerily calm as ever. "Not to mention the three silver crowns I loaned you last week. I have a few jobs you could do if you don't have the coin on hand. They may be a bit bloody, but that's nothing you're not used to, eh?"

"It'll have to wait," said Lannick. He abandoned his search of his clothing and set about looking for the duplicate key he kept stashed in a knot of wood.

"It'd be best for you if I didn't have to wait overlong," said Silas, almost sadly. "I'd hate to have to ask one of my other lads to pay you a visit."

"That won't be necessary," Lannick said brusquely as he found the key and turned the lock. "I'll have it for you this week."

"You'd better," Silas said, turning away toward his pawnshop. "Life can be too short for waiting."

Lannick shook his head and entered his squalid room, slamming the door behind him. He picked his way between piles of refuse buzzing with flies, then stepped atop his soiled sleeping pallet. Above the pallet, behind a plank in the ceiling, he found it: an embroidered green cloak bundled about his most valued possessions, the last tangible connections to his past.

His pulled free a decorative longsword, an elegant blade etched with runic marks and still honed to a deadly precision despite years of disuse. The locket, which held hairs plucked from the heads of his dead children. And the box of richly lacquered wood, adorned with the script of the elder tongue and containing a bracelet of black iron. He thought of taking it with him, but knew it would be safer in its place. He wrapped the cloak about the box and returned it to the nook in the ceiling. He would return for them, someday.

He pulled the locket around his neck, sheathed his sword and slung it on his hips, and departed.

A new life awaits. Perhaps something more akin to my old one.

He opened the door only to be met by a gauntleted fist to the face. He reeled, then was jerked from his quarters and shoved. He tumbled down the stairway and smacked his head on the street. He staggered to his feet, hand finding the hilt of his sword.

"Take him!" cried General Thalius Fane, his burned face as grotesque as Lannick remembered. The general smiled smugly. "Wound him only, though, for I'd like to finish things myself."

Flanking General Fane were six of his Scarlet Swords, hard-eyed men draped in ebony chainmail and crimson cloaks. A seventh was descending from the stairway, wiping Lannick's spittle from his fist. They were the general's personal attachment. Not Rune's finest soldiers, but certainly its most vicious.

Lannick drew his sword, backing away from the soldiers toward the dead end of the street. The odds were against him, but he would never surrender to this man. At last, he had a chance to exact real vengeance for what wickedness the general had visited upon him those many years before.

The soldier from the stairs was the first to charge him. He held a broad-bladed axe in massive hands. Lannick noticed the man moved clumsily, so he crouched low. The oaf broke into a run. When he came close, Lannick lunged sideways, just beneath the swing of the axe. Lannick took a sharp, backhanded swipe with his sword as the man hurtled past. His blade cleaved into the soldier's hamstring, just below the hang of the chainmail tunic. The oaf crumbled to a heap, wailing like a baby.

Lannick flashed a grin as an old feeling rose within him. He'd been an exceptional swordsman, long ago, but since then he'd done little more than Silas's dirty work. It'd been years since he'd fought a man capable of defending himself. Yet, the movements of real combat were readily remembered, and he was invigorated. With a little luck he could best these dogs, even hung-over. Then he'd take the general, slowly and painfully.

He fell back into the street's dead end and readied his blade, eying the Swordsmen. Two drew steel and began walking toward him, wary looks in their eyes. One was a giant of a man with a wild beard, the other short and swarthy. Lannick decided to rush at them as well, and closed the distance in an instant. When he was nearly upon them he dodged to the side of the street. Their mail was heavy and slowed them. Lannick redirected a blow from the bearded giant and spun about the giant's back. He whirled to the swarthy man and found his throat with his blade. The Swordsman fell to his knees and clutched at the spewing wound. Lannick kicked him, yanking free the sword and sending the man into the giant's legs. The giant toppled forward and Lannick separated the crown of his head from the bottom.

Lannick felt a slight step slower than he'd been years before, but reckoned he was still fast enough when faced with armored men. He grinned again. *I just need to keep from being hit.*

He turned to the remaining men, his sword dancing dangerously. General Fane wore a look of abject madness, his dark eyes nearly crossing. But then, abruptly, his features relaxed to an easy grin.

Lannick's head nearly exploded from the blow, his vision going white and his ears clanging from the concussion. The pain was immense and he collapsed. His head swam and his world started fading to darkness, and he struggled to retain consciousness.

Dark, painful moments followed. He felt something under him, a boot perhaps, forcing him to his side and onto his back. *Damn my wine-addled brain!* It had to have been the one he'd hamstrung but hadn't killed. He eased open his eyes to the sight of General Fane caressing his sword with black-gloved hands, mad eyes inspecting the markings on the blade.

"This is no pauper's weapon," Fane said, his voice no longer a shriek but a whisper. "Nor is it that of a worthless drunk. If I'd not seen you use it, I would have accused you of stealing it. This is a rare thing, a hero's prize. Who are *you* to wield such a thing? Do I know you?"

Blood pooled in Lannick's mouth and he coughed wetly. "No," he lied. "But your daughter does."

Lannick's head exploded again. He felt broken teeth with his tongue. Opening his eyes proved difficult, and even in the shade of the leaning buildings the light seared his sockets.

"You fool!" Fane said, the shrillness returning to his voice. As his face slowly came into focus, Lannick noticed the general's lips trembling. "Do you think I care that much for my daughter? Do you?"

Lannick tried to muster a clever retort, but just then

the general drove a boot in his gut, driving the wind from his lungs.

Fane's eyes flared and he thrust Lannick's sword into the ground. "Under other circumstances I would have let my soldiers ravage her, one after another after another, if I thought it would buy me an advantage. But you... You have ruined things in a way you cannot comprehend."

Fane crouched low, pulling Lannick up by the throat until their faces nearly touched. It was not the striated, stretched burns covering the man's face that disturbed Lannick, but the eyes. The general was a madman, and there was not an ounce of goodness in his soul. He felt his blood run cold, certain this moment was his very last.

"She was to be a virgin," the general spat in Lannick's ear. "The Necrist said no other sacrifice would do..."

The general shoved Lannick back to the ground, stood and smoothed his crimson surcoat. "Keln?" he said, gesturing to one of his Scarlet Swords.

"Shall I kill him, sir?" came a coarse voice.

"No," said Fane. "I believe I know this loathsome cur, and have a use for him. Take him to the brig. Tell them he's there on my direct order, and let the guards know he's not to be harmed. By them, anyway." He chuckled grimly. "The rest of you can clean up these bodies."

2
ANOTHER EXORCISM

THE DUST MADE Zandrachus Bale sneeze, and the sneeze stirred up more dust. The depths of the ancient library were rife with the stuff; a thick glaze coated every shelf, every table, and every book. Bale dragged his tongue upon his forefinger and then trailed the finger across the spine of his tome. The brown paste rendered looked quite revolting. He waggled the finger and flicked it toward the floor, recalling a scientific treatise postulating that dust was comprised largely of human parts. Hair, skin, and who knows what else.

Perhaps little bits of my sneezes.

For a moment he studied the misshapen globule on the floor. The shadows of the flickering candlelight danced about it, making it seem almost alive, and all the more unsightly. Bale had a weak stomach, yet often found himself enraptured by the grotesque. Certain smells, sights and textures delighted him as much as they repelled. He thought for a moment of retrieving the pasty blob for further inspection, but then remembered he had a book to read. *Faultain's Study of Anatomic Anomalies.* He'd left off with the chapter concerning superfluous teats. He rubbed away a dribble of snot from a nose he'd always felt to be several sizes too large, then settled in to read.

"Bale!" The voice echoed through the cavernous hall for long, irritating moments.

Bale shrunk low in his chair and drew the brown hood of his robes over his head of long, graying hair. He knew any attempt at disguise was ridiculous, for rare was the day he couldn't be found in the library, dodging his duties in favor of studying old tomes on history, spellcraft, and minor perversions. Nevertheless, he resolved to ignore the summons and play the part of an insolent child as long as it suited him. He'd long grown weary of people and the mundane cycle of their days.

Of course, it wasn't long before he was found. It was Prefect Kreer, as always. The tall man, at least three decades Bale's senior, preened over him, jaundiced eyes staring down the long drip of his nose. "Acolyte Bale," he said tiredly. "A member of His Majesty's staff has requested an exorcism."

"You mean *another* exorcism."

Prefect Kreer raised a bushy brow. "The Faith has become an object of mockery to you, has it?"

Oh, not the Faith. Just those who practice it. "Of course not, Prefect. It's just the High King and the residents of the castle seem to have grown overly zealous of late."

"Our Sanctum has served the Crown for centuries, even in matters of seemingly small import. The Faith instructs that the High King carries the blessing of the goddess Illienne, and it is this blessing that ensures the well-being of Rune. Are you refusing an act of service to our divinely blessed High King? To Rune?"

"Of course not, Prefect. I live to serve." He bowed his head low, his big nose pressing upon a diagram of a third nipple in his book. He had to admire the artist's hand. *All in the name of science, of course.*

"Your tone is one of mockery, Acolyte Bale, and the Sanctum does not look kindly upon jesters or blasphemers. Do you have further complaints? Something I should address with the Dictorian?"

Bale straightened in his chair, doing his best to appear reverent. Crossing Prefect Kreer would only mean assignments to foolish tasks, and upsetting the head of their order, Dictorian Theal, could mean expulsion.

I'd never survive outside this place.

"Nothing at all, Prefect," he said. "I apologize for any perceived insolence. May I inquire as to the nature of the possession?"

"One of the scullery maids fears the castle's kitchens are haunted by a demon. Her description leads me to believe the interloper is a rodent." His purple lips wrinkled to a smile. "But one can never be certain."

Torches lit the stonework corridors of the Abbey, and windows were small and infrequent. The design made for poor ventilation and a haze of foul smoke, but one of the Sanctum's precepts was that the less distracted one was with the outside world, the more focused one's pursuit of truth could be. It was one of the few precepts Bale had never found cause to question. The outside world seemed a frightening place full of violence, hardship, and, worst of all, people.

It was a tedious walk from the library to the apothecary, with the latter situated deep within the Abbey's halls. Mishaps with reagents and potions were not infrequent, so the location had been chosen to prevent catastrophe. A wise choice, Bane reckoned, but it meant passing by several of his brethren in the hallways and exchanging feigned pleasantries. *How I hate people.*

After a winding route through the Abbey's maze-like passageways, he arrived at the counter of the apothecary. The withered, bespectacled acolyte who manned the counter seemed a kindred spirit, in that he avoided eye contact and discussion as adeptly as Bale. Bale had to clear his throat three times before the alchemist removed his attention from an array of glass globes full of colored liquids and swirling fumes.

"Rat poison and drimroot," Bale said simply, wondering if he'd said too much for the alchemist's liking.

The alchemist grumbled something Bale took to be an acknowledgement and trudged up a ladder servicing the tall shelving behind him. Shelf after shelf bowed from the weight of decanters, vials, powders, casks and dried herbs. The alchemist grabbed a small, brownish sprig then snatched a jar from one of the upper shelves. He descended the ladder, handed Bale the dry sprig then meted out a few granules from the jar into a pouch.

Bale gave a curt nod and left. It occurred to him that he'd made dozens of trips to the apothecary over the years, but they'd never exchanged words beyond the requested concoctions and had never traded names. It seemed a perfect relationship.

He retrieved his traveling cloak, staff, and a book from his cramped quarters and departed. It wasn't until he'd arrived at the Abbey's outer door that he noticed the book's title, *On Digestion and the Production of Feces*. Hardly the sort of tome to contain the sacred commands of an exorcism, but chances were the scullery maid wasn't the literate sort. A smile slipped across his weary face.

A light spring rain stirred up the scent of the sea, yielding a smell much like days-old fish. Bale rubbed away drips of rain from his large nose and inhaled deeply. He found the odor not altogether unpleasant, but loathed the notion of enduring the outside world at midday. The streets were sure to be crowded in spite of the weather. Yet, he had a job to do, so he set out upon the wet street with plodding steps.

The Abbey stood in Ironmoor's Nearer Ward, a collection of time-worn structures. These stone shrines had served as the homes of Rune's great seats of power for time immemorial. The Abbey of the Ancient Sanctum of Illienne, the Grand Court of the Magistrate Examiners, and the House of Minor Laws.

Old tombs jealously guarding treasures disregarded long ago by the rest of the world.

He rounded a corner and spotted the hulking form of the High King's castle, the Bastion. Atop its tall tower loomed the gold statue of a dragon. Bale figured on a clear afternoon he'd be walking now in the cast of its shadow. But not today, when the city appeared a ruin of gray stones cowering beneath a gray sky.

The Bastion was near yet distant. Deralor the Mad, seventeenth High King of Rune, had ordered the construction of several walls surrounding the Bastion in concentric circles, with the breaches alternating between north and south on each circuitous wall. Bale grunted his frustration, knowing that although a stronger man could likely hit the castle with a thrown stone, it'd take him quite some time to walk there. The rain was cold and miserable.

The streets were crowded by all manner of official, emissary, bureaucrat, and magistrate. The sort of folk unmoved by the rain, chins held high, cloaks of oiled leather sparkling with inlaid jewels and voices booming with patent hubris. There was talk of imminent war with Arranan and their mysterious Spider King, the interminable trade dispute with the Merchant-Lords of Khaldisia, and rumors of discontent among Rune's eight thanes. Each boldly proclaimed solutions, only to be shouted down by others in their company. Bale shambled between the knots of people, trying hard to ignore the jostles from their gesticulations.

Even Bale's fellow acolytes seemed like pleasant company when measured against this ilk. He passed one richly dressed magistrate regaling his listeners with a bad joke about the sexual proclivities of High King Deragol and the true reason he'd not yet sired an heir. Bale roared with mock laughter, long and loud, and enough to draw the magistrate's reprobating glare. Bale widened his eyes, stuck out his tongue, and then quickened his pace.

The crowds waned as Bale neared the Bastion, the bickering officials giving way to red-sashed guardsmen and hooded servants. The guards at the gates knew him on sight, he was sure, but waited for him to present his sealed warrant before parting their crossed halberds. They didn't question his errand, but Bale could hear their whispered derision. They laughed about the castle being haunted, as there was no other reason an old kook from the Abbey would visit with such frequency.

"Spooker," one called after him. Bale continued walking, having heard the insult many times before.

He passed through the massive portcullis of the last gate and entered the Bastion's grounds. Even to Bale it was an impressive sight. Meticulously trimmed pathways meandered through a decadent garden containing flowers of every shape and hue. In spite of the heavy clouds overhead, the young blossoms of spring were brilliant.

Beyond the gardens stood the Bastion, the massive castle of Rune's High King. The castle proper was an angular bulwark of stone, all stout walls and battlements the color of the sea stirred by storm. Somewhere in its depths was the Godswell, said to be the very place at which the gods Yrghul and Illienne descended into oblivion many years ago. The Old Faith instructed that the final battle of the War of Fates had been fought upon this very ground.

At the Bastion's center rose the Tower of Lords, an incredible structure of sculpted masonry and one of Rune's true wonders. It stretched more than three hundred feet from its base to the great golden dragon at its peak. Gilded reliefs covered its outer wall, depicting the High Kings and their triumphs. There was Deranthol, the first High King, standing with Rune's greatest heroes, the immortal Seven Sentinels, to receive the Blessing of Illienne the Light Eternal. Next a relief depicting them with swords aflame, striking down Illienne's old foe, the dark god Yrghul the Lord of Nightmares, then the two gods descending to oblivion. There was Derand, son of Deranthol, with Rune's eight lesser kings—or 'thanes' as they were known—kneeling before him and pledging fealty. Then Derganfel the Purer, riding with the thanes and battling the Sentinels as they tried to wrest the throne from him, and another portraying the Sentinels' banishment. Upward the reliefs went about the tower, a visual history of ten centuries. The last, just more than two-thirds the distance to the tower's crest, depicted a stylized King Deragol standing ever vigilant over a peaceful land.

A display rife with falsehoods, but inspiring nonetheless.

Bale's chest swelled as he regarded the images. The older reliefs told of times altogether different, when true goodness mustered against true evil. Many members of the Sanctum believed good and evil sat at opposite ends of a balancing scale, and if one dipped the other rose. The more evil in the world the less good, and the converse. Bale thought differently. He guessed the true goodness in men's hearts, the kind that kindled self-sacrifice and real courage, only manifested in the face of true evil. At all other times, like now, it sat dormant, smothered beneath layers of ambivalence.

Along either side of the flagstone path to the Bastion's main entrance stood two rows of crimson-sashed guardsmen, faces veiled in the traditional display of humility in the presence of their divinely blessed king. Bale passed swiftly and uneasily between their silent forms, approaching a great door bearing the dragon emblem of Rune. He began ascending the granite stairway leading to the door, but just then one of the guards beside him jolted as though rudely awakened from a slumber.

"Halt, sir!" the guard huffed through the thin fabric of his translucent veil. He was a portly sort, the same oaf who'd confronted Bale during previous visits to the castle. "You will state your name and your business with the Crown."

Bale rolled his eyes and presented his warrant. "Acolyte Zandrachus Bale of the Ancient Sanctum of Illienne the Light Eternal. I am here at the summons of the king's staff, whose business I am not compelled to discuss with you."

The guard suppressed a yawn and waved Bale along. "I'll fetch Chamberlain Alamis. I'm sure he'll be thrilled at the news of your return."

Chamberlain Alamis was a tall reed of a man, impeccably groomed and dressed in an elegant robe of blue silk. He wore no cover upon his face or head, which Bale found an odd departure from the customary display of deference to Rune's High King. The man's pale eyes studied Bale with unsettling intensity, and he bowed mechanically as Bale approached. He shook Bale's hand limply, then gestured toward a long hallway and they began walking.

The interior of the Bastion was even more impressive than its imposing exterior. It was an ancient place of impossibly long hallways of polished stone, lined with flickering candles, priceless relics from conquered lands and storied weapons of old heroes. The walls stretched upward and arched toward soaring ceilings so high they were lost in shadow. It seemed a place worthy of great kings and old legends, and even Bale's stalwart cynicism wavered upon viewing the marvel.

The chamberlain leaned toward Bale. "I apologize for yet another intrusion upon your *dearly* valuable time, Acolyte. I'm quite certain you have matters of far graver import demanding your attention. However," he leaned closer, as though to avoid unwanted ears, "High King Deragol has been quite, um, *eccentric*, and it seems to be catching."

Bale found it strange that the chamberlain himself would preside over his visit, but thought it best to play along. He nodded deeply and rubbed at his chin, doing his best to portray the calm, thoughtful appearance he guessed people expected from members of the Sanctum.

Alamis halted abruptly and remained still until a hooded official had passed them. He then seized Bale with a hard grip upon the shoulder and pulled him uncomfortably close. "Your faith binds you to protect the Crown, yes?"

Bale found the chamberlain's penetrating, pale eyes unnerving. "I serve the Faith, and thereby the throne and the kingdom."

"Queen Reyis suffered another miscarriage last winter. Her eighth. You are aware of this, yes?"

"I am," Bale said, trying to pull free of the tall man, "but the royal couple's difficulties with conception are well known. My order trusts Illienne the Light Eternal will bless them with a child, and ensure the bloodline of High Kings remains intact. It is a matter of faith."

"Perhaps. But what is not so well known is the effect this has had on the High King. Alas, he's gone quite mad."

Bale had heard hints of this in recent years. The High King was approaching fifty and there was growing concern he would not be able to sire an heir. "His tragedies would weigh upon any man."

"But this is not *any* man, Acolyte. This is Rune's High King, the most powerful man in all the world. Your order proclaims that this man is possessed of divinity, the great blessing of Illienne. Think what would happen if our enemies knew High King Deragol had been reduced to a blubbering fool. Already some of the thanes raise questions they wouldn't have dared in previous years." He drew closer, painfully so. "These are the most dangerous of times, Acolyte. Our enemies are bold and numerous, and present both without and within our land. Perhaps even within these very walls."

"You have my word, Chamberlain. The Sanctum will do everything we can to help. I should summon my superiors. They should meet with the High King to see if this illness can be cured."

Chamberlain Alamis's eyes narrowed. "No. You will not. Between his bouts of blathering, the High King has decreed he wants nothing to do with the Sanctum. I am sure this is simply a tragic consequence of his state, but for the time being his wishes must be honored lest he succumb to greater madness."

Bale did not reply, instead shifting his eyes about to avoid the chamberlain's unnerving glare.

Alamis paused for a moment, then nodded. "Very well. You will relay these directives to your order. What he, and I, require of you and your superiors is *trust*, Acolyte. Trust when I speak, I speak for High King Deragol. Trust I serve him, and have his implicit authority. Trust me, and bring me word of any *hint* of treason. Trust, and do not question." He regarded Bale for an instant longer and then released his grip.

Bale rubbed his shoulder. "We live to serve. We would never betray the Crown."

Chamberlain Alamis resumed his march down the hall, his pace brisk. "Excellent. To the kitchens, then."

Bale followed, finding the thought of dealing with rats preferable to dealing with people.

The scullery maid seemed a simple woman, stoutly built, chubby faced, and dressed in the plain, hooded robes of palace servants. She seemed also an earnest sort, and her accent marked her as hailing from the coastal farms of the Waters of World's End, far to the north. Bale had read such folk were renowned for their forthrightness, although not their intelligence.

She seemed frightened, and in her melodic speech recounted arrhythmic taps on doors, unattended objects moving about the kitchen during late hours, and squeals and shrieks from the larder. She then fell silent and glared disapprovingly at Alamis.

Perhaps not the brilliant sort, but certainly a sound

judge of character. "There is more you'd like to discuss?" Bale ventured.

The scullery maid whispered a curse and gestured toward the chamberlain.

Bale turned to the chamberlain, who was returning the maid's glare with a bemused smile. "It would be best if you left us, Master Chamberlain. Discussions on the subject of possessions and demonic manifestations are most delicate in nature, and require the complete confidence of the witness. It seems this woman has more observations she can only discuss in private."

Alamis looked suspiciously at Bale, his pale eyes narrowing in seeming appraisal. "Very well," he said at last.

Bale noticed the scullery maid's eyes nervously follow the chamberlain as he glided across the steamy expanse of the kitchen. The chamberlain stopped and leaned against a sturdy table and began paring his nails with a small knife. He seemed sufficiently beyond earshot, so Bale urged the maid to continue.

She gripped his hand almost painfully. "There is more, spooker." She grimaced. "I'm sorry. I meant Acolyte. I mean no disrespect."

With a nod he urged her to continue.

"I don't confuse no rats for devils, sir," she said quickly. "I am no fool, and I know there is evil afoot in this place. I risk my life in doing this, but I could think of no other way to get word to you."

Bale shot a glance across the kitchen and his eyes were met by the chamberlain's sneer. Bale had only just met Chamberlain Alamis, but knew already he neither liked nor trusted him. His influence with the throne was well known, and if the High King were truly mad then the chamberlain was very likely running the castle, if not the whole of Rune. *To run afoul of this man would be most dangerous. Yet...* Something stirred within Bale, a bravery he'd rarely possessed. He breathed deeply and exhaled.

The maid pulled at his cloak, her eyes pleading. "Can you help me?" she asked.

Bale nodded, thinking of something his teacher, Lector Erlorn, had once told him: *"Character is doing what you don't want to do, for reasons you cannot avoid."* He held the woman's eyes for a moment. "I will keep your confidence, even at my peril," he said.

"I can't bear the weight of secrets," she whispered, pressing a piece of folded parchment into Bale's hands. "Especially dark ones."

Bale winked as he tucked the paper inside his robes. "Now," he said with a quick thump of his staff. He secretly produced the sprig of drimroot and squeezed it tightly, producing a great puff of pleasant-scented, white smoke. It was a simple trick, but a minor miracle to those unfamiliar with alchemy. "Let us dispel these wicked spirits!"

3
MURDER TO MAKE

KARNAG MAK RAGG squinted in the morning sunlight, flint-colored eyes surveying the vast valley of oaks and poplars draped with mist. The Ghostwood, at the southernmost edge of the kingdom of Rune, struck him as similar to the wind-bitten highlands of his youth. Both were hard countries, unforgiving and full of predators.

Like me.

He pressed himself upward to stand and shook fresh blood into brawny limbs. Morning meditations were a ritual common among his people, used to seek hidden truths or consult with ancestors long dead. Karnag was not given to such nonsense, but found the meditations stilled his restless mind. With his waking hours rife with violence, he needed what calm he could find.

"Awake at last, eh?" asked Drenj from the mouth of a small tent at the opposite end of the hilltop clearing. He was a Khaldisian from far to the south, his brown tunic sagging from his form to reveal olive skin covered in tattoos. "I was beginning to think you'd learned to sleep on your knees. Like a camel."

Karnag ignored the young man's remark and set about readying his weapons. He often grew weary of such prattle, borne by nerves or bravado and bearing no meaning. Such words were breaths wasted rather than saved for combat.

"Are you certain I can't lend you a knife?" the southerner said, dragging a whetstone down the length of his curved Khaldisian steel.

Karnag brushed aside the thick braids of his black hair and studied the weapons he'd laid on his bedroll, all agleam in the morning sun. Six daggers balanced for throwing. Two swords, one short for tight quarters and the other a long, two-handed blade for cleaving men apart. A hunting knife he'd used for gutting deer that fit neatly in his boot, and a blackjack for laying out a man without spilling blood. "I'm certain," he said.

"Do you figure on using *all* of those things in a fight?" asked Drenj.

"Careful, lad," said Tream, a dark-eyed thug with rotting teeth. "You're new to this company, and Karnag's not the sort to be trifled with. Least of all by a skinny whelp like you. He's a damned nasty killer, boy. Nastiest of them all."

The Khaldisian seemed undeterred. "Are they trinkets for decoration?"

Karnag scowled, his patience wearing. "They all have their purpose."

"You have only two hands, you know," said Drenj,

laughing overlong at his joke as though encouraging the others to join him.

"And you have but one mouth," Karnag said, "but you blather on as though you have ten. Perhaps my hands are as potent." He snatched a dagger and flung it hard and true. It cracked into the center support at the mouth of Drenj's tent, mere inches from the youth's head. The tent collapsed about him in turn.

The company of hired killers laughed heartily. Drenj cursed and yanked the linen away from his form, his kohl-lined eyes narrowing. "Are all of you northerners like this? Savage ingrates with thin skins and thick heads?"

Fencress Fallcrow, a raven-haired woman clad as ever in black, sauntered across the clearing. She was a hard lass, rough-featured and muscular, yet had a roguish charm with her sapphire eyes and biting wit. She stopped near Drenj and flipped a copper coin at him. "And are all of your kind painted like whores? I fear you make even me feel like a man, Drenj."

"Not much of a stretch, eh?" said Paddyn, a scrawny lad with grubby skin and a missing front tooth.

The company laughed again, all save Karnag.

Karnag slid his daggers into the sheaths sewn into the blood-red leather of his jerkin. He straightened and his countenance darkened. "Shut your mouths and saddle the horses," he said, sweeping his eyes across his four companions. "We have murder to make."

The old forest creaked and yawned, with veils of white moss swaying from the boughs like haunting wraiths. The thick canopy strangled away all but the brightest beams of sunlight, and narrow hunting trails twisted through the brush-choked floor in a maddening webwork. Distant beasts howled in the gloom.

Karnag vainly sought obvious hoof-prints amidst muck and brush, while Drenj found markers in the form of every bent blade of new grass and crushed spring clover. The young man located the tracks with ease, forcing Karnag to admit that, in spite of Drenj's mindless tongue, he was a skilled woodsman.

"How far away?" Tream asked, urging his chestnut mount close behind Karnag.

Ahead of them, Drenj looked upward and appeared to locate the sun through the heavy weave of trees. "We should manage to travel perhaps half again as fast as the Lector and his retinue. I'd wager we'll be upon them by nightfall."

Tream leaned forward in his saddle, as though he could spy the Lector and his companions in the distance. "Trample and torch their camp, eh?"

"No," said Karnag. "That would invite chaos. We'll gut the Lector in his sleep."

Tream looked at him wide-eyed. "The man is a member of the Sanctum, its Lector no less! They say in the Old Faith the Lector speaks the word of Illienne the Light Eternal, the very goddess who guides the kingdom of Rune from her grave!" Worry pinched his pimply brow. "It'd be better for us all if we didn't gut this man like an animal."

Karnag shook his head. Tream had a decent sword arm but his head was made of mush. "I'm sure people say all sorts of things about the Lector. And we've been hired to kill him. Do you think your soul would be spared if the man burned to death or if his brains were squeezed loose by your horse's hooves?"

Fencress chuckled behind them and Tream turned to give the black-garbed woman a hard look.

"Perhaps it would!" Tream chided. "I mean, if the Lector happened to catch fire, it wouldn't be *me* doing the killing."

Fencress giggled again. "Well, if you were to stab him," she said, humor dancing in her blue eyes, "it wouldn't be you doing the killing, either. You could blame it on your sword."

Karnag glared at them and in an instant they fell silent.

After a time Tream cleared his throat to speak, his eyes downcast. "This is no *ordinary* man we hunt, Karnag. I mean…" He paused and picked at his brown, pitted teeth. "I mean this is the sort of thing that could curse us, if you believe the Old Faith. Curse us forever."

Karnag stared at the man in silence. Tream stared back but his watery eyes quickly broke away. "We are hired killers," Karnag said, and no doubts quailed in his heart. "We were cursed the moment we first accepted coin to kill someone who'd done us no wrong. Accept your path. Revel in it."

Three days had passed since Karnag and his four hired killers had left the town of Raven's Roost, two days after the Lector. They'd ridden hard, for time was against them. "*You must slay him before he reaches the mountains,*" their patron had demanded. That gave them another two days'

ride before the Lector would reach the Southwalls, Rune's southern border. It was time enough to do it right. They traveled lean and needed none of the comforts required by a man of the Lector's pampered station. Signs of his passage were growing fresher, more obvious. The task's conclusion was becoming a certainty.

Near mid-morning they came upon the ruins of an ancient shrine in a clearing along the trail. Drenj's skills as a tracker proved infallible, and he discerned that the Lector and his entourage had paused at the shrine less than a day prior. The horses were lathered from their ride, so Karnag called for a respite.

The shrine was a mess of moss-covered stones, indistinguishable from the remains of any other ruin but for the unique construct. Karnag had seen its like before, and the markings of the Old Faith were known to him. Eight stone pillars in a round with a well at their center. It seemed a fine place to test the company's mettle.

Tream dismounted and spoke in a hushed tone. "This is an old shrine, from before the faith was rewritten. Eight pillars. One for the High King of Rune, and the others for the immortal Seven Sentinels. The well is for the Godswell, the place where the gods descended into oblivion." He approached one of the pillars and laid his hands upon it. "Reminds me of the rhyme my mum used to sing:

Illienne named eight on the eve of her death,
Rune's high king and seven more blessed,
Aspects of god each gifted in gloom,
And together cast Yrghul down to his doom,

The king's line reigned with the god's light grace,
Whilst seven stood watch to guard men's fate.

There were more rhymes, of course. But that one was my favorite. Always made me feel safe, somehow."

Karnag looped the reins of his steed about a branch then ambled through the jumble of stones to the well. He coughed once, twice, and again. Loudly. When he sensed the company's eyes upon him, he lowered his trousers and began to piss. Several heartbeats passed before the stream sounded its arrival at the well's depths.

Tream charged forward with arms outstretched, as though to snatch the piss in his hands. "Fool! You fool! That's a Godswell! This is holy ground!"

Karnag finished and turned to Tream, who stood with mouth agape.

"This," Tream said, breathless, "is holy ground."

Karnag slapped him hard across the cheek. With his other hand he snatched a knife from a scabbard stitched into his jerkin and pressed it against Tream's stubbly throat. "Then I piss on the dead gods," he growled.

Tream fell back and slammed against one of the pillars. "You cannot do this! This is a shrine to the Old Faith, from before it was corrupted and the Sentinels were banished! I can't allow this blasphemy!"

"Blasphemy? Against what? Against whom? I've disgraced holy ground. What is more, I've slaughtered hundreds—*hundreds!*—of men. I've killed women and children. I've set fire to homes with families barred inside. I've had people mutter prayers with my sword at their throats. Did the dead gods stay my hand? Even once? Did the dead gods strike me down? No. Your faith is nothing more than a sad way to endure the cruelty of life, to claim there is some divine 'plan' guiding things. There isn't. There is only you against everything else, and your reward for surviving is determined only by what you can take."

Tream blinked and looked skyward. "Dead gods forgive him!" he breathed. "Karnag, you cannot speak this way! Not here!"

Karnag shook his head and grabbed Tream by the shoulder. "I cannot trust you with this task, Tream. You're too weak. You've said these things here, yet you'd have me believe you'll stand by idly when I place my blade at the Lector's throat? Ha. We are murderers. If there are such things as gods, how could they abide villains such as we? Do you think it matters who we kill? Or how we kill them? Or," he laughed, "where we piss? We are wretched people, and if there are heavens above they will most certainly be shut to us. I set my own fate. If your faith tells you otherwise, then go home." He turned Tream about and shoved him toward the horses. "Be gone."

Tream stumbled several steps before turning to face Karnag. "My coin," he said, his eyes wet and pleading. "What of my share of the coin?"

Karnag measured the four in his company. He knew Tream wasn't the only of their number rotting with doubt. He'd seen Paddyn, their skinny archer, mumbling prayers when they'd caught sight of the ancient shrine, and the grimy lad averted his eyes now. Fencress Fallcrow, a cold-hearted assassin who'd never voiced any qualms about her dark work, kept a religious totem strung about her throat. *"I prefer my bets to be of the hedged variety,"* she'd once told Karnag. She was a good friend—perhaps Karnag's only—and could be trusted, but her heart certainly held some measure of doubt for this task. Drenj was newest to their company, but Khaldisians were said to think paying tribute to gods was naught but a waste of good coin.

"I need neither dissent nor hesitation," Karnag said, voice rising so to be heard by them all. "Any holding quarrels with our task should return to Raven's Roost. Such a person will have no ill feeling from me, and I'll gladly pay a third of their share upon my return. However, if you do remain, and your beliefs become a hindrance, you'll be the first person I slay after the Lector."

Drenj looked at him incredulously, waving his long-fingered hands wildly. Karnag leveled his eyes at him in hopes of silencing the protest, and the Khaldisian shut his mouth.

The others remained quiet. Karnag studied them each in turn. Even Fencress seemed pensive in that moment, twirling a strand of her black hair and looking askance. The whole of the company appeared to be waiting for someone to voice a decision.

"A third of his share," Karnag said.

"But Karnag!" It was Fencress, rising from her seat on a stone. Her thoughtful look had been replaced by a playful grin Karnag was pleased to see. "If I left I wouldn't get to kill anyone. Besides, think how dull this whole venture would be without my charm?"

"Death's dancing mistress!" cheered Paddyn, slapping his hands on trousers that ruffled like empty sacks on his thin legs.

Fencress offered a genteel curtsy, her arms moving in a flourish. "The very same."

The company laughed. It sounded as much like relief as good humor. Thereafter they resumed their casual banter. All but Tream, who kept to himself.

After a moment Tream turned about and strode toward the horses. He pulled himself astride his mare and turned the horse on the path, toward the way from which they'd come.

"I'm sorry, Karnag," Tream said. "I've fought at your side many times. But you're right. I can't do this." He looked away and rubbed at his eyes before continuing. "You're getting involved in things much bigger than us, and to be honest it scares me. My mum prayed every night to the goddess Illienne. My da called her crazy, and I may have a time or two as well. But I'm not about to wager my soul on the chance the woman was dead wrong."

They rode in silence the remainder of the morning. No one voiced questions about Tream's departure, and there were no questions about their task, either. Karnag hoped the matter was settled, and those who'd stayed could be counted upon.

The forest about them was dense and the oaks and poplars squeezed the trail. Maintaining their pace proved difficult. The horses slowed to pick their way through brush strewn across the path, and low-hanging limbs made the group leery of a gallop.

The pace seemed to make them more aware of their surroundings. They were jumpy, and Karnag noticed their hands straying to their blades with every crunch and crash in the forest. Even he started once when an owl alighted from a tree to snatch a rodent in its talons. Karnag cursed his nerves, reminding himself he was the predator, not the prey.

"A thousand silver crowns is a lot of coin," said Drenj, his voice jarring in the quiet.

Karnag turned to see the Khaldisian rubbing long fingers together. Karnag grinned, amused by the lad's avarice. He also found himself glad for once to have the distraction of small talk. "I'm not so sure we'll see any more than the four hundred we were paid in advance," he said. "You think I've ever offered to pay even a partial share to a man who didn't finish a job?"

Drenj cocked a black brow. "It had crossed my mind that you had lost yours. I was wrong for doubting you." He paused, his smooth face twisted in thought. "Do you really doubt we'll see the rest of the money?"

"It seems possible. Tream may be a dullard, but the man was right when he said we're in a mess bigger than ourselves. Things like that don't usually end as expected."

"You think we'll be swindled?"

Karnag shrugged his broad shoulders. "Perhaps worse. The Lector is a powerful man. Not the sort whose death will be treated lightly. There will be consequences. What's more, the man who retained us might not be the sort to trust us with the knowledge of this deed. He may want his secrecy preserved by knowing we guard it in our graves."

Drenj slumped in his saddle. "You're not planning on returning to Raven's Roost to try to collect, are you?"

"I may," said Karnag. "I may not."

The Khaldisian's face brightened. "Why not just run with the coin we've already been paid?"

Karnag hadn't considered that option. He was quiet for a moment, contemplative. He recalled his meeting with their patron, a thin man with a face hidden in the hood of his black robes. His voice had been that of a serpent. Karnag did not fear other men, but this one had unnerved him.

Drenj flailed his arms. "Why not run?" he asked, dark eyes pleading.

Karnag looked hard at the young Khaldisian, his gaze a reprimand, then settled back into his saddle. He fingered the hilts of his various blades and found comfort in them. Purpose.

"Four hundred crowns is a small fortune," Drenj said. "One hundred crowns a man. Enough almost for a dozen head of fine cattle. We could pocket the money without spilling a drop of blood. If you're certain our patron will double cross us, then why shouldn't we do this?"

Karnag drew his short sword from its scabbard and held it straight before him. He would drive this blade to the hilt through the Lector's belly while the man wept in agony. Perhaps the Lector was holy. Perhaps killing him would invite the wrath of the dead gods.

But therein resided the challenge, the allure, the glory. By killing the Lector, Karnag would prove his measure. He would kill to prove he *could*.

"Why shouldn't we?" Drenj's voice was frantic.

"Because I do not do these things for the coin."

Drenj shook his head dumbly. "It's the coin that justifies these abominable deeds. The coin feeds my family and buys me a better life. It gives me a reason. Without the reason there is only depravity."

"You sound even more the whore than you look."

Drenj's eyes snapped back to Karnag. "I daresay you are not a good man."

Karnag chuckled and spat. "Good? I do not quibble with my conscience, nor do I try to divine the whims of dead gods. My 'goodness,' if there is such a thing, is defined by my usefulness, my effectiveness. I am a slayer of men, and in that I endeavor to be the very best of all."

After midday they came upon the remnants of the Lector's next encampment, a swath of trampled ground in a clearing. Karnag counted eleven empty wine bottles, and the amount of discarded food was enough to feed several men. He smiled, thinking how soft these men were, how easy the task suddenly seemed.

He found the carcass of a roasted pheasant near a fire pit and shooed away the flies buzzing about it. "The Lector eats well," he said, picking a chunk of meat from the bones.

Paddyn scratched his short, sandy hair and squatted low to the ground. "Perhaps a dozen men," he said, his voice whistling through his missing tooth. "And at least as many horses. More than we thought."

"These are soft men, Paddyn," Karnag said through a mouthful of meat, "and no match for us. You need not fear."

Drenj inspected the fire pit. "The ashes are still wet. The Lector and his men got a late start, then lingered here for lunch. This fire was doused not long ago."

"We're close, then," said Paddyn, green eyes searching the forest about them.

"Aye," said Karnag, leaning back against a poplar and tossing away the bones of the pheasant. "We'll let the horses rest for a while. We'll wait and come at them in the night while they're sleeping off another feast."

"You're right, of course." Drenj said as he retrieved a discarded bottle and drained its contents. He looked at Karnag and smiled sheepishly. "Or we could run off with the advance we were paid."

"You know my answer to that. You're welcome to ride to Raven's Roost with Tream, where the two of you can wait for me to pay you a third of your share."

"I don't take it you'd come," said Drenj.

"Never."

Karnag lurked in the darkness, masking himself in the trees near the camp's perimeter. It was much as he'd expected. The Lector, a thin and ancient man draped in white robes, knelt close to a fire with hands knotted in prayer. His men bantered loudly, faces glazed with the grease of cooked meat and teeth stained by too much wine. Counting the Lector there were eleven in all.

Karnag turned to his company, making sure they'd not fled or strayed too close to the camp. Paddyn's gap-toothed grin shone in the dark, an expression Karnag reckoned was one of anxiety. "Keep your mouth shut," Karnag snapped. Paddyn shot him a puzzled look but complied.

The company had grown restless as they'd waited in the dark, their unease obvious. Karnag noticed Drenj's eyes wandering back to the direction of their horses, a few hundred feet away. Few truly relished the moment of the kill.

"We do this," Karnag growled.

He returned his attention to the firelight, studying the Lector and his party. The Lector seemed frail and unacquainted with the demands of travel. The man shivered in spite of the spring night's warmth and the heat of his fire. His robes were frayed and he bore bruises hinting at a spill from horseback. He sat with his eyes squeezed shut and his mouth moved in a murmur of prayer.

Beside him squatted a manservant, head cocked in constant regard of the Lector. Behind them were several dark-robed men with the reverent bearing of clerics, likely acolytes of the Ancient Sanctum. They seemed contemplative sorts, speaking infrequently as they read in the firelight or gazed at the night sky. They would prove no trouble in combat.

Five loudmouthed louts wore coin purses and rusty weapons on their belts. Karnag reckoned they were hired strongmen. They were big men, but unscarred and fat-handed. Tavern brawlers, enough to scare off brigands but little match for trained killers. Karnag thought it odd the Lector of the Sanctum would not travel with royal soldiers, but he wasted no thought on politics.

Finally, there was a square-jawed man far from the fire, a green cloak pulled tightly about him. He did not laugh at the men's jokes nor did he partake of the wine offered to him. Karnag detected the outline of a weapon beneath the cloak, and reckoned the man knew how to use it.

"Paddyn," he whispered, "if things go amiss, I want an arrow through that man's heart."

The young archer nodded firmly, making a decent show of steady nerves.

Karnag turned his eyes back to the camp. He fingered the hilts of his blades, each one in turn. His moment was coming.

Soon.

It was not long before the Lector retired to his tent. Shortly after, a rhythmic snoring sounded. The manservant slept on a bedroll adjacent to the tent, the clerics in their own tents, and the strongmen passed out around the fire. The cloaked man did not move.

"Is he standing watch?" Drenj whispered.

Karnag found a stone and flung it to the far side of the camp, producing a minor racket. The cloaked man's hand moved to his weapon and he turned his head. "He'll have to sleep at some point," Karnag said. "We'll wait."

Two hours passed. The campfire dimmed to a smolder. At last the cloaked man stood, but only to retrieve an armful of firewood from the clearing's far edge.

"When will he sleep?" Drenj said. "Should we rush him?"

Karnag shook his head. The thought had occurred to him, but the confusion certain to result was not likely to produce good results. Chaos, by definition, was the bearer of the unexpected, and any good killing required a plan.

More time passed. Karnag was reluctant to have his company position themselves, worried the cloaked man would detect their movements. Instead, they waited as the sliver of the moon crept across the sky.

Finally, the cloaked man arose again and strode toward the sleeping strongmen. He prodded one awake, and the big dullard grumbled as he staggered upright. The oaf grabbed a half-emptied bottle and plopped upon a fallen tree. The cloaked man disappeared in the darkness on the far side of the encampment. Karnag didn't like that he couldn't see the man, but then murder was rarely an easy thing.

Within minutes the strongman was swaying in his seat. Karnag motioned for Paddyn to move along the edge of the encampment to find a clear shot at the cloaked man. He gestured to Fencress to position herself at the opposite side of the camp. Drenj, however, was succumbing to sleep. "Stay here," Karnag said, figuring the Khaldisian was better asleep than half awake.

Karnag focused on the fire's dance. His heart slowed and his body stilled. His mind drifted, and he recalled the day in his youth when he was forced to flee his northern highlands. His father had dishonored their clan in battle. *"Coward,"* the chieftain had proclaimed, spitting on the funeral pyre as the body burned. His mother and sisters were raped and slaughtered, as was custom, and he and his brothers were cast from the highlands.

Karnag had defined himself that day. He would never suffer the same fate. He would become the deadliest slayer the world had ever known, and one day he would return for the chieftain's head.

Such thoughts calmed him.

He arose, ready. He counted his blades and refastened the straps of his jerkin and scabbards. He then set out, creeping around the encampment's perimeter and staying just beyond the yellow fingers of firelight.

He caught the eyes of Paddyn and Fencress in the gloom and nodded to them both. The three of them had worked together on many occasions and knew their business.

Karnag crept low to the ground, timing his footfalls with the rhythmic snores of the Lector. No one stirred. The camp was serene, the only movement that of the teetering guardsman on the fallen tree. Karnag noticed the lout still caressed a wine bottle in slackening hands. He knew he could not tarry, suspecting it was only a matter of moments before the bottle dropped and clattered on the ground.

At last he reached the rear of the Lector's tent. It was closed and tied down, presenting a triangular wall of linen. He withdrew the hunting knife from his boot and poked a hole at the level of his knee. He then worked the opening with his fingers, again timing the fabric's rip with the man's snoring. In time he'd formed an entrance.

He sank to the ground and pulled his torso into the shadows of the tent. There was the bald head of the Lector, the man on his back and snoring deeply. Karnag would sever the jugular and carve out most of the man's throat. It would prevent the Lector from calling out, but the body would convulse and blood would spray. There was a reasonable chance the nearby manservant would be awakened by the struggle, so he would need to be killed as well.

Karnag grabbed the Lector's dry scalp and held the head in place. The man slept soundly. He readied his blade and guided it to a point above the Lector's throat.

Just then there was a clamor. The strongman had dropped the bottle. A low groan followed as the lout oriented himself. "What?" A pause, then the sound of the oaf shuffling upright. Clumsy at first, but then the sound of urgency. "Who goes there?"

Someone had made a mistake. Karnag shook his head and plunged his blade deep into the Lector's gullet. He shoved the knife all the way through the spine, then pulled it across the width of the man's neck for good measure. The man jerked and quivered, and warm blood gushed from the wound. It was messier than Karnag would have liked, but there was no longer time to be neat.

Suddenly there came a rumble like the sound of a thunderhead, then a swift string of words. *"Necrista traellus a abridalusi Yrghul y ogo alliata,"* hissed a strange voice. *"Illienne cradus e Warduren renden e sallem orn argo apocha."*

Karnag blinked. The words had come from the Lector's lifeless form. And the man's lips had not moved.

Were these words spoken aloud, or whispered only in my head? How?

The manservant stirred. "Sleep…" the manservant grumbled. "Go back to sleep…"

"Wake up, boys!" came the bellow of the strongman. "It seems we've caught ourselves a bandit!"

Chaos. Precisely the thing Karnag always prepared against. He pressed the strange words from his mind and withdrew from the Lector's tent, into the dark.

A glance at the encampment revealed what had transpired. Drenj stood frozen in the firelight, arms laden with purses he'd swiped from the sleeping strongmen, and the strongmen were awake and encircling the Khaldisian. Karnag noticed Drenj's breeches were discolored. He'd pissed himself. Karnag cursed under his breath. The greedy lad must have figured he'd steal a few coins and run off, leaving Karnag and the rest to deal with the consequences.

In an instant Fencress was within the camp, darting amidst the strongmen like a flickering shadow with her twin blades drawn. There was the sound of steel on steel and the thrumming of Paddyn's bow. Then the manservant began screaming and there was commotion from where the clerics slept.

"Ah, hell," Karnag said, jerking his short sword free of its scabbard.

He moved toward the encampment but then glimpsed a swift movement to his right. He spun about to see the cloaked man facing him in a wide stance, blade poised overhead. *A genuine swordsman*, Karnag thought, a wicked smile crossing his face.

In the twenty-odd years since he'd left the highlands of his youth, Karnag had learned from many teachers. A Harkane blademaster, a guild assassin, a Scarlet Sword of Rune. None had taught him anything more valuable than his time as a slave forced to fight by his merchant master in the slums of Riverweave. The fight wasn't always won by the strongest or the quickest. Rather, the advantage was held by the first recognize the stakes. The first to know—to truly understand—the contest was to the *death*. To life's utter end, with no second chances.

Karnag roared as he charged, not a battle cry of the highlands but something more feral. The cloaked man shifted into a defensive posture, trying to protect life rather than take it.

At that moment Karnag knew the fight was won.

The cloaked man steadied his blade crossways before him, readying to parry a strike. Karnag obliged, swinging his short sword in a tight arc. With a clang he pinned the man's blade low. The man tried to slide free to his right, the side of his sword hand, just as Karnag expected. Karnag pulled loose a dagger with his free hand and punched it toward the man's gut as he tried to shift away.

Impossibly, the man forced aside the blow with the hilt of his blade, which now glowed with a faint greenish hue. The man jumped into the camp's clearing and moved his blade slowly before him. Fencress, Drenj and the two remaining strongmen struggled behind him, but the man's attention remained solely upon Karnag.

"You fool!" the man wailed. "Do you have any idea what you've done?"

Karnag's eyes darkened. He dropped his sword and his hands sought the long hilt of his two-handed blade, *Gravemaker*. This was a killing he would relish.

The man traced a circle with his steel. "So the enemy resorts to hiring common killers now? No matter. The Sentinels will receive the Lector's summons, and you and your vile ilk will not stop the vigilant."

The man screamed and rushed at Karnag, forcing him backward with a barrage of strikes with his blade. Karnag deflected the blows with swift movements of his sword, waiting to sense either a rhythm or the man's fatigue. His moment would come.

Karnag shoved the man forward with his weapon, trying to force him off balance. The man stumbled for an instant and Karnag thrust his sword at the man's chest. Again, though, the man moved with inhuman quickness, a green blur against the backdrop of the campfire. He recovered just in time to fend away the strike.

The man pressed again, redoubling his attack. He was strong and quick and Karnag's sinews burned. Karnag retreated a stride, toward the trees. A thought occurred to him just then, and he foresaw the fight's conclusion. He took another stride backward, placing himself just beside a stout tree.

The man struck with overhead sweeps of his weapon, shouting words without meaning. And then it happened, just as Karnag had anticipated. In his fury the man struck wide, his sword biting into the trunk of the tree.

Karnag grinned as the man wrestled with his weapon. He tightened his hands about the hilt and then swung *Gravemaker* in a deadly arc overhead. He caught the man's hip, the sword cleaving deep and severing the man's leg. The man cried out and collapsed at Karnag's feet. Karnag leered over him, watching as dark blood pooled on the ground.

The man choked as he fumbled with his mortal wound. He looked at Karnag with sad eyes. "Why?" He choked again, his face twisted with pain. He groped for his missing leg and his voice was measured as he settled into shock. "The Sentinels… They must be summoned…"

Karnag spat and looked at the man grimly. "Not by you, it seems."

The man choked back a sob. "Why do you do this? For the High King? For the Necrists?"

"No, lad. For a few hundred coins."

The man shuddered and sobbed. Karnag took a tall step over him and strode into the light of the campfire, *Gravemaker* before him.

There were a few who yet stood.

4

THE ABSURDITY OF HAVING HOPED

ZANDRACHUS BALE HUNCHED over a candlelit desk in the darkest corner of the Abbey's library, lost in thought. What had been requested of him was daunting, and he felt profoundly inadequate.

I am too weak an instrument.

He pulled a long strand of graying hair from his eyes and tucked it behind his ear. He folded the scullery maid's note into a tight, tiny triangle, as though he could make it disappear. Then he unfolded it, as though the words could change. He reckoned he'd done this a few dozen times, and the parchment frayed at the folds.

Repetition grants comfort to the troubled mind.

He rubbed away a dribble of snot from his overlarge nose and read the note again, slowly and deliberately. Not surprisingly, the message still read the same. He chuckled at the absurdity of having hoped it would be different, somehow.

"*The King is being poisoned. That's why he's gone mad, and why he's making no babies. He is in grave danger. Beware of the chamberlain. He speaks much with a man whose face is made of stitches.*"

He thought for a long moment on that last sentence. He'd studied in the library's darkest depths, and had read accounts of an ancient sect of necromancers loyal to Yrghul the Lord of Nightmares. Necrists, whose faces were said to be stitched together from the flesh of their sacrifices.

Could she have been referring to a Necrist?

Nonsense, he thought. The Sanctum's scholars held that the Necrists had been defeated long ago. They were now widely regarded to be as much myth as anything else, and the thought of one communing with Rune's chamberlain inside the very walls of Ironmoor was ridiculous.

The woman's likely cracked in the head.

Nevertheless, Bale admired the scullery maid's pluck. She'd risked her life in delivering the note, and under the very nose of Chamberlain Alamis! Bale knew he could never have been so courageous. He held a deep dislike for the chamberlain—he disliked most if not all people—but to act so directly against the man required something wholly more, something he simply lacked.

Bale reckoned the woman's courage deserved to be rewarded, somehow, and he thought of taking the note to his superiors. But then he thought of Prefect Kreer laughing nasally in his face, and knew he'd be best served to gather more compelling evidence before taking things further.

But must I do that? To protect the High King?

The Faith instructed that the line of the High King of Rune was sacred and the Sanctum was bound to protect it. Bale was a skeptic when it came to most things. He would never place his trust in people, and he knew people—people in power most of all—were given to twisting the truth to serve their own ends.

He did, however, believe in such things as goodness and righteousness. He knew implicitly there were truths greater than the truths of men, and it was only in the pursuit of such truths that the betterment of men could be found.

He believed also in Illienne the Light Eternal, or at least in the *idea* of her. He believed in the notion of eternal goodness, and believed there was something of her that survived her descent into oblivion a millennium before. Not necessarily a power or an influence, but an ideal that inspired the hearts of men in their darkest hours. Not many folk believed such notions, but Bale *knew* them to be true.

The Faith held that Illienne blessed the first High King of Rune, Deranthol, and the Kingdom's seven greatest heroes—known now as the Sentinels—with measures of her divinity. It was through this blessing the dark god Yrghul, Lord of Nightmares, was deceived and drawn into oblivion with Illienne. Doctrine taught that the Godswell, a place deep within the Bastion, was the site of that descent, and that the High Kings were blessed with the unique power to touch that place, to guard over it. The High Kings were blessed to rule by Illienne herself, and the Sanctum was bound to serve the royal line as a result.

Bale questioned many precepts of the Faith, and this was one. He reckoned he'd spent years digging about the library, satisfying one curiosity or another. He'd read countless histories, certainly enough to know that many of the men who'd sat upon Rune's throne were despicable creatures, utterly lacking any touch of goodness, much less godliness. Some old scrolls told that High King Derthane cast his second-born son from the Tower of Lords when the boy proved too sickly for his liking. A few ancient scholars mentioned that High King Derreft shared a bed with his own mother until she'd died at the ripe old age of sixty-seven, then for six weeks after that. A largely redacted document from the Magistrate Examiner mentioned that High King Derashtor was suspected in the murders of dozens of prostitutes.

These are the men I should be compelled to protect?

The *accepted* histories held that the Seven Sentinels lusted for power and tried to usurp High King Derganfel the Purer, many hundreds of years ago. But Bale had read older, more credible accounts holding that it was the High King who grew mad with jealousy, and thus decided to banish the Sentinels rather than share his power. Bale tended to believe the latter.

As he contemplated these things, Bale wondered whether Rune truly would suffer if the High King died without an heir. He wondered whether the alternatives to the High King's line would prove any more depraved, any more bereft of righteousness. The chamberlain had a slippery feel to him, certainly, but would Rune truly be condemned with his rump polishing the throne?

Bale read the note once more. He examined the clumsy, almost childlike script of the scullery maid. Though she'd seemed an earnest sort, Bale reminded himself she was likely a simpleton whose position granted her only a sliver of understanding when it came to the goings-on within the Bastion's walls. A word misheard or a statement taken out of context would certainly cause all sorts of unfounded speculation.

He again folded the parchment into a tiny triangle and tucked it into one of the pockets lining his robes. *Is any of this worth the danger it would entail?* He sat for a long moment and then puffed out the sputtering candle on his desk.

Likely not.

It was a pleasant afternoon, the rare sort to compel Bale to wander outside without any real reason to do so. He found his walking staff and a book, *Arythail's Poetics*. Not the sort of study in which he typically indulged, but he was in need of distraction.

The Abbey's courtyard garden was a tranquil enclosure of flowering trees, pleasant-scented herbs and exotic plants, and secluded benches. A few robed acolytes sat or strolled in silence. Speaking was forbidden here. There came only the sounds of birds warbling, a breeze rustling amidst the trees, and the distant, muffled discord of the city beyond the Abbey's walls.

Bale settled on a stone bench in the shade of a white-bloomed dogwood and withdrew his book. It was a worn volume of indeterminable age, an antique which had squatted in the library's recesses for perhaps hundreds of years. Bale wondered how many hands had caressed its leather, how many dead acolytes had cracked its spine. He held the tome in the crook of his arm and savored the musty odor wafting from its brittle pages.

After reading through a few poems he concluded he enjoyed the feel of the physical volume far more than its contents. He was no student of verse, but it seemed to him that Arythail was given to forced rhymes and trite imagery.

He began turning the pages more rapidly, perusing titles and opening verses rather than digesting the poems whole. After a time he admitted that, in spite of its quaintness, Arythail's poetry was impressive for the sheer breadth of its subject matter. The poet mused on love and hate, charity and vengeance, and the travails of both paupers and kings. There were verses of pure fancy, and others recounting the events of history with surprising insight. One, *A Dirge for Erkelon*, caught his eye. He read it through, down to its final stanzas:

The beasts besiege with hearts of black
Whilst tears wander a well-worn track
Set by the smiles of long ago.

"If" calls the herald of remorse
Never daring a righteous course
From tower's height he falls to death below.

He'd read of Erkelon, the last lord of the Gray Gates. It was said he'd permitted the hordes of Yrghul to pass through the Southwall Mountains in the War of Fates, a thousand years before. Although Erkelon knew the cause of Illienne to be righteous, he wavered, fearing much the retribution that would come from the Lord of Nightmares. He allowed Yrghul's men to march unchallenged through the mountain passes. Once through they sacked Erkelon's fortress and slaughtered its people. Erkelon, overcome with grief, leapt to his death as his fortress burned.

Bale closed the tome slowly and rested his hands upon its worn cover. *Is such the fate of those who abide the advance of evil?*

He sat, contemplating. After a time he stood and smoothed his robes, only to catch his hand against the outline of the folded parchment tucked within them.

Not the distraction I needed.

He straightened his weary back and withdrew into the shadows of the Abbey.

5
BETTER THAN DEATH

LANNICK RECKONED HE'D been in places far worse. The cell seemed only half as filthy as his quarters, the room's arrow-loop window permitted a picturesque view of Ironmoor's bustling harbor, and prison food was a sight better than rumored. *At the very least, it's better than death.*

In the two weeks he'd been in the brig, his wounds had mended some. The shivering sweats he'd endured in the first week had also dissipated, although Lannick still craved a drink more than the air he breathed. He'd begged the guards for a cup of wine or even a flask of rotgut, but was rebuffed nicely the first time and not so nicely the second. He hadn't yet mustered the courage for a third request, worried as he was they'd make worse the pain that still lingered in his ribs from General Fane's boot.

Despite denying him libations, the soldiers were positively gentlemanly as far as prison guards were concerned. Lannick supposed it had something to do with the place being a military prison. He figured his captors were of the mind that the inmates they held were a more civilized lot than the murderers and cutpurses rotting in a common jail. His chest swelled a bit at the notion, but then upon further thought he chuckled and winced.

He sat at the edge of his bed, eying the door for a long, nervous moment. Morning was the least pleasant thing about the place. He awoke every day with a cold pit in his guts, certain the day would be his last. However, General Fane had yet to pay a visit, as had his Scarlet Swords. He'd heard the guards mumble that the situation with Arranan was not going well, which Lannick trusted was keeping the general and his brutes occupied. His sense of dread had diminished slightly with every new morning's sunrise, and he was almost beginning to allow himself to hope.

Perhaps I will survive even this.

This day seemed a particularly fine one. Lannick arose and pressed his face against the arrow-loop to catch the sun's warmth. To the east, half a league distant, a myriad of colorful, broad-sailed ships filled the harbor's blue waters. Trading ships from every corner of the world. He sighed wistfully, remembering his plan to escape Ironmoor aboard such a vessel. He imagined he'd be drunk on sailor's rum about now, swaying gently in a hammock below deck.

As he surveyed the harbor he counted a number of military vessels, sails emblazoned with the gold dragon of Rune. Most were moored to the docks, met by lines of red-sashed soldiers. Indeed, he noticed the docks swarmed with soldiers, thousands of them, hastily making their way aboard the ships. Even confined in his cell, Lannick envied them not at all. He'd seen quite enough of war.

A knock shook the cell's thick door, and a shallow bowl of boiled oats skittered beneath. Lannick called out, and an instant later a pockmarked face filled the door's barred portal. "You'd better not be asking me for that whiskey again," the guard said.

"Why of course not, good Horus," Lannick replied, as though the accusation were utterly ridiculous. "Just an honest question, soldier to soldier." He'd noticed that Horus, though humpbacked and lazy-eyed, relished any implication that he was a fighting man rather than a prison attendant. "Why all of the commotion on the docks? It looks like an entire Column is setting sail. Will you be disembarking as well?"

Horus seemed perplexed by the question, and it took him a moment to straighten up and fix his good eye on Lannick. "Well, no. They don't need me. Not just yet, anyways. But some of the thanes aren't answering the call to war, so I guess you never know…"

"Some of the thanes?"

"Brandiss the Thane of Stormfall, for one. There's talk he won't commit his oath-bound. Claims he's under threat of invasion from those sheep-herding highlanders and won't risk it. And there's others, too. Thane Meledin of Farwatch won't send a single soul to the front, saying he fears an incursion from the sea. And—"

"The Sea Lord himself?" said Lannick, mostly to himself. He was surprised to hear Thane Meledin, such an old friend of the High King, would withhold his support of the Crown in wartime. Lannick's head hadn't swirled with politics in years and he wondered how much things had changed while he'd been slumped over a bar. "Well, if you're called to war, Horus, you'll have to regale me with stories of your heroics when you return. Some grand tales those will be, I'm certain."

Horus grinned slightly, his good eye glazing over momentarily. "Yes. Yes, you're probably right."

"So it's really war, then? Looks like a lot of men moving about."

Horus glanced back and forth, making like he was scanning the hall for eavesdroppers. "Word is things aren't faring well. Not well at all. We took custody of a man last evening. Said the Arranese killed the commander of the Gray Gates and sent his head right to Riverweave. What's more, they've slaughtered nearly every garrison in the Southwalls and are crossing the mountain passes, if he's to be believed. General Fane's ordered the whole Third Column to Riverweave. He hopes to crush the invasion before the Arranese can head north, but there's many men who're certain to die before he gets there."

"Well, let us both hope our dear general is triumphant. I'd pity the Spider King of Arranan if the general saw need to unleash your fury."

Horus grinned again, and he cupped the side of his mouth as though to shield his words from others. "We keep a stash of wine and some harder stuff in the mess. If you can promise me it's just between us, I'll bring you a bottle."

Lannick belched loudly. It was the sort of long, guttural belch that could only be summoned from a fully sated belly. Horus had exceeded his promises admirably. Half a well-seasoned, roasted chicken and a wedge of sharp cheese. The meal paired well with the bottle of spiced Khaldisian wine Horus had brought. Uncorked, even! Lannick had guzzled the first half, but intended a more leisurely conquest of the rest.

The reminders of his confinement were everywhere, yet the wine liberated him. Dark thoughts vanished, the pain of his wounds was readily ignored, and his straw-filled cot seemed an indulgence of comfort. He hummed an old traveler's tune, gesturing with his bottle at the song's lulls and crescendos.

For the first moment in days his head wasn't haunted by ghosts of regret. Thoughts of his "old life"—as he'd come to think of it—were suddenly less painful, and the dark void in his heart felt momentarily filled.

Lannick thought of laughter. His children's laughter. He thought of snatching his oldest boy and flinging him upward, of the boy's wide grin as he did so. He thought of the chuckles of his infant twins as he pranced clumsily about before them, arms waving as he pretended to be some great sea serpent threatening them with tickles. Of his beautiful wife watching it all with an admonishing smirk on her face, telling him he was being silly.

Lannick's hand drifted to the locket about his neck and he smiled. This feeling was fleeting, he knew. Eventually the thoughts of his family would turn to the harrowing image of finding them murdered and mutilated, and his chest would tremble with heartache.

But for this moment, he heard laughter.

Three-quarters through the bottle of wine Lannick's stomach lurched and groaned loudly. He'd subsisted on prison gruel for two full weeks, and reckoned his innards were not ready for the sudden digestion of rich cheese, roasted meat and potent wine. Another groan and an uncomfortable swell in his buttocks sent him rushing to the foul-smelling bucket in the room's darkest corner. Just as he perched himself astride the bucket, his door rattled with knocking.

My wine! His eyes darted to the foot of his cot, where sat the bottle in clear view of the door. He cursed his stupidity, knowing the wine would be seized as contraband and his arrangement with Horus would come to an abrupt end.

"Prisoner!" said a gruff voice. Lannick couldn't see through the door's portal from this angle, but knew the guard was not Horus.

"I'm, um, indisposed here," Lannick said loudly, hoping to pull the guard's attention to this side of the cell. "Could you grant me just a few moments? I'm worried this is going to be something most foul."

"Indisposed?" asked the faceless voice. "What kind of smart talk is that? This had better be no kind of trickery."

"No trickery, sir. It means I'm taking a crap."

"Oh. Right. Indisposed, of course. I'll leave you to yourself then, for a short bit anyways."

"Thank you," Lannick said, and he meant it. He would have enough time to finish his precious wine. He sighed and finished his task on the bucket.

There came a shuffle from outside his door. "And prisoner?" said the guard. "You'll be wanting to clean yourself up something nice. You have a visitor."

Fane. Alas, all good things must meet their end.

The guard shackled Lannick's hands and led him from his cell. Lannick's eyes were wide as he walked, as much with curiosity as fear. It was his first real chance to take full account of his confinement. When he was thrown in his cell two weeks prior, his eyes had been swollen and crusted with blood so he hadn't seen much of anything then.

He realized he hadn't missed much, as the brig had seemed a better place from the inside his cell than from without. Dark passageways, sputtering torches, and every manner of rank odor and agonized cry. It was frightening and disheartening, a place of torment and terror. A pained howl sounded from a cell beside him, a shriek that hardly seemed human. Lannick shivered and reckoned that if breaking the spirit was the place's purpose, it was most certainly suited to accomplish it.

The guards, too, lent a burden to the place. They were soldiers suffering from disabilities, lamed by combat or otherwise, doubtless deemed liabilities on the battlefield. The guard before him dragged his left foot as he walked, and had but two fingers on his right hand. The other guards they passed wore cruel stares, seeming as much prisoners as jailers themselves.

Lannick cleared his throat. "Excuse me, sir. Might I inquire as to the identity of my visitor?"

The guard grunted. "I don't know. I was told to fetch you. I was also told to do it right quick, so I figure it's somebody important." He turned his thick head and eyeballed Lannick. "You'd best hope the time you wasted shitting causes no trouble for me."

"I thank you again for your kindness, sir." This guard seemed to possess nothing of Horus's good nature.

Nevertheless, Lannick reckoned he'd best be courteous to the man, as he certainly felt no desire for another beating. *Not before General Fane has his turn, anyway.*

The passageway gradually widened and windows to the outside world broke the monotony of the stone walls and heavy doors. They passed a hearth room and a large mess area, and Lannick guessed some prisoners were regarded as less threatening than others. A knot of inmates crowded about a mess table, laughing heartily as they bantered with a guardsman. It sounded almost like casual talk amongst free men.

"Captain?" shouted someone from the mess table. "Captain Lannick?"

Lannick turned suddenly to see one of the men waving wildly. He felt a flush of shame color his cheeks. He cast his head down and pretended not to hear the man.

"It *is* you!" the man said. "Boys! That there is Captain Lannick deVeers! The hero of Pryam's Bay! The Scourge of Tallorrath, we called him! The High King himself declared him a Protector of Ironmoor. Isn't that right, Captain?"

Lannick kept moving, hoping the guard would do the same. He did, much to Lannick's relief. Soon they were out of the mess hall.

The guard turned again to regard Lannick. "That you? A captain?"

"No."

Not anymore.

"Your visitor's in that room," the guard said, gesturing to the door.

Lannick felt his guts wrench. He'd known this would

come from the moment Fane leered over him two weeks before, the man's grotesque face stretched to a sick grin. Lannick's tongue felt suddenly thick in his mouth and the remaining taste of wine sickened him like poison.

The guard eyed Lannick with a crooked brow and beady eyes. "No tricky stuff," he said. "No taking anything from anybody, and don't even dream of getting out of here. I'll be waiting just outside, and I'll be watching. I'm fully prepared to run you clean through if you get any grand ideas."

"You needn't worry about that. I suspect my visitor will dispose of me long before you have the chance."

The guard snorted. "Save your clever talk for your visitor." He pressed the door open with one hand and yanked Lannick by his shackles with the other.

Lannick stumbled inside the small room. It was brightly lit by a large window of stained glass at its opposite end, and his eyes struggled in the light. A dark figure sat at a solitary table in the room's center.

My end awaits.

Lannick felt a hand pressing him, forcing him into a chair opposite the figure. "Sit down, prisoner," said the guard.

His eyes adjusted after a moment, and he realized his visitor was not General Fane. Not at all.

A woman sat tranquilly at the table, her hands folded before her. Although not classically beautiful, the sight of any woman, at this moment, was nearly enough to make Lannick swoon. Her dark hair was cut short, in a practical fashion. She wore simple clothes of earthy colors, all greens and browns. Lannick was mystified.

She smirked and arched her brow over eyes of warm brown. "You don't recognize me, do you?"

Lannick squinted at the woman as he fumbled through his memories. Did she have him confused with someone? She was utterly, completely unfamiliar. "Of course I do. How ever have you been?"

"Well, ever since our little encounter two weeks ago, I've found my life to be rather hectic."

Encounter? Damn my wine-soaked head! "Uh, I'm terribly sorry. How can I help?"

Her smile broadened. "You've already helped quite enough, thank you. We met two weeks ago, that night. You *do* remember my name, of course?"

Lannick's jaw dropped as the gearwheels of his mind finally clicked into place. She was the friend. The friend of General Fane's daughter. *Of course! But did she ever give me her name?*

"Alisa," she said with a knowing look. "And you are Lannick. I realize you were somewhat altered during our last encounter."

Lannick grinned despite the awkwardness of the situation. Even though he'd been completely drunk that night, certain images had proven indelible. Rare was the man who could lay claim to such romancing such a beauty. "Yes, of course."

She regarded him seriously. "'Yes' you remember my name, or 'yes' you were altered?"

Lannick's grin vanished and he placed his head in his hands. "I'm sorry," he said. "I haven't been quite myself since we last met."

"Worry not." She reached across the table and pulled

his hand close to her. Her voice dropped to a whisper. "Your captors will not permit us much time, so I need to get straight to the heart of things. I saw something that night, Lannick. Something that has drawn me here."

Lannick's eyes nearly crossed as he listened, for he had no idea what she meant. *Is this woman mad? Has she come to court my affections again?*

With her free hand Alisa pulled Lannick's loose sleeve upward. Slowly it peeled back, until his mark was revealed. The watchtower and the elder word "*Variden*."

"The Vigilant Ones," Alisa whispered.

Lannick's eyes widened. He tried to pull his arm away but she held him fast. When she finally released him he snatched his arm back as though it'd caught fire.

"We toil each of us in secret," she said, "but we are never alone. The Vigilant ever stand guard."

"What?" Lannick asked, dumbfounded.

Alisa undid a button on her sleeve and pulled the cloth back to the crease of her elbow. About her wrist was a bracelet of heavy black iron which Lannick recognized as a Coda, the sacred instrument of the Variden order. And further up, upon her forearm, was emblazoned the same watchtower emblem. She sighed softly, then rejoined Lannick's stare. Her brown eyes seemed to blaze. "The spirit of Valis moves within all the Variden, Lannick. It must have been the will of that spirit that caused me to choose you that night. I will return to save you."

6

THERE IS POETRY

"BLOODY WORK THAT was," Fencress said. She was the only one who'd spoken freely with Karnag since they'd murdered the Lector and his company. Drenj seemed ashamed of the mess he'd made of things, and Paddyn's stare hadn't left the ground.

"Aye," Karnag said. "Murder usually is."

Fencress grinned, her blue eyes dancing in the shadows of the black cowl she often wore. "I think when you kill that many men, it becomes something other than murder. But *what*, precisely? Assassination strikes me as implying the killing of just one man. So does execution. Slaughter sounds like we've just gutted pigs or cows or some such farm animals, and I don't fancy the ring of it."

"What about killing?" ventured Drenj.

"Too common," said Fencress, waving her hand as though shooing a fly. "Too broad. Too… clumsy. I like to believe there is poetry in our work, and it is just a matter of giving it voice. What say you, Karnag? After all, it was you who did the very most of it."

Karnag liked Fencress, but more for her skill with a blade than for the prattle of her tongue. "I'll leave the poetry to you."

They rode on in silence. The forested path seemed less taxing now that their task was done. Karnag found himself enjoying the warmth of the afternoon sunlight filtering through the canopy above them. He was breathing easier, and his restless thoughts had given way to a calm satisfaction.

As he'd anticipated, they'd not suffered the wrath of dead gods, the skies had not shaken, and the Lector had bled like any other man. There were those words he'd heard from the Lector, but aside from the strangeness of their utterance there'd been no terrible consequences.

Drenj cleared his throat behind them. "Maybe massacre?"

Fencress breathed sharply and then paused for a moment, as though she'd forgotten the earlier discussion. She turned about in her saddle and clapped her gloved hands. "Quite well done, Khaldisian. *Quite* well done. It was, indeed, a massacre. A *massacre*!" She slapped her knee as though struck by an epiphany. "You see, Karnag? There is poetry."

That evening they found a clearing atop a low rise and made camp. Agreeing a modest feast was in order, they sorted through the stash of wine and foodstuffs they'd found in the Lector's traveling crates. Paddyn managed to down a wild pig, and after gutting it they roasted it with onions over their fire.

Paddyn made most of the preparations, going about his work quietly and alone. Of all the company that remained, Karnag reckoned the young bowman was most affected by the events of the previous night. He was a rough-looking lad but just barely old enough to be called a man, and Karnag guessed he'd fallen into this business only through the worst kind of desperation.

"What ever are you doing, my friend?" Fencress shouted to Paddyn.

The lean bowman froze, holding a wine bottle over the spit to allow the liquid to drizzle on the pig. "Marinating."

"Urinating?" exclaimed Drenj, waving his hands and starting toward the pig. "On my supper? You northerners are as barbaric as the spice merchants claim!"

"No," Paddyn said with a gap-toothed grin and a welcome show of humor. "Marinating. With the wine. Flavoring the meat, is all."

"You're a fool nonetheless, boy!" Fencress shouted, rattling an empty bottle. "The dead don't drink. The libations should be saved for the living!"

Paddyn's smile broadened and he poured the wine liberally over the carcass.

The pig was done just before nightfall. They sat circled about the fire and ate as quickly as their jaws would allow. It was the best meal Karnag had tasted in weeks, perhaps longer, and the pork was tender and delicious, much better than the salted meat and molded cheese he'd eaten in the saddle.

Once the pig was picked clean the company settled back and spoke in carefree tones. Their anxieties over killing the Lector and his men seemed to subside.

"So, Karnag," said Fencress, "what was it like? Killing the Lector I mean. He has to have been one of the greater names to have perished at your hands."

Karnag shrugged. "The same as any other. He bled and fell still." He'd not mentioned the strange words to the company, and reckoned he never would. Even now he wondered if the sound had been real or imagined.

"Poetry, indeed," Fencress said mockingly. "I always knew you were much more than a mere murderer."

The talk soon drifted to money, as it often did. Karnag listened as the killers spent money they'd not yet been paid. It was a source of distraction, so he didn't bother to interrupt.

"I'll start with a new set of clothes," said Fencress, fingering her cowl. "Perhaps something ladylike for once."

"Oh yeah?" Paddyn said, stoking the fire with a bent stick. "I'm hiring a big, fat whore. The kind capable of burying me in her gigantic tits." He made a burbling sound and shook his head to and fro.

Fencress feigned offense with a hand over her mouth. "You speak of such things in front of *me*?"

"Maybe I won't when you look all ladylike," said Paddyn. "But then I might try a go with you when you do."

Fencress smiled but her hands fell to her twin swords. "Those who've tried that have lost their cocks or their lives, and sometimes both. Which will you lose?"

Karnag grunted and spat. "Enough. There'll be plenty of ways to spend your coin in Raven's Roost."

Drenj looked up from the fire, wiping his hands on his breeches. "We're heading there, then?"

Karnag picked a piece of meat from his teeth. "Aye."

"But you said you hadn't decided," said Drenj. "You said you thought we'd be cheated, or worse."

Karnag eyed the Khaldisian squarely. "If we'd cut but one man I might be happy with the four hundred crowns we were tendered in advance. But thanks to the greed and stupidity of one of our number, we slaughtered eleven."

Fencress cleared her throat. "Massacred, you mean."

Drenj laughed loudly, seeming to desire a shift in subject and tone. Karnag, though, would not suffer it. "We should have left you to deal with that mess by yourself, Khaldisian. We should have watched as those brutes carved you to pieces."

Drenj lowered his head. "I am sorry, to all of you. I drifted asleep. When I awoke the three of you were nowhere to be seen. I didn't know whether you'd slain the Lector and left me. I saw those men sleeping and thought it would be an easy robbery."

Karnag spat again into the fire. "I haven't given you your share of the coin yet. I may find need to alter the terms of our bargain."

Drenj stiffened, his dark-lined eyes narrowing. He said not a word for the balance of the evening.

Karnag's night was fitful. Any sense of calm abandoned him, and he jumped with every crunch of brush and groan of tree limbs. His hand frequently found the hilt of his short sword, and at last he decided to bring it into his bedroll to clutch it as he tried to sleep. He cursed his nerves as a weakness, and resolved to be their master. He breathed hard and squeezed his eyes shut.

Eventually sleep found him, but it was a restless sort haunted by horrors. A frantic, hissed phrase echoed incessantly through the depths of his dreams. *"Necrista traellus a abridalusi Yrghul y ogo alliata. Illienne cradus e Warduren renden e sallem orn argo apocha."*

He awoke with a start and could hear the phrase still. They were the Lector's undead words, he knew. Although he felt he'd barely heard them when they were first spoken through unmoving lips, they were emblazoned upon his mind. He knew not their meaning, but knew they would never be forgotten.

He sought to summon his earlier bravado, closing his eyes and focusing on the memory of driving his steel into the Lector's throat. He would not be troubled by the fears of faith. He resolved that the memory of that night would not be feared, but embraced. He was the Lector's slayer, his conqueror.

After a time he opened his eyes to the sight of a sky filled with stars. He gripped the hilt of his sword, and felt the disquiet leaving him. He sensed the blade understood him, for he shared its purpose.

He turned in his bedroll to face the dying embers of the fire, following the drifts of short-lived sparks and moonlit smoke. He looked upon the glow for a time and thought of himself as the fire, that which consumed all else. In that, he found comfort.

At dawn they awoke to the thunder of hooves. Karnag scrambled from his bedroll and grabbed his short sword. He stood, trying to make sense of the commotion. He saw the blurred shapes of several riders in succession as they raced down the trail toward Raven's Roost.

He noticed their own horses were spooked, wheeling wildly and nearly breaking free of their reins. He found Paddyn and gestured for him to tend to the horses, then he slipped through the trees to the path.

The riders who'd passed were already well distant, but from their dress they appeared to be ordinary folk, not bandits or fighting men.

"They must be in quite the hurry," said Fencress, emerging from the trees to stand near Karnag. "Didn't even stop to say hello. How *utterly* rude."

Shouts sounded from the opposite direction of the trail. Karnag turned about and within moments caught sight of several more riders charging hard along the path.

"Off the road!" the lead rider screamed as he approached. He was an older man in rough-hewn clothes, pots and pans strapped to his pack and clanking as he rode. Behind him came a brown-robed woman on horseback, and behind her a boy a few years shy of manhood.

"What madness is this?" Karnag shouted as they passed.

The older man did not voice a reply, instead making a shooing motion with his hand. The woman, too, ignored them. The boy looked at them with eyes wide, but did not slow.

"Why do you flee?" Karnag screamed after him.

The boy twisted his head once he was beyond them. "The Arranese! They're coming across the Southwalls!"

Karnag and Fencress watched until the riders faded from sight and then withdrew from the road.

"War," said Fencress, "can be a most profitable thing for people with our talents."

Karnag nodded. "We'd best reach Raven's Roost before the Arranese put their torches to the place. We'll take what's owed us and then plan things from there."

They set out immediately after seeing the riders, but progress on the trail came slowly. There was every manner of obstacle and setback, including a downed tree and a flooded creek. Worst of all, an illness had spread among the horses. By mid-morning the horses moved clumsily on trembling legs, and the company grew wary of the beasts stumbling.

"This is not a good omen," Paddyn said, the dread returning to his face. "It is said the dead gods can punish in such ways."

Karnag threw down the reins of his steed and gave Paddyn a fierce look. "The only punishment you need fear is mine, boy. Any talk of dead gods and magical curses and other such nonsense left this company the moment Tream did."

Paddyn averted his gaze and did not reply.

They resumed their slog down the trail but their efforts did not last long. The horses became lathered with sweat and grew skittish. They were getting worse.

Soon the horses refused water and wouldn't respond to commands. Paddyn tried draping a blanket over his mount, but the horse shook it off and in doing so knocked the young man into a tree. The company dismounted.

"These beasts will not live out the day," Drenj said, holding his horse by the bit of its bridle and inspecting its mouth. "I've seen this sickness before."

Karnag regarded his own horse, noticing a reddish mucus dripping from its muzzle and crusting its panicked eyes. The Khaldisian spoke truth.

"We should give them a rest, some clean water," Fencress said. "We can't be sure they'll die."

"Perhaps," said Drenj. "But the late stages of this sickness are not kind to these animals."

"Grab what items you can carry," said Karnag. "I'm slaughtering these beasts." He stripped his horse of its baggage and pulled *Gravemaker* from its scabbard.

He set about dispatching the horses in turn while the others looked on grimly. The animals slobbered and shook as they died, and the last, Paddyn's dappled mare, jumped wildly as Karnag approached. The others turned away as Karnag ran the length of his blade through her ribcage, toward the heart. A great groan came from the mare as Karnag pulled the blade free. She shivered and slumped to the earth.

After Karnag had cleaned his hands and arms of blood they shouldered their packs and set upon the path once more.

They left the beasts to rot.

7

MURMURED
DISCUSSION

ORD OF THE Lector's murder reached the
Sanctum's Abbey in the dead of night. Rumors
swirled of a green-cloaked stranger having
sought a private audience with one of the Sanctum's
elders, Prefect Gamghast, and it was said the two had
spoken for hours. Gamghast apparently whispered the
dire account to the other prefects, whereupon Prefect
Borel was said to have fainted.

By first light every denizen of the Abbey knew of
the tragedy. They rushed to the long tables of the dining
hall where they fretted together over plates of fruits and
breads, speaking solemnly about the news.

Bale's heart sagged upon learning of the tragedy, for
he'd counted the Lector—the Sanctum's second-highest
ranking member—as perhaps his only friend. The two had
enjoyed many conversations in the Abbey's garden, and

the Lector had instructed Bale in subjects and spellcraft other acolytes were told were forbidden. He'd also allowed Bale occasional access to his private library, a wealth of arcane texts Bale had devoured beneath candlelight. He would be missed.

Bale never breakfasted with others, or enjoyed any other meal with other people, for that matter. Yet, his curiosity over the awful circumstances of the Lector's death had dragged him to join the collection of acolytes in the dining hall. Bale shied from their nervous talk and scanned the tables to find a place near the elder members of the Sanctum. He assumed the appearance of caring only about peeling his orange and perked his ears to eavesdrop.

For a time, words among the small collection of elders were few. Prefect Kreer pulled at his long nose and picked at his gnarled knuckles, saying nothing. Prefect Borel, a man almost perfectly round in shape, sniffled and rubbed tears from his eyes with fat thumbs. Prefect Gamghast, now the Sanctum's second most senior member behind only Dictorian Theal himself, pondered a great leather-bound tome. His face was so deeply lined with wrinkles it struck Bale as a seaside crag, and his wild, white beard the crash of waves against it.

Murmured discussion resounded from every corner of the hall, but the prefects sat in somber silence. Bale began to wonder whether he'd be better served by lurking nearer another table. After a time he'd finished the last wedge of his orange, and thus had lost the necessary prop to excuse his presence in the hall. Frustrated, he smoothed his robes and stood, and began making his way to another location.

Just then, Gamghast shut the tome with a thud and cleared his throat. Bale searched quickly about and snatched an apple from a large plate sitting amidst another huddle of acolytes, all of whom turned to regard Bale contemptuously. Bale glowered back, then licked the apple to stake his claim. He held out the apple toward the acolytes for an instant in a mocking gesture, then licked it again.

Would anyone like it now? I thought not.

He dashed back to his table and assumed as casual a posture as his awkward actions would permit. He produced a small knife from the pockets of his robes and began peeling the red skin from the apple in slow strokes. The task was halfway done when at last the men spoke.

"Our dear Lector is dead," said Kreer, his wheeze of a voice sounding even weaker than usual. "The Sanctum has suffered its greatest loss."

"This is the worst of news," said Borel through a choke of tears. "It is a sad day when any of our number depart this life, but the Lector? And in so foul a fashion? It is too much to bear. We are lost without him!" He blew his nose into his handkerchief.

Gamghast pulled at the wisps of his beard and drummed his fingers against the cover of his book. "Yes, he is dead. It is heartbreaking news and we will honor his passage. But there is only so much time for grief, brothers. We require *answers*, and we require them in swift order if we are to honor the mission of our order. Why was the Lector traveling so close to the Southwall Mountains? So close to Arranan? He'd claimed he needed to attend to matters concerning his sister, but his family's lands lay far to the north, near the Waters of World's End. Why would he see a need to hide both the purpose and destination of his journey? From even us? These things trouble me..."

Kreer's chin eased upward, allowing the tall man to peer down the length of his nose while regarding the others. "I would argue our faith instructs us to assume a far-sighted purpose behind the Lector's actions, especially mere days after his death. Certainly a more distant time would be more suitable for questioning his actions."

Gamghast waved his hand dismissively. "Yes, yes, yes. I'm well aware there is none so righteous as Prefect Kreer. But please, Kreer, spare us the sanctimony. There are urgent concerns to address, difficult puzzles to solve. I'll not be hamstrung in those endeavors by your heightened sense of piety."

Borel whimpered and his prodigious belly shook with quiet sobs. "I know there are questions needing answering, but must we discuss these things while the body is still warm?"

"The Lector died at least a week ago," said Gamghast impassively. "Rather, he was *murdered* at least a week ago. The body has long since cooled."

Borel sniffled and seemed to compose himself. "He was a truly kind and faithful man. The very best of us all. The sort all of us should endeavor to emulate. He was the very source of our faith!" He made a quick, intricate gesture with his hand, a blessing in the name of Illienne. He retrieved his handkerchief and blew his nose with vigor, sounding much like a trumpet. "We are lost and adrift without him!"

Gamghast nodded impatiently and continued.

"He had hired soldiers and was accompanied by several acolytes. Why? What is more, the death of that many does not seem the random work of highwaymen or burglars. Nor does his death seem like the result of soldiery, as his throat was slit as he slept. Who would seek to murder our Lector? If the killer knew of the man's importance to our order and to our faith, then a grave threat may be stalking us all. Indeed, all of Rune."

Bale thought for an instant of the scullery maid's note, of her warning about Chamberlain Alamis. He placed the apple on the table and felt for an instant the fold of the note within his robes.

Kreer shifted about and pursed his thin lips, as though tasting his words before speaking them. "I say this not to disparage the man, but to aid in the investigation of his death. It is known the Lector had developed a penchant for banned books, old histories and such. Think of the time he spent digging through old scrolls in the library and elsewhere. Old things, things dealing with the Sentinels and with Yrghul the Lord of Nightmares. Dictorian Theal warned him not to explore too deeply those works, for fear of drawing unwanted attention."

"They'd been at odds, lately," said Borel, burrowing a corner of his handkerchief into a dripping nostril. "Dictorian Theal and the Lector I mean. It seemed to me there was some disagreement between them. Some form of tension."

Gamghast scratched at his ear. "Dictorian Theal has always been most concerned with the succession, of what would happen when the Lector died. Too concerned, if you ask me. He's always worried about where the spirit—"

"Blasphemy," muttered Kreer. "Dictorian Theal is a most holy man. You should know better than to say such things."

"Is he?" said Gamghast. "Are you suggesting he is more divine than the Lector himself? Who is it that speaks blasphemy among us, Kreer?"

Kreer snorted. "Mind your tongue. You never know who is near." He suddenly turned in his chair. "Acolyte Bale! You know something of these banned texts, don't you?"

Bale was caught completely unawares. His eyes widened, his lips stammered, and his hands trembled. He missed his apple entirely with his paring knife and the blade nicked the tip of his thumb. "Ouch!" he howled. The knife and apple clattered noisily across and off the far side of the table, and Bale sucked at his bleeding thumb.

Borel produced his discolored handkerchief and offered it to Bale with a kindly expression. Bale accepted it and tried to find its cleanest part, but quickly discovered this was a choice among lesser evils. He gave up, and pressed the mostly moist cloth about his thumb. "I'm sorry," he said too quickly, the words tumbling over themselves. "You posed a question?"

"Banned texts," Kreer said. "You know of the Lector's interest in banned texts, do you not?"

"He was curious, as is every fertile mind." He breathed deeply and slowed himself. *Of course I know. I've read nearly every one myself.* "He said he needed to know the circumstances of the Sentinels' exile, needed to scrutinize the old texts. There was no blasphemy. He was an intellectual man, seeking only to study the foundations of our faith and thereby reaffirm that faith." He smiled frailly. "It is as our maxim instructs: 'Through Faith, Wisdom, and through Wisdom, Faith.' The Lector would often say faith is not faith at all if it cannot weather inquisition."

Kreer huffed, staring hard at Bale. "A man of true faith knows there is no wisdom in lies."

Gamghast rapped the cover of his tome, signaling an end to further discussion. "We will inquire further, later. I will inspect the Lector's chambers to see if there are any hints to guide our inquiry. Borel, do we know who accompanied him? No? Then I ask you to find out. Kreer, I suggest you take charge of the Rites of Passage. Dictorian Theal will be in prayer until sundown, at least, and we would be well served to have preparations underway by the time he emerges."

Bale stood to excuse himself. "Prefects, seeing as you have nothing further for me I shall—"

"Hardly," said Gamghast. "You will meet me in my quarters before lunch, at noon. We will discuss in detail your knowledge of the Lector's studies."

Bale bowed stiffly and left the prefects. He was several tables away when he remembered he'd left his knife and apple. He returned to retrieve them, taking care to avoid the eyes of the prefects as he approached.

He caught sight of a glint of metal, and noticed his knife and what remained of his apple beneath a table. He tried to toe them free but they were too far away. Cursing, he bent low on creaking knees and reached for them.

"But what of his confession?" said Kreer, his tone urgent.

The confession? Bale froze, ignoring the protesting aches of his joints.

"Yes," said Borel, his voice quavering with worry. "What of his confession? What of his last wisdom and, more importantly, of the passing of the *spirit*? Should we not concern ourselves with that above all? If he did not utter his confession, could his spirit have been stilled forever?"

"His throat was slit," said Gamghast sullenly. "The account I received from... from our friend last night was that no words were spoken. I fear his wisdom—and Illienne's—is lost to us. The spirit seems unattached or stayed, and that's the most troubling news of all."

Bale tapped gently upon Gamghast's door as noon tolled from Ironmoor's many belfries. He didn't want to knock too loudly, or he'd eliminate any chance of the prefect *not* hearing him.

He paused for a moment, listening. There was, as he hoped, no answer. *Oh, I'm terribly sorry, Prefect Gamghast! I arrived precisely at noon as you instructed, and knocked several times. When there came no answer I assumed you'd been able to answer your questions without my assistance...*

He grinned and tapped again. The tap was so faint he reckoned only a church mouse would hear it. Again, no answer.

Oh, very well. Perhaps another time, my dear Prefect.

Bale turned from the door, only to be confronted by the sight of Prefect Gamghast lumbering down the hallway, arms laden with books.

"Acolyte Bale," Gamghast said matter-of-factly.

"Prefect Gamghast," Bale sighed. "A pleasure to see you."

Gamghast eyed him suspiciously. "Acolyte Bale, you *do* realize honesty is expected of all members of the Sanctum, particularly when dealing with their superiors."

Bale opened his mouth to speak, but couldn't quite find the words. *The man is entirely correct: it is indeed a distinct* dis*pleasure to see him. Dare I say that aloud?*

"Come," said Gamghast, gesturing for Bale to open the door. "I am a practical man, and have no need for false flattery or pious pretense. Our Lector has been murdered, in a place far from his home. I need to know what could have driven him there, what information he could have discovered, and whether such information could have placed him in peril. I need to know if anyone heard his confession—his last words—and where that person has gone. Assist me in setting a course to track those answers, and you will be free of me."

Gamghast's quarters reflected his practical nature. A small bed, two squat chairs crowding a small table, a half-burned candle, a reading glass, a washbasin, and a wardrobe. There were no trappings of his station, no baubles or lacquered scrolls lauding his rank of prefect.

Perhaps the man is not all bad.

Gamghast gestured to one of the chairs with a nod, and brought the two stacks of books down upon the table with a heavy thud and a puff of dust. Bale assumed his chair and the prefect eased himself into the other. Bale took a moment to study the titles etched across the spines of the books, and recognized them all as banned. He'd read many of them, but the last copies of the others were rumored to have been burned long ago, by order of the High King.

"Tell me what you know of the Sentinels," the prefect asked.

This is a dangerous discussion. Bale folded his hands in his lap and let his eyes wander the room. He'd always been a terrible liar. *Best not look the man in the eye.* "The Sanctum regards the Sentinels as guilty of betraying their sacred pact with Illienne. They sought to usurp the throne and rule the Kingdom rather than protect it. That is why the Sanctum proclaims High King Derganfel the Purer was righteous in banishing them from Rune, and why we have helped rid the holy places of their remembrances and our books of their references."

Gamghast stroked his white beard. "Yes, yes, yes. But my question did not seek the Sanctum's *official* position on the Sentinels, but rather what you know of them. Let us not waste each other's time, Bale."

Bale regarded Gamghast. The prefect's face was stern, but not unkind. Yet, Bale was reluctant to place trust in anyone. He'd discussed these things with the Lector, but reckoned all other members of the Sanctum thought such conversations to be blasphemy. "It is sacrilege to deny doctrine."

Gamghast slapped the table. "Damn it, man! You sound just like that pompous fool Kreer." He gazed out the small window above the table and inhaled deeply. "The Sanctum is waning, our influence diminishing. The rest of the world thinks of us as charlatans who do naught but proclaim childish fairy tales and hoard useless old secrets. We've become a mere whimsy of royalty, an order asserting the divine right of a High King whose bloodline seems to most no nobler than that of ordinary men. Is such the extent of our faith? Is such the limit of our purpose?"

Bale looked on earnestly. He was always comforted to find another who shared his concerns.

Gamghast leaned across the table and peered over the stack of books. "Do you wonder, Bale? Do you ever wonder if we stand on the wrong side of things? If the Sentinels were the righteous ones, and it was the High King who betrayed *them*? Perhaps the time approaches when we will need to reassess the tenets of our faith."

Bale examined his hands and picked at a hangnail. "Erlorn and I—or rather I should say the Lector and I—spoke at times about such things. A dozen or so years ago he caught me in the courtyard reading *The Shadows of the Warduren.*" Bale pointed at one of the volumes in the stack before him. "That one. He asked me why I'd be reading such a thing, and whether I agreed that such books should be burned. I posed to him nearly the same questions you just posed to me. He just smiled and nodded, and from then on he tutored me in more potent spellcraft, and granted me access to his collection of outlawed histories. Many of these," he said, making a wide sweep with his hand, "and more."

"Very well," Gamghast said, nodding deeply. "Unlike others in these halls I do not declare such studies to be blasphemy. Yours or the Lector's." He stared long at Bale. "I assure you, this discussion is ours and ours alone."

Bale smiled. He knew the prefect spoke truth.

"So, I will pose again my original question. What do you know of the Sentinels?"

"The historical accounts differ on the events leading to their banishment. The popular histories, of course, recite that Thaydorne, the greatest hero of the War of Fates and the most powerful of the Sentinels, grew jealous of the High King. It is said he marshaled men loyal to his purpose and attempted to overthrow the High King. Some of the Sentinels stood loyal to the Crown, but others united under Thaydorne's banner once the battle was joined. It is said Derganfel the Purer met Thaydorne and his warriors on the battlefield, and routed them. And it is said he was merciful, and in consideration of Thaydorne's great service to Rune he spared his life. But, he knew Thaydorne and the rest of the Sentinels—even those who'd been loyal—would never remain content to serve mortal men. Thus, he banished them from Rune, whereupon the Sentinels were stripped of their divine gifts and lived the rest of their lives as mortals. It is said they died."

"And what say the unpopular histories?"

Bale found himself smiling again. "I'm certain you're aware most such histories were ordered burned, often in great piles in the garden of the Bastion."

Gamghast nodded toward the books. "It's a fortunate thing we don't heed every edict of the Crown."

"Indeed," Bale said, rubbing his hands together excitedly. "Those histories say it was Derganfel who grew mad with jealousy, and he desired glory above all things and despised sharing the citizenry's adulation with the Sentinels. Many then regarded the Sentinels as the great saviors of Rune and the vanquishers of Yrghul. People thought of them as gods, and Derganfel would suffer it not. He grew mad in his lust for power, and cast all the Sentinels from his sight. Thaydorne and others resisted, but ultimately accepted the banishment."

"And what became of them?"

Bale pressed a finger to his lips. "The histories are less specific on that point. Very little is known of who or what the Sentinels were, to begin with. The accounts agree the Sentinels and the High King were granted measures of divinity by Illienne. But what power was imparted, precisely? The High King and his line are said to be the only mortal men who can touch the Godswell, and thus they have long claimed possession of divine righteousness and infallibility in their rule... They may be able to touch the Godswell, yes, but do they possess divine righteousness? Rubbish. Even the most faithful among us should view such claims with great skepticism."

"But what of the Sentinels?"

"These banned accounts hold firmly that they retired to quieter lives, but lived on, in some form of immortality. Some of the more persuasive scholars posit that the 'measure of divinity' manifested in different ways among them. Some were granted an ability to survive death, in a manner of speaking, by imparting their memories or abilities to another. Others, chief among them Thaydorne, were said to be truly immortal. Each was said to possess a unique and profound power, portraying a separate aspect of Illienne's godliness. Thaydorne was known to possess great strength of arms. Lyan was just. Valis was ever watchful. Castor was—"

"Castor was said to possess great wisdom, and to receive the ongoing instruction of Illienne as it echoed through the black void of oblivion. That," said Gamghast, his eyes piercing, "is why he's served as the Sanctum's Lector for these many centuries."

Bale's jaw dropped and he shook his head. He paused and was about to resume speaking as though the words had not been spoken. They were too jolting to be true.

"Our Lector."

Bale paused again, glaring at the stacks of books. *More secrets untold, and not even a whispered hint of their existence.* "But… How?"

Gamghast eyed him for a long moment before continuing, as though waiting for the concussion of a blow to subside. "Castor was immortal in one of the senses you described: in the sense his wisdom would pass to another vessel upon death, and that vessel passed that wisdom on in turn. This cycle has continued for nearly a millennium." Gamghast grimaced slightly and pulled at his beard. "It is a secret known to very, very few. Myself, Borel, Kreer, Dictorian Theal, and now you. It is a secret confided only to those he most trusted. Such a thing could never become known to the High King, you understand."

Bale was dumbfounded. "That one of the Sentinels has lived here for centuries, in the very shadow of the Bastion, in defiance of the banishment?" He shook his head, the strands of his gray hair forming a veil across his face. "I cannot comprehend this."

"I felt much the same when I was told, many years ago. But it was described to me thus: those Sentinels who'd remained loyal to the High King would not break those oaths they swore to Illienne. They felt bound by those oaths to protect the kingdom of Rune, and even the betrayer who sat on its throne. So, they served in secret. And the Sanctum was formed as part of that effort. We were loyal to the High King in word and deed, but all the while we have preserved a secret history, kept alive a secret flame. We serve two masters. Often their ambitions are conjoined. And when they are not, we keep our efforts discrete."

"I cannot believe this." Bale said, rubbing at his eyes.

"Erlorn saw fit to trust you. He was giving you keys to unlock the true secrets of the Sanctum. The powerful magics we hoard and, more importantly, the *truth*."

"But he's been murdered! Can it be a Sentinel has died? Is such a thing possible?"

Gamghast's face knotted. "These are questions I cannot answer, not yet. His spirit passed by virtue of the utterance of his confession, his last words of wisdom. We don't know whether anyone, or no one, heard the confession and thus was chosen as Castor's vessel, his successor. These things trouble me."

"What must we do?"

"You will fetch your walking staff and don your traveling cloak."

Bale pulled his face from his hands, his heart welling with apprehension. *By the dead gods, please do not cast me into the world, among people! I am a miscreant, a misanthrope!* "Where would you have me go?"

"Find his resting place. The Lector seemed bound for Arranan, a nation with which we are on the very brink of war, for reasons he did not disclose. We know not the identity of his killer. Worst of all, we know not the words of his confession, nor have we detected the manifestation of Castor's soul in another. Answers, Bale. I want you to deliver answers. Use the ways Erlorn taught you."

"I am no horseman, and my stiff knees will not permit a long walk. Certainly there is someone else?"

"Nonsense. A strong purpose makes an easy road."

"But—"

"I will hear no more. I've arranged your passage by sea, all the way to Riverweave. You leave in three days."

Bale awoke the next morning at the sixth hour, the belfries loudly announcing the time. He studied the bricks of his ceiling for a while, lost in his thoughts. The world was different this day, as though all things had been upended.

My suspicions have been confirmed. The Sentinels live. Why then am I so plagued with doubt?

He pulled himself out of his bed and stretched his creaking frame with a groan. He eyed for a moment his reflection in his small mirror, his lanky limbs a frail support for his bone-colored nightshirt, and wondered how he could manage the task that'd been asked of him.

He moved closer to the mirror, noticing the crow's feet lining his hazel eyes. How long it had been since he'd ventured beyond the walls of Ironmoor? Nearly half of his forty years had been spent as a member of the Sanctum, and the vast majority of that time had been spent sequestered within the halls of the Abbey. He felt safe here. Protected. Beyond the walls he would be vulnerable.

What will become of me?

Gradually he set about readying himself, washing his

face and hands in the small basin of lemon-scented water. His hands were delicate. The most work they'd performed in years was turning the pages of books. He imagined his hands growing white knuckled while desperately grasping the rough ropes of a galley at sea, trying not to be pitched overboard. He became nearly seasick at the thought of it.

Damned be the day I was cast from the family farm.

It was late morning when Bale left his quarters. His anxieties nagged him, and he rushed through the Abbey's winding halls until at last he reached Gamghast's quarters.

He pounded hard upon the prefect's door. "Gamghast! I have need of you!"

There came no reply for the span of several heartbeats, and Bale held his breath. At last, he heard the squeak of the knob and the door swung open. Gamghast stood in the doorway and Prefect Borel sat at the table behind him.

"Acolyte Bale," said Gamghast, his dark-rimmed eyes and drooping features betraying profound exhaustion.

Bale peeked over Gamghast's shoulder, eyeing Prefect Borel. The rotund man sipped at a mug of tea, his look one of utter confusion. Bale returned his gaze to Gamghast, and spoke in a whisper. "Does he know?"

"He does. It is safe to speak in his presence. Close the door and come inside."

Bale slipped inside and pulled the folded note from his robes. The scullery maid's note. He pressed it firmly into Gamghast's hand, much as it had been pressed into his own. "I am sorry, Prefect Gamghast. I should have come to you with this earlier, but I was afraid and weak of will. I also had suspicions as to the veracity of the allegations, and felt the matter merited further inquisition before it could be pursued."

Gamghast eyed him warily as he unfolded the parchment.

"Read it."

Gamghast scanned the missive, then did so once more. "Who gave this to you? Whose words are these?"

Bale shook his head. "A scullery maid in the Bastion. I know not her name. I was summoned for an exorcism several weeks ago—strange noises in the larder or some such nonsense. It turned out to be a ruse, merely a means for the woman to contact a member of the Sanctum. She handed me the note in the very presence of Chamberlain Alamis."

Gamghast turned and handed the note to Borel. "Prefect Borel, you were at the Bastion just a few days ago, were you not?"

"Indeed I was, although the chamberlain allowed me nowhere near the High King or the Godswell," he said, setting his mug upon the table. He looked up and regarded Bale for a moment, his wide mouth wrenching into a frown. "He's forbidding us any contact with the High King. I was allowed only to perform the Rites of the Dead upon a young scullery maid who'd taken an unfortunate tumble down the stairs to the larder. Snapped her neck in two. I had no reason to question the story at the time, but now..."

Bale felt his guts run cold. He thought of the woman's pleading eyes and earnest nature. *If I'd only acted sooner!*

Gamghast stared at him firmly. "Now that you know who we serve, I trust you will relay any concerns or suspicions more quickly in the future. Perhaps lives will be saved next time."

Bale nodded, ashamed. "I'll know to trust you next time, Prefect."

Gamghast turned and looked to Borel. "Brother, your misgivings about Chamberlain Alamis were not unfounded, nor were your suspicions of the movements of our enemies."

Bale felt suddenly uncomfortable standing amidst the two prefects, his hands becoming clammy and his spine aching. Just then, the clanging ring of ten o'clock sounded, startling them.

Gamghast pressed a heavy hand upon Bale's shoulder. "We will handle this. You should have brought this to us sooner, yes, but I am certain you know that now. It seems we have many foes prowling near our gates. Know we are not without weapons of our own, and we have allies loyal to our purpose. Castor was not the only Sentinel with disciples, and others loyal to our cause will assist us." He turned back to Borel but then turned again. "And Bale," he said. "You must find the answers we need. Much now depends upon you."

8
SCOUNDRELS
AND OUTLAWS

TREAM CLICKED HIS tongue, urging his chestnut mare up the road to the sun-bleached walls of Raven's Roost. Instead, though, the horse whinnied and stamped, refusing to move. The mare had been skittish ever since they'd parted ways with Karnag and his company, causing Tream to wonder whether she'd guessed his unscrupulous intentions.

"Aw c'mon, Fancy," Tream said, scratching the mare's withers. "Our lives are about to get a good sight better than they've been. Trust me, girl. Things won't be hard for long." He slapped her flank and at last she pressed up the gravelly road toward the gates.

Raven's Roost squatted atop a wide, rocky outcrop, the former site of a massive prison and gallows. Now, the place was home to the same sorts of scoundrels and outlaws it once hanged. It was a place of solace for the most wanted, because just about every fellow in town had a price on his head.

Tream had resided in the town for years, finding he fit quite well among the town's unsavory denizens. He had a terrible temper and was good with a blade. That left him ill-suited for soldiering, especially after he'd gutted his commanding officer and been forced to flee the army. But, those qualities made him a fine settler of scores and a dependable bodyguard for the chiefs of underground society. Raven's Roost had given him a place to sell his skills, and, in turn, earn a measure of respect.

"Welcome home," said the toothless guard manning the rusted gate.

Tream smiled, suddenly feeling his own brown teeth were quite the luxury. The guard was a frequent player of deadman's dice in the local taverns, and had lightened Tream's pockets on a few occasions. "Don't get any ideas of taking more money off me. I don't mean to be here long."

The gates opened to a mud-packed street, lined by cattle traders and smithies. The heat from the forges did not mix well with the scent of the cattle, and only a faint breeze stirred the air. It made for an oppressively hot stink, and Tream rode several dozen yards before the road ascended and he was able to breathe freely.

He guided Fancy down a cross street, narrower and only slightly less muddy. There were seamy taverns jammed with patrons, even though it was still a while before sunset. Rough-looking harlots called from the balconies of the inns, some shouting for Tream by name. He waved at them dismissively and kept his head down, realizing it was best to avoid attention under the circumstances.

After a few more turns he arrived at the mouth of a shaded alleyway. At its end sat his usual spot, *The Dead Messenger*. He tied Fancy's reins to a post and patted her twice for luck. "Get your rest, girl," he whispered in her ear. "We may be riding hard tonight."

The Dead Messenger wasn't bustling with as many folk as the other taverns, and those who frequented the place were generally a villainous sort. Tream took account of the small crowd before moving inside the heavy shadows of the common room. He recognized much of the clientele as his competitors—assassins and cutpurses awaiting their next jobs. They gave him their typical dark stares and curt nods, and returned to their tankards.

It was always those few he didn't recognize who made him jumpy. There was a green-cloaked ruffian at the bar whose eyes lingered on him a bit overlong for his liking, so he chose a seat at a small table farthest from him. He knew there was ever the risk someone would seek revenge for another he'd killed, or perhaps a young rogue would try to make a reputation for himself by challenging his betters.

Dark work brings dark rewards, they say.

"Ale?"

The croaking voice startled Tream, and his hand shot to the hilt of his sword. He sighed in relief when he saw it was Handsome, the tavern's droopy-eyed, harelipped barkeep, looming over him. Tream nodded politely. "Two hands of your finest, if you please."

Handsome grunted in reply and shuffled to the casks

lining the back of the bar. He soon returned with a mug nearly a foot tall. "Two hands of the good stuff, Tream. Enjoy it while it lasts. We may not see any more of it for a while, with the rumors of war, and all." He glanced curiously to either side of Tream. "Where is the rest of your lot?"

Tream lowered his head and gave his best mockup of a sad sob and snort, but worried after he'd done it that it'd sounded much like laughter. He shook his head dramatically and pounded his fist for further effect, and snorted again.

That's more like it.

"Tream?"

He rubbed hard at his eyes, trying to redden them before returning Handsome's gaze. "I'm sorry, Handsome. The thought of it just *pains* me so. They're dead, Handsome. All of them *dead!*" He faked a blubber. "Saw it happen with my very own eyes!"

Handsome stumbled back with a gasp. "All of them? Karnag and Fencress, too? How?"

"Every last one of them. Skewered like pigs. I had to finish the job alone."

"You know I don't like asking questions of you fellows, but who did this? What kind of job did you take?"

"Our mark was a person of some repute, and had men with him, fighting men. Serious trained soldiers. They caught us off-guard." He picked at his fingernails and sighed heavily. "It was a black, black day. I was just finishing off our mark when they came at us, out of the wild. They killed Karnag and the rest. Only by the grace of the dead gods did I manage to take them down and make it back here alive. The last survivor."

Handsome's gaze narrowed. "The *last* survivor?"

Tream rubbed his eyes harder and faked a sniffle. "It was horrible, Handsome. What I would give to have them back among the living..." He stared out the small, thick-paned window, trying to appear forlorn. "I'd trade every last crown I have coming to me." He looked at Handsome tentatively, and was relieved to see the barkeep's look had drifted away from him.

"That's a real shame." Handsome breathed in slowly and was quiet for a moment. "Karnag dying is some bit of news. He was as wicked a man as I've known, and I mean that in the best of ways. And that Fencress was a tough girl—not many of them in our business—and I'll miss hearing her witty talk around this place." He pulled a rag from his pocket and rubbed at his eyes. His voice dropped to a quiet sigh. "I reckon you'll be needing to meet with your patron, to get paid and all."

I've fooled him! "Why yes!" Tream reflexively slapped a hand over his mouth, realizing he'd sounded too eager. "I mean, it would be a real shame if the efforts of my brave friends went unrewarded. Any coin I receive will be like a shining tribute to them."

"I'll send word you've returned. As I recall, your patron was a curious sort. Impatient, too. Stay here for a while. I suspect we'll get his reply before nightfall."

Tream was halfway through his fourth two-hand mug of ale when Handsome approached him, wearing a serious look on his ugly features.

"A fellow just left a note in the Blood Box."

The Blood Box was nothing more than *The Dead Messenger's* repository for contracts and coin exchanged between patrons and their hires, but the way Handsome said it seemed ominous. "He didn't just deliver the money?"

"Afraid not." He handed a sealed note to Tream.

"You know I can't read, Handsome."

Handsome opened the note and scanned it quickly. "It says to meet at Old Gallows Rock at tenth hour of night."

"Ten o'clock? Dead gods, man." The ninth hour had sounded a good while before, and it wouldn't be long before the belfries were ringing again. Tream lifted his mug and swilled the remainder of his ale. He smacked two silver crowns on the table and shouldered his way past Handsome and out of the bar.

There was no moon out, and the streets were dark as death. Fancy grew nervous as they approached Old Gallows Rock, until at last she refused to go any farther. Tream thought of pulling the beast by her reins for the last hundred yards, but then decided instead to tie her to the arm of an old statue. "Don't go anywhere, girl," he whispered, patting her twice for luck.

He picked at his rotting teeth, as he often did when uneasy. He tried whistling as he walked, but found it sounded overloud in the dark. Eventually he settled on keeping one hand on his sword, the other hanging free, and his mouth shut. The ale had calmed him somewhat, but not nearly enough.

There were few folk on the streets at this hour,

particularly in this part of the town. Old Gallows Rock was at the center of Raven's Roost, in the middle of a vast square cornered by a soldiers' barracks, an empty library, and the court of the town's Magistrate Examiner. All were parts of the prison that used to dominate this town, years before. Tream cast a crooked smile when he thought of that, knowing how these days the King's Law was scarcely enforced in the place. There were times, though, like now, when he wished there were more honest guards marching the streets.

Tream grew more nervous as he walked, realizing he knew nothing of their patron. Karnag had said little of his initial meeting other than to tell the company the terms of the bargain. One thousand silver crowns to be paid upon finishing the job. It was an enormous amount of money, a number Tream couldn't dream of counting. Yet, the thought was anything but comforting. Tream was used to dealing in small squabbles. A brother of a dead man seeking vengeance upon the killer. A gambling debt satisfied by the breaking of bones. A home ransacked over suspicions of an affair. These were easy things, understandable things.

This job, though, had been something else entirely. It bothered Tream, as he'd thought from the outset the job was too big to be safe. It spoke of motives far fouler than simple revenge or street justice. He spied the black outline of Old Gallows Rock and his stomach grew sick with nerves.

He reached the stout expanse of rock just as the tenth bell clanged from a nearby belfry. Its flat top was just taller than him, so he had to walk around its broad base to inspect its other aspects. He walked timidly about the rock several times, but there was no one to be found.

After a time Tream reckoned it was best to just keep still. He'd look less jittery that way. He found a low protrusion on the rock and sat on it, tapping his fingers on the hilt of his sword.

Occasionally there was torchlight moving elsewhere in the square, but it seemed to be just folk scurrying down side streets or walking briskly along the square's perimeter. None of the lights approached him.

The hour grew late, and Tream began to worry Handsome had misread the note. After all, the barkeep likely wasn't much brighter than Tream himself, and it was certainly possible the man had mistaken the hour or the place. What was more, Tream did not care for sitting on Old Gallows Rock at this time of night or at any other. He was a superstitious sort, and didn't reckon the souls who'd died at the place would enjoy his backside using the rock as a bench.

Tream inhaled deeply and resolved to walk about the rock once more before leaving. He knew he'd need to leave Raven's Roost quickly, but it seemed one more night in the place would be necessary.

He bowed his head, shutting his eyes and squeezing his hands together. *Beloved Illienne, let it be time enough. Please damn me not for the worst of my deeds.*

When he opened his eyes he nearly soiled himself in shock. He'd heard not a thing, but standing before him was a figure robed from head to toe in black, its face concealed by a drooping hood.

"I am sorry to have kept you waiting," the figure said, its voice a hiss.

"Ah," Tream stammered, standing abruptly. Instinctively he tried to take a step back, but thumped against the bulk of the rock instead. "Ah, no trouble at all." Tream squinted, trying to catch sight of the figure's face within the shadows. He could discern nothing.

The figure pressed closer. There was a sour odor, like the smell of rot, wafting from it. "You completed the task? You slew the Lector?"

"Of course I did," Tream blurted, his words almost stumbling over themselves as he spoke too quickly. *Coin*, he thought, trying to calm himself. *This man owes you a lot of coin.* "We met our end of the bargain, and I lost a number of friends as a result." He wiped beading sweat from his brow and let his hand drift to his sword.

The robed form took a step back, to Tream's relief. "Yes, you did meet your end. I've received confirmation of the Lector's murder."

By the dead gods! They did it!

"However," the figure continued, "I am hoping you have more for me than simply the news of his death." Pale, long-fingered hands adorned with silver rings emerged from the sleeves of the black robes, and pulled back the hood to reveal a face. It was a pale, hairless face of indeterminate gender, split neatly in half by a thick, black stitch. The flesh on either side of the stitch wriggled and stretched unnaturally.

Tream fought against a horrible, swelling fear. *Think only of the coin! The coin!* "W-we were h-hired to kill the man, and we d-did. There was a p-price for our work."

He straightened to his full height, doing his best to appear intimidating but his bowels groaned and felt ready to spill.

"Rewarded you shall be," the figure said quietly, smiling to reveal yellow teeth. "Yours was a great step toward a greater end."

"Y-you promised a th-thousand silver crowns."

The figure stood silently for a moment, tapping its long, ringed fingers together. "You do not trust me." It reached inside the robes, and produced five slim cylinders of gold. "Khaldisian gold ingots. Together they are worth even more than the balance of my debt. The amount entire is yours, if you can answer my questions to my satisfaction."

Tream's hands trembled as he held them outward. The gold glinted in the dark. It was more money than he'd ever seen in one place. The figure offered him one, and he snatched it desperately. He inspected it in the same way he'd seen pawnbrokers inspect the stolen jewelry he'd fenced. It was heavy and etched with strange symbols. He bit it with his rotting teeth, as he'd seen pawnbrokers do, but realized he had no idea what that was supposed to reveal. *Tastes like gold, I reckon.*

"What did he say?" the thing asked.

"Who?"

The figure cocked its pale, stitched head. "The Lector. It is said the Lectors of the Sanctum always utter something upon death, something of great importance. What did he say?"

Tream shrugged curtly, his eyes not wavering from

the small fortune in the figure's hands. "He said nothing, I'm afraid."

"It was your blade that slew the Lector, yes? And there were no other survivors? Then you *must* have heard something. Some words, a phrase, perhaps more. Perhaps you did not understand what it meant at the time."

Tream kept his eyes on the gold, but his free hand found the pommel of his sword. *He suspects I'm lying.* "I really must be—"

Suddenly a shadow dashed before Tream's eyes, forcing the black robed figure to the ground. There were heavy thuds and grunts and a mad scuffle in the dark, and the ingots fell clanking to the ground. Tream looked frantically up and then behind him. Someone had leapt from Old Gallows Rock and onto his patron.

He quickly bent low and seized the gold, pressing the ingots to his chest as he stood. He then watched as the attacker was suddenly thrown, landing with a heavy thud nearly fifteen feet away. *Impossible.* The black robed figure then shot to its feet, its hideous, split face twisting with a perverse grin.

The attacker stood also, slapping dust from his breeches. Tream squinted hard, and in a moment realized he recognized the man. The green-cloaked ruffian from *The Dead Messenger*. The man pulled a long sword free of its scabbard, the sound of it piercing the dark. He uttered something in a tongue Tream did not comprehend, and the sword hummed as a faint, green flame spilled down its length.

Sorcery! He'd heard tales, but such powers were thought to have left the world long ago.

In answer to the challenge, the black robed figure spoke in harsh, misshapen words both low and guttural. Broken sounds that pained the ears. Tream felt too frightened to move and watched as blackness coalesced about the creature's ringed fingers. The space about the figure darkened to a foul gloom, as though all the night's shadows were summoned to its call.

The man in green leveled his weapon at the figure, the flames brightening and curling up his arm. "Your kind has seen its last days, Necrist," he shouted. "This murder of the Lector will stir all the light to action, and we will crush you and all your kind."

"It is you who faces doom," the Necrist said. It cast its hands downward and the dark shadows flowed from them. "We have delved deep into the old hells and have found *power*. We are coming to take what is *ours*."

Serpentine strands of black formed in the space about the green man, entwining about his legs. He hacked at the shadows with his fiery blade and they diminished but did not disappear.

Tream's eyes burned with dripping sweat and his hands quivered. *Cursed! This work was cursed! Forgive me, mum, for ever doubting you!*

The green-garbed man uttered another string of words and the entanglement of shadows broke apart for an instant. He leapt free and rushed toward the Necrist, brandished his flaming blade.

Tream thought suddenly of his mother's sweet, soothing voice. Of the soft lullabies she sang, telling of the dead gods and the threat of the things they'd left behind.

Of the Sentinels, the Necrists, and other secrets. He thought of these things and wrenched free of his stupor.

The Necrist retreated several steps and was swallowed by the wreath of black shadows surrounding it. It appeared as a cloud of absolute blackness, shifting and swelling as though possessing physical form.

The green-cloaked man charged forward, his sword a bright blaze. He swept the weapon in ferocious arcs, assailing the blackness and rending the dark shadows. The combat pressed close to Tream, and he leaned back as far as Old Gallows Rock would allow.

Just then, the black figure emerged from the swirl of shadows, its back toward Tream and only an arm's reach distant.

Tream reached for his sword and yanked it free, suddenly thinking of his mum's deep faith. He looped his free arm—clutching the gold—over the figure's head and about its neck, and drove the sword clean through its gut.

A horrid howl came from the thing, a frenzied shriek which sounded like something being sucked away rather than shouted out. Tream released the hilt of his weapon and the Necrist collapsed in a heap. It hissed and writhed and clawed at the ground before it fell still. Tream pulled back his hands in disgust, almost dropping his gold in the process.

The blackness dispersed immediately, the shadows finding again their dark recesses.

Tream breathed heavily. He tucked the ingots in his pocket and scampered several steps clear of the thing.

"You," said the man in green.

Tream recoiled, almost having forgotten the man's

presence. His heart quailed with fear. He sidestepped along Old Gallows Rock, his back pressed against its surface.

The man took several steps forward, his blade dimming as he approached. "You killed the Lector." His tone was measured and menacing. "I heard your every word, both here and at *The Dead Messenger*."

Tream shook his head frantically. "I killed no one," he said, tears clouding his eyes. "You must believe me, sir. I did not kill the Lector."

"Ha!" the man said, grabbing Tream by the dirty collar of his shirt. His black eyes glimmered with anger. "You think I did not hear your exchange with the Necrist?"

Dear Illienne, don't let this be the end of me! Tream sank to his knees, blubbering. He pressed tears away from his cheeks and stammered as he spoke. "I-I'm a coward, sir. I am a l-liar and I am a coward. I did not kill the Lector, but I know the men who d-did." He wiped snot away from his lip and sobbed. "My mum's faith kept me from doing it. I came back here to collect the reward before the real killers could."

The man spat. "So, you would have me believe you were a liar then, but are not a liar now. You must think me a fool."

Tream grabbed at the man's cloak. "I swear to you! I swear to you I had not the heart to kill him, and I'm not bold enough to lie to the likes of you." He pulled away from the man, casting his eyes downward. "It was Karnag Mak Ragg. He'll come back to this place, and Handsome knows him well." He hung his head. *Forgive me, friends.*

The man raised a boot and kicked Tream back against

Old Gallows Rock. He leered over him, holding his sword close to Tream's face. Tream tried to look away from the man's penetrating gaze but could not.

"You are a pathetic crook," the man said, withdrawing at last. "You do speak the truth." He kicked Tream again, causing him to topple to his side. "You helped save my life, so I will spare yours. But I will not countenance the sight of you. Be gone, and may Illienne grant you what you deserve."

Thank the dead gods I am spared!

Tream scrambled away, falling over in the process and then stumbling upright in desperation. He fumbled with his pocket and found the gold still rested within. He clutched it firmly and smiled and wept all at once.

Then he ran. He ran and did not look back. Most of all, he feared he would see Karnag there, with teeth bared and eyes ablaze with fury. Tream knew such a man would never forgive. Not in a dozen lifetimes.

9

HOW LIFE ENDS

A THUNDEROUS POUNDING RESOUNDED
from the door of Lannick's cell. He started from his
deep sleep, nearly rolling out of his straw cot in a
panic. The sound seemed almost unreal, like a remnant of
a bad nightmare. He scratched at his head with both hands,
trying to gather his wits and adjust to the sudden shock of
the waking world. It was very late at night, or very early in the
morning, and certainly not an hour for entertaining guests.

My grand escape? Has it arrived at last? "I'm—" was all
he could manage before the door was thrown open.

The orange flicker and greasy smoke of torchlight
spilled into his cell, followed by two dark silhouettes.
Large men, armed and armored and draped in red cloaks.

The Scarlet Swords. Alas, a far cry from my lovely Alisa.
Lannick put on his bravest face and rose from his bed.
"Well met, gentlemen! How ever may I help—"

The butt of a quarterstaff slammed into his gut,
throwing him across the floor's damp stones and leaving

him breathless. His chest rattled and he gasped. His lungs felt like deep bellows he could not fill. He turned and rose to his hands and knees and gasped again. He sucked hard, wheezing with the effort. At last there was breath.

Just then the staff cracked across his temple. He was knocked flat against the floor. His head rang and pounded with pain. He crawled clumsily to the wall and pulled his knees against his chest. The figures before him were a blur of red and black, and it seemed a third had entered the room.

A heavy boot crushed his foot. He felt one toe break, perhaps more. Pain seared his body. He groaned, which made his temple throb. He pressed his hand to the side of his head and felt a tender knot rising.

A knee smashed into his chin, and his skull smacked against the wall behind him. He swooned again, blinking through tears and struggling to focus.

This is how life ends.

"I think that's enough for now, Keln," came a voice, shrill like scraping steel.

General Fane. Lannick did his best to still his nerves, pulling his head upright to face his tormentor, his nemesis.

"Leave us," Fane said, gesturing with the torch at his Scarlet Swords. The two armored figures trudged from the room, leveling hard stares at Lannick as they exited.

Fane looked especially grotesque in the sputtering torchlight, the swell of his burned face mottled and stretched. His mad eyes twitched in their dark sockets.

"Now," Fane said, his tone mocking. "You didn't think I'd leave Ironmoor without saying my heartfelt goodbyes, did you?"

Lannick gritted his teeth. He found he could not speak.

The general leaned closer. Lannick thought for a moment of spitting in the man's face, of finishing things with a dramatic flair, but his jaw cracked and would not open. Blood dribbled from his nose and across his lips, and a coppery froth was the best he could manage.

"Ah, it seems my men were overzealous in their task. Forgive me." He straightened and took a step backward, smoothing his surcoat with a gloved hand. "I really wished only to talk."

Fane paced before Lannick for a moment, his polished boots clicking rhythmically on the stone tiles. He eyed him with patent revulsion. At last he paused, placed the torch in an iron sconce by the door and stooped gracefully to sit on the end of Lannick's cot.

"You have no idea the inconvenience you've caused me," he said, eyes darting about the cell. "I should kill you, you know. A less calculating man would certainly strike that course, and claim vengeance in the traditional fashion."

Lannick rested his forearms on his knees and leaned against the wall. His tongue was swelling and painful—he'd bitten it. He moved it about his mouth and regarded the general. He was a smallish man, hands drifting often to the trappings of his station: the decorative blade, the dangling medal, the embroidered lining of his scarlet cloak. *A pompous, self-impressed prick, and a sadistic one at that. Would that our places were switched, Fane, for I would take profound joy in your demise.*

Fane straightened and regarded Lannick. "But I am a most calculating sort. I have achieved my position not through brute strength or expert swordsmanship, but through resourcefulness, through sheer cunning. I have learned when one way is shut there are other passages available to achieve one's ends, if one but possesses the intellect to chart them. I have been cornered, I have been besieged, I have been outnumbered. But I have never been broken."

Lannick shrugged. He'd hoped to display a dismissive gesture, but instead his limbs moved slowly and with a painful protest. He rolled his bleeding tongue about his mouth.

Fane stood and pulled his sword free of its scabbard. It was a long rapier with a gilded guard and grip. "You ruined a plan of mine, or, should I say, a component of that plan. You defiled a sacrifice that was to have been virginal. A sacrifice that would have greatly aided my ambitions, that would have brought me power." He took a swift, whistling swipe with the rapier.

Lannick winced and tried to press back, but the dank wall braced him.

"As I've said," Fane continued, "other passages always open to the keen of mind. Oh, I remember you, Captain deVeers." A smile twisted his hideous face. His mad eyes danced. "For one man to endure so much seems a great inequity. A great fall from grace, the murder of his family at the hands of my Scarlet Swords, years spent living with regret, and now a death certain to be rife with suffering. Ah, but perhaps this is justice for your treason? To think, if you had bedded any other man's daughter, you might be visiting the bitch right now for another turn between the sheets. If you had crossed any other man those many years ago, you might be standing now in my place."

So much for a quick death. Lannick hung his head, for he knew what would follow. He heard the click-clack of Fane's boots as the general approached, and he offered no resistance when the general eased his battered chin upward with the flat of his blade.

"The Necrists were delighted when I told them I could deliver them a Variden. One stripped of his protections, one whose mind they could pry apart for its secrets. They thought this suitable consideration for my bargain." His smile vanished. "They will strip your body clean of its skin and your mind free of its sanity, until you can endure no more and surrender the last of your order's secrets. You will be forced to betray all you hold dear. And then you will die."

Lannick forced the sword from his throat with the back of his hand. The blade was honed to a vicious sharpness and it cut flesh as he pressed against it but he cared little.

"They will come for you soon enough," said Fane. "You may have hours or you may have days, but they will come. They will use what they learn from you to hunt down the rest of your order, and dismantle the very foundations of Rune. You can take solace in knowing you have served well as my unwitting accomplice, Lannick." He returned his blade to its sheath and walked smartly to the door.

Fane chuckled as he retrieved his torch. "Most, including myself, thought you were long dead. It seems such thoughts will be proven correct soon enough."

10
THE PROBLEMS
AT HAND

PREFECT GAMGHAST SAT quietly in his small chambers, focusing for a moment on the drifting dust motes illuminated by the late afternoon sunlight. He'd found concentration was a difficult state to achieve of late. He was often distracted by the mundane or consumed with worry, and in either case unable to set his mind to the problems at hand. *If only our most difficult challenges were set upon us when we still possessed the vigor of youth.*

On the desk before him was a blank sheet of parchment, a quill, and an inkwell. He'd been contemplating the instruments since noon, but had been unable to capture his thoughts with written words. Instead, he'd fussed with the unruly wisps of his white beard, cracked his knuckles, and picked at a chipped corner of his desk. *Is this how I'll meet my end? Lost in thought and incapable of action?*

He seized the quill and dipped the nib into the inkwell, decisively. He held the quill poised over the parchment, the ink dripping and pooling into an ever-widening splotch as he waited for words to coalesce in his head. But, after a time, he realized such gestures would not give shape to his muddled ideations. He returned the quill to the inkwell.

His eyes drifted again to the motes of dust. He watched them float and flutter, shifting with even the slightest movements of air and lacking any purpose or direction. *I will not be thus.* He inhaled sharply and knotted his brow, urging his thoughts to assume some sort of sensible order, some pattern from which he could decipher meaning.

A list, he insisted. *I shall begin with a list.*

He retrieved again the quill, drawing the excess ink from the tip by wiping it over the mouth of the inkwell. He cleared his throat and pressed the quill to the parchment. "The Necrists," he wrote at the top of the sheet. He stared at the words, watching the ink soak into the fibers of the parchment until it achieved a dull, deep black.

It was known Yrghul had followers and successors in the same manner as Illienne, and the Necrists were regarded as the Sanctum's foil. In the years after the gods' descent to oblivion, the Necrists laid claim to this inheritance from Yrghul, declaring themselves heirs to fell powers and the last practitioners of profane enchantments. But after a time they all but vanished, becoming little more than a dark rumor. In bleaker times, they were a fashionable scapegoat, with charlatans proclaiming that the Necrists were cursing the Kingdom as a measure of revenge for their dead god, Yrghul. In other times, they were almost forgotten. Their practice of secrecy made them a myth.

Yet they'd persisted. The Sanctum's archives contained accounts of clashes with the Necrists, and descriptions of their foul sorceries. Rumors of stillborn children bearing unnatural marks. Accounts of the possession of souls by vile demons. Rumors of Necric rituals, with the cultists communing with the dead god Yrghul through pools of blood. There were stories that their arts caused their own flesh to rot, and that they practiced grafting to their bones the skins of their sacrifices. But so much of it was only rumor.

Gamghast drummed his fingers on the desk and dipped the quill again into the inkwell. His eyes wandered for an instant to a shelf on his wardrobe where he'd stashed the scullery maid's note. *Is it possible they've operated beneath our noses, and have incited treachery at our very doorstep?*

"The chamberlain," began his next line, "is poisoning the High King. He speaks much with a man whose face is made of stitches."

A face made of stitches. They graft the skins of their sacrifices to their bones. It must be a Necrist.

He dropped the quill in the inkwell and pushed away from the table. He pulled his cloak about his shoulders, grabbed his staff, and looked wearily out his window.

It seems I must start by stalking the chamberlain. To think, a prefect of the Sanctum taking to skullduggery and skulking in shadows. Bale, I trust your investigation is more dignified.

Bale braced himself against the railing of *Losander's Revenge* and expelled the sour remnants of his lunch. The mess splattered upon the indigo waters below, leaving behind a green flotsam. Bale smacked his lips and spat thickly, thinking this would not be the last time he fell sick at sea.

"Ho there, spooker!" yelled a soldier. "You can't make sea legs with magic, eh?"

The nearby group of red-sashed soldiers laughed loudly. Bale turned his head from the railing and gave them an angry look. They only laughed louder, pointing fingers and elbowing each other.

"Ah," Bale said with a level tone, "the easy amusements of stunted minds. Hilarious, I'm sure." As he spoke, he noticed a long string of spittle and snot dangling from his chin and twisting wildly about in the wind. He wiped it away with the sleeve of his robe, and tried to display his most ferocious scowl.

They continued laughing.

Bale then noticed the string of viscous mucus had anchored itself to his sleeve, and continued its mad dance. It was at least a yard long and sparkled in the afternoon sun. He shook his arm but it would not dislodge.

"A new flag for our ship!" laughed a thick-bearded soldier.

"Run the spooker up the mast!" said a balding one.

How I hate people. Bale stumbled backward and steadied himself against a tall coil of hempen rope. He gave the soldiers one last glare before walking unsteadily to the companionway and descending below deck.

The voyage across the Sullen Sea had been a rough one. The sea was known for the wicked rocks lurking just beneath its surface, and for the swift storms that whipped at sails and churned the sea's dark waters. There had been times when *Losander's Revenge* careened dangerously, nearly capsizing, and others when it groaned and shook while narrowly avoiding the sea's sharp rocks.

Bale lay in his hammock below deck, squeezing shut his eyes and swallowing frequently in an effort to keep from vomiting. His stomach lurched with every tilt of the ship and shudder of its hull. The rocking hammock only made things worse, for when he opened his eyes it seemed the ship was moving in one direction and he in another.

But at least down in the darkness of the ship's berth, at this time of day, he was mostly alone. If there was anything that disagreed with him more than travel at sea, it was doing so in the company of soldiers. They taunted and intimidated him. He despised their ilk, and cursed Gamghast for arranging travel aboard a military vessel. *Certainly there are less odious methods of traveling southward.*

He found himself becoming disoriented by the sways of the ship and felt he needed something to subdue his nausea. He stumbled out of the hammock, nearly falling face-first into the floor's timbers as the hammock tipped. There were a few soldiers sleeping nearby, but to Bale's relief they did not stir. He could only imagine their derisive jeers if he'd awoken them with his clumsiness.

He found his pack hanging on a hook and carried it to a table near the berth's only lantern. He thrust his hands inside the pack, identifying its contents by feel, and retrieved a sleeve of leather rolled and bound with a bronze clasp. He undid the clasp and unfurled the sleeve across the table, revealing numerous pockets containing the reagents, powders and herbs he'd secured from the Sanctum's apothecary. He opened a slender pocket and from it withdrew a sprig of hagsweed. He chewed it, grimacing at the bitter lather it yielded. After a moment, though, his stomach began to settle.

Once indoctrinated in the precepts of the Old Faith, all members of the Sanctum learned the arts of healing. Infections, plagues and rots were anathema to them, for such things marked the work of Yrghul and a corruption of Illienne's creation. And so, it was their sworn duty to rid bodies of their ills. For centuries they'd been regarded as healers of the highest order, and even now in their decline they were often sought to address maladies of all sorts. Already Bale had been asked by the ship's captain to test the ship's casks of drinking water, after a soldier came down with dysentery.

He remembered how the soldiers had regarded him with mocking reverence once he declared the water safe to drink.

Next time I should poison the casks.

The hagsweed quelled the roil of his stomach. He caught the scent of cooking, and after he'd returned his pack to his hook he wandered into the galley adjacent to the ship's berth. Therein, a portly crewman attended a kettle filled with a soup of brown broth, carrots and hunks of white fish, and next to it was a basket filled with hardtack bread. The crewman mechanically dipped a wooden mug into the kettle and handed it to Bale without a word.

Bale nodded, grateful for the lack of communication, and grabbed a chunk of the bread. He settled against a table in the galley's corner and dropped the bread into his soup, remembering how he'd nearly cracked a tooth on the hardtack the night before.

The companionway trembled from the boots of soldiers as a group of them descended into the berth. *Time for supper, and time for me to take my leave.* Bale ducked out of the galley and squeezed past the soldiers with his head down. Once the companionway was clear he pulled himself above deck and found a quiet spot on the ship's forecastle.

Bale sipped at the mug and chewed the tough, crusty bread. The soup was salty and thin, but the warmth of it made tolerable the chill winds of the sea. *Perhaps the stuff will even stay in my stomach this time.*

The sea before him shimmered beneath the moon and stars, an ever-changing canvas of black and silver. Off to his right, perhaps a league or two distant, was the murky outline of Rune's coast. There was the occasional firelight of a seaside town and lantern glow of a fishing boat, but otherwise all lay in darkness.

He drained the last of his soup and chewed his remaining bread. As he did, he found his head clearing for the first time in many days. He felt his thoughts were finally freed from his stomach, the soldiers, and the swaying of the ship. He thought of his mission and of the events that had led him to this moment.

What would draw the Lector so very far south? What was it he sought? He was a Sentinel. He pulled a lock of gray hair away from his eyes and tucked it behind his ear. *What would a Sentinel have sought so near to Arranan, a nation with whom we may soon be at war?* There would be few answers among the corpses, but perhaps there would be something. A note, a map, perhaps one of Erlorn's banned books. *Something…*

The sound of boots trudging up the small ladder to the forecastle disrupted Bale's contemplation. He swallowed the last thick bits of bread and turned. A short fellow ascended and then smoothed his smart surcoat. His gaze fell immediately to Bale.

"Aha!" the man said in a harsh, high-pitched voice. "Our very own stowaway spooker! I knew I'd find you at the place farthest from my men."

Bale made no effort to rise or greet the man in proper fashion. He returned his attention to the sea.

"I'm sorry," the man continued, "but I've failed to introduce myself." He thrust forward a gloved hand. "I am General Thalius Fane, commander of all the armies of Rune."

If the voyage hadn't been unpleasant already, it certainly was once Bale met General Fane. The general was an intimidating sort, not in the roughhousing, mocking manner of the soldiers, but in the way he seemed to coolly appraise every remark and subtly assert authority. He was also hideous, with most of his face covered by burn scars that looked much like dried drips of wax from a candle. Bale could not help but study the striations and swells, which invariably led to a weighty pause in discussion and a distasteful glare from Fane.

The day after Fane had found Bale on the forecastle the general insisted Bale meet with him at daybreak. The general had evicted the captain from his traditional quarters at the rear of the ship, so their time was spent talking over a stout table in the well-appointed, windowed room. Aside from the company, it was far more comfortable than his hammock in the berth.

Breakfast consisted of toasted bread, boiled quail eggs, and sliced tomatoes—none of which Bale particularly enjoyed—and innumerable questions concerning the purpose of Bale's journey. Bale quickly discerned the general knew a great deal of the Sanctum and its history, and had already received the news of the Lector's death. *He will be a difficult man to deceive, and a vengeful one if he catches me trying to do so.*

"It's a dangerous time for a man such as you," Fane said, cracking a speckled egg on his silver plate. He looked at Bale with black eyes. "To travel south, I mean."

"The Lector was a most holy man," Bale said, speaking too quickly. He tried to slow himself, regarding his breakfast with his best portrayal of a casual demeanor. He plucked an egg from a silver bowl in the table's center and began rolling it about the rim of his plate with a fingertip. "There are sacred rituals which must be observed."

"Of course, Acolyte. But a solitary man, particularly one so *unprepared* for violence as yourself, venturing into the very teeth of war? Certainly prayers are heard with equal clarity whether they are uttered in the Abbey or at a gravesite?"

"He was a revered member of the Sanctum. He deserves honor in death. Such is our way."

General Fane took a bite of his egg. The yolk spilled across his lips and dribbled through the neatly trimmed hair adorning his chin. "I'll soon have tens of thousands of soldiers standing in the shadows of the Southwalls. As a gesture of my sympathy for the Sanctum's dear loss, I could have them deliver the Lector's body to your very hands. You need only find a room at one of the many inns crowding the harbor of Riverweave and wait for my promise to be fulfilled. Such would surely be a task more suited to one of your... substance." His lips curled to a thin smile, his scars stretching and becoming pale.

Bale studied the scars with some fascination but then detached his eyes from the disfiguration. *What to tell such a man? It is said a small string of truth can mislead more than an entire fabric of falsity*. He rubbed at his chin, pretending to address an itch. "My mission entails more than merely ensuring the Lector's corpse is not picked clean by crows. Sacred rites, er, oils for the body, and such things. The body could become corrupted with movement."

"Your *mission*? That seems an odd word for an acolyte, but certainly something understandable to a man of my vocation. Is there something you hope to find amidst those mutilated bodies?"

Bale kept his eyes on his plate, maneuvering the egg around a slice of toasted bread. He was quiet for a moment before answering. "I know not."

"Such bravado!" General Fane said, his shrill voice sarcastic. "To venture so *boldly* into the vast unknown, with only a faint feeling of purpose! Perhaps I should thrust a weapon in your hand and have you fight alongside my Scarlet Swords!" He rapped his knuckles on the table, and Bale met his stern gaze. Fane's smile turned to a scowl. "You have been permitted passage on *my* ship, allowed to travel among the soldiers of *my* army. Let us dispense with any notions of evasion and smallish talk, shall we?"

Bale's finger trembled for an instant. The egg rolled free and settled against the bread. "You have my gratitude, General Fane. Indeed, the gratitude of all the Sanctum. I assure you, I spoke honestly. I do not know what I will find."

"That is not an answer to my question, spooker. I asked you what it was you *hoped* to find." He wiped his mouth with a napkin, hastily and indelicately. "Put another way, what is the *question* you intend to have answered with your mission?"

"I am simply an acolyte, General Fane. In many regards I simply follow the instructions of others."

Fane slammed the napkin in a fist against the table. The wood shook and the plates jumped. He leveled a finger at Bale and his breath shuddered. "Perhaps my reputation has not yet penetrated the cloister of delusion that is the Abbey. I am not one to anger, Acolyte. That fact should be considered most of all by those I could so easily destroy."

Bale pulled a strand of hair from his face and tucked it behind his ear. His hand was shaking. *I am too weak an instrument!* He rubbed at his eyes, as though they were irritating him even though they were not. "We must know who killed the Lector. It is that, and that alone."

Fane's black eyes glittered. His grin returned, and he retrieved his napkin and draped it gently upon his lap. "Does the Sanctum believe a corpse can disclose its killer? If so, then perhaps the powers of your kind have been understated." He set about cracking another speckled egg. "Rune has so very many enemies. The Arranese are but one, an obvious one surely, but there are other knives at our back. There are other powers more... ancient." The egg broke upon the plate, the yolk spreading in a pool of yellow. "You know of whom I speak, don't you?"

General Fane must not know my suspicions. "If it is the Necrists you speak of, you'd be better served reading fairy tales and speaking with fishwives. Their 'myth' has followers, certainly, but they are hardly the powerful necromancers of old. I would not identify them as a true threat."

"Are they not?" General Fane arched a scarred brow. "Perhaps you are right. But there are others yet, aren't there?" He picked the bits of broken shell away from the slimy eggs on his plate. "Certainly the Sanctum has not burned every book that posited an unpopular position?"

He knows much. But how? Bale found he could not help himself. "Do you speak of the Sentinels?"

"I have traveled to the farthest reaches of Rune, and beyond. I have seen much and heard many things. Rumors of things long thought dead, of things forgotten entirely. What do you believe became of the Sentinels, after they were banished those many years ago? Where is it they went? To whom did they tell their secrets? And might there be secrets that preceded even them?" He pinched a bit of egg white between his fingers and studied it briefly before eating.

Bale stared at the general in silence.

"I am an ambitious man, Acolyte. There are powers in this world beyond the understanding of mortals, held in ancient relics and in the blood of rare beings. If we could but decipher those secrets, we could possess those powers. A man with such powers could make the entire world anew, and bend the fates to his will."

Dead gods, get me free of this man. "Such ambition can be dangerous, General. There are paths mortals should not tread."

Fane's black eyes twitched erratically. "Are there, indeed? Or are we simply too afraid to dare those paths? I have learned the Spider King of Arranan may have discovered such secrets. Should we surrender these advantages to our enemy?"

Who is it, General, who is truly our enemy?

11
VIOLENCE

KARNAG MAK RAGG threw open the door to *The Dead Messenger*. He was weary from the road and his troubling dreams. The words he'd heard since passing through the gates of Raven's Roost rankled him. *"Tream was here just days ago, and said you were dead!"* Karnag reckoned he knew what had happened and a hot anger welled inside him.

"Dead gods!" shouted Handsome, the barkeep. He rushed to the door and nearly tumbled over a chair in his haste. "You live!"

Fencress moved to stand at Karnag's side. "Tream told you otherwise, did he?" she said. There was none of the usual levity in her tone.

"Aye," said Handsome, gesturing toward a table. "Ale?"

Karnag spat at the table. "Did he take the money? Did he betray us?" He spoke loudly, and those in the tavern fell silent.

"I-I believe so. He told me he killed your mark, that you and the rest were cut down, that he was the sole survivor. It seemed an unlikely story, but I had no cause to question the lad." He shook his head. "A foul thing to do, that. I'm sorry."

Karnag felt as though fire burned in his veins, spreading out from his chest and coursing through his limbs. *The feeling returns.* Ever since he'd slain the Lector, it seemed as though something had possessed him. He'd battled with his dreams, where words haunted him, and his waking hours were uneasy. He gritted his teeth to the point of nearly cracking them and squeezed his hands into fists. With sudden fury, he brought a fist down upon the table, smashing the wood to splinters.

Handsome's eyes darted about and his lips trembled. "Karnag, there is no need for violence here! Dead gods, you know me! I didn't think I could question Tream. You'd worked with him several times, so I reckoned he had your trust."

Karnag fingered the hilts of his blades, each in turn. "Where is he?"

"I have no idea, I swear to you. Your patron sent him a note, asked him to meet at Old Gallows Rock. That's the last I saw of him. I only arranged the meeting because I thought you were dead. You have to understand that, Karnag! I would never betray you!"

Karnag grabbed Handsome by the throat and slammed him against the tavern's sandstone wall. His eyes darkened and he gave him a fierce look. "You should never believe news of my death unless you bear witness to it yourself, and then you should question your eyes. Where is he?"

Handsome flailed and fumbled with Karnag's iron grip. "H-Hargrave," he gasped.

Karnag eased his grip, allowing Handsome's feet to touch the floor.

"Hargrave," the barkeep said through wheezing breaths. "He told me once his brother had a farm near Hargrave." Karnag withdrew his hand and Handsome sucked in air. "There's a chance he'd head there," he said. "I've built my business on keeping people's secrets, but you've been wronged. I'll break his trust if it means regaining yours."

Fencress placed a hand on Karnag's shoulder. "If a man is on the run, he runs most often to family, they say."

The narrow streets of Raven's Roost were choked with refugees fleeing the threat of war. Karnag pressed through the throngs of bedraggled folk and their mangy animals, his company in tow.

"Dead gods!" called Fencress, shouting over a braying donkey, "I thought this place smelled like shit before. What do you reckon it smells like now? What smells worse than shit?"

Karnag said nothing. He no longer had humor within him. He kept moving through the crowd, forging a path through the rabble with an icy glare and powerful movements. An old man stumbled into his path, and Karnag shoved him hard against an overladen cart.

"Death," said Drenj from behind, voice barely loud

enough to be heard over the din of the crowd. "Death smells worse."

"You are a veritable poet, my young Khaldisian friend! Oh, the songs we'll write once we've settled in some seedy tavern to count our coin!"

After a moment Karnag felt the black-clad woman's eyes upon him. "What is it?" he grumbled.

"New horses?" she asked. "Hargrave is a good two days' ride southeast, perhaps three."

Karnag grunted and continued his march, turning a corner and heading toward the town's stockyards and smithies.

Fencress edged to Karnag's side. "We're spilling a lot of blood for the coin we've been paid. What's more, Tream may not be as dimwitted as we suspect. He could prove a hard man to find."

Karnag regarded her. Fencress had for years now been a trustworthy companion, his only friend even, but work such as this tested everyone. "I'll ride to the world's ending to find him," said Karnag. "I leave no score unsettled."

Fencress nodded in reply. "I'm at your side, of course." She glanced over her shoulder at Drenj and Paddyn. "But what of them?"

Karnag chuckled grimly. "Neither of them will want to be sitting behind these walls when war arrives. The Khaldisian's greed will keep him loyal, at least until the crowns are in his hands. Paddyn is young and scared, but he's more frightened of crossing me than helping me."

"Such are the ties that bind," said Fencress, smirking.

The crowds thinned near the city's gates. In the shadow of

the wall they found a horse trader, his stall holding a sad collection of steeds. Six bony beasts, each more emaciated than the last. Their merchant sat with legs raised upon a table near the street, lounging in the shade of the stall. He had a fat belly and smiled smugly as he looked up from the bowl of olives balanced on his yellow shirt.

Drenj passed wordlessly by the man and moved to the horses, checking their teeth and hooves. After a moment he turned back to Karnag and nodded.

"How much for the lot of them?" asked Karnag.

The merchant stood and his smile broadened. "War is on the way," he said, stroking a long mustache. "They say folk should be fleeing north." He made a sweeping gesture with his hand. "A healthy horse is the fastest method of travel. But, they are hard to come by now, and highly valued."

"Your price, merchant," said Karnag. "We have no time to tarry."

"Three hundred silver crowns." His eyes drifted across each of the company, as though appraising opponents in combat.

"Three hundred?" demanded Drenj, arms flailing. "That is many times a fair price!"

"These are hard days, gentlemen!" said the merchant, rolling his eyes as though bothered by the insolence of children. "I have but six horses to sell, and that is my price. The Arranese may soon be at our gates. What would be the value of such horses, then? Trust me, my price now is a bargain compared to what it could be in just a few days."

"We have a deal," said Karnag, dropping three heavy purses on the table.

"Madness!" yelped Drenj, his dark-lined eyes wide with shock. "Think of the coin, you ingrate!"

"I appreciate a customer who knows value," said the merchant, drawing open the purse strings and fingering the coins with a smile. "The horses are yours. And, as a gesture of my good faith, I'll throw in their tack."

Drenj stormed across the hay-covered ground to stand before Karnag. "Are you mad? You've just spent the bulk of our advance for a slim chance to recover the rest! You realize if we don't find Tream we'll be left with next to nothing for our troubles? He has wronged us all equally, Karnag. Vengeance would be a fine thing, but this is business."

Karnag regarded the Khaldisian stoically. "I've told you," he said in a level voice, "I do not do these things for the coin."

"But I do! And you've just squandered nearly all the money we had in hand!" He paced about the stall. "I've been away from my family for weeks, I've undoubtedly missed other opportunities for easier, more reliable work, and now I'm being asked to ride south again, toward an invading army, on the meager hope Tream is picking his rotting teeth on his brother's farm?"

"I know he's there." *I can see it.* He shut his eyes for an instant, and heard the sound of Tream begging for his life. *It will happen thus.*

"Ah yes," Drenj said, "Karnag Mak Ragg, the great slayer of men. Tell me, do you smell his blood? Can you taste his fear? Tell me just how is it you *know*? Tell me you haven't just cast aside our coin on nothing more than a hint from that hare-lipped barkeep?"

Karnag tapped the hilt of his short sword. "You are free to go, Khaldisian. Just as Tream was."

"Not without my share," he said, squaring to Karnag.

"Gentlemen!" said the merchant, moving between the two and placing his hands upon their chests. "Please, if you must quarrel, do it elsewhere!"

"Out of my way," Karnag growled.

The merchant spat, offended. "I'll not be treated this way by scum such as you!"

Karnag slapped the man across the face. "Out of my way."

The merchant stood in shock for a moment, rubbing a flushed cheek. He then withdrew a bejeweled dagger from his belt. "I rescind our bargain! Best of luck finding healthy horses within five leagues of this city!"

Karnag struck the merchant square upon the jaw, sending him sprawling onto his table with a shower of silver coins. The merchant tumbled backward and off, into a pile of hay. Karnag gave Drenj a dangerous look and then strode to stand over the merchant.

"Guards!" the man screamed, staggering away from Karnag while sweeping straws of hay from his shirt. "Guards!"

Karnag lunged forward, driving the merchant into one of the stall's wooden posts. The post snapped and the two men crashed to the ground near the horses.

Karnag pressed himself upward and drove a knee into the merchant's chest. Bones snapped and the man gasped in shock. He struggled beneath Karnag but to no avail.

Karnag grabbed the merchant's head in his hands. "No man commands me," he said through gritted teeth, "and none dares betray me."

Fencress screamed from somewhere and there was a clamor of shouts and steel.

Karnag roared and he squeezed tightly. The merchant gurgled and his eyes bulged and he squirmed desperately. Karnag felt hands pulling at his shoulders but he would not be moved. *I yield to no man.*

He roared again, and a feeling rose within him. A feeling from deep inside, from a place beyond thought and instinct, from his very essence. It rose and swelled, filling him completely. A spirit, a power, an invulnerability.

His hands flexed and dug into the merchant's sweaty skin. Then, Karnag shouted a word he did not know, in a tongue not his own. A loud crack sounded, and the man fell still.

Karnag stumbled back and stood. He regarded the corpse, split asunder from the crown of the head to the center of the gut. Blood and brains spilled from his skull, and broken ribs pierced his chest and poked through the yellow linen of his shirt.

He regarded the carcass and realized a wide grin had split his face. *I can slay by will alone.*

Hands tugged at him and heard his name called as though from far away. Over the span of several heartbeats the sounds grew louder. Someone came into his field of vision, a face frozen in a rictus of horror.

"Karnag!" It was Fencress, her face spattered with blood. "Dead gods, man! What have you done?"

Karnag allowed himself to be pulled away from

the merchant's stall by Fencress as Drenj and Paddyn frantically gathered handfuls of the spilled coins and what few horses they could. A dead guardsman lay near the stall, his guts cut open. Bells clanged as the city's alarm sounded, and Karnag caught sight of several red-sashed soldiers scrambling toward the stockyards.

They pulled their horses hurriedly through the city's gate, its guardsman whimpering and holding up his hands as they passed. Screams of terror sounded from behind them.

Fencress yelled at the men to mount the horses bareback, to worry about the tack for the beasts later. "Get clear of this place, now!"

Karnag did so in a daze, his movements slow and dreamlike. The wicked smile did not leave his face.

They rode hard and came to a clearing half a league south of Raven's Roost and dismounted their steeds. No one said a word as they fitted their horses with bits, bridles and saddles.

"A warning would have been a nice thing," said Fencress, her face displaying her usual bemusement but her eyes something else. "We have little left of our supplies."

Karnag shrugged. "We're bound to cross refugees on the road."

"Simple criminals, then?" said Paddyn, spitting through the hole left by his missing tooth. "Is that what we've become?"

Karnag gave him a black look. "Did you ever think of yourself as something more?"

They were quiet and climbed astride their horses once more. Karnag turned and regarded the road behind them, shadowed by leafy trees and gently rising toward Raven's Roost. The alarm bells could still be heard, faint and distant. On the road, perhaps three hundred yards away, was a lone, green-cloaked rider.

"A guard?" asked Fencress. "Perhaps a friend of the merchant?"

Karnag shrugged and turned his horse slowly about. He straightened in the saddle and breathed deeply. He fingered the hilts of his blades, each in turn. *No matter. Let them come.*

Shivering, Karnag pulled his moth-eaten blanket to his chin and rolled over to face the dead remains of the campfire. His teeth chattered and his body trembled as though he stood upon the snow-laden highlands of his youth. Yet, it was a warm night, and his companions rested peacefully in their bedrolls nearby.

He rubbed at his neck, and his hand came away slick with sweat. He wondered for an instant whether he'd fallen ill, but then thought of the horse trader, his corpse broken and awash in blood. And then were those words— those of the Lector—threading through his thoughts. *No. I fight with something else entirely.*

He squeezed shut his eyes and searched again for that place within him. He slowed his breathing and disregarded the chill in his bones, settling deep within himself. He sought that center, that focus he'd drawn upon just before the killing. It had seemed a sense of utter certainty, a willful embrace of death and all its cold consequences. It had seemed then so familiar, like something he'd known he'd held within all along, but had never been fully able to touch. It had seemed like his very soul.

He searched, but within were only the words. The maddening words whose meaning was utterly incomprehensible. Over and over again they came, at first as soft as a lover's whisper but growing steadily louder. *"Necrista traellus a abridalusi Yrghul y ogo alliata. Illienne cradus e Warduren renden e sallem orn argo apocha."*

He opened his eyes and smacked his head, as though he could knock the words from his skull. His eyes found the stars above and he breathed deeply the night air. He took in the world around him, the heavy boughs of the old trees, the groaning sound they made as the wind moved through them. The faint rustle of leaves. He pulled in all the perceptions he could discern, but still, through and over it all, the words resounded.

They grew louder still. *"Necrista traellus a abridalusi Yrghul y ogo alliata. Illienne cradus e Warduren renden e sallem orn argo apocha."* He could not pull his thoughts from their utterance, and could not bend his mind to think of other things.

Soon, they were like a thunderclap, as loud and forceful as the most violent storm. He tossed aside his blanket and pressed himself upright. It seemed as though the whole forest shook with the noise, yet his companions slept soundly still.

The words were heard by him alone.

Louder and louder they came, until all other thought was drummed from his mind. His vision went to blackness and his head rang. *"Necrista traellus a abridalusi*

Yrghul y ogo alliata. Illienne cradus e Warduren renden e sallem orn argo apocha."

His head seemed ready to split with the reverberation. He reeled with agony, squeezing his hands to his skull in hopes of keeping it whole.

"No!" he roared. He fell back to the ground, writhing in his struggle to force the sounds from his head.

"Karnag?" called someone, the sound distant and drowned by the words roaring through his mind.

"No!" he screamed again, gnashing his teeth and cracking his jaw.

After a time he rose, defiant.

No.

And then there it was. The feeling. It began deep within him, in his very center. Faintly at first, but growing ever more intense.

The chill fled his form and the shivers subsided. He felt within him a warmth, a strength, a conviction. A truth. The feel of it invigorated, and he surrendered to it and reveled in it. His heart became a cauldron, spreading white-hot fire through his limbs.

I am the predator, the taker of lives. I am the executioner and decider of fates. I shall not succumb to the will of another.

The words of the Lector diminished and grew silent.

I have become their master.

12
THE DEEP SHADOWS

ANNICK SHIFTED UNCOMFORTABLY in his straw cot. Every last bit of him hurt, and he'd been unable to eat for days. Horus had been kind enough to deliver the occasional bottle of wine, but even that did nothing to remedy his aches, much less his profound despair.

What pains can I bear, when even the wine fails to dull them?

Ever since his encounter with General Fane his sleep had been fitful, as it was this night. He lay with eyes open, watching the barred portal of his door, the thin moonlight streaming from his window, and the deep shadows pooled in the corners of his cell.

He knew they were coming.

General Fane was right: the Necrists would torture him for as long as he could endure, until at last he was broken and revealed to them everything. He would be forced to surrender the identities of all the Variden, the

Vigilant Ones. They were the surviving disciples of Valis, one of the seven banished Sentinels, and he would betray them all.

He thought of the lacquered box he'd left in his quarters, and how foolish he'd been to leave it there. It was his Coda, the bracelet of black iron given to him when he'd taken the oaths of the Variden—the same bracelet Alisa had worn when she'd come to visit him. The Codas had been gifted to the order by the Sentinel Valis, and were the key to their power and survival. All the Variden wore them, for the Codas sealed their secrets, and preserved knowledge upon the death of the body. Without it, Lannick would stand naked before the sorcerous inquisitions of his enemies.

He shifted again in his cot. He would not sleep this night, he knew. The memories of his old life, of his countless failures, were growing too tangible. When his family was murdered he'd disappeared. He'd abandoned his order, buried the symbols of his affiliation and spent his time sulking in taverns. He'd drank and drank, desperately trying to wash away all regrets. At last, he became lost. Lost to his enemies, his order, and himself.

But here, in prison, his past had found him once again.

He kicked aside his blanket. He felt unsteady, plagued by the vague dizziness of insomnia. His eyes trailed again to the door, waiting for it to open. *Waiting for death.*

He knew the Necrists would not come for him during the day, bound as they were to darkness. But if he could avoid them for but one more day, then perhaps there was some narrow chance. Perhaps Alisa would come to rescue him as she'd promised. He pulled himself from his cot and shuffled to the cell's arrow-loop window. The sky was dead black, still a long while before dawn.

As they had for several nights, his thoughts focused on his meeting with Alisa. It seemed now a lifetime ago she'd visited him. *"I will return for you,"* she'd said.

Could she save me? It was the memory of those words that kept alive the frail fire of hope within him. *Perhaps only the hope of a hopeless fool, but hope nonetheless.*

If she could come for him before the Necrists, he could grasp a chance at safety, at survival. He could recover his Coda, rejoin his order, and redeem himself. His life could regain the purpose it had been so long without.

He knelt before the window and pressed his head against the wall's wet stones. His eyes burned with tears.

Sweet Illienne the Light Eternal, let the sun rise!

"Lannick."

The word was softly spoken, just barely more than a whisper. Lannick drifted from the throes of a rare slumber. His ears perked for a moment, but there came no other sound. He pulled his blanket to his shoulders and shifted in his cot.

"Lannick."

A woman's voice. He turned in his cot and cracked open his eyes. The cell was dark and empty. He looked to the window and saw the sky had shifted from black to a deep purple. Dawn would come soon. He looked to the barred portal in his door, but all was lost in shadow.

Do I dream?

And then he saw it. In the shadows near the foot of

his cot there was a deeper, darker blackness. It seemed less a thing than the *absence* of a thing—a void, a nothingness, a rip in the world.

Terror seized him and Lannick retreated until he was pressed firmly against the wall. *I have nowhere to run.* "Help me!" he croaked. His voice was hoarse and the pain in his jaw made the words difficult to shape.

There was a pale glow from the center of the void and the sound of shuffling movement. Something was emerging from blackness. The void shifted spasmodically and expanded, growing to consume the whole of the cell between the cot and the door.

"Lannick."

A tall figure emerged from the blackness, thin and elegant and cloaked from head to toe in what seemed a black veil. Behind it came three squat shapes, each half the size of a man, shambling and misshapen.

"Help me!" Lannick shouted more loudly, but it was still little more than a moan, unlikely to draw the attention of the guards. He huddled in the cell's corner and pressed harder against the wall, madly hoping the stone would swallow him whole.

The tall figure glided gracefully to within an arm's reach of Lannick, and with slender hands parted the veil to reveal a face so ghostly pale it seemed almost luminescent. It was a face delicately featured, a woman's face that would have been beautiful but for the thick, barbed stitch extending from hairline to chin, splitting it precisely in half.

I know this face! It was stretched and pitted as

compared to when he'd last seen it years before, and its hue was now the white pallor of death, but…

Dead gods!

"Lannick," the woman said. "I hope this face pleases you." She smiled, causing the stitch to buckle and twist grotesquely. "General Fane was kind enough to reveal to us the location of your wife's grave."

Dead gods! What horrors must I suffer?

She gestured to the three abominations behind her. "And the graves of your children."

Lannick sobbed and shrieked in revulsion as the ghastly malformations grinned at him, their faces sick perversions of his children's. They came at him and pulled with gnarled hands, grabbing him by his ankles and dragging him through the dark rift and into the cold netherworld beyond. They giggled all the while.

Let me die!

Ahead of them walked the tall Necrist, leading them into the blackness. "We have found the flesh *remembers*," she said. "You must have provided some amusement to your children."

Lannick choked on his tears and gnashed his teeth. *Sweet Illienne, damned be the day I forsook you! Forgive me!*

The abominations chuckled and babbled like babies.

The Necrist turned her head, displaying an unnatural smile. "It must be heartwarming for you to lay eyes upon them again. Touching how the flesh remembers such emotions…" Just then she stopped and barked strange words in a guttural tongue.

The abominations skittered to Lannick's sides and lifted him, pressing him upward and restraining his arms. Lannick wrenched about in the chilling blackness surrounding him, but he could not break free. As he struggled, the Necrist came to stand over him, her face mere inches from his own.

"No," Lannick wept, vainly trying to look away from the warped but still familiar face.

The Necrist's smile broadened, becoming an expression almost feral, a wide swath of yellow teeth and purplish gums. The face was so familiar, yet so awfully monstrous. "Your wife's skin carried memories as well." She bent close, the skin venting a putrid odor of decay, and then she pressed against him.

Lannick squeezed shut his eyes and wept and wailed, so terrible was the feel of that cold face against his own. *Sweet Illienne, no!*

He shuddered with sobs as the Necrist smothered his mouth with a lingering kiss.

Lannick rubbed tears from his eyes and choked down a sob, determined to hold dear his sanity. *Such madness!* Then he sobbed again and wiped at his mouth with a tear-wetted hand, desperately trying to wash away a stain he felt certain was there.

They dragged him onward through the netherworld, and Lannick had no idea how far or how long the journey had been. All about him was an endless blackness of shifting shadows, and the only sensation of movement was the cold chill flowing beneath him. The horrors he'd endured made the journey seem ponderous in length, but as his wits gathered he realized he'd been gone from his cell only briefly.

I will not be so easily broken, he vowed, rising to his elbows. He studied the shadows upon shadows lining the unearthly tunnel. *A shadowpath*, he remembered. It was said the Necrists could move unseen among contiguous shadows, accessing the furrows in the world's substance forged ages ago by the dark god Yrghul. Yrghul, the Lord of Nightmares, had used the shadowpaths as a means to corrupt the dreams of humankind. His disciples, the Necrists, used them to travel in ways invisible.

Dead gods, where are they taking me?

Lannick struggled to peer ahead through eyes rheumy with drying tears. He tried to avert the backward gazes of the misshapen dwarfs, and struggled to shut his ears to their macabre, mimicked sounds. *Shodafayn*—shadow men—the navigators of the shadowpaths. They leered at him over their knobby shoulders, chortling and drooling with sick, stolen faces.

Suddenly the Necrist halted, wheeled about and shouted harshly at the Shodafayn. One of them ambled crookedly to her side and held its hands outward, pleading. The Necrist spoke in angry tones, pointing at the creature and gesturing at the path ahead. There, before them, the shadows were dissipating, retreating from a pinpoint of light.

Something's amiss.

The Necrist growled and waved a hand. The Shodafayn responded by rushing toward the light source, now the size of a keyhole. It squatted close to the light, hands upon its hips and muttering as it inspected the anomaly.

At last the misshapen thing turned and spoke, its tone

apologetic. The Necrist huffed and nodded curtly in reply. The Shodafayn's brethren shuffled to its side.

The three abominations gathered together and whispered. Gradually their murmurs assumed the measured cadence of a chant, and the words the intonations of sorcery. They turned toward the break in the darkness and set about prodding and tugging at its edges with their knotty hands, moving with surprising dexterity. The light expanded as they pulled, and grew to cast a frail illumination into the blackness of the shadowpath. It shimmered and shifted, and what lay beyond was distorted as though seen through a thick pane of stained glass.

Within moments the rift was as wide as several men. The Necrist barked a brusque command, causing the Shodafayn to scurry from the light and return to Lannick. They grabbed him again at the ankles and dragged him swiftly, closer and closer to the flickering breach.

And then through it.

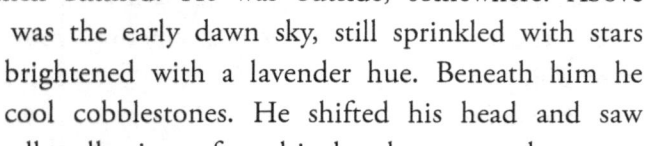

Lannick blinked. He was outside, somewhere. Above him was the early dawn sky, still sprinkled with stars but brightened with a lavender hue. Beneath him he felt cool cobblestones. He shifted his head and saw a small collection of multicolored tents and wagons laden with crates and sacks. There came the sound of chickens clucking.

I know this place. Ironmoor's Old Market.

He tried to force himself upward to sit but was pressed back to the stones by a silken boot. Above him stood the

Necrist, the black veil of her clothing hiding all but her pale hands. *Thank the dead gods I need not look at her face.*

"Our journey has not yet ended," she said, turning her head about as though looking for something. After a moment she returned her attention to Lannick. "Oh, the things we have planned for you," she said through the cover of her veil. "It is a rare gift to find a Variden without the protection of his Coda. We will rip apart your flesh and your mind, my love."

There sounded a sharp chirp of a bird from a nearby rooftop. Another answered. The dawn sun brightened the sky.

The Necrist hissed something, a curse perhaps.

She's nervous.

Lannick turned his head as subtly as he was able, mindful of the Necrist's presence. A dozen or so feet away, one of the misshapen Shodafayn crawled on hands and knees along the edge of a tent, sniffing at the mud-clotted cobbles with a nose that once belonged to Lannick's eldest son.

Dead gods, kill me.

He shuddered and put a hand to his brow. He knew what his circumstances required, but he was weak, stiff, and drained of nearly all life. He felt as though no blood flowed within him and no life filled his limbs, as much a corpse as a man. He wished so much he could summon something, some inner reserve of strength to fight or flee, but there was no hope for such dramatics in his present state.

He pulled his head just off the stones, but could manage no more. His eyes strayed again to the hound-like

Shodafayn, smelling at cracked rocks and frayed cloths, searching for something.

Lannick remembered it then. The shadowpaths were passages through the netherworld, but were mirrored in the world above by contiguous shadows—shadows cast by the roof of a house, melding into another cast by a cobble, to another cast by a discarded broom, and so forth. As shadows shifted in the world above, depending upon the position of the moon, stars, and objects, so did the shadowpaths. The disciples of Yrghul could travel unseen for as long as shadows joined others, but a break in the line of shadows left them to travel in the world of men.

It was clear the Necrist had not expected this interruption in their passage, and had accused the Shodafayn navigators of making a mistake.

Perhaps their path amidst the shadows has been purposefully altered.

Suddenly something squealed like a pig being slaughtered. Lannick turned and saw one of the other Shodafayn fumbling at an arrow stuck in its throat, trying vainly to stop the spout of black blood from the wound.

"Don't move!" the Necrist hissed at Lannick. She mumbled a string of broken-sounding words and made intricate gestures with her hands.

Sorcery. Lannick struggled upward but realized his arms would not move. He looked down to see the shadows bleeding from between the cobblestones to form bindings upon his wrists. They bit at his flesh like ice.

There was a commotion off to his side, and Lannick

saw another of the Shodafayn pinned against a wagon wheel by two arrows lodged in its chest.

The Necrist remained near him, scanning the market's wide square and the rooftops at its far boundaries. She shouted at the last of the Shodafayn, which continued sniffing along the flap of a tent. The Shodafayn croaked in answer, and began scratching at the ground as though digging a hole.

"Good," said the Necrist, "you've found it." She turned back to Lannick. "Come!"

Lannick felt the bonds at his wrists dissolve, and pressed upward with the waning, desperate remains of his strength. Too late. The Necrist seized him by his matted mop of hair and pulled hard. He groaned in pain, and found he could do nothing but scramble backward in the Necrist's tow.

An arrow whistled by and clattered against the stone cobbles inches from Lannick's bare foot. Then another.

The Necrist barked another urgent command, her tone frantic. Lannick tried to turn to see ahead of her but the movement made his scalp feel as though it were ripping apart. He felt a trickle of blood upon his forehead.

Another cry sounded and the Necrist halted abruptly. Lannick felt her hand pull free of his skull, and he lunged away as quickly as his beaten body would allow. He came to rest at the broken wheel of a wagon and turned timidly about.

From behind the nearby traders' tents emerged several figures, all wearing green cloaks and brandishing weapons tinged by flickering flames.

Variden.

171

The Necrist faced them, her pale hands outstretched and gathering the shadows surrounding her. Just beyond, the Shodafayn tore open a rift of swirling shadow with its stunted arms, and in an instant the rift jerked and expanded to several feet across.

"Hold fast, you fiend!" one of the Variden shouted. The Variden were close now, close enough for Lannick to recognize some of their once-familiar faces.

The Necrist cursed in the foul tongue of its kind, and whipped about to regard Lannick. She seized an edge of the veil covering her face and pulled it aside, revealing again the face of his dead wife, knitted together with a black stitch.

"Another time, my love," she said with a sickly sweetness, her face contorting to a wicked grin. She then turned and dove headlong into the shadowy rift, disappearing into the blackness with the Shodafayn following closely behind.

The air about the breach shimmered and shook, and then the hole collapsed upon itself, leaving only the gently swaying tent flap brushing the cobblestones.

"Lannick!" cried a voice. It was Alisa, her large brown eyes catching the first beams of the morning sun. Behind her stalked two more Variden, grimly regarding the two corpses of the Shodafayn and the perversions upon their faces.

The faces of Lannick's infant twins.

Lannick collapsed against the cobblestones and wept.

13
THE LAST KING

PREFECT GAMGHAST STRODE through the Bastion's cavernous hallways, his boots and heavy staff drumming a rhythmic *click-click-clack* upon the marble tiles and echoing throughout the vaulted sprawl. He peered out from the sagging hood of his brown robe, eyeing the musty tapestries, the exaggerated sculptures, and the vast gulfs of unnecessary space. *It is a shameful, corrupting thing when the powerful rule amidst such excess.*

The Bastion had stood for centuries. It had been expanded to serve Rune's pride, it had been burned to the ground by enemies, it had been built anew, it had been gutted when one High King desired to eradicate the memories of a predecessor. The countless alterations had left the place with innumerable secret passages, uneven halls, and dead ends. It was a place difficult for Gamghast to traverse with any air of purpose or certainty, and he feared his confusion showed.

The Bastion's hooded, scurrying functionaries regarded him with cocked brows and narrowed eyes, displaying varying degrees of suspicion and derision. Gamghast quickly lost count of the number of times the word "spooker" was whispered in his wake. Nevertheless, as he'd hoped, none of them confronted him or questioned his presence in the hallowed halls of the High King's castle, and his exchange with the veiled guards outside had been brief.

He hadn't seen High King Deragol in quite some time, but was familiar with the rumors of his condition. The High King was no longer a young man, and had not yet produced an heir. It was said his wife had suffered many miscarriages, and his mind was tortured by grief. Gossipmongers mockingly referred to him as "The Last King," anticipating he'd prove to be the last of his line.

Gamghast paused in the center of the yawning chamber at the juncture of several hallways and gazed upward at nothing in particular. He'd gathered information on Chamberlain Alamis and he'd followed the man for several days outside the castle, but he'd learned nothing. Gamghast realized he had no gift for snooping, so today he'd try a different tack. He'd rely upon old customs to secure an audience with the Last King himself.

A murdered Sentinel. An heirless King. Such are the trials of our times.

He heaved a sigh and continued his trudge through the great halls of stone.

Gamghast rounded a corner and immediately caught

sight of the tall figure standing between two gaudy vases at the end of the hallway, dressed in opulent, blue silk. His head was uncovered, in blatant defiance of tradition. His pale eyes held Gamghast's firmly as he approached, his look one of genuine contempt only slightly offset by a thin smile.

Chamberlain Alamis, Rune's most venomous serpent.

"Prefect Gamghast," said the man in a voice that carried in spite of its seemingly quiet quality. "What an unexpected surprise. I understand you've come for an audience with the High King? Let me assure you, His Majesty is in no condition for visitors, particularly the unannounced kind. If your visit concerns the well-being of Rune," he said with a wave to a nearby door, "then I'd suggest you and I speak in the sitting room."

Gamghast smoothed the wisps of his white beard. *Tread carefully.* "Chamberlain Alamis," he said, bowing slightly. "As you know, our dear Lector was taken from us just weeks ago. He met regularly with His Majesty, in fulfillment of the Sanctum's mission. Our charge is to ensure the welfare of the kingdom of Rune, and the person who sits upon its throne. It is my task to continue the Lector's service to our King."

"Truly?" the chamberlain asked, his smile tightening. "Let me see," he said, tapping his pointed chin with a forefinger. "Ah, yes. I do recall your Lector meeting with His Majesty a few months ago, and, if memory serves, this was an annual event. A meeting at the Godswell, correct? To perform whatever charlatanry your kind practices. Are you here to engage in such nonsense? If so, then another time would be preferred."

"The Faith is still sacrosanct within these walls, Chamberlain. It is through the Faith that the High King's power—and yours—is granted."

The chamberlain's eyes narrowed, his smile one of bemusement. "Do you recite these platitudes for my benefit, or for your own?" He clucked his tongue, chiding. "It must be a difficult thing, clinging to old beliefs no one else shares, knowing your kind is widely regarded as doddering old fools." He drew closer, and his voice dipped to little more than a whisper. "There are times, Prefect, when old branches must be pruned, so that newer ones can thrive. *Now* is such a time."

Gamghast straightened his spine, bringing his eyes level with the chamberlain's. "Mine is a sacred calling." He dug into his robe and produced a sealed scroll and shook it before him in a fist, nearly smacking it against the chamberlain's smoothly shaven cheek. "This is my warrant, signed by High King Deragol himself on the very day he ascended to the throne. I need not your permission to call upon him!"

The chamberlain was a picture of calm and the thin smile did not leave his face. He breathed deeply before speaking. "You can dispense with the histrionics, Prefect. I, for one, believe your Sanctum meddles in dark magics behind a convenient veneer of religion. I can think of no greater hypocrisy than yours." He tugged at the cuffs of his sleeves and his shoulders sagged. "That said, who am I, a mere steward, to deny your task?" He bowed, gesturing to the hallway to his right. "This way, my dear Prefect."

The throne room of the High King was as impressive

a thing as Gamghast had ever beheld. It was a massive, circular expanse, at least a hundred feet in diameter, with great buttresses ringing the round of the wall and meeting somewhere far above to form a domed ceiling. The granite floor was leaden in hue and cast with a map of inlaid gold portraying the whole of the known world, with the kingdom of Rune at its center. The gold inlay glowed, reflecting the light of innumerable, aromatic candles lining the chamber's edge. There were no windows to be seen, and there was the smoke of incense hanging in a low haze. The heavy scent caused a catch in the back of Gamghast's throat and he coughed.

At the room's far end stood a dais, at least six feet in height and perhaps four times that wide, atop which was the throne. It was a tall chair of ivory, and the Old Faith instructed it was formed from shards of bone pulled from the mortal shell of the dead goddess Illienne the Light Eternal. The throne sat empty now, yet the power of the Crown was palpable in its place.

"This is your first time here?" Chamberlain Alamis asked, thumbing the cleft of his chin. "Ah. Of course it is. I apologize. I forget you are only a prefect, accustomed as I am to dealing with people of more… significance."

Gamghast let the comment pass. *Engaging him now serves no purpose, and only augments the dangers of my task.* He avoided the chamberlain's pale eyes, focusing instead on the room's wall. Ancient relics and treasures of great value adorned the wall, just beyond the ring of candlelight. Antiquities from as far back as the War of Fates, when the gods Illienne and Yrghul descended to oblivion and left the world to men. Swords, shields, and articles of clothing from great and powerful figures.

Alamis paused as though to allow the room's grandeur to weigh upon the prefect. He fiddled with a button at his collar before setting off toward the throne with long strides. "This way is the throne, Prefect."

Gamghast followed, gathering his robes from his ankles in a fist as he struggled to match the tall man's pace. As he walked he could not help but study the inlaid map decorating the granite floor. He moved northward according to the map's orientation, from the vast desert wastes at the world's ending, through the uncharted jungles of Rimgald to its pirate-infested coast, across the narrow stretch of the Ebony Sea, through the Bowl of Fire, into exotic Khaldisia along its border with fierce Arranan, near Arranan's ancient city of Zyn, home of its secretive Spider King. In a few more strides he was crossing the peaks of the Southwall Mountains, and as he did he reckoned countless Arranese warriors were doing the same at that place in the world. Then he was within Rune, across her old forests and into the holds of the thanes. Through the southern holds he crossed, then to Ironmoor and north to the hold of Farwatch. He glanced to the map's east and saw the island kingdom of Tallorrath and farther still the glint of proud Harkane, its honor-bound people ever at war. Onward he walked, through the high countries and mist-covered Stormfall, hold of Thane Brandiss, then to Rune's vague border with the untamed highlands, then at last the Waters of World's End.

At the head of it all, upon the crown of the world, was the foot of the great dais and the throne of the High King.

The chamberlain came to a stop a few feet away from the first stair of the dais. "The throne of Rune's High King," he said, his voice rising to fill the great hall, "The seat of the entire world's dominion for a thousand years. Imagine," he said, his tone longing, "all the kings and warlords and thanes who've bent their knees before this chair to lick the boots of the High King. Think of all the great powers emasculated in the shadow of this seat."

"Or," Gamghast said, eyeing the throne, "from another perspective, all of the ways in which Illienne's blessing has manifested, and the righteousness it has worked through imperfect instruments."

Alamis moved closer to the dais, and then ascended several steps. "That is what your faith instructs, is it? That a dead god blessed a line of kings, and it is by virtue of that they continue to rule? How quaint. How convenient." He shook his head and smirked before taking another few steps upward, more than halfway to the throne. "A fine story for children, perhaps, but I prefer to believe things are thus only through the art of *taking*. Whether by force or compact or swindle, Rune has taken. It has taken and thus it has reigned." He ascended the final steps and stood next to the throne, stroking the ivory armrest. "Who is to say Rune cannot have power taken from it?"

"Those are perilous words, Chamberlain," Gamghast said, clearing his throat of the tickle of incense.

Alamis smiled and eased into the seat of the throne, tapping the armrests. "Are they? Perhaps they are, but it is not *my* ambition I imply. It is yours."

"Nonsense," Gamghast said, clearing his throat again. He looked about the chamber and noted they were entirely alone. "Chamberlain, I am here by sacred warrant to speak with High King Deragol. I have no time to waste in parley with you."

"Oh, I disagree, Prefect. I think you will find we have need for much discussion, and those discussions have only begun. With things being such, I would urge you to speak honestly. The matter of your treason could be more gently regarded with an earnest confession."

"Treason?" Gamghast coughed and pounded the butt of his staff against the floor, causing it to shiver in his hand. "That is an odd charge coming from you, Chamberlain."

The chamberlain leaned forward in the throne. "I am a shrewd man, but I would not have guessed you'd be so bold as to come charging into the Bastion, brandishing that wrinkled old scroll. I had thought to level these accusations in a more formal manner, but your brash request to see the High King compels me to act."

Gamghast shook with anger and he tugged at his white beard. "This talk is no more than drivel. Now bring me to the High King!"

Alamis abruptly stood and his countenance darkened. "It is I!" he shouted, the sound reverberating through the massive hall. "It is I who commands the throne! It is I who rules in the stead of our mad king! And it is I who accuses your order of high treason!"

"We serve the High King!" Gamghast roared, taking a stride up the dais. "Your charges are rubbish, and by inventing them you cast dishonor upon the Lector's death!"

Alamis's eyes seethed as he looked upon Gamghast from the top of the dais. "Do not dare attempt to deceive me, Prefect. I have many eyes and many ears. Missives can be intercepted, and even the quietest discussions overheard."

Gamghast spat on the ground and turned to take his leave. "You have overstepped your station, Chamberlain. There are others on the council who will honor my request."

"Prefect! I have not dismissed you."

Gamghast turned, readying a response, but paused when he noticed the chamberlain withdrawing a note from within his blue garment.

Alamis held the note before him, an accusation. "I have proof, written in the Lector's own hand. A plea to the Sentinels that they return to Rune, ready to make war." He shook his head. "Most believe the Sentinels vanished long ago, but we know better, don't we, Prefect?"

What does he know? Could he know the Lector's true identity?

"Your Lector's actions stand in direct violation of the ancient edict banishing the Sentinels from Rune. He was summoning them! The Sentinels, the very ones who tried to usurp the throne those many years ago! Has your Sanctum grown so bold as to believe you can ignore history and the rule of law? To believe you can draw old traitors within our walls?"

Gamghast breathed deeply. "The Lector served the High King, just as all members of the Sanctum are bound by faith to do. I am most certain he acted in defense of Rune. If he called for the aid of what were once our greatest heroes, then the question is why? I would gladly offer my assistance to your investigation, as the Lector's actions clearly speak of an urgent danger to us all."

"Strange," Alamis said, inspecting the note. "If your Lector was acting in defense of Rune, why then was the message intended for Zyn? Why was it being sent to the capital of Arranan, the very nation with which we are at war?" He leveled his eyes at Gamghast. "Your Lector meant to betray us all."

What could this mean?

The chamberlain began descending the dais. "Lector Erlorn not only disregarded the edict of banishment, but he sent word to Rune's most ancient traitors, summoning them to battle. And now, as though on cue, Arranan invades our borders! Your Sanctum has grown so mad with ambition that it has chosen an alliance with Rune's enemies, and invited this invasion." He tucked the note within his robe. "If I so choose, I could have every member of your sad order arrested and executed for treason. Do you wish to press me on this, Prefect?"

Gamghast's face sagged. "Chamberlain, you have me at a disadvantage. I am willing to assist you, if you'd just allow me to inspect the note."

Chamberlain Alamis descended the last stair and came close to Gamghast. "Every man who deals with me is at a disadvantage, Prefect. Rune bows to the banner of the High King, but I am the true ruler of this realm. Mine may not be the head that wears the crown, but mine is the fist that wields the power. You and your kind will stay clear of the Bastion. The days of your meddling with the High King are at an end."

Gamghast realized his mouth had fallen open and he snapped it shut. "But… It is our holy charge. Our reason for being."

Alamis smiled wickedly. "Ah, my dear, pathetic Prefect. I pity you. It is always a shame when the old realize they are no longer needed. You can almost see the life drain from their eyes when they realize the workings of the world have passed to younger, more capable hands. Stay clear of this place, Prefect. Stay out of the way." He brushed a finger against the Gamghast's shoulder, as though removing lint. "Pass quietly into the night."

14
FEAR

FENCRESS FALLCROW GUIDED her skinny gray mare along the tree-darkened path which ran atop the bank of a shallow stream. The water ran noisily, making conversation difficult. But then, none of them had spoken much at all since they'd fled Raven's Roost two days before.

She rode at the rear of the company, just behind Drenj and Paddyn. She smiled wryly as she watched them. The two swayed slump-shouldered and silent in their saddles, not daring to exchange even glances, as though they struggled mightily with something in their souls. *Ah, the difficult moral conundrums of killers.*

At the group's lead, perhaps thirty or so feet ahead, rode Karnag. His broad back seemed a fortress wall, adamant and impregnable, and the weapons slung across it served a grave warning. Fencress had always held profound respect for the highlander's skills in combat, but now there was something else mingled with those feelings. *Fear*.

She tugged at the black leather of her cowl to bring it low over her brow, hiding her blue eyes in shadow. She had a knack for gambling, and her many games of deadman's dice had taught her much could be learned from the eyes. It'd be best if Karnag couldn't read hers.

Fencress reckoned she'd killed more than a hundred men. She'd killed folk of all sorts, from deadbeat debtors to petty royalty, from simple farmhands to warriors of great renown. She'd killed with blades, axes, fire, poison, and even a pot of boiling rabbit stew. Most of those killings had been at a close, almost intimate distance, such that she'd been able to watch the life drain from the eyes of the dying. Yet, she'd never seen a man die in a fashion remotely like the horse trader in Raven's Roost.

Fencress had heard of rare magic, as well. The old tales told of great sorcerers wielding the fires of the dead gods, speaking with the dead, and moving in ways unseen. It was rumored the old codgers of the Sanctum could heal the sick by prayer alone, and summon the lost spirit of Illienne to aid in their protection. But those tales were of sorcerers and spookers, folk who pored over dusty books and arcane objects in studies lasting decades before such secrets could be plied. *How could Karnag command such a power?*

She'd poked at his memory with countless, cynical challenges, but she could no longer question what she'd seen. Karnag had ripped a man apart, from cock to crown, with nary more than a *word*.

Fencress had sensed a change in the man even since

they'd massacred the Lector and his men. Karnag seemed set with a grim purpose, and the taking of lives was no longer a means to a greater end but an end unto itself.

Fencress's horse stopped suddenly, uncertain how to navigate a jumble of tree roots stretching from an old poplar to the creek below. Fencress scratched the space between the mare's ears and patted her neck, encouraging, and after a tremulous step she was across the obstruction and on the trail once more.

"It's alright, girl," she said. "The path is frightening to us all."

<hr />

That night they found a clearing atop a rise and made camp in silence. Karnag chose a spot near the campfire, where he sat motionless and stared at the flames. Fencress and the rest gave him a wide berth, choosing to remain within their tents or near the horses.

For what she knew was overlong, Fencress tended to her mare, picking barbs and bugs from her mane and feeding her chunks of a bruised apple Fencress had found discarded on the path. In truth, she was wary of being near the highlander, and didn't fancy the thought of the fellow's conversation. She turned from his horse and saw Karnag's silhouette atop the rise and aside the fire, and couldn't help but finger the religious totem—the rough, wooden carving of Illienne's golden sun—dangling from her throat.

She thought of the look in Karnag's eyes just after they'd left Raven's Roost, just after he'd killed the horse trader. They hadn't been the eyes of her old friend. Instead, those gray eyes had been lifeless, as though the soul no longer lit them. She'd seen the eyes of cold-blooded killers, even in the mirror at times, but this was a different gaze. *The look of the dead.*

"Your horse is as clean as the day she tumbled from the womb," came a quiet voice in the darkness.

Fencress whirled about, her hand finding the hilt of one of her twin blades and pulling the weapon loose. There was Drenj, standing on the other side of the horse and scratching its shoulder with his long fingers.

"You just nearly lost that hand," hissed Fencress, sliding the weapon back into its sheath.

The Khaldisian nodded his head toward the rise. "You and I should speak."

Fencress walked to the other side of the horse to stand beside Drenj. "Carefully, Khaldisian," she whispered. "After what we've witnessed, I'd reckon any talk among us that doesn't include Karnag would be viewed as conspiracy."

"I've spoken with Paddyn," he said. "We're ready to abandon this madness and head north to Riverweave. We'll take all four of the horses, to ensure a good start ahead of Karnag."

"That is inviting death. I've known Karnag for years, ever since…" she said, her voice trailing off. She'd known Karnag for a dozen years, ever since he'd killed three bastards trying to have their way with her after catching her drunk and unarmed in Riverweave's slums. She paused. The young Khaldisian hadn't earned the right to know that. She held his eyes with a steady look. "He'd kill you for such a thing even if he were right in the head, which he isn't now. Haven't you seen how he's changed?"

"I *have* seen how he's changed!" he hissed. "And that is precisely why we must be rid of him. It is inviting death to stay at his side." He shook his head, eyes downcast. "I have followed him only for the coin, but even that has lost meaning in his shadow. He's unstable, Fencress. He has made me terrified of the night." Fencress nodded, for she knew of what the Khaldisian spoke. Karnag's sleep, if it could be called that, was tortured, and the highlander whispered incessantly in a strange tongue while he slumbered. The night before, he'd screamed out in seeming terror, shrieking madly at some unseen horror.

Drenj shivered, as though shaking off a chill. "He will kill Tream, and cover the town in his blood. But what else? What other havoc will he wreak? Who knows how many others will die in the wake of those deeds, how many others will be caused to seek revenge upon him? 'Dark work brings dark rewards,' they say in Raven's Roost. The place at his side is a dangerous one."

"Perhaps," Fencress said, frowning. "But of all the enemies we could have right now, he may be the very worst of them."

Drenj was silent for a moment, scratching the horse absentmindedly. "You may be right, Fencress, but he won't stop with Tream."

"Perhaps he won't. Perhaps he will. Perhaps things will be finished after Hargrave, and we can all parts ways as friends." She smiled slightly. "Those are long odds, but the best bet isn't always the safest one. I'll not consider abandoning a friend such as Karnag until I've seen how the dice roll."

The next morning the skies were solemn and greeted the company with a chilling rain. Rocky earth and mossy tree roots crowded a path slick with muck, and the ride grew treacherous. More than once Fencress nearly toppled into the swift-moving stream from her horse, and the company quickly reached a consensus to dismount and guide the beasts by their reins.

At midmorning their path met a stout bridge and the wider road that crossed it. At the intersection stood a rotting signpost, upon which was scratched a marker. Hargrave was but five leagues distant.

The horses seemed to delight in the road's firmer footing and the company remounted. Their pace quickened and the horses became playful. Fencress's mare splashed ahead several paces on the puddle-filled road, and soon Fencress found herself just a few feet behind Karnag at the group's lead.

She made no effort at conversation, and instead sat with eyes fixed on the road ahead as rain dripped from her cowl. It was a straight path, shaded by an overhang of trees, and Fencress reckoned she could see several hundred yards along its gradual upward slope. Beyond that, through the forest's canopy, she could discern the distant, black smear of the Southwall Mountains against the gray sky.

"A killing ground," said Karnag, his voice an unnerving monotone. "In days this road will be awash in blood."

Fencress nodded, hoping it would suffice as a reply.

Karnag gestured at the road ahead. "The Arranese army has chosen this as one of their passageways into

Rune. The road heads right to Riverweave, and the High King's army is too late to mount a stout defense. The southern garrisons will take arms but they will be overrun, and the Arranese will take the whole of the south, from the Southwalls to the Sullen Sea, before they tender their terms. Already they've crushed the mountain garrisons and are marching upon this very road, putting villages to the torch and men to the sword."

"You know this?" Fencress asked, unable to resist engaging the highlander in spite of her better judgment.

Karnag turned in the saddle, his bent face battered from a hundred battles. His gaze was just as Fencress remembered it from that awful day with the horse trader: heavy lids drooped over lifeless eyes. He stared at Fencress with those dead eyes for long moments before answering. "My dreams."

Fencress looked away and lowered her head. The thought of such things was disquieting, unnatural.

"I have seen it," Karnag said. "Just as I can see Tream now, sipping at a tall tankard of ale before him at the town's only tavern."

"Karnag," said Fencress, squeezing her horse's reins in gloved hands until her knuckles ached. She breathed deeply before continuing. "How can this be? I am not the sort to fear others, but lately I've seen things that have left me a bit... unnerved." She steeled herself and turned to Karnag. The highlander's eyes no longer held hers, but had drifted to the road ahead. "You are my friend. What's happened?"

"There is a call I hear," Karnag said quietly, the heavy braids of his black hair dripping with rain. "A whisper in my head. If I struggle to listen to it, it fades away, but when I am quiet I can hear it clear. It tells of paths before me, of things yet to come, and of my hand in such things. I can do naught but harken to it, for it tells my destiny."

Fencress kept her eyes down, staring at the wet road and pulling again at her cowl to keep it low.

Long odds, indeed.

The road ran straight through Hargrave, a tumbledown hamlet huddled against the banks of Cladderback Creek. A fat sow and her piglets rolled in a muddy puddle in the middle of the road, snorting noisily. Lining the edges of the road were two dozen or so homes and shops of rotting wood. If there were folk who hadn't fled the town already, then they'd shuttered themselves tight within. Aside from the pigs, the town's only movement was that of its creaky watermill, beside which squatted its only tavern, *The Wain and Paddle.*

Karnag slowed his horse as he reached the town's edge, and Fencress turned about to regard the others. The Khaldisian nodded meaningfully and made a pull at his horse's reins, winking as though to tell Fencress he was ready to turn the beast about. Paddyn sat near him, rubbing his grimy face while keeping his eyes downcast. Fencress reckoned the young fellow was more confused and frightened than the rest of them, and was worried the lad's bow would be of little use in trembling hands.

Down the road behind them, barely visible, was a solitary rider on the road, clad all in green. *The same who followed us from the gates of Raven's Roost?* Fencress shook her head. *Damned jitters.* She brought her mare even with

Karnag as the highlander pulled his steed to a stop. She noticed Karnag's eyes were fixed on the faded shingle marking the tavern, and the highlander sat quietly for a time before dismounting.

"Tream is there, inside," Karnag said firmly, stretching his legs as he stood. He tightened the leather straps of his jerkin and then his hands seized the hilt of his two-handed sword, *Gravemaker* as he called it. The weapon slid from its sheath with a harsh scraping noise which sounded loudly amidst the drumming rain and snorting pigs.

"You have a plan?" Fencress asked, her voice sounding more timid than she would have liked.

Karnag turned and looked up at the mounted company with those lifeless eyes. "I am going to kill Tream."

"Just like that?" Fencress asked.

Karnag's heavy brow knotted. "Is there something else?"

Fencress pulled at her cowl, feeling helpless and hopeless. She stared at her gloved hands as she knotted the reins about them. "Karnag," she said uneasily, "we've done a lot of hard work together, and we've always had a plan. Shouldn't we case the tavern, take count of its exits, and take a peek through the windows? Tream's worked with us and knows how we do things. He's a misguided lout, but he's not entirely stupid. We should take care with such things."

Karnag was already nearing *The Wain and Paddle*, his great sword drooping from his right hand and drawing a lazy line in the mud. The highlander stooped to peer through a window of clouded glass, and then, without warning, he smashed through it with his forearm.

Drenj kicked his horse next to Karnag's, grabbing its reins and turning to Fencress. "We must leave!" he said, grinding his teeth together. "Now!"

There came a commotion from within the tavern, and someone inside hurled a cleaver out the broken window. It grazed Karnag's shoulder and plopped harmlessly into the mud.

"Tream!" Karnag shouted, his deep bellow seeming to shake the tavern's timbers.

"Now!" said Drenj more urgently, shaking the reins at Fencress.

"No," said Fencress, watching as Karnag lumbered to stand before the tavern door. "I cannot betray him."

"Tream!" the highlander roared again, his voice painful to the ears.

Just then there was the slam of a door being thrown open from the tavern's opposite side, overlooking the creek. A tumble and a loud splash and then the sloshing of boots through water.

Karnag rushed through the tavern door and a chorus of shouts erupted from inside. There was the ring of steel upon steel, then the thuds and whimpers of folk being cut down.

"Get around this place," said Fencress, almost to herself. She yanked the reins and drove her heels into the flanks of her skinny horse, spinning it about. She steered the mare to a gap between the tavern and the mill, around a rick of firewood and some barrels and then to the bank of the creek.

There he was—Tream—clad in a garish red shirt and

running hard across the creek toward the opposite bank. "Paddyn!" Fencress shouted. "Take him down!"

In a moment Paddyn was beside her, hissing as he nocked an arrow to his bowstring. "You're sure?" he asked.

"No," Fencress confessed. "But we haven't a choice."

"Sweet Illienne have mercy upon me," Paddyn whispered. He let fly the arrow, but it splashed in the water a few feet ahead of Tream.

"To the abyss with you both!" came Drenj's voice from behind them.

Fencress turned about and regarded the Khaldisian blackly. "Perhaps you'll meet us there some day, after Karnag comes for you next."

Drenj's face was a mask of anger as he wiped rainwater from the dusky skin of his brow. "This is madness, woman!" he yelled. He threw down the reins of Karnag's horse and spat, then drove his horse to a gallop north along the road.

There was another splash from the back of tavern. *Karnag.* The highlander crashed across the creek with long strides, speaking in a low tone those strange, broken-sounding words he'd uttered in his sleep. Fencress suddenly felt pity for Tream. *This was a bad gamble for you, Tream. Things will not end well.*

Paddyn's bow hummed as he loosed another arrow. This time the shot was true and the arrow smacked into Tream's back, just above the loop of his belt. Tream cried out and collapsed, clutching at the arrow with one hand and reaching for the creek bank, just a few feet away, with the other.

Karnag slowed his pace and watched as Tream howled

in pain. He walked, unhurriedly and inevitably, to stand over Tream in the knee-deep water.

"Karnag!" Tream squealed, his hand struggling with the arrow in his back. "I thought you were dead, I swear it! I apologize! Please, Karnag! I apologize!"

"That's it, Karnag!" Fencress shouted hopefully. "A lesson learned! Ask him to hand over the money, give him a good scar to remember, and let's be done with this!"

"She's right!" said Tream, sitting upright in the creek, face twisted with fear. "The gold. I left it in the tavern. A coin purse behind the ale cask. It's yours, of course. I never would have taken it had I thought you'd live," he said, gesturing clumsily. "For the life of me I thought the dead gods would strike you down for what you were about to do. Please. Please don't kill me…" He burst into tears.

From somewhere far off there came a low rumble. At first, Fencress thought it was thunder, but it was too rhythmic, too consistent. *War drums.*

Karnag turned to face southward, his expression unreadable and his eyes hidden by his thick braids. He stood there with an eerie stillness for long moments as the rain fell about him and Tream blubbered at his feet.

"Be done with it, Karnag!" shouted Fencress, trying to sound calm and cheery. She reminded herself of how she'd bluffed her way into small fortunes at deadman's dice, trying to stoke her confidence. "He's confessed his crime, offered to hand over the coin, and Paddyn's given him a wound he may not survive. Let us leave him and get clear of this place!"

A sinister smile crept across Karnag's face as he turned back to Tream. "You hear it," he said, his voice just loud enough to carry. "War. All of those soldiers and all of the blood they will spill. Marching to make a ruin of Rune and a sacrifice of its people. The rivers will run red, the fields will be sown with corpses. Yet, the great sum of their deeds will not move the scales when weighed against mine. I," he said, heaving his arms above him, *Gravemaker* poised to strike, "have become Death itself."

"Karnag!" cried Fencress. *At least give him a quick, clean death.*

The highlander brought down his sword, not upon Tream's neck but upon his foot, fixing him to the creek bed like a great nail and bringing a thick swirl of red blood to wash about the water. Tream clawed at his face and pulled at his hair, whether out of agony or fear or relief Fencress did not know.

Karnag walked about him in a circle, moving with the drums' cadence. He muttered words barely audible but entirely incomprehensible, squeezing his hands into fists and then slackening them again, over and over. Fencress had seen Karnag kill many, many men, and he'd always done so with a cold efficiency. He'd cared not for the manner of men's deaths, only that they died. This, though, was different, for there was a careful method to this, a reverence. *A ritual.*

Paddyn tugged at Fencress's sleeve. "We must stop this, or we must run! This is wickedness! If the dead gods haven't cursed us already, they will surely curse this!"

Fencress pulled her eyes from the scene before them and looked at Paddyn. The young man's face was as wet with tears as it was with rain. *Faith can be a frightening thing.* Fencress nodded and tugged at her horse's reins to turn it around.

An ear-shattering shriek drew their eyes back to the creek. Karnag stood over Tream, holding the bloody remains of what appeared to be Tream's arm. Tream sat shaking in the water, his mouth agape and seeming to draw breath for a scream. Karnag's smile widened and he tossed the stump into the creek with a chilling nonchalance.

"Wickedness!" said Paddyn.

Then Karnag's hand was upon Tream's head, entwined in the mess of his greasy hair. He continued on in his mutter, brandishing that sick grin upon his battered face. Tream appeared to try to speak but formed no sound.

Fencress shivered, cold to her very bones. Her hands went numb and she dropped the reins of her mare. She could do naught but watch the grotesque display before her.

Karnag looked skyward and cried out a word in that strange tongue. His smile broadened and his teeth shone and he growled a savage growl. The massive sinews of his arm flexed and his knuckles whitened upon the crown of Tream's head.

There came a cracking sound, like a tree splitting in a storm, and Tream's tongue spilled from his mouth and his eyes rolled back in his skull. Then his head separated from his shoulders in a spray of blood and tissue.

Karnag hefted the disembodied head above him, displaying it as he would a great prize. He turned it upon himself, as though to look Tream in the eyes once more, then cast the head to the creek bank just below Paddyn and Fencress. It came to a rest with a thump, staring wide-eyed at them from a crook in a tree root.

Fencress stared back at Karnag, feeling her face drain of all color.

"I," said the highlander, "have become Death."

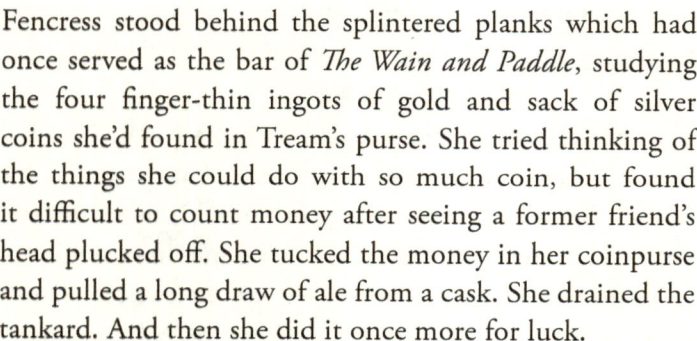

Fencress stood behind the splintered planks which had once served as the bar of *The Wain and Paddle*, studying the four finger-thin ingots of gold and sack of silver coins she'd found in Tream's purse. She tried thinking of the things she could do with so much coin, but found it difficult to count money after seeing a former friend's head plucked off. She tucked the money in her coinpurse and pulled a long draw of ale from a cask. She drained the tankard. And then she did it once more for luck.

She turned from the bar and regarded the corpses littered about the tavern. Five rough fellows were sprawled about, surrounded by pools of sticky blood buzzing with flies. She stepped over the body of the closest one, a farmhand clutching a rusty knife, and moved into the tavern's kitchen.

The kitchen smelled as much of death as the common room, and Fencress found the carcasses of a few squirrels or rats and a dog stuck on a spit and only halfway cleaned. She chuckled in spite of the gore. *Even with a wealth of gold, Tream, you still ate like a shit-headed scoundrel.*

Paddyn had been rummaging through the larder and emerged cradling a sack of potatoes, a bottle of vinegar, and a few turnips. "There'll be no kingly feast during our journey, but there're a few things I can do with this and perhaps some venison and herbs." He looked apprehensively about the kitchen and then peeked into the common room. "Is Karnag…"

"No," said Fencress, gesturing toward the broken window. "He's still outside."

"Waiting for us?" Paddyn stuffed the provisions into a burlap sack he'd found and crept toward the window.

"Or the whole Arranese army, by the looks of him. I'm not sure."

Paddyn stared outside, his expression fearful. "He's facing south, just cleaning his sword. Do you reckon he'll hunt down Drenj, like he did Tream?"

Fencress shrugged. "I fear I can predict that fellow no better than I can the roll of honest dice. But odds are his blade won't stay clean for long."

Paddyn scratched his head. "What's going to happen, Fencress? You've known him for years. How long before Karnag kills us, or the dead gods curse us?"

"Sounds like the Arranese are slaughtering everyone in their path, so we'll not be heading south, and I don't reckon the guards will welcome us back in Raven's Roost just yet. It seems the reasonable thing to do is to head north to Riverweave and hope the High King's soldiers mistake us for refugees when we pass. That, or find an old friend of mine in the Ghostwood not too far away. Old Crook. You'd like him."

"Has Karnag spoken of this?"

"No, but then his mind doesn't seem much concerned with survival," Fencress said, joining Paddyn at the window. In the middle of the road, fifty or so feet to the south, stood Karnag, menacing in his silence. He was pulling a rag down the length of his sword *Gravemaker*, giving it a dull gleam in the rain. In the distance the war drums sounded.

Fencress started to turn about but a movement caught her eye. Opposite the road, behind a rickety house and a line of brush, there was a bearded fellow clad all in green, creeping close to the ground and moving northward along the forest's edge.

"Someone's watching us," she said. *And our kind doesn't take kindly to prying eyes.*

"I see him."

"It was a good distance, but I saw a fellow leave Raven's Roost just after us, wearing those very same colors."

"A scout for the army?"

"Perhaps," said Fencress, squinting to keep sight of the figure as he moved low along the tree line. "I'd thought he could be a guard, but then no guard from Raven's Roost would've bothered following us this far south during wartime. Yet," she said, "everything that's happened since we killed the Lector has left me thinking of things with a bit more care than I used to. It'd be best to ask the fellow a question or two, just to make certain."

Paddyn pulled his long bow from his back. "Do we tell Karnag?"

Fencress snorted, amused. "I said we should ask the fellow some questions, not pop his head off like a wine cork. Head out back and get your horse. Make your way to the town's northern edge and keep your eye on him, but do it casually so as not to look suspicious. I'll tell Karnag we're foraging for supplies and that we'll meet him up the road."

Karnag stared down the road, his flint-colored eyes fixed to a point dead south. He remained still as Fencress approached.

"There," he said, his voice devoid of emotion, "a vanguard of the Arranese army. Seven men on horseback moving this way. They're scouting the area ahead of a horde ten thousand soldiers strong."

Fencress followed the line of Karnag's stare but could see nothing. The road, though straight, was obscured by a thick haze from the rain.

Karnag inhaled deeply. "They're hungry for blood. They had a taste of it in the mountains but it sated them not."

Fencress looked again down the road. There seemed to be the faintest outline of riders but she could not be certain. "We should leave this place. Paddyn and I found a few supplies in the tavern but not nearly enough. We're going to toss the homes and then make ready to leave."

The highlander said nothing.

"We'll leave here, then?"

Karnag eyes drifted skyward and he seemed to laugh softly. "My thirst for blood has not been sated, either. The Arranese should have a proper welcome to Rune."

"I never figured you a patriot, Karnag."

"This is my land. I will not abide trespassers."

Fencress huffed. "You're no soldier, Karnag. You don't intend to fight the High King's war for him?"

Karnag remained silent.

"Seven trained men with an army behind them means poor odds for us. What's more, we have no stake in this fight. We serve no cause but our own. We need to get clear of this place before we're crushed between two armies."

The highlander turned to her and stared, his expression blank. "You will leave here, along with the others. I have been called to another path."

Fencress found her hands seeking the hilts of her twin blades. Speaking with Karnag was a dangerous dance now. He was random and violent, like a great force of nature. "Karnag... We have been through much, you and I. This is how we leave things?"

"Our paths diverge, now. Go."

The look in Karnag's eyes told Fencress argument was futile, but she could not leave her questions unanswered. "The whispers in your head? You worry me, Karnag. Has so much changed? What is this you've become?"

Karnag's gaze was unwavering. "Something powerful. Something eternal. And with my sword I will recast the fates of all men. To what end, I do not yet know, but the answers will be written in blood. I have foreseen it."

"How can this be? You are no sorcerer."

"No. I am more."

"But what? What are you, Karnag?"

Karnag said nothing, but stared at Fencress with the eyes of the dead.

Fencress knew then there was no use talking to the man, and no chance of reasoning with him. She suppressed a shudder and broke away from Karnag's stare. Paddyn was a hundred yards up the road, ambling ahead on his horse and making a good show of inspecting the ramshackle buildings lining the road. "What of the gold?"

Karnag grunted, his sound one of disgust. "I care for

it not at all." He returned his eyes to the road. "You will leave me now."

"Karnag…"

"I have need of you no longer."

"But…" Fencress stopped short. The look in Karnag's eyes made her realize he was no longer the person she once knew. There was no use in saying some poetic fare-thee-well or long goodbye, and no sense in trying to help the man. Karnag appeared far beyond that. Fencress turned about and found her horse, her heart heavy with sadness as she moved away.

Fencress brought her horse alongside Paddyn's at Hargrave's northern edge, near a rundown home with a hole in its roof. "You've watched him?" she asked.

Paddyn nodded at the road ahead. "Aye. He's up the road a few hundred feet or so, weaving between the trees lining the road. I figure he has a horse tied up somewhere, and probably one faster than ours."

"We can track him. This country's too hard for him to try to ride in the wild, so I'd wager he'll stick to the road. Any sign of Drenj?"

"Nothing, but if what you're saying is true then he's likely on the road as well, perhaps only a league or so ahead."

"We'll find him and give him his share of the coin," said Fencress. "He'll know not to head back to Raven's Roost, and Riverweave makes the best sense of any place right now."

Paddyn was quiet for a moment before speaking. "You spoke with Karnag?"

Fencress turned in her saddle and looked back. Karnag stood in the same spot. He'd unsheathed *Gravemaker* and was moving the great sword about in a practice form, thrusting it forward, swinging it in a wide arc, spinning it in a circle overhead. Beyond him, Fencress could now see the forms of riders on the road south, clad in the heavy hides and flowing cloaks favored by the Arranese. The war drums continued to sound from far away.

"Did you?" Paddyn persisted.

Fencress turned to face north along the road and pulled her cowl low over her eyes. "I spoke with a man named Karnag, but I'm no longer certain he's the man who was my friend." She shook her head. "Let's ride."

15
PROTECTOR OF IRONMOOR

ANNICK STARED INTO the mirror, absent-mindedly scraping a whetstone over his knife. He'd never been a particularly handsome fellow, but he was a good sight uglier nowadays. There was the pinkish scar that'd pinched his cheek for the past few years now, a reminder of a drunken brawl he could hardly remember. And now there was the chip in his front tooth—useful for whistling, perhaps, but it lent him a half-witted look. He tried closing his mouth, but things didn't quite fit together with his jaw now shifted askew. His nose was bent also, but in the way opposite his jaw.

He regarded his misdirecting, damaged face and smirked. *At least no one will know where I'm headed.* He laughed, but the painful catch in his ribs brought a quick end to that.

He brought the knife to his throat and cut away at

the stubborn remains of his beard. He pulled the blade from his neck, watching how his hands shook unsteadily. He grinned again, thinking of the irony of accidentally slitting his own throat after surviving the horrors he'd endured. *Perhaps a most fitting end for Captain Lannick deVeers, Protector of Ironmoor.*

He cleaned the blade in the washbasin and placed it on the shelf below the mirror. He then moved upon painful limbs to the room's table and found there his jug of red wine, delivered just as he'd requested. He filled a cup and sipped it slowly, judging it best to show restraint this early in the day. It was delicious, far better than the stuff Horus had slipped to him in his cell. After a moment he tilted it back, finding he could not help but drain the cup.

He walked to the room's window and opened wide its shutters. He breathed in the morning air, noticing how differently it smelled here than it had in his cell. No longer did the air carry the salty scent of the sea or the greasy stink of the brig. It was a cleansing odor, and Lannick felt old strength returning to him as he pulled it in.

The landscape before him was all rolling hills, trimmed hedges, and tilled fields. At least a dozen leagues from Ironmoor and all the things that haunted the place. A donkey brayed in the field below, pulling a plow ahead of a brightly dressed farmer. Beyond them, a home of red brick squatted atop a hill, its chimney puffing smoke. Lannick imagined a family breakfasted within, sitting before their hearth's crackling fire as it chased away the morning chill.

It was the sort of place he'd dreamed of having in

happier times, perhaps retiring there after years of loyal service to the Crown. A safe place. A simple place with only simple troubles.

There came a sharp knock at his door.

Such dreams are dead.

They sat about a table in the inn's common room, eating the breakfast of cheese and berries in relative silence. Lannick ate quickly, but even after he'd finished he found it difficult to move his eyes to any place other than his plate. He felt ashamed of how he'd spent the bulk of the last decade, how he'd turned his back on his order, and how he'd cursed their names while drunk in countless taverns, blaming them for failures he knew to be his alone.

A hand brushed against his. *Alisa.* She'd not been a Variden when he'd disappeared all those years ago, and she leveled no accusations. It was comforting to have her near. The other two—Ogrund and Wil—had been there, and being near them was disquieting. Lannick could sense their hard gazes upon him and hear their unspoken indictment: "*A Variden never abandons his watch, honoring his cause eternal.*" It was said the Sentinel Valis had given the Variden that very charge, first and foremost, when he forged the order centuries ago.

And I violated it.

"You have suffered much," Alisa said, her voice soft.

Lannick looked upward. Alisa's large, brown eyes were filled with a warmth Lannick had forgotten people could possess. It was nearly enough for him to disregard the presence of the other two beside her. *Nearly.*

"I searched for you for a year," Ogrund said in his

gravelly voice. He looked as he ever did, squint-eyed with only the vague rumor of a neck between his shaven head and muscular shoulders.

"We thought you dead," said Wil, his face round and soft but his eyes fierce.

Lannick cleared his throat. "I pretty much was, if that provides any consolation to the two of you."

Wil sniffed derisively. "Dead drunk, perhaps. Your reputation as the kingdom's greatest drunkard has become known to us, but you'll not excuse betrayal so easily."

Ogrund raised his chin, as though he squinted so hard he could not otherwise see. "How can a man waste so many years of life, knowing each to be a blessing from Illienne the Light Eternal?"

Lannick looked back at his plate and found a crumble of cheese. "I'm not proud of what I've done, and I need not be patronized."

"Ah," said Wil, bowing his head. "Our deepest apologies, then. We'll not speak of the fact we've spent the last nine years waging a secret war against the Necrists, desperately trying to protect Rune, while you've been guzzling wine and courting harlots. We'll not talk of how our old foes have gained in strength while we've had to hide and peek about like church mice. We'll not mention how you betrayed us to General Fane and then abandoned us when he and his Scarlet Swords hunted us down like dogs."

Lannick bristled. "I betrayed no one."

Wil rubbed at his cheek, scowling. "No? A remarkable coincidence, then. You see, just after you were charged with treason, Fane and his brutes stalked us, taking four of our number. Meanwhile, you, it seems, were sitting safe and sound in an alehouse. It seems to me you bargained away our lives for your own."

Lannick leveled his gaze at Wil. "Safe? My family was murdered. Only the High King's pardon because of my service prevented me from being jailed or killed. And Fane? He discovered my affiliation with the Variden on his own."

"Did he? And whatever drove him to do that, I wonder?"

"I did not provoke him, Wil."

Wil laughed mockingly. "No? Forgive me, Lannick, but as I recall, you soaked in all the praises, smugly accepting the title of 'Protector of Ironmoor' from High King Deragol in spite of our strict edict of secrecy. You may as well have spat in Fane's face from that pedestal. Where is your trinket, I wonder? Your little decorated blade for winning the High King's favor?"

"Fane took it," Lannick grumbled. "Took it after his dogs beat me down."

"You were foolish, Lannick," said Ogrund. "Your Coda *found* you. It found you for a reason. You were chosen to observe the army from within, not to lead it."

"You claimed glory," continued Wil, "and in doing so provoked an enemy. What gave you the notion that a Variden accepting such a prominent honor was a sound idea? Did you not foresee how that would shame the general after his blundered attack on Pryam's Bay and his capture? How embarrassed the commander of the High King's armies would be, having to applaud as his rescuer—the most obvious reminder of his mistakes—was revered by the High King and credited with victory? Did you not think he'd seek to humble you?"

"I was careful," said Lannick. "I was always careful in keeping my identity as a Variden a secret."

"And what of your Coda? Any fool could see it brandished upon your wrist, and any man with enough ambition and access to the Kingdom's archives could discover its meaning."

"I never would have thought he'd dig so deeply."

Wil smacked the table. "Yet he *did*, didn't he!"

"And what," added Ogrund, "became of that Coda? Did you pawn it for wine, or perhaps lose it in a game of dice?"

Lannick gritted his teeth, ignoring the pain in his jaw. "It is secure, Ogrund. Unlike the corpses of my wife and children."

"Gentlemen," said Alisa. "Lannick's been through much. Perhaps the time for this talk has not yet arrived."

"This is difficult for you," said Alisa.

Lannick stared at his new boots, already covered with dust. "Walking?" He took a few quick steps down the winding, sunlit path. "Not at all. None of my wounds was so grave as to hinder my graceful stride. My toe may have been broken, but I reckon every bit of me is so thankful to be free that I hardly notice it at all."

Alisa smiled, although Lannick perceived her expression carried a hint of sadness.

They walked along the path in silence for a time, much to Lannick's liking. It had been a long while since he'd taken a walk for the sake of walking, and a long time since he'd chosen to spend an afternoon out of doors rather than perched upon a barstool with a bottle before him.

He admired the neat walls of piled stones lining the path, the tilled fields beyond them, and he inhaled, savoring the scent of things growing. But soon his thoughts drifted to the jug of wine in his quarters and the casks of ales crowding the wall at the rear of the inn's common room.

I could enjoy such things in moderation, perhaps? He shook his head. *I shouldn't go back to that life.* Then he shook his head again. *Well, not all the way back, anyway.*

"I did not mean walking," said Alisa. "I meant this place." She gestured back toward the countryside inn which served as a safe house for the Variden. "I meant Ogrund and Wil. And me."

Lannick heaved a sigh and scratched at his head. He'd cut his hair short, as he'd done long ago, and his fingers moved freely across his scalp rather than becoming entangled in a matted mess. It was the short fashion worn by soldiers, an appearance he'd avoided ever since his family was butchered. He sighed again.

Alisa touched his arm, her gesture unassuming. "I imagine you have no shortage of questions for me."

"I reckon I have a few," he said, turning to look at Alisa. "Why me? Of all the men in Ironmoor, why did you choose me that night with Fane's daughter?"

"The spirit of Valis moves within all the Variden. It must have been his design. There was a *reason* I discovered you, and helped set in motion the events that pulled you from that life you were living."

"Bah," Lannick said. "You couldn't have been thinking that at the time. Why did you pick me out of that crowd?"

She shrugged. "You seemed the sort who'd be willing."

"I seemed desperate, you mean."

"You seemed the sort who wouldn't ask questions, and wouldn't pose a threat if things went awry."

Lannick sank to a seat on the stone wall. "Desperate and weak, then."

Alisa didn't answer.

"You know," he said, "when I was mercilessly beaten by Fane and his Scarlet Swords, I gathered a few things."

"I am sorry for that, Lannick. Fate can create terrible events as it unfolds. I wish it hadn't led you to such pain. When I noticed the Variden symbol on your arm, when you were naked—"

Lannick waved dismissively, embarrassed by any discussion of the details of that evening. "When I was being beaten I gathered General Fane intended to sacrifice his daughter, that he had some plan requiring her virginity."

"An exchange with the Necrists. The life of his virgin daughter in exchange for some dark power. We know not the details, as their blood rites and other methods of communication remain a mystery to us."

"And you needed someone to upset the deal?"

"Yes."

"That was all, then? You intended me to be used and then discarded? And that's why the girl was playing along?"

Alisa took a seat beside Lannick and held his gaze with her large eyes. "I'd told her of her father's bargain,

Lannick, and she was willing to do anything to avoid death. That was all. It was a simple plan, and the most obvious way of spoiling the sacrifice without confronting General Fane or the Necrists directly. I never would have guessed you'd object to your role in the scheme. You saved her life, Lannick, if it makes you feel any better. She was beaten, but not killed."

Lannick's head sagged. "That's good to know, but that evening caused my life to take quite an awful turn."

She rubbed his shoulder, roughly. "You'd best toughen up, Lannick, for things will get no easier. There is a storm coming, a war for the ages. As Wil said, our old enemies have grown stronger. Rune has weakened, and has few allies to protect it. Even some of the thanes refuse to honor their oaths to the Crown. Old allies like Thane Meledin and Thane Brandiss withhold their oath-bound soldiers. The Lector of the Sanctum—the Sentinel Castor—was seeking out the other Sentinels when he was slain. To what end? One of our number, Karab, was killed along with him. I fear the coming days will be fierce and fraught with peril. Your strength will be needed, but not your self-pity."

Lannick looked away, back down the path and toward the inn. There was the faint smell of a wood fire in the air, and Lannick reckoned the innkeeper was preparing supper. His thoughts turned again to his wine.

"Lannick," Alisa continued, her voice quiet, "Wil told me of your family, of their murder at the hands of Fane and his men. Of how you disappeared thereafter." She placed her hand on his. "I cannot pretend to understand the hurt you've felt or the depths of your depression. But there comes a time when one must let go of regret. The past cannot be rewritten."

Lannick felt his expression darken. "Such platitudes are easily spoken, especially by someone who hasn't suffered."

"You have to choose a better life, Lannick. Seize this chance fate has granted you."

His hand found the locket about his neck, the one containing hairs from the heads of his children. It had always served as a comforting remembrance, but this time it brought a swell of awful images to his head. He thought of the Necrist and the misshapen Shodafayn digging about in a gravesite, hacking off the faces of his wife and children. He blinked.

"Lannick?"

He said nothing, and instead stood and walked with long strides back to the inn. Alisa called after him but he did not answer.

Once in his room he found his wine had soured somewhat, but he did not care. He swilled it down in hearty gulps until the jug was empty.

He sat at the edge of his bed and wept until sleep took him.

The inn was a safe house for the Variden, with a generous supply of provisions on hand, and the innkeeper hadn't raised any questions when Lannick visited the storeroom and retrieved an armful of items. *At least there's one soul in this place who doesn't ask me questions or level accusations.*

Lannick inspected the assortment lined across his bed and lit by the sunlight of early morning. He admired the traveling cloak, brown and plain-looking and a contrast to the deep forest green traditionally worn by the Variden. The linen shirt and leather breeches beside it didn't fit just right, but were close enough so as not to pinch or sag. There was a leather belt and a matching purse to be worn upon the hip. Next to those rested a knife, a roll of string, a wedge of cheese and a few apples. There was a coin purse, also, which Lannick grabbed and jingled to ensure that the many silver crowns inside hadn't found their way out. There was a flask he'd filled with whiskey. *Just to help me sleep, of course.* And lastly there was a sword, simple and sharp and clean.

Lannick dressed, stuffed the small items in the satchel and stretched the cloak across his shoulders. He thrust the sword in its scabbard and it hung across his thigh. His boots were new and the hard leather bit but he reckoned they'd be broken in before he reached the gates of Ironmoor, a dozen or so leagues to the south.

He stood for a moment, looking in the mirror. He sucked in his gut and straightened his spine, and for the first time in years felt he looked like a person of substance, not some drunken wretch or lowlife scoundrel. *Perhaps Alisa is right. Perhaps I can choose a better life.*

As he turned to leave he realized the flask of whiskey still lay on the bed. He thought for a moment of leaving it, but then seized it and dropped it into his purse.

Just to help me sleep.

He was perhaps a quarter mile beyond the door of the inn when he heard the drumming of hooves on the road behind him. He lowered his head and kept walking.

"Lannick!" It was Ogrund's voice, low and hoarse.

Lannick ignored him, hoping for an instant Ogrund would allow him to leave without any more talk.

Ogrund pulled his bay horse to a walk alongside Lannick and leered at him with his squinted eyes before speaking. "You took the oath, Lannick."

Lannick continued his march in silence.

"Are you renouncing your oath, then? Again? Even after we rescued you? Your Coda found you for a *reason*, Lannick. You cannot abandon us."

Lannick spat and shook his head. He kept walking.

"No one has ever left the Variden, Lannick. Wil may not be able to say it, but I can. We need you. There are portents, omens. Something is afoot and it is something of grave import. The Necrists are emboldened. They attack us openly, something they wouldn't have dared in the past. They have grown more powerful, and their ambitions have grown accordingly. And worst of all, the Sanctum's Lector was murdered—a Sentinel slain! You were one of our best, and you swore an oath to fight such evil."

Lannick stopped and looked up at Ogrund, the morning sun perched over the man's thick shoulder and setting his edges aglow. "You speak much of our oath, Ogrund, but nothing of its consequences. What wounds have you suffered? Have you lost family? Have you been tortured, had your children's faces ripped from their skulls and worn like ballroom masks? What would our oath mean to you then?"

Ogrund was quiet for a moment, his eyes barely more than slits. "Our oath is everything, Lannick. We honor the cause eternal, even in the most difficult of times."

"I have other debts to honor now," Lannick said.

"Where is it you will go? Will you return?"

"To Ironmoor. As for your other question, I do not know. But I can assure you I'll go nowhere else, and Alisa should know where to find me if you're searching."

"You cannot betray us again," said Ogrund.

Lannick stared at him, his face burning and his brow knotted. "I never did in the first place."

Ogrund scowled and turned his horse about. "You saved my life on a handful of occasions, Lannick. For that, I'll wait until afternoon before I tell the others of your departure. But then you'd best consider us square."

"Fair enough," said Lannick, setting off again on the road.

"And Lannick?" called Ogrund after him. "Stay clear of the deep shadows. The Necrists know men by the scent of their flesh and the shadows they cast, and they don't ever forget."

16

VISITORS

ANDRACHUS BALE STUMBLED behind General Fane as the man stormed off the deck of his warship and down the gangway, a dozen of his Scarlet Swords in tow. The general halted abruptly, gesturing with a gloved hand to a small crowd gathered at the far side of the docks. They were clad in little more than rags, and were shouting protests over the conscription of men and the seizure of property.

"Not at all the greeting I'd anticipated upon reaching Riverweave," said Fane. "Especially after days spent on the Sullen Sea. I would have expected an outpouring of gratitude upon my arrival."

One of the crowd hurled something, possibly a tomato, which landed with a splatter less than a dozen feet from the general's men.

Fane eyed the crowd for a moment, straightening his surcoat and adjusting his gloves. "Keln," he said to a cruel-eyed, red-haired swordsman at his heel, "teach this rabble to respect their betters, particularly the sort here to save them from the Arranese. Choose the eldest male."

Keln nodded his understanding and strode toward the small crowd, his heavy boots thundering upon the timbers. The ragged crowd grew louder as he approached, howling obscenities and shaking their fists.

They were a hundred or so feet away and Bale could not discern the soldier's words over the din. Whatever he said stirred the mob to a heightened frenzy and soon they were hurling more than insults. Bale saw several protesters strike Keln with handfuls of feces and rotting vegetables. The Scarlet Swordsman did not waver.

After an exchange of angry shouts, Keln ripped a man from the crowd by his shock of white hair. In an instant, Keln had swept his blade from its scabbard and brought it down upon the man's neck. His head was severed clean, and Keln tossed it toward the crowd like a challenge. They fell suddenly silent and withdrew several paces.

Bale grimaced and choked back the bile rising in his throat.

"Such are the lessons of war," Fane said, and resumed his march ashore.

Bale found Riverweave far different from the tall belfries and leaden stone of Ironmoor. The city sprawled across the boggy delta where Rune's two mightiest rivers, the Drimrill and the Silverflow, emptied into the sea, and as much of the place floated upon massive barges as sat firmly upon the ground. Wooden buildings of every color lined a vast maze of canals and tight streets, and the place seemed to have more bridges than a man could count. It was a notorious meeting place of all the world's cultures, a grand bazaar where every good and service imaginable was available if one but had the coin.

Bale thought it'd be an interesting place to visit at any moment but the present, where war had seemingly turned the city into a tinderbox. The citizenry harried the refugees clogging the city and scuffled with the soldiers seizing their homes and supplies. Fane's soldiers reacted with their swords, and blood was spilled in the streets. The governor had taken issue with Fane's methods, but the argument was settled when the general declared the governor a traitor and had him strung from one of the city's many bridges.

Bale hurried to keep pace with Fane and his Scarlet Swords as they marched along a causeway beside the Silverflow. Nervous eyes watched them from nearby windows, and ahead was an arching bridge from which a number of bodies dangled.

"Damned traitors," Fane screeched. He looked to Bale. "Does my method of justice perturb you, spooker?"

Bale grimaced but decided against voicing any objection.

"Alas, some men have the stomach for what must be done, and others do not," Fane said, smiling with satisfaction. "But as for other matters, my offer still stands. You stay here, and I will send a detachment to secure the body of your Lector."

"I greatly appreciate your generosity," said Bale, "but there are certain rites which need to be performed, certain rituals at the situs of passage."

"Threats are everywhere," said Fane, gesturing across

the river to a home consumed by flames, its residents fleeing a group of soldiers wielding swords and torches. "I don't expect a man such as you comprehends the stakes of a war between great nations, or the vicious lengths to which ambitious men will go to achieve victory."

Bale looked askance at the general, observing how the man walked with his chin raised, his black eyes constantly appraising his surroundings. *Oh, I think I can guess how vicious an ambitious man can be.*

One of the crimson-clad soldiers walking ahead of them shouted, and Bale peered over the man's shoulder to see a throng of ruddy-skinned refugees crowding the path ahead. Several of the Scarlet Swords rushed forward and roughly removed them from the causeway, tossing the refugees into the river amid loud protests.

"Those people," Fane said, waving a hand at the refugees flailing about in the river, "could be Arranese spies for all we know. Victory in battle requires the most rigid discipline, the most steadfast resolve. Any soldier or citizen failing to obey orders to the very letter is a danger, and must be corrected or eliminated. My orders were clear: all denizens of Riverweave must clear the causeways, bridges, and docks while the soldiers disembark. Those mongrels are fortunate they weren't put to the sword. I *am* merciful, you must know."

Bale pulled a strand of hair away from his eyes and tucked it behind his ear. Fane was an increasingly frightening presence, and Bale was sickened by the man's capacity to treat innocent citizens of Rune—the very people he was charged to protect—with such cruelty. His stomach knotted and felt ready to spill its contents. "You are indeed merciful and just, General."

General Fane grinned, the deep furrows of his scars stretching and growing white. "But we digress. As I said, my offer still stands."

"I thank you but I must refuse."

"Do you? You realize the savagery of the enemies we face, and that you will be afforded no protection from my army once you leave my side? There will be none to save you from the Arranese pouring from the passes of the Southwalls."

Bale bowed his head. "It is my hope the Old Faith will light my way."

Fane laughed. It was a series of clipped, sharp huffs and snorts.

Even this madman's laughter is tailored with military precision. "I meant that with all sincerity, General."

"Did you?" he asked, cocking his hairless brow. "Of course you did. Well, if that is the case then I must give you an order," said Fane.

"An order? General, I am no soldier," said Bale nervously.

"No, you are anything but. Nevertheless, you are within my jurisdiction now, as Riverweave and all points south have become a war zone and as such are subject to martial law. As a citizen subject to this law, you are bound to observe my commands. Do you understand?"

Sweet Illienne, please heap no more burdens upon me. I am too weak an instrument!

"Do you, Acolyte?"

Bale nodded, worried any word he uttered would ring of deception. His stomach churned.

"Excellent. When you have finished with your *mission*, as you've termed it, you will return to me and you will disclose the details of your findings to me. Every last detail."

Bale's head spun. *I am such an awful liar! Dare I assure him I will?* He swallowed a mouthful of spit and nodded, again finding gestures far easier than words.

"Very well," said General Fane, coming to a stop. "As a reward for your loyalty I am sending my very best swordsman to accompany you. Keln?" he said, turning to the fierce-looking soldier behind him. "Please accompany the acolyte, and see my orders are followed to the letter. Keln, remind me to speak with you over my supper this evening regarding the details of this assignment, and the two of you can leave at first light tomorrow."

Bale shifted about in the straw-filled mattress in the servant's quarters, unable to sleep. He turned to his side and looked with revulsion at the sticky, red smear on floor's planks. *The former occupant did not leave willingly. I sleep in a dead man's bed.*

Fane and his men had tossed the governor's family and staff from his mansion, and Bale had been assigned a room not far from the general's own. The general had acted as though it had been a gesture of profound kindness, but Bale knew better.

The air had a chill to it, something that shook him to the bones. He rubbed at his arms with a shiver. The flickering light of fires and the din of chaos filtered through his shutters from the troubled streets outside. Looters and angry citizens clashed with soldiers, and the streets resounded with glass shattering, folks shouting, and houses burning to the ground. There came also the rings of steel and the cries of the dying.

At last Bale concluded he would not sleep, so he pulled himself out of bed and adjusted his nightshirt. He tiptoed around the wide stain of blood, opened his door, and walked down the long hallway. He didn't bother to acknowledge the soldier who just so happened to be seated at the hall's end, and just so happened to decide to follow him down another hallway and then down the winding staircase to the mansion's first floor.

Bale walked to the kitchen, dimly lit by a sputtering candle, and found a kettle of tea suspended over the ashes of a dead fire. He found an earthenware cup and filled it. The tea was only lukewarm but it was flavorful, like flowers and oranges mixed together with a hint of foreign spices.

He looked about the kitchen, taking account of the pots, cleavers and knives. He thought again of the long ride ahead with Keln, and snatched a knife from a wooden cutting block. He gripped the handle and tucked it inside the sleeve of his nightshirt. *One never knows when such a thing will be of use.*

The red-clad soldier entered the room just after, his presence bringing a flush to Bale's cheeks. The soldier didn't seem to notice, though, and poured a cup of tea from the same kettle. "Can't sleep?" he asked.

Bale avoided the man's eyes and nodded. "Just fighting off a chill," he said and left the room, retreating up the staircase.

He hurried along the first hallway's length, but then

slowed as he noticed light emanating from the cracks of a door. As he walked near it he heard voices. He craned his neck and moved his ear close to the doorframe, curiosity seizing him.

There were indeed voices, one of which had the unmistakable scraping pitch of General Fane.

"You have asked much of me, and I will deliver," came Fane's voice. "Just as we bargained. But I demand assurances."

There came another voice, a low hiss, and the air grew noticeably colder with the sound. "We will succeed. The Lector is dead, and that has crippled the Sanctum just as our master foretold. The High King will join him in death soon enough. Our other enemies have dwindled drastically over the centuries, leaving precious few capable of opposing us. Our efforts will succeed, for we have seen it written in the blood of the dead."

It seemed to Bale the light dimmed and the air grew colder, bringing to his mind the stories of the Sanctum's most ancient enemy. He shuddered. *A Necrist? Impossible.*

"I have come to accept many aspects of your faith," said Fane, "However, I am by nature a skeptical man. Certainly you appreciate that men often require assurances of more... substance? Understand that once we move forward with this, I have everything to lose should you and your colleagues fail in your task."

The hissing voice sounded again. "The blood does not lie. It is just as our master has foretold."

There was a thud, the sound of a fist striking a table. "I've heard quite enough of this wizard's talk," growled Fane. "I am the only man in Rune who can accomplish what you've requested. If you wish to count upon my services, then my prize must be delivered. Now. And only thereafter will your demands be met. Certainly you realize my station affords me many advantages, and my loyalty cannot be purchased with mere promises."

Again the hissing voice. "One of my brothers journeys to Riverweave as we speak. He carries with him the Auruch, and you will have it before your army marches. We will have then honored our promise, and we will be watching to make certain you honor yours."

An Auruch? Bale knew the word—it was a word in the elder tongue for an item of great and dangerous power, something left by the Elder God before he gifted dominion of the world to his children. The Sanctum had accounted for some, but not all, of the objects. *Our task grows ever more perilous.*

"Very well," said Fane. "Remember, though, this game must be played with subtlety, lest the High King's council take action. I hold much sway, but great losses will breed impatience and distrust. There will need to be diversions."

The other voice spoke. "We have a… *friend* on the council. You will be granted a lengthy leash."

Bale took a step back and examined the door. It had been damaged, likely when Fane and his Scarlet Swords removed the governor and his staff. It rested cockeyed on its frame, and near its bottom was a gap from which light spilled. Bale dropped to a crouch, ignoring the complaints of his knees, and pressed his face close.

Within the opulent room—a well-stocked library— sat General Fane. Facing him, with its back to the door, was a figure robed in black, the back of its bald head crisscrossed with stitches.

Bale froze and his jaw fell agape, realizing his suspicions were true indeed. *Dead gods, it is a Necrist!*

"Be assured, General Fane, that what is told in the blood of the dead will come to pass. When the High King dies—and he *will* die—there will be none left of his line to protect the Godswell. That gate will be open to us, and we will pry from it the power of our dead master. And when we do, you will be rewarded beyond measure."

Their master? Yrghul? Bale's hands trembled and there came a clunk. He'd dropped the knife on the floor. Gnashing his teeth, he scrambled and retrieved it and then nervously returned his gaze to the library.

Fane was peering over the black-robed figure, eyes trained to the door. He shifted in his chair and moved to stand.

Just then there came the thuds of boots from the nearby staircase. Bale's head wheeled but quickly he gathered himself and stood, tucking the knife up his sleeve and bolting down the hallway with footfalls as quiet as he could manage.

He pulled his door shut and turned the lock, his hands shaking. He slipped into bed and pulled his blanket to his chin, clutching close the knife and praying the Sanctum's most secret, most powerful prayers to Illienne to plead for safety until dawn.

They set off at sunrise, navigating cramped streets and bridges strangled by fog and filth. It seemed every rustic and rogue from the Sullen Sea to the Southwalls had sought refuge in Riverweave, their few possessions lashed to their backs or heaped upon their withered animals. The door of every home and inn was barred, so they lay strewn along the roads or stuffed in the alleyways, ghostly shapes haunting the haze.

Bale was uneasy on horseback. The beast, a white stallion better suited to bearing great heroes rather than old spookers, obeyed none of his commands but adhered to Keln's every grunt and gesture. It was an uncomfortable, lurching ride, and did nothing to settle his already queasy stomach. He swallowed thick spit and did his best to keep down his breakfast.

His nerves were still rattled from the previous night's events, most particularly General Fane's visitor. His head whirled with thought, wondering how deeply the Sanctum's ancient enemy had infected Rune. He thought of the scullery maid and her note, which now seemed so very long ago. *General Fane and Chamberlain Alamis, perhaps the two most powerful men in Rune, in league with our black foe. Fane soon to be in possession of an Auruch. A plot to draw Yrghul's power from the Godswell.*

These are indeed the darkest of times.

His horse lurched suddenly around a corner, threatening to toss him into a narrow canal that smelled distinctly of rot. Bale regained his balance and pulled his focus back to the task of remaining upright.

Keln rode ahead of him, his hair pulled back in a tight knot and matching in color the crimson cloak draped over his shoulders. He was a taciturn companion, which was a small measure of relief. He kept his eyes forward with the exception of the occasional backward glance to make certain Bale still followed. Their gazes locked more than once, and Keln's stern glower conveyed a clear message: "*To the letter.*"

It was a long ride through the sprawling city and they arrived at the wall just as the belfries announced seven o'clock in the morning. The wall was a moss-covered jumble of old stones just taller than a man, and it seemed to Bale it would offer little protection if the Arranese horde made it this far north.

But then, who is the real enemy?

Two soldiers wordlessly unbarred the gate as they approached, throwing it wide to reveal a flat, misty expanse to the city's south. Upon the wet plain beyond the wall was the encampment of the High King's army, a collection of white tents so numerous it escaped calculation. There was the smoke of a thousand fires, the ring of blacksmiths' hammers, and countless soldiers milling about in the mist, tending to armor and weapons and making ready to make war. Bale sensed the High King's soldiers would be waging a devastating battle very soon, and reckoned there was a reasonable chance his journey would leave him caught in the battle's throes.

This will be the death of me.

"Where to, spooker?" asked Keln gruffly.

Bale was quiet, the scope of the scene before him causing him to tremble. His heart thumped heavily in his chest and throat and he swallowed hard.

Keln turned about in his saddle to regard Bale, his jaw shifting as though chewing a gristly piece of meat. "I asked you a question, and I'll not have you waste any more of my time than is necessary."

"I-" Bale stammered. "I- I am sorry. South by southwest, several days at least." As he put this distance into words it occurred to him again just how long and unpleasant his journey would be, and how very far away he was from home. He breathed deeply and tried to slow the rapid beats of his heart as they set out south upon a wide swath of road.

Prefect Gamghast awoke in the dead of night to a rapping on his door. He fumbled about for a moment before orienting himself and rising from bed. He grabbed a candlestick and breathed a word of power, one of the secrets given to the Sanctum by the Sentinel Castor, and a flame sprung to life upon the wick. He unlatched his door and cracked it open.

"Hullo, Prefect," said the man at the door. It was Wit, a gangly simpleton to whom they'd given shelter and assigned more menial tasks including the night watch. "You, ah, have a visitor."

"Who would call upon me at such an hour, Wit?" Gamghast asked. Every resident of the Abbey had been anxious since the Lector's death, and nighttime visits from acolytes seeking counsel were not uncommon. An outsider, though, was.

Wit bowed his shaggy head. "S-sorry. I didn't get a name."

"No?" Gamghast pressed a hand to his brow. *Alamis? Has the chamberlain decided to make good his threat?* "A soldier? One of the High King's guards? A tall man with pale eyes, perhaps?" he asked with urgency.

"Ah, no. A woman."

"And she asked for *me*?"

"By name, sir. She's waiting in the vestibule."

Gamghast cursed as he drew his robes over his shoulder and grabbed his staff. "The next time there's a visitor at the gates, identify them before throwing wide our door. These are troubled times, boy."

"She smelled nice, Prefect. Like noble folk. I don't think she means you harm."

"So you are able to identify danger by smell alone? Imagine that. Perhaps your considerable talents are being wasted and we should advance your studies in spellcraft!" Gamghast huffed, shouldered Wit aside and trudged into the hallway.

"She didn't seem like trouble, Prefect," said Wit, walking close behind Gamghast.

"Yes, yes, yes," he said, waving a hand dismissively. "In peaceful times I would be comfortable with your instincts, Wit. But these are not peaceful times. Rune is besieged, both from without and within, and our enemies do not always choose to reveal themselves as such. Doubt your every instinct, and question all who claim to be your friend."

The halls of the Abbey were quiet this time of night, though Gamghast noticed a number of doors with cracks aglow, betraying candlelight in the rooms beyond them. *Few find sleep easily in these times.* He'd told Prefects Borel and Kreer of the threats made by Alamis, and suspected Borel in particular had difficulty keeping the news to himself.

He shook his head and smoothed his robes, wondering at the identity of his caller. Ever since the news had reached Ironmoor of the Arranese crossing the Southwalls, the Sanctum had been beset by requests for prayers and exorcisms. Many claimed to see demons or hear the howls of haunting ghosts.

They arrived at last at the Abbey's vestibule, a wide area of simple chairs and solemn statutes and artifacts, a place meant to convey the Sanctum's longevity and reverence to all who entered its doors.

Seated in one of the chairs was, indeed, a woman. She was dressed in simple robes, but her proud bearing suggested she was accustomed to something more elegant. Her blue eyes rested above high cheekbones, all framed by long, flaxen hair just beginning to give way to gray. It took a moment, but Gamghast recognized her, and as he did he nearly swooned. He fell awkwardly to one knee and heard Wit doing likewise behind him.

"My queen!" he said, bowing his head low.

"Get up," she said, her voice smooth and commanding. "Get up, you old fool! I'll not have the whole of Ironmoor knowing I'm here!"

"B-But..." Gamghast stammered, "w-what may I do for you?" His head spun, wondering what would compel this woman to seek his company. He had been present at her wedding to High King Deragol, as had all the Sanctum fifteen years prior, but that was the only time he could recall being in her presence. *What could she want of me?*

She rose from her seat, again gesturing for him to rise. "Is there a place we might speak?" She gestured to Wit. "Somewhere private?"

Gamghast struggled upward, pressing upon his

creaking knee for leverage and doing his best not to groan in discomfort. "Of course, of course. There is a sanctuary just over there. If you will but allow me to lead the way? Or, considering your station, is it proper for you to lead?"

She looked at him coolly.

"Very well," Gamghast said, gesturing for her to follow. "This way."

Thirty or so feet away he found the door to one of the Abbey's many sanctuaries, quiet rooms reserved for prayer or study. There were chairs set at the room's corners, and tapestries lining the walls. The room was lit, as always, by a fire in a stone cylinder at the room's center, a symbol of the Bastion's Godswell. He held the door open for Queen Reyis and then shut it quietly behind her.

Here, in her presence, Gamghast became aware of his disheveled appearance. He licked his hand and frantically tried to smooth the wild wisps of his beard. He smacked at the wrinkles of his robe but the exercise was futile. "I apologize, my queen. I am an old, simple man, unused to visitors of your stature. To what do I owe this most unexpected honor?"

She found one of the chairs and after pulling it closer to the fire she sat. "I am a keeper of the Old Faith, Prefect, as difficult as that has been of late."

"I am honored to know that, my queen. We members of the Sanctum live to serve the Crown, and thereby Rune, and it is always inspiring to learn someone in the Bastion is praying with us."

She nodded. "I may be the only one. The Bastion is not a place of devotion, Prefect, unless the devotion is to the throne. It is power that is worshipped there, not principle."

Gamghast sank into a chair and adjusted his robes. He knew not how to address Queen Reyis, nor could he guess at why she would call upon him. He decided to remain quiet.

Queen Reyis was quiet as well, her blue eyes fixed upon the flame at the center of the room. Her shoulders slouched, and in this light Gamghast could see her face was creased with worry.

"Forgive me if I overreach, my queen, but something troubles you?"

She smiled, warmly and brilliantly, though Gamghast guessed that was from practice rather than genuine emotion. "Why ever do you ask, Prefect?"

He scratched his knee. It still ached from kneeling. "A midnight visit to the Abbey by Queen Reyis of Rune is not a common distraction for me. I am guessing there is some purpose behind it, some counsel sought here that is not found in the Bastion. I am here for you."

"I was told you were a wise man, and your insight does not disappoint." She leaned closer. "I was also told you were trustworthy. You understand no one can ever know I was here, nor can you ever speak of what I am about to tell you. My bodyguards are outside, Prefect, and they can be a most vicious lot."

Always threats these days. Have people forgotten favors are asked, not demanded? His shoulders sagged. "You have my word."

She looked at her hands twisted in her lap and her

smile vanished. "You have heard of my... difficulties, yes?"

Gamghast nodded. "The health of the Crown is of utmost importance to us, my queen, even if High King Deragol does not call upon our services as often as the High Kings of old." He cleared his throat. "The answer is yes, my queen. We know of the miscarriages."

"Eight," she said, looking away and holding her chin high. Gamghast thought there was the glint of a tear welling in her eye. "Eight miscarriages."

Gamghast's thoughts turned to the scullery maid's note: *"The King is being poisoned. That's why he's making no babies and he is in grave danger."*

"The pregnancies never lasted more than three months." She scowled and shook her head. "Then I would burn with an unbearable pain, and bleed and bleed until I was near death. I learned to dread every pregnancy, to fight away tears when I missed my first cycle."

He felt a sudden need to reach out, to comfort her, but withdrew. "I know it can be troubling, my queen. We have various things in our apothecary, roots and herbs and concoctions to place the mind at ease, to give a person a feeling of well-being."

Queen Reyis turned back to regard him, a thin smile on her lips. "I am pregnant once again, Prefect. I am in my fourth month, further along than I have ever been."

"This is most excellent news, my queen! I congratulate you!"

"Perhaps it is excellent news, but I have lost hope. I still check my bed sheets every morning for blood. I'm afraid, Prefect. I'm afraid I will prove a disappointment to my husband and my kingdom once more."

"With prayer, with the grace of Illienne, anything is possible. You must not despair."

She pressed her hands against her belly, smoothing the loose clothing to reveal a swell. "I cannot bear such a loss again, and everything we tried previously ended in failure. Thus, with your consent, I will call upon you regularly. You can monitor my progress and provide what ministrations you can. Yours is said to be an order of healers, and I ask for the application of your skills. As well as your earnest prayers."

Gamghast nodded as earnestly as he could. *If I am to help save Rune, it seems it will be as its most unlikely midwife.* "I would be honored, my queen."

"It is settled then," she said, rising to stand. "We will be discrete, as I have not made this news public nor have I even told my husband. You will call upon me regularly at the Bastion, under other auspices."

Gamghast remained in his seat, knotting his hands together. He breathed deeply. "That poses a concern, my queen. The last time I entered the Bastion, Chamberlain Alamis denied my request to call upon His Majesty."

"Did he, now?" asked Queen Reyis, her expression one of genuine surprise. "Has he grown so bold?" She was quiet for a moment before speaking. "I will provide you means of visiting me secretly."

"That would be useful. The chamberlain has threatened me with charges of treason."

She frowned and her hands clenched into fists. "Worry not, Prefect. The royal family still has some sway within the walls of the Bastion. I will deliver word to the guards I trust most, and you will be granted a means of entry. And I have long been friends with the Magistrate-Examiner. If Alamis makes good on his threats, I'll let the Magistrate-Examiner know what the Crown thinks of the charges." She rose to leave.

"Thank you, my queen," Gamghast said. "Just one more thing. Take none of the medicines or elixirs given to you by members of your staff, or of the chamberlain's. Be careful even with your food and drink. It is imperative you trust no one. I will arrive tomorrow with my ministrations."

17

THE SHORT ODDS

FENCRESS FALLCROW CREPT in the darkness, her twin blades drawn. She moved softly between the trees, pressing her boots gently beneath her. She'd killed many this very way, quiet and quick. As shaken as she was by the events of the past few weeks, she reckoned she hadn't lost the gifts of a true assassin. *Quiet as the grave.*

There ahead, no more than forty feet away, was the green-cloaked fellow, himself stalking in the darkness. Beyond him, perhaps another twenty feet distant, was Drenj, sleeping in the warmth of firelight. Fencress smiled, amazed at the Khaldisian's recklessness in lighting a fire so close to the road and in the middle of a war.

The trees thinned and the brush grew heavier, stubborn stuff that was difficult to move through silently. Fencress breathed easy and found her rhythm, matching the man's footfalls with impeccable timing. After escaping from slavery as a youth she'd trained as an acrobat and as a dancer—her steps were nimble and muted. *I will be no more than an echo.*

As the green-cloaked man approached Drenj's campsite he slowed. Fencress noted the man's longsword was slung upon his left hip, suggesting he was right-handed. She was surprised the blade remained in its scabbard, but then the Khaldisian showed no signs of stirring.

The man moved into the glow of the fire and stood, seeming to appraise Drenj and perhaps his belongings. He appeared utterly unaware of Fencress's presence, but Fencress made certain to silence her stride, dancing on tiptoes through the brush while she found the quietest path. *Careful, now.*

She looked toward the road, searching for Paddyn. The youth was damned good with a bow, but downright clumsy when it came to more intimate murder. She'd directed the archer to find a spot opposite the camp, and to put an arrow through the green man's throat if things got out of hand. She saw no sign of him, but figured the short odds were the boy hadn't run off and left her. It was no guarantee, but then Fencress was used to taking chances.

The green man sank to a crouch just before Drenj. Fencress reckoned his still-sheathed sword meant he had no intention of killing the Khaldisian, and if this were a robbery he would have been searching his purse rather than his expression. Regardless, the man had followed them for days, and good intentions rarely required stalking.

The man moved his hands over Drenj, as though

warming them over a fire. His mouth shifted but Fencress could hear no words. His eyes were closed, and he seemed to assume some sort of trance.

Spellcraft?

Fencress wagered now was the time, guessing the man would have difficulty discerning the sound of footsteps from Drenj's snore and the crackling campfire. She quickened her pace, making her way round the campsite so as to come at the cloaked man from behind. *Lickety-split, nice and quick.*

Her strides were smooth, and her feet found the quietest parts of the brush. She tugged at her cowl, pulling it low over her eyes, and figured the only parts of her that would catch the firelight would be her blades. The rest would be blackness.

She was close now, close enough for her to discern the rise of the man's shoulders as he breathed, close enough to count the wrinkles in his clothing. She focused on the soft part of the head where the jawline met the neck. She would press her blade there, hard enough to cut flesh but not so vicious as to nick the jugular. She'd draw just enough blood to get the man's attention.

Fencress came to the encampment's edge, drew a deep breath, and charged forward. She made no more sound than a rush of wind. Yet, the man must have heard something as he whirled about, not to his right as Fencress had anticipated, but to his left. *Better still.* Fencress slammed into him with full force, pinning the man's sword arm beneath him and driving his head to within inches of the fire's glowing embers. She knelt upon the man with all her weight and pressed a blade to his

240

throat, shaving clean a few dirty whiskers in the process. Fencress was by no means a big brute like Karnag, but she knew where bodies were weakest and what made them hurt. This fellow would not rise unless permitted.

Drenj gasped and scrambled about beside them, stumbling back several steps to get clear of the fray. "Fencress?" he said, his tongue thick with sleep. "What is this?"

Fencress gave the Khaldisian a wink before returning her attention to her prey. The man struggled dumbly beneath her, clearly caught off guard and shaken with shock. He kicked about, but then Fencress made use of her second sword. She pressed the point against the fellow's jewels. *A right-thinking man won't move if doing so means ripping his jingles.*

She clicked her tongue, scolding. "Hush, now," she said.

The man looked wildly about, into Fencress's eyes, upward at the fire, downward to the blades. He pulled his head back, trying to pull his throat free of the blade, and Fencress let him. The man suddenly cursed and howled.

Fencress sniffed. "Awful odor, isn't it, friend? Nothing has quite the same stink as burning hair. Forgive me for not warning you earlier, but your head is quite close to the fire. Then again, you probably sensed that already?"

The man struggled, desperately trying to work his right arm free from beneath him. He growled and glowered like some feral beast and then began muttering strange-sounding words.

Fencress shook her head in admonition. She withdrew the blade from the man's throat for the briefest of instants, and popped the pommel hard into that small dip between the base of the neck and top of the breastbone. The man gasped, as Fencress knew he would, and then struggled for breath. Fencress smiled, then found a new, untouched part of the man's throat to press her blade upon. "You'll be shaved clean at this rate. I'd suggest you lie still, and not move that tongue of yours with any ill intent."

The man gritted his teeth and shook his head, saying nothing. He stared at Fencress hard, right in the eyes like he meant something by it. Fencress realized then the fellow would not give up his secrets easily and she grinned. Breaking brave men was always more entertaining than breaking the weak ones.

"Kill him!" shrieked Drenj, his long hands flailing as though shooing away a ghost. "He meant to kill me!"

"Not just yet," said Fencress. "I'll not put an end to the drama so quickly. I spent much of my later youth performing in a circus, and I'll not dishonor my old troupe by abandoning all sense of theater. What sort of sorry performance would that be? I want applause for my work."

Just then there was a commotion in the trees and Paddyn emerged from the darkness. "Rope?" he asked.

Fencress nodded. "Good and tight. This lad seems to be a witch of some sort, so keep his hands bound and his mouth gagged. I don't want him talking unless he's answering my questions."

Paddyn knelt beside them and cut a strip of cloth from the man's cloak. Fencress eased the blade from the man's throat to allow the archer to gag him, then eased her weight off him to allow room for the rope. At that moment, the green man shifted quickly to his side, yanking his right arm from beneath him and moving to bring his hands together.

Fencress acted swiftly, cracking the man's temple with the hilt of the sword in her right hand and then pinning the man's arm with the flat of the blade in her left. The man went limp and his eyes rolled back in his head.

"Well, then," Fencress said, pulling herself to stand and sheathing her blades. "It appears we can work at our leisure. Our prisoner won't be waking for a while."

Drenj walked closer and kicked a clod of dirt at the man's head. "He tried to kill me! What sort of monster tries to kill a man in his sleep!"

Fencress thought of the Lector and chuckled, but let the comment pass. She took time to inspect the man, noticing his sword was one of quality, and noticing the outlines of two other knives beneath his green jerkin. They were the sort of weapons that would be carried by one who knew how to use them. The man also seemed accustomed to roving far from home, as his boots were worn but well-tended and he had two satchels stuffed with durable provisions. He also had an odd band of black iron about his wrist, inscribed with strange symbols. *A sorcerer's trinket?*

"Remove that," Fencress said, gesturing at the bracelet. "And Paddyn? Tie him up tight and blindfold him as well. Odds are this fellow's trouble."

"I'd guess another two leagues," said Drenj, standing in his stirrups and peering down the narrow trail. "Assuming your directions are correct, and assuming the Arranese haven't found the place already."

Fencress walked beside Drenj and his horse, squinting in the morning sunlight. She pulled her own horse by its reins, as they'd slung their prisoner over the mare's back. "They won't find it. They'll hold to the wider roads. An army can't move through a forest this dense, so I reckon Old Crook will be just fine. A rugged old goat like that doesn't suffer in war. He profits."

"I hope you're right," said Paddyn from behind her. "But I should tell you I smell smoke on the air, and I'd swear the breeze is carrying the sound of war drums."

Fencress sniffed at the air and also detected the faintest odor of smoke. "Perhaps that smell is just Old Crook cooking that terrible squirrel stew he used to make."

"You know this man well?" asked Drenj.

"You could say," said Fencress. "Old Crook ran *The Dead Messenger* years ago, back when I was a much younger lass. He was the one who invented the whole notion of the Blood Box, a way to keep patrons and those of us who did their dark work from ever having to meet each other. Folk felt safer that way, and Old Crook charged a percentage for playing the middle man. After a time he'd made so much coin he grew tired of hoarding it, and left the inn to Handsome and retired in the south. He kept his whereabouts mostly secret, telling only those few of us who'd helped him earn the bulk of his riches. Over the years it's been a good spot to hide when things have gotten hairy."

"Does Karnag know of it?" asked Drenj, speaking the name like a curse.

"Aye," said Fencress. "Karnag made Old Crook more coin than any other, likely double. I'd have to say he was Old Crook's favorite, as that old bastard admired that Karnag was never shamed by his work and never seemed to do it out of desperation. And by the dead gods he was good at it, the best killer in the whole of Rune. It was Karnag who first introduced me to Old Crook, more than a decade ago."

"He's stirring," said Paddyn, gesturing to their prisoner.

Fencress smirked. "Best not talk of where we're going, then. You boys will have to trust me."

"Who comes?" called a rough voice from atop a wall of earth and timbers. "Best put your hands up, nice and easy, afore my lads loose their arrows."

Fencress looked about the heavy forest surrounding them and saw three bowmen lurking amidst the trees. She figured there were at least twice that many elsewhere, judging from the many groans of bowstrings drawing.

She surveyed the surroundings and then stepped forward, bowing low with a flourish. "At ease, gentlemen! I am none other than Fencress Fallcrow, assassin extraordinaire, thief of great renown, and noteworthy purveyor of wit and wisdom alike. Tell Old Crook I'm here to collect an old debt."

There was silence for long moments. Paddyn and Drenj shifted nervously in their saddles, and Fencress maintained her bow so long that her back started aching. Paddyn shot a glance at Fencress, an anxious look upon his grubby face. Fencress winked, doing her best to appear unfailingly confident.

"We should leave this place," whispered Drenj.

There came just then from the wall a guttural laugh which gave way to a hacking cough. "An old debt?" the voice croaked, and then there was the sound of its owner struggling to clear his throat. "To Fencress Fallcrow?" More laughter and coughing. "The Fencress I knew was always a funny lass, so maybe you're talking straight. And the others?"

"Well if it isn't Old Crook himself!" said Fencress, smiling widely. She gestured to her right. "May I present Paddyn of Barrendell, son of a simple farmer. He was a forthright young man who labored on his father's hardscrabble farm. Little did he know his pa had a gambler's soul, so the young fellow was forced to find work at *The Dead Messenger* to spare his dear pa from debtors' prison. And to my left is Drenj, a Khaldisian who came to Rune seeking his fortune, but found love before he found honest work. Soon he'd fathered three whelps and only did the dark work to put food in their mouths. Before long he discovered that the path of dark deeds is a steep, downward one, and it's never easy to turn back."

"Touching stories, all. But will they help defend these walls if the Arranese stumble upon us?"

"I'll vouch for them both."

"And the sack of shit on your horse? It doesn't look like you've brought me a nice set of tits in exchange for my hospitality. No offense against yours, of course."

"Alas, no," said Fencress. "We have a prisoner. This fellow followed us all the way from Raven's Roost. I know not his name, but I'm hoping we can make use of your facilities to find out."

"Anything for an old friend," said Old Crook. "Speaking of friends, where's your usual companion? I haven't seen Karnag Mak Ragg in years."

Fencress's grin withered at the mention of the name. "That's a sore matter. The sort of thing I'd prefer to speak of only among dear friends, Crook."

"Very well. Lads, open the gate!"

Fencress took a long draw from her mug, draining the last of its contents. It was cider, and a strong cider at that. She'd had only one mug and already her head had the tingles.

"Good stuff, eh?" asked Old Crook, taking the mug and moving to refill it at the cask set near the wall. "I make it myself. Takes me back to my days as a simple old innkeeper." He chuckled and returned the mug to Fencress, assuming a seat across from her at the circular table.

They sat alone in the comfortable room, a place of dark wood constructed upon the limbs of a massive oak. Narrow windows were carved into its circular wall and offered a full view of Crook's Hole, as Old Crook called his place. It was a sprawling compound of interconnected structures situated among, between, and upon the forest's thick trees, and all of it surrounded by a wall of wood and earth. Old Crook always kept a number of hard lads, and harder lasses, on retainer, so the place seemed sound as a fortress.

Old Crook took a sip from his mug—a bit too much—and it dribbled over his thick lips and jutting chin. He wiped it away with the back of his hand, revealing fingers even more crooked than Fencress remembered. Old Crook had told her once he'd been caught stealing bread as a boy, and that the shopkeeper had broken every one of his fingers to teach him a lesson. Fencress figured the story was a load of horseshit, as were most of her own, but reckoned it was a clever way of explaining the name "Crook" as something other than a moniker for a criminal. *Anything to make us seem better than the heartless scoundrels we really are.*

"So what of Karnag?" Old Crook asked. "How is he?"

Fencress sighed and stared into her mug. "That's a difficult question. One I have trouble answering even to myself. He... He's not the same. I worry for him."

Old Crook looked at Fencress, his dark brow easing from its usual glower. "We are friends, you and I. Some of you I thought of as children I'd never been able to father myself. You and Karnag most of all. You needn't fear words with me, lass."

Fencress nodded and sipped her cider. "We took a job from Handsome, a big money job which would allow us to take things easy for a good long while. It was a dangerous one for certain but Karnag thought we were up to the task." She grinned. "You know Karnag. The man hasn't a shred of fear in him, and always has something to prove."

"A murder?"

"Of course. But not just any old murder. We were hired to kill the Lector of the Sanctum. Anyone holding to religion would say the Lector's one of the most powerful people in all of Rune, perhaps all the world." Fencress paused, letting the weight of the words settle.

Old Crook's face was unreadable. "You're the ones who killed the Lector of the Sanctum."

"The very same, and in the forest not too far from here. It was a lot of coin, more than we'd ever seen."

Old Crook took a long drink and then looked curiously into his mug, as though surprised to find he'd emptied it. "Folk can make a great pile of coin by sticking to the little things, so long as they're willing to work hard. I always warned you and the rest not to get mixed up in things bigger than yourselves."

Fencress felt shame coloring her cheeks. "You did, Old Crook. I wish we'd listened."

Old Crook moved to the cask and refilled his mug. He then stood by a window and stared out in silence for a time before speaking. "We all start life accepting whatever crap our parents choose to feed us. Me? My mum, like most mums, taught me the Old Faith, or at least whatever scraps of it she'd learned as a child. I soon found I wasn't much for it, but then I don't figure you *can* be for such things in a profession such as ours. But as a man gets older those things no longer seem so... outlandish. You see things. You feel things shift inside you, a change of heart, or maybe just a *wanting* to have a change of heart. You begin to get the feeling there's more to this world than just men and their madness." He sighed and returned to his chair.

Fencress hunched over her mug and took another long drink. "I can't say I take such things lightly anymore, either. Not after what we've been through."

"Karnag? He lives, yes?"

Fencress nodded. "He lives, but he's changed, Crook.

The murder itself was nothing of note, aside from being an utter mess with more people dead than we intended, just as such things sometimes are. But after that... After that Karnag was different. He spoke in a strange tongue, at first when he slept, and later when he killed a man. He possessed some kind of power. When we returned to Raven's Roost to collect what was owed us, Karnag killed a man with a *word*. We headed south to Hargrave, a couple of days from here, and he did it again, only worse." She tapped her mug on the table. "I've seen sorcery, but this was something else. It was as though he could *will* the death of men, and he seemed to make a ritual of it. I fear he's cursed. Cursed in the oldest, worst of ways."

Old Crook looked toward the window and tapped his crooked fingers against his mug. "That's a sad thing, Fencress. Folk like us shouldn't meddle in those things. I believe one of my lads found the site of the murder. The body was *black*, Fencress. All black and powdery like something burned. Yet, there was no sign of a fire being set to the body. His clothes and the sheet about him were untouched, still white and pristine in the places not soaked with blood. It was as though all life had been sucked out of that body, leaving it no more than a hollowed-out husk. I saw it myself, and when I did I knew the man to be some high ranking member of the Sanctum. I had the remains thrown into a pyre with the rest of the dead, out of respect for my mum. I've no need of devilry on my doorstep."

Fencress frowned. "I can make no sense of this, but I know I can't leave Karnag like this."

"You need to help the lad."

"I can't imagine where to begin. He's my friend, but I deal in murder, Crook. Not madness."

Old Crook's brow arched thoughtfully. "You said your prisoner followed you from Raven's Roost? And you'd just returned there to collect your coin?"

"Aye. We noticed him on our tail just after Karnag had one of his… episodes. I'm guessing the fellow also saw what Karnag did in Hargrave. After that he decided to head north, and we grabbed him."

Old Crook's face twisted into a grin. "Maybe he knows a thing or two?"

"He seems like a tough sort. I'll need some time with him to get the answers I need."

"Maybe not as much time as you think. My lads are softening him up right now in the stockade, for practice and such. I figured you wouldn't mind."

The stockade of Crook's Hole was a deep, wide pit in the ground, its walls all black soil held back by wooden planks. Fencress entered it from the ramp dug out of one of its corners and regarded the prisoner shackled to a post in the center. She walked round the man, still blindfolded and gagged, and noticed blood dripping from a dozen fresh wounds. The fellow shuddered with frantic breaths, and his blindfold was damp with tears. *Old Crook's lads know their business.*

Fencress moved behind the man and began untying his gag. The prisoner recoiled and whimpered, seeming to fear another beating. "Hush," Fencress said. "There will be no need for violence so long as we understand each other."

The man settled back against the post, his breathing becoming more even. After a moment he nodded.

"Very well," said Fencress, removing the man's blindfold and walking to stand before him. She bowed politely. "I am Fencress Fallcrow, and I am equally willing to serve as your executioner as I am your liberator. The choice, friend, is yours. And you are?"

"Merek," he answered, his voice ragged and hoarse. His nose was flattened and blood trickled from both nostrils and through his greasy beard.

"Let me apologize, Merek, for the circumstances of our first encounter, and this, our second. However, I do not take kindly to being spied upon, nor do I fancy seeing one of my friends nearly murdered in his sleep."

"I intended no harm."

Fencress twirled a strand of black hair that had fallen from her cowl. "A convenient explanation to make, now that you find yourself in this predicament. The way I saw things—and I have very sharp eyes—you were crouched over him as he slept, your hands ready to wrap around his throat." She waggled a gloved finger at him, scolding. "Friends don't treat each other so, do they?"

"If I'd thought to kill your friend I'd have gutted him with my blade while he slept."

Fencress measured the man's eyes, searching for the tics of a liar. The fellow's gaze was unwavering. Fencress was certain the man was hiding something, but he wasn't lying about this. "Perhaps you're no murderer, but that doesn't mean you didn't hold ill intent. You practice witchcraft, do you not?"

"I am no witch," Merek said, his eyes narrowing.

"Not a witch, eh? Does the term insult you? Tell me, then, what you are? I recognize sorcery when I see it."

The man looked away, his bloody chin held high.

"Do we no longer understand each other, friend?" Fencress tucked her hand into one of the pockets of her cloak and retrieved the iron bracelet they'd taken from the man. It was an odd thing, etched with strange writing and its surface seemed to reflect no light. "I've fenced my fair share of jewelry, and this strikes me as much more than a mere bauble."

Merek looked hungrily at the object, momentarily struggling against the heavy chains that bound him.

"Ah," said Fencress, moving closer. "You want this?"

Merek cast his eyes downward and was still. "Yes," he said quietly. "You must let me go. There are things afoot, great forces at work. You must set me free!"

Fencress drew one of her blades and pressed the point against the fellow's forehead, easing his head upward. "You are in no position to make demands upon me, friend. I do not trust sorcerers, which means I do not trust you. I will ask my questions only once, and if you have any desire to leave this place with your head, you will answer them earnestly. Do we understand each other?"

Merek's eyes sharpened, and Fencress felt herself being appraised. She met the gaze with her hardest stare and pressed the blade more firmly against the man's forehead, drawing blood.

Oh, I am not bluffing.

"We understand each other," said Merek.

"Tell me why you followed us, all the way from Raven's Roost."

"You were there to collect the bounty for killing the Lector of the Sanctum."

Fencress said nothing.

"But your companion had already done so. I met him, and I met your patron. Do you know who it was who retained you? Do you know you were hired by a Necrist?"

Fencress gave an impassive look. The term was only dimly familiar, and Karnag had never said who'd retained them. "I did not."

Merek grimaced. "You have no idea what you've done. Your actions have shifted the balance in a great and secret war. The Lector was… Suffice it to say the Lector was a man possessed of tremendous power. For his life to be forfeit for mere coin!" He blinked hard, his eyes suddenly wet. "Your leader. The highlander. He was the one who slit the Lector's throat, wasn't he?"

Fencress nodded. "And how is it you know this?"

Merek breathed deeply. "I saw what happened in Raven's Roost, with the merchant. I also witnessed the killing of your companion in Hargrave. The highlander has become possessed by something. Something much greater than himself. And he has neither the discipline nor the desire to contain it. My order deals with such things. The old powers. The dead gods."

"You can help him?" Fencress asked, easing her sword from the man's head.

"I can."

Fencress returned her sword to its sheath but held his gaze. "You stray even once, friend, and I will run you through."

"I will help your friend."

Fencress knew trusting this man meant playing the odds, but then the only player who'd never win was the one who refused to throw the dice.

Karnag Mak Ragg moved through the night, slowly and with dark intent. He'd lost count of the number of men he'd slain, of the times they'd begged him to spare their lives, of the times he'd denied their pleas. He looked at his thick arms, so stained with blood he wondered whether they could ever be washed clean. Or whether he'd ever want them to be.

The Arranese had come to Rune seeking death, and he would grant it to them. He would slay Arranan's soldiers, and he would draw to him their king. He would take the lives of many men, and would ascend to the heavens atop a mountain of corpses.

He no longer slept, but the dreams remained. He needed to but shut his eyes and still himself to hear the voice, that seductive call which spoke to him of things that once were, and of things yet to come. When he alighted from such a trance he could read the fates of men in their faces and could see their actions long before they occurred. It was as though their thoughts and their futures lay open to him, and their lives were his to conclude. There was a righteousness, a certainty of purpose, in being the end of men.

There was an encampment ahead, seven Arranese warriors sent to harry Rune's army. They had built no fire, but Karnag could see them all the same. Tall and lean with angular features, almond-shaped eyes, and ears peaked nearly to a point. They sat in a tight circle, calloused hands close to their weapons.

"The Gravemaker," one of them said in an accent, drawing the word out and sharply annunciating its sounds.

Karnag smiled. He'd heard the Arranese utter this word before, after he'd shouted the name of his sword when they'd fled before it. They'd taken it to be his name, which was just as well. He and the blade were one.

"He stalks this wilderness," the man continued. "My brother Bashka saw him, two days ago when his war band stopped to water their horses. He came suddenly upon them. A demon. A devil. Bashka said he beheaded every member of his war band, all except for him. He drank their blood and laughed as Bashka ran away." He sighed heavily. "I fear him more than all the armies of Rune."

Another man laughed. "Do you fear this Gravemaker more than you fear our Spider King or his sorcerers?" asked another.

"Yes."

"Then you are a fool, Aleki," said the other. "There is no such thing as this Gravemaker. Your brother was afraid, and his eyes deceived him."

"You insult my tribe, Jelan," said Aleki, moving to stand. "My brother is no coward."

Coward. Karnag snarled at the mention of the word. He recalled his own clan's chieftain leveling the same accusation against his dead father, many years before. He remembered the chieftain uttering the word as he spat upon the funeral pyre, just before raping and slaughtering Karnag's mother and sisters and then casting him and his brothers from the highlands. The word rang in his skull, and Karnag turned his eyes to the accuser. *You have cast your fate. You will die this night.*

"I did not call him a coward," said Jelan, defensively. "Fear plays tricks on the eyes. Now sit down and be quiet, before a *real* enemy hears you."

"My brother is no coward," repeated Aleki, sitting. "If he says he saw the Gravemaker, then I trust him as though I'd seen him myself."

"I too have heard of this demon," said an older man. "Eight days ago, when we first marched upon the road, we sent a vanguard of seven men ahead of us. We came upon a village and there they were, all seven of them dead. But it wasn't the work of soldiers. They'd had their heads and arms ripped from their bodies. I looked for tracks, and there was only one set of footprints trailing away from the bodies."

Karnag smiled once more. He remembered this. He walked closer to the circle of men, easing his great sword from its sheath.

The Arranese continued speaking, oblivious to Karnag's presence. He was close enough to smell them, the strange oils they used upon their skin.

He closed his eyes and stilled himself, listening for the call. After an instant he heard it, a warm whisper which filled his mind and expanded him. He reached out with his thoughts and among the shifting scape of futures he discerned the deaths of these men.

He sharpened his mind and could see it. He would leap into their circle and would cleave away the heads and shoulders of three of them in one sweep of his sword.

The others would tremble with shock, stammering and stumbling as they fled from him but they would struggle in vain. He would hack apart and mangle three of those who remained, seizing their lives before they could give voice to their agony. He would be a black storm of fury among them, and he would shower the earth with their blood.

It happened thus.

The last he let live. He stood over him, his bones still humming with rage. He breathed deeply, suppressing the call which yet sounded in his head and then sheathed his mighty sword.

"Flee, Aleki," Karnag said, "and tell your brother he is no coward. All men are wise to fear me."

Aleki ran without a word.

18
REQUIEM

LANNICK STOOD BENEATH the leafy eaves of the old oak, solemnly regarding the desecration at his feet. It was here, on this hill once part of his father's farm, where he'd married his wife on a midsummer's morning. And where he'd buried her and their children in the dead of a winter's night.

The ground before him was upturned, a deep hole torn in the earth. Within the hole were four corpses, ripped from their linen wrappings and discarded in a haphazard pile. Their faces had been shorn from their skulls, leaving masks of ruined, grinning bones.

Lannick descended into the grave and pulled aside the first corpse, that of his elder son. He'd given the bodies ancient Variden rites which preserved the flesh and protected the soul, and thus they felt just as they had that night nine years before. Cold, stiff, but still horribly familiar.

He retrieved an armful of the shredded linens and

took the body upon his lap. He looked skyward as he wrapped the bands of cloth about the boy's face and neck, not daring to look upon the eyes still resting in their sockets.

As he did this he did not weep. His eyes burned but there were no tears. Instead, he moaned. Softly at first, but soon it was a throaty howl. To his ears it was pain given sound, a dirge of despair so profound it could not be bound by words.

He did this again and again, and again once more. His young twins, his beloved wife. As he wrapped their bodies his hands found their wounds almost of their own accord, those hollows in the flesh left by the weapons of General Fane's Scarlet Swords. His hands shook as they crossed over those damaged parts, but he continued his grim work until the four bodies were once again laid in order, with reverence.

He then dug at the dirt and threw it in clumps upon them, clawing and scraping until his nails cracked and his fingers bled and his arms felt ready to fall from their sockets.

At last he stood. The day had given way to evening, and there was a chill upon the air. He pulled his cloak about him and kept a silent vigil until the moon rose over the land, bathing the gravesite in a ghostly light.

He straightened his shoulders and recited his loving farewells in his head. His hand found the locket about his neck, and he retrieved it from beneath his shirt and detached it. He then knelt and pressed the locket deep into the dirt. He held his hand there for a moment, thinking of the horrors suffered by these who he'd loved most.

He arose, and with one last, silent goodbye he turned and left the place.

My revenge will be their requiem.

It was midmorning when Lannick caught sight of Ironmoor, a great mass of gray stone crowded against the edge of the sea. He'd spent so much time within its walls he'd nearly forgotten how imposing the city appeared from without. It was surrounded by a wall four times as tall as a man, and the steel of soldiers pacing its battlements glinted in the sun. Beyond those walls the city rose, higher and higher upon a broad hill before coming to a crest at the Bastion. Thereupon, the Bastion's majestic Tower of Lords stretched to the sky, the statue of a gold dragon shining upon its peak.

Home. Lannick's expression twisted, not quite a smile and not quite a frown, but whether this was due to mixed emotions or the crookedness of his face even he wasn't sure. He'd long desired a new beginning, a new start for his life, and now he had it. *But at such a dear price.*

The pain of the previous night had left him empty. He felt as though he'd buried more than his family in that grave, and knew now he would no longer measure his love for his family by the depth of his anguish. He would measure it by his deeds.

For the first time in a long while he felt his stride driven by a hint of purpose. He thought of the years he'd spent grieving, then of the years he'd wasted thereafter using that grief as an excuse. He'd shed those chains, now, he hoped. His was not the hand that had murdered his family. He'd betrayed no one. And his purpose now was to give proof to these truths and deliver justice to those who were guilty.

When he arrived at the city gates he found them shut. A massive portcullis blocked his entry and the two soldiers manning it eyed him suspiciously as he neared.

"We're at war, stranger," said the shorter soldier. "Identify yourself and your business in Ironmoor."

"Ironmoor is my home," said Lannick, straightening to his full height. "And I am no stranger. I am Captain Lannick deVeers, Protector of Ironmoor."

This drew a hearty laugh from the guards, but the shorter one moved to open the gate. "Well, judging by the look of you, you're no Arranese warlord, and that's good enough for me."

Lannick went first to the Hollows, the city's hardest quarter. It was a weave of squalid streets crowded by shanties, and seemed rougher than Lannick remembered. The place was filthy and the air carried the reek of rot, refuse, and unwashed flesh. The folk trudging through the streets looked a sight more desperate than before, and seemed as ready to exchange pleasantries as knife a fellow in the back.

He looked upward, squinting at the sun high overhead. Midday, just as he'd planned. He reckoned the shadows would be at their slimmest, giving him the best chance to retrieve what he needed.

He did not see many familiar faces, and those folk he did recognize didn't seem to recognize him. Perhaps it was the short haircut or the clean clothes. *Or the fact that I'm not stone, stumbling drunk.* In any case, anonymity was a welcome thing.

At last he rounded a corner and came upon a dead-end street where sat a brothel, a pawnshop, and above the shop his dwelling. A few tired-eyed prostitutes called out as he passed, asking if he was new to town and whether he was up for a tangle between the sheets. One even called him pretty. He politely waved and shook his head as they displayed their wares, and continued across the street. *If they'd lavished me with such flattery a month ago perhaps I wouldn't be in this mess.*

He ascended the rickety staircase alongside the pawnshop and found his door covered with notes from the pawnbroker, Silas, threatening eviction and demanding payment. He looked sideways down the stairs, half expecting Silas to come charging out of his shop, but remembered that at midday Silas generally took his "lunch" at one of the nearby brothels.

He swept the notes aside and tried the knob. The door was locked, so there was some measure of chance his possessions hadn't been stolen. Beside the door was a knot in the wood, and within the knot was his key. He turned the lock and paused for an instant, feeling for once a stranger to the place rather than its resident.

The sordid chamber still carried the sour stink of a bad drunk. It was littered with empty bottles, loaves of moldy bread, and no fewer than a score of skittering cockroaches. There was a washbasin of stagnant water, a mattress covered with stains, and a chamber pot in dire need of emptying.

A sardonic grin slipped across his face. *No wonder I lived like such a sorry sot for so long. Comfort is ever the enemy of ambition.*

Lannick set across the room with apprehensive steps, each stride slower than the last. It had been nine years. Nine awful years filled with guilt and misery. He stopped, uncertain. Then he spat and clenched his crooked jaw, ignoring the grinding sensation and cursing his self-doubt. He thought about his family. *I buried my failures with them. It will do no honor to their memory if I keep running away.*

He moved to the room's opposite side with an inspired urgency, not daring to give his doubts another chance to gnaw at him. He stepped atop the mattress and stretched upward, pressing free the loose board in the ceiling and reaching his hand inside the hole. And there it was, the bundled cloth of his old cloak. He pulled it free and then stooped to sit on the edge of his mattress, holding it upon his lap with timid hands. A cloak wrapped about a box. *To the eye, such modest things.*

After a time he undid the ties of the simple cloak he wore and he stood, letting the garment slide from his shoulders. He then unfurled the green cloak and regarded it. It was worn and weathered but retained its color: a forest green edged with silver embroidery. The embroidery was a swirling script, an ancient spell told to the Variden by Valis, the Sentinel of Rune. Lannick could not decipher the words, but knew they imparted to the wearer certain protections against the dark.

With a swift movement Lannick slung the cloak across his shoulders and waited, almost fearfully. After all these years he almost expected the cloak to make him *feel* something, some change in his substance, some shift in his thinking. But there was nothing, and the cloak felt much like the ordinary one he'd just discarded. After several heartbeats he sighed, allowing the tension to leak from his form.

He then turned to the box. It was small, such that it could be held comfortably in one hand. But this was no mean thing, he knew. He lifted it from the bed and held it before him. There was an unnatural heaviness to it, an unexpected heft for so small a thing. The box, too, was etched with script, this spell one of concealment meant to hide the box from unwelcome eyes.

At last he opened it, revealing a thick bracelet of dull iron. *My Coda.* There was sunlight streaming from the window, but the Coda reflected none of it. There were markings carved upon its surface—another spell— and the Coda was said to be comprised of a hundred thin layers of that black metal, each one etched with a different invocation.

But these were no simple enchantments, no pale imitations of the forces that had forged the world. These were ancient commands in the very language of the dead gods. This was a thing possessed of true magic, a divine potency given form.

His hand hung above it, trembling, for long moments. He'd last worn his Coda the day he buried his family. He'd been branded a traitor for belonging to an order devoted to a banished Sentinel. After the murders he renounced the Variden, blaming the slaughter of his family upon his association with them. He thereby gained the High King's pardon for his so-called crime, but not his forgiveness. He'd vowed then to never again walk that path, and he'd broken the Coda loose with a smith's hammer.

Times change, and people with them. He gently lifted the Coda from the box. It unhinged as he did so, leaving a space through which he could thread his wrist. He held it just over his wrist, slightly behind the hand, and paused again.

He knew if he did this he would be bound to the Variden once more. The Codas were forged by the Sentinel Valis, who poured into them all remnants of his divine power. Valis had made the instruments so that he could uphold his oath to protect Rune, even after the death of his mortal form. His power would live on through his followers, the Variden. The Codas granted every Variden the ability to work formidable spellcraft while obscuring them to their enemies. The Codas also created a link by pulling the Variden toward a common purpose and preserving for the order each mind's knowledge after death.

"*We toil each of us in secret,*" Alisa had said, "*but we are never alone. The Vigilant ever stand guard.*"

Lannick paused before returning the Coda to its case and snapping the box shut. Lashing the Coda would join his thoughts to the other Variden. Although he would remain free to make his own decisions, the others would sense his actions and he would be pressed to follow the order's purpose. He thought then the Coda could be as much a shackle as an instrument of power, and he wasn't yet ready to be tethered to the cause.

He thought too of Wil's statement. Wil had mentioned

that four of the Variden were slain by Fane and his men once Lannick's affiliation had been discovered. Perhaps he could try setting some things right before placing others at risk.

He stashed the box in the satchel upon his belt and made ready to leave.

Not just yet.

The Wanton Vicar looked the same as ever, its squat wooden structure leaning tiredly against the ruins of a cathedral. Lannick stopped before pulling open the door, wondering how different things might have been had he not wandered into the place that evening not so long ago. He sniffed, shook his head, and walked inside.

It was a light crowd, as it generally was this time of the afternoon. A couple of shady-looking men played deadman's dice in a corner, silver coins scattered across their table. At another table a few richly clad sorts, merchants likely, sat in hushed conversation. The place smelled of garlic and beef, and Lannick suspected a stew was simmering in the kitchen.

Behind the bar was Brugan, wielding a rag in a thick hand as he polished the bar, wearing a grin Lannick knew was almost ever-present. The big man's ugly face had never seemed a more welcome sight. His nose was perhaps more flattened than it had been the last time they'd met, lending his face an almost sunken shape. But his good cheer remained.

"Take a seat wherever you'd like," Brugan said, his eyes not straying from his task.

"Do you have a seat at the bar?" Lannick asked, mirth finding its way to his face.

"I said wherever you'd—" Brugan stopped midsentence when his gaze found Lannick. "Dead gods! Lannick? Can it be?"

Lannick remained beside the door, his smile widening. *Old friends are a comfort to the soul, no matter what they look like.*

"It *is* you!" said Brugan, rushing from behind the bar. He seized Lannick by the shoulders and then wrapped his burly arms about him, squeezing tightly enough to make Lannick wince at the wound in his ribs not yet healed. "I feared the worst, and thought you were dead."

"I live, Brugan," said Lannick, pressing free of the burly man. "I'm okay."

Brugan regarded him with a cocked brow. "You look… different. You've had some rough days, I'm sure. I promise you, Lannick, I did not betray you to Fane and his brutes. But my serving girl Lacy walked in and they put a sword to her throat. She wouldn't give your name but told them you lived in the Hollows when they made her bleed. She's not to blame."

"I know, Brugan. No one's to blame but me. I'm sorry for bringing my troubles to your door."

Brugan shrugged. "Friends need to do that sometimes, especially when they have nowhere else to go." He gestured to the bar. "Now enough of such talk. Grab a seat. Wine? This one's on the house, my friend. And maybe a good number more."

"No, no. Just hot tea, if you have it."

Brugan looked at him dumbstruck, as though

Lannick had sprouted a second head. "Tea it is," he said, and disappeared into the kitchen.

Lannick eased onto a stool at the bar, his usual spot. He assumed what he felt was an all too familiar pose, elbows on the bar, shoulders high, head hung low. He wondered just how many evenings he'd spent in this very spot, draining cup after cup of wine until his thoughts softened and his regrets washed away, at least until he awoke the next morning with his head pounding. Regardless, he couldn't help but allow his eyes to drift to the many bottles of wine and whiskey lined behind the bar, as well as the casks of ale near the tankards and cups. *Greetings, my old friends.* He thought for a instant about calling out to Brugan to forget the tea, but just then the barkeep emerged from the kitchen with a steaming mug.

"Careful," Brugan said. "It's hot." He stood there for a moment, quiet, and Lannick could feel the man's eyes upon him. "You've changed, if you don't mind me saying. And I don't just mean your new nose."

"I reckon I have," said Lannick. "Pain and heartbreak will do that to a man."

"I won't ask what happened to you. I'm sure you'll tell me when and if you want to, and I'm sure it was nothing pleasant. But whatever happened, I'd say it's chipped some new edges into you."

Lannick nodded and took a tentative sip. The tea was spiced with cinnamon and clove—an expensive blend from Khaldisia. It was just the sort of kind thing Brugan would do for him on occasion.

"Should I take anything from the fact that you're wearing a new sword?" Brugan asked.

"I lost my old one, and figured I'd have need for a blade fairly soon."

"Perhaps sooner than you think. That filthy pawnbroker Silas was sniffing around here for you, a couple of weeks back. Said you owed him a lot of money. I told him you owed me even more, and to let me know when he'd found you." He winked.

"I'm good for it, this time. But the sword's not for Silas." He scowled. "The sword's for the bastard who's tormented me for the last nine years."

"At last? By the dead gods, man, it's about time!"

Lannick closed his eyes and smelled the rich vapors from the tea. The odor bit pleasantly. "Unfortunately my nemesis is hundreds of leagues away, battling the Arranese."

"He'll return here at some point. If he survives the war, that is. Have you heard talk of the war?"

"Here and there. Sounds as though things aren't going as planned."

Brugan snorted. "That's a kind way to put it. A couple of southerners, mercenaries by the looks of them, were in here last night. They said the Arranese have yet to lose a battle, that they've crushed Rune's armies at every turn. At this rate they'll take Riverweave within the month, if not sooner."

Lannick frowned and sipped his tea. "General Fane's a slippery sort. He's likely hatched some plan to lull the enemy into thinking they've won, and thus lead them into a trap. He'd do that, you know. He'd let many men die as part of a deception. 'Necessary losses,' he'd call them."

"That's what the High King's council has to be telling

themselves. They'd have replaced any other commander by now and had the man hanged for such failure. But, then, Fane holds more sway with the council than ever."

"Dead gods, that's an awful thing." Lannick fixed his eyes to Brugan's. "Well perhaps I'll just disguise myself and enlist, and volunteer to go straight to the front. I can still use a sword better than most, and I'd get my chance before long. I'd get close to Fane at some point, and do what I should have done a long time ago."

Brugan stooped closer, and there was a fire in his eyes. He slapped a heavy hand on the bar. "You could do more than that, Lannick. There are rumors of a revolt among the soldiers, of seasoned fighters deserting instead of following Fane's orders. Fane's not a sane man, and soldiers are beginning to realize it. It's just the same as Pryam's Bay. You remember it, Lannick. You remember that look in his eyes, and the way the men turned."

"Oh, I remember that look. I've had the pleasure of gazing upon it rather recently, as a matter of fact. Right after his Scarlet Swords gave me this lovely new face."

Brugan slapped the bar again. "And I recall how that war was won. You were the hero, Lannick. You won the battle of Pryam's Bay and saved Rune from ruin. The 'Scourge of Tallorrath,' they called you. You did all of that, with the help of a few of your friends, of course," he said with a smile.

Lannick studied his mug of tea. "What are you suggesting, Brugan?"

"There are men willing to fight who won't fight for Fane. Thane Vandyl, Thane Meledin, and Brandiss Thane of Stormfall still stand aside. Meledin for one holds a debt to you from Pryam's Bay, and my guess is he'd honor it. The High King's council demanded two columns of soldiers be kept in reserve—they're not complete fools. If those thanes were to take up the cause—"

"I'm not that man anymore. I'm no proud hero the thanes would trust."

"No? Was it so very long ago? Are we such different men now?" He sank lower, bringing his face even with Lannick's. "Men *would* follow you, Lannick. Those deserters? The men running from Fane? They're massing, Lannick. They still serve Rune, but won't march for Fane. We could join them, rally them, and march with them. And when we do march, the thanes will take notice. Nobles value debts like no other, for they see debts as the currency of power. If Meledin heard you were marching against Fane, he'd get involved. The others would be bound to, after him."

Lannick waved a hand dismissively.

"There are still many soldiers who remember you, who respect you. Folk who *knew* you were no traitor, and knew you were only punished because of Fane's mad jealousy." He straightened. "You could win this war."

"That's not me anymore. I can't pretend to be who I once was. Not after all that's happened."

"You're a different man, Lannick, but that doesn't mean you need to be less of one. I've watched you sit here and crumble under the weight of your grief. I'd watched it happen for so long and with such inevitable certainty that I'd given up trying to save you. But I see that old spark in you again, Lannick. Something's changed. Take hold of it. Grab this chance before it escapes you forever."

Lannick nodded. "You're halfway right, Brugan. I'll admit I've spent years blaming myself for what happened to my family. Years poring over the consequences of every decision I'd made, examining all the ways I could have changed things by not doing this or by doing that instead." He shook his head. "I'd been thinking about it all wrong. And I'd been laying blame on the wrong man. I want my revenge, Brugan. But let's leave it at that."

Brugan fixed Lannick with a hard eye. "What better revenge could there be? What better way for you to destroy Fane than to take from him all his glory? All his power? To strip him of everything he holds dear, just as he did to you? Then, at last, when he cowers at your feet in shame, you take from him his life. By the dead gods, Lannick, it's time for the old ghosts of Pryam's Bay to return. It's time for us old, broken down heroes to finally set things right."

Lannick smiled but the expression was fleeting. "It's a pleasant thought, Brugan."

"It can happen. We can *make* it happen. You know you aren't the only man Fane wronged, Lannick. You had the worst of it, but he wronged every man who stood at your side. We were decommissioned after the war. All of us 'heroes' were cast aside, with no glory or reward or honor. Replaced by every mindless bastard willing to remain loyal to Fane." He pounded his fist on the bar. "Any member of your company who protested was thrown in the brig for a year or more, as a lesson. We were fighting men, Lannick, and Fane took from all of us the only living we knew. There are a good number of lads who'd love to push that man from his pedestal, and climb up there themselves. A lot of lads who won a war but were treated like dogs instead of soldiers."

Lannick took another sip of his tea. "I don't know, Brugan. That's a large task, but I'll think about it."

"Well then I'll await your orders, Captain," Brugan said. He clasped his big hand upon Lannick's shoulder. "Just don't let me down again."

The sun was sinking behind Ironmoor's western edge when Lannick left *The Wanton Vicar*. Long shadows stretched across the cobblestoned street. Lannick stopped and prodded his satchel, finding the outline of the box holding his Coda. Its presence provided some comfort, but not nearly enough.

Temple Street was nearly empty in spite of the evening's pleasant weather. There were a few ne'er-do-wells ambling between the nearby taverns, but the street was far quieter than Lannick had hoped. He reminded himself Rune was a nation at war, but couldn't resist tugging his cloak tightly about him as he walked.

He examined every face he passed, seeking signs of rotting or stitched flesh. His eyes strained as he peered at every shadow, looking for shapes emerging from the darkness. He thought of his torturous journey through the shadowpath, and wondered if he'd ever again feel at ease in the night.

He felt a sudden chill settle upon him and did his best to shrug it off. It came upon him again and he paused, thinking of the Necrists. He cursed, and then steeled his gaze and set his jaw, assuming every outward appearance of bravado in hopes it would grant his soul a similar strength. *Purpose is one thing, but courage is entirely another.* He redoubled his pace, walking with a firm, unwavering stride. He needed to find an inn, a place where no one would think to find him, and figured the best place was Ironmoor's bustling harbor.

He found a wide thoroughfare through Ironmoor's finer neighborhoods. The taverns gave way to fancier storefronts, and there came the calls of merchants urging prospective customers that the war in the south meant a limited supply of exotic goods. Many customers milled about, their hands poised near their purses.

Lannick walked easier, finding the presence of others a welcome relief. Even as emboldened as the Necrists had seemingly become, he reckoned they'd never confront him amidst so many others. He paused occasionally, inspecting the storefront displays of Khaldisian silks and spices, thick wools from near the Waters of World's End, and carved woods and ivory from Harkane. What value such things held at wartime was a mystery to him, but puffy-faced and perfumed customers desperately haggled for them nonetheless.

The crowd grew as he walked, but so did the shadows as the light retreated from the sky. Lannick pressed ahead with greater urgency, moving amidst the throngs of people and gripping the outline of the box holding his Coda.

Then he stopped. Ahead of him, perhaps thirty yards away and moving closer, was a tall figure draped in black robes. At this distance he couldn't discern any details of the person's face but he was in no position to take chances.

He located an alleyway weaving between two buildings and dashed toward it.

The alley was cast entirely in shadow, the narrow space between the large buildings nearly shutting out entirely the fading light of the evening sky. It seemed cold, also, and a stiff wind whipped through the divide. He could not see the far end of the alley, but the air smelled of livestock so Lannick reckoned he was approaching the Old Market. He pressed forward, hoping there would be more people there.

"*Lannick, my love,*" called a soft voice. Not just a whisper, but a icy breath in his ear.

He whirled about but there was no one. Only the dark shadows of the alleyway. He turned and ran at a full sprint, leaping over the crates and garbage littering the alley. At last he broke into the wide square of the Old Market. Hundreds of people milled about the tents and stalls, packing up their goods or striking the day's last bargain.

Lannick set off in the direction of the harbor. He glanced repeatedly over his shoulder, seeking the black-robed figure, but there came nothing of the sort. After a time he wondered whether the troubles of the last month were causing his head to play tricks.

Soon the road was descending to the sea and the air was scented with brine. He looked again behind him and saw nothing, and slowed his pace. He inhaled deeply though his crooked nose and then breathed out, feeling his shoulders sink. *My head is a mess.*

As he walked he opened his satchel and retrieved it. Not his Coda, but the flask of whiskey he'd taken from the safe house days before. He opened it and brought it to his lips, his hand suddenly shaking. He took a long draw and felt the familiar burn in his throat.

Just to help me sleep.

19
A SIMILAR MONSTER

ANDRACHUS BALE SURVEYED the forested valley before them and the black outline of mountains beyond. The Ghostwood was an old forest, untamed by men and rumored to be haunted by uneasy spirits and stalked by all manner of dangerous beast. It was known to be place full of peril and seemed as far from the cozy corridors of the Abbey as any place could ever be.

Bale wondered again if he'd ever make it home.

They stood on a rocky outcropping overlooking the valley, and from this vantage Bale could see smoke rising in gray pillars far to the east. There was also the echo of distant drums and the faint ring of weaponry, and Bale was certain he could feel the ground trembling beneath him.

War.

Thankfully, Keln had proven a skilled woodsman, catching the scent of war parties on the wind, and discovering the subtle signs of their passage in brush and soil. The Scarlet Swordsman had found trails that kept them at all times on the flank of the Arranese army, and at a great enough distance that Bale had only caught a glimpse of Arranese soldiers on one occasion. *And then I nearly soiled myself.*

What Keln possessed in forestry, though, he lacked in camaraderie. Bale was never one for talk and much preferred keeping to himself. This, though, was an angry silence, a quiet tension they shared. Keln regarded him with varying degrees of suspicion, disgust, and abject hatred. Bale could not recall being less comfortable in the presence of another, short of General Fane himself.

"South?" Keln growled.

"Yes, yes," answered Bale, speaking too quickly and tucking a strand of hair behind his ear with a nervous hand. "Well, south by southwest, actually. The spells I've cast revealed signs of the Lector's location, and although the Arranese have forced us to depart from it to some degree I believe we're still on the right course. I'm not entirely sure of the precise distance, but—"

Keln shouldered past Bale with a grunt, nearly knocking him over. "I needed no more than a yes or no, spooker," he said, pulling himself astride his massive black horse. "I have no desire to hear any more of your nonsense than is absolutely necessary."

Bale nodded and followed, and after several clumsy attempts he found himself atop his white stallion. The horse followed Keln without a word from Bale, making clear who was its master. They descended a switchback trail from the outcropping, into the deep forest.

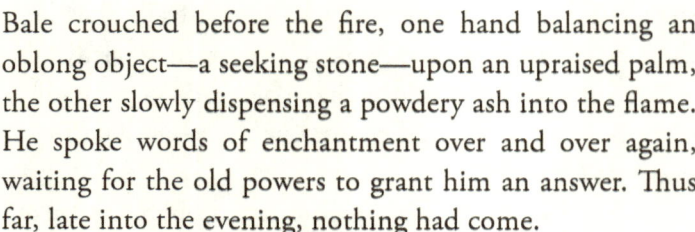

Bale crouched before the fire, one hand balancing an oblong object—a seeking stone—upon an upraised palm, the other slowly dispensing a powdery ash into the flame. He spoke words of enchantment over and over again, waiting for the old powers to grant him an answer. Thus far, late into the evening, nothing had come.

Keln sat opposite the smoldering fire, hunched forward and drinking from a wineskin. He took a swig and spat upon the fire, causing the small flame to hiss and diminish.

Bale cleared his throat, frustrated. "I cannot accomplish this without the fire," he said.

Keln grunted and spat again. The flame vanished.

Bale hurriedly huffed at those embers that yet glowed, and at last a flame kindled. He looked up at Keln, who wore a smug grimace. "I said I need the flame to make this work. This will only take longer if you insist upon wetting it."

"You spookers are such fools," Keln said, shifting about before settling against the mossy trunk of a fallen tree. "Lost in your little world, ignorant of the reality about you. Your entire lives spent with books and prayers. Ha. You are a useless bunch, capable of no more than frightening children and simpletons." He took another swig from his wineskin. "Look at you. So weak and afraid, so utterly lost outside the walls of your Abbey. You wouldn't have lasted a day in this wilderness without me."

Bale glared hard into the soldier's eyes before averting his own. He did not answer, and instead concentrated again upon the seeking stone. After a time he resumed casting the ancient Spell of Divination. Lector Erlorn had told him it was one of the Sanctum's most potent incantations, the first given to them by the Sentinel Castor. If one possessed a part of a thing, one could divine the thing's location anywhere in the world. The part would seek the whole.

He scattered a pinch of ashes onto the fire. They were the ashes of the Lector's hair, pulled from a comb he'd left at the Abbey, and hopefully enough of a bond to his person to make the spell succeed. As he did this he stared at the oblong stone in his other hand, waiting for it to shift to reveal a direction. He chanted quietly, speaking the words of power.

Keln spat again, jolting Bale from his task. "Tell me, spooker, do you have any idea where the Arranese war bands are raiding this night?" he asked. "No? Nor do I, which is why it's best not to signal them with a big, blazing invitation. I wouldn't at all mind seeing you gutted in your sleep, but I'll not have that happen to me. Keep the fire low, or keep no fire at all."

Bale did his best to ignore the Scarlet Swordsmen, clearing his mind of all but the stone. After a long while, the seeking stone shifted almost imperceptibly in his hand. Then it jerked and shifted again and came abruptly to rest, disclosing the direction. He clasped his hand about the stone, seizing its energy and willing his mind to seek the pole to which it was drawn. He stilled himself and shut his eyes, and soon his conscious mind rose above the eaves of the forest. His thoughts found a path beyond the wooded expanse and he envisioned a clearing far away, a place where his answers would be found. The flame flared suddenly.

"Dead gods," said Keln. "Have you no sense?" He kicked at the campfire, sending a shower of sparks and embers at Bale.

Bale yelped and jumped upward, frantically brushing the burning bits from his robes. A few holes grew in the rough cloth, smoking and glowing a deep orange. Bale patted them out and after a time was satisfied he wasn't about to burn to death.

He looked at his thin hands, noticing he'd dropped all but a pinch of the ashes. He'd be unable to cast the spell again with any measure of potency. He sank to a seat and hung his head, wondering if he'd be able to remember the incantation's disclosures, or whether he'd forget the precise direction and become lost in the wild.

Keln laughed gruffly and settled again against the trunk. He took a long drink from his wineskin, eyes glittering dangerously in the dark. "You needn't worry, spooker. You haven't much time left."

Bale regarded Keln, his brutish appearance and the many trappings of soldiery. *How I despise this man, and those of his like.* He so resented those who intimidated through physical presence, who threatened with raw violence, who had no conception of complexities they could not resolve with their fists.

He looked again at his frail hands, squeezing the last flakes of ash with only a mockery of strength. As he stared, his thoughts turned to memories of his youth, to images of his father's hands. They were a stark contrast to his own, thick and calloused from working the plow and corralling the pigs. He thought of those hands upon his throat when Bale's prolonged bout with red fever had left him too weak to help with the harvest. He recalled those hands pummeling his mother for teaching Bale to read when she could have been patching the leak in their thatched roof. He remembered those hands as they'd seized him by the shoulders when he'd inquired after spellcraft, and how they'd cast him from the home forever as an embarrassment to the blood.

Bale's eyes returned to Keln.

This man is a similar monster.

The forest was cut by a myriad of hunting trails, tight paths winding through the old, creaking trees. The trails held only briefly to a particular direction, and Bale found it difficult to maintain the fixture of his destination in his head. The heavy foliage made it hard to discern his heading by the sun, and after a time he was looking for the location of moss on trees and struggling to remember what he'd read about such a thing revealing direction. *Moss always grows on the southern side of trees. Or is it the northern?*

"You know where we're headed, spooker?" asked Keln, as though guessing Bale's thoughts.

Bale nodded assuredly, although he wondered how long it would take the Scarlet Swordsman to realize his deception. He'd gathered Keln wasn't as cunning as General Fane, but he reckoned the man was just as capable of bringing his life to a uniquely miserable end.

"The horses need rest," Keln said. "There's a clearing ahead. We'll stop there."

Bale looked ahead and saw nothing but the deep green of the forest. "I don't—" he began, but then saw a pillar of moss-covered stone through the trees.

Soon they were upon the clearing, and within it stood a ruined relic of an older time. Eight stone pillars rising in a circle, one for each of the Sentinels and another for the High King. In the center of the pillars was a well, crumbling at its edges and strangled by ivy.

Bale dismounted and rushed to behold the ancient shrine. He touched each of the pillars and then rounded the Godswell, awestruck. "This must be many centuries old," he whispered, "or built by someone who understood the folly of the High King."

Keln grumbled something as he set about tying the horses to the nearby trees.

Bale walked reverently about the rustic shrine. His mind wheeled and he tried to temper the pace of his thoughts, taking time to inspect the details of the structure. Seven pillars for the Sentinels: Castor the Wise, Valis the Watchful, Lyan the Just, Thaydorne the Strong, Sienne the Quick, Kressan the Kind, and Pastine the Nurturing. Then one more for the line of the High King.

He felt breathless. He'd read many books concerning the Sentinels, yes, but to see them venerated by a physical monument was something else entirely. It seemed a validation, a lingering proof of the Sentinels' prominence in the Old Faith. This place was a relic of an older, nobler time, for all known structures like it had been razed when the Sentinels were banished from Rune.

He stood before the pillar bearing a faded carving of Castor's old symbol, the eye within an eye. *Wisdom, the ability to behold unseen truths.* As he studied the symbol a feeling grew within him, an overwhelming sense the Lector had been at this very place before his death. For a moment he could *feel* Erlorn's presence and he stepped back, coming to rest upon the lip of the Godswell.

He was shaken from his reverie by a hand upon his shoulder. He turned to see Keln, a finger pressed to his lips. Keln nodded toward the ground, and Bale followed his gaze. There were spots of what seemed to be blood near the base of one of the pillars. Blood newly spilled. As he looked he saw other driblets nearby, a trail of them leading toward the brush at the far side of the clearing. Keln gestured for Bale to retreat toward the horses, and Bale complied without a word.

Keln moved slowly toward the brush, drawing his sword from its scabbard as he did. "I am not a patient man," he said, his tone threatening, "and I do not enjoy playing children's games. Come out of the brush at once, or my sword will be coming in."

There was a crackle of twigs snapping and leaves crunching. The brush rustled and shifted, suggesting the movement of a large form. After a moment, though, the brush grew still again.

"Show yourself!" Keln growled, sinking to a predatory stance so menacing Bale found himself more frightened of the Scarlet Swordsman than whatever it was lurking in the brush.

Just then two men, wretched and wounded, stumbled from the brush. Keln threw them to the ground where they collapsed into a heap. Their chainmail hauberks were ripped and stained, their armor plates battered and broken. They wore the red sashes of Rune, though judging from the agonized looks on their faces they no longer wanted any part of the kingdom's war.

"Stand up, soldiers," Keln said, his sword dipping but still at the ready.

"Mercy," groaned one of the soldiers, struggling to rise to a knee. The other remained prone, drawing rattling breaths. Bale recognized the men were badly hurt, and likely suffering from infection. He frantically pulled his travel pack off his shoulder, knowing they required the healing arts.

"Stand up, boys," Keln said, rolling the prone soldier over with the toe of his boot. The man had three dark wounds in his chest, each of them wet with blood.

"These men are badly hurt," Bale said, starting forward. He stopped just as quickly, though, when Keln regarded him with a vicious gaze.

"You will stay clear of this, spooker," he said, derisively spitting out the last word. "On your feet, soldiers! That's an order from an officer."

At last the soldier who'd gotten to his knee forced himself upward upon unsteady feet. His eyes were feverish, his lips split and bleeding. Bale noticed a wound in the man's side, the chainmail there shredded. The wound was bandaged, but the blood had soaked through.

Keln regarded the man sternly. "Do you always respond to orders so slowly, soldier?"

The soldier looked at the clasp fastened upon Keln's red cloak and snapped to attention. He hurriedly nudged the prone soldier with the toe of his boot. "Piter," he said. "Get up! This fellow's a captain!"

"Identify yourselves."

"S-Sir," the soldier stammered, "I am Corporal Stevran, of the First Division of the Third Column. Him there," he said, "is Private Piter, also of the First of the Third."

Keln lowered his sword near Piter's throat. "You're deserters?"

"Dead gods, no, Sir," Stevran said, his voice thick with emotion.

Keln's expression softened unexpectedly. "What is it, son? What brings you here, so far from the fighting?"

Stevran swooned and nearly fell, but Keln caught him by the arm. "We were routed," Stevran said. "Routed at Blackvale."

"The entire division?"

Stevran nodded. "What was left of us, but at least six hundred soldiers. General Fane himself arrived to lead us. Told us he wanted to take Blackvale, telling us it would cripple the enemy if we did. I'd scouted Blackvale days before, and knew it to be nothing more than an abandoned town with a few dozen starving cows. But by the dead gods he wanted it." He began weeping.

"Slow down, son," said Keln, his voice gentle. He directed Stevran to sit. "Don't worry. You're with friends now."

"Thank you, sir," Stevran said, sinking to a spot near the motionless Piter.

"Tell me what happened."

Stevran sniffled, his eyes fixed on his wound. "The general ordered half the division into Blackvale, while the rest of us held back." His eyes were distant and he was quiet for a moment. "The road into the place was narrow, with steep hills on either side. The Arranese knew we were coming, and they'd set an ambush with fire, oil, and archers. Our men were funneled right to the points of their swords. Half our division, slaughtered to the very man. And we just watched it happen."

"And then?"

Stevran pounded the earth with a fist and blinked away tears. "General Fane ordered us in after them, telling us there was strength in numbers. Telling us the dead gods favored us. Ha." He sobbed and rubbed snot away from his nose. "We didn't stand a chance. We fought atop the bodies of our countrymen, the ground slick with their blood." He swooned again and seemed about to faint.

Bale pressed forward. "He's suffering from a terrible infection. He's been gravely wounded. I should tend to these men or they will die."

Anger colored Keln's face and he gritted his teeth. "You will do nothing of the sort, spooker. Mind yourself."

Bale did as instructed but with great reluctance. *How I hate this man!* The soldiers would die if he didn't act. His hand moved to his robes, finding there the knife he'd stolen from the governor's palace in Riverweave. *Sometimes saving a life means taking another.* His mind raced with the possibility, wondering whether the neck or the back would be the better place to stick the thing, whether he would be able to move subtly enough to be thought of as harmless. *Do I possess the courage?*

Keln returned his gaze to Stevran and spoke again with a kind tone. "It's alright, son. Speak freely. We're just talking soldier to soldier."

"There…" Stevran began, but his voice failed him. He breathed deeply and began again. "There's talk, sir. Most of the soldiers are too scared to spread the word, but it's made it round. Soldiers are saying the general's gone mad, sir. There's whispers he's talking with devils, speaking to a black skull he keeps in his tent. I know a man who saw it himself."

Keln stood in silence, his expression unreadable.

"The men are afraid of him. They say he's possessed by a demon and soldiers are talking of revolt, sir. One of our captains questioned the general before we marched on Blackvale, but the general had him put him to the sword. Right before us. Then we marched, just as we were told." He shuddered. "There was so much blood… Piter and I barely escaped with our lives. We fled, hoping to find help." His legs were seized with a sudden spasm and his whole body shook. For an instant the life seemed to drain from his eyes.

"You had no other choice," Keln said, his tone paternal. His eyes, though, flared with cruelty.

Stevran choked back a sob. "Could you help us? There're other soldiers heading northeast, to the Silverflow River and regrouping. Soldiers who'll fight for Rune but not for the general. We could win this war, for the High King. But I fear the general has come undone…"

"You were right to tell me this, soldier," said Keln, placing a hand upon Stevran's head and wiping his thumb across his brow. "At ease, now," he said.

"Aye, sir," Stevran said, his face drooping with exhaustion.

Then Keln seized the soldier by his hair and plunged

the sword into his throat. Stevran gurgled and gasped, falling backward. The sword slowly glided free of his gullet, replaced by a font of blood.

"No!" Bale shrieked, leaping to the soldier's side. But it was futile. The boy was beyond any help, his heart sputtering its final beats.

Keln shifted and stuck Piter with the sword. The body did not move, and Bale figured the lad had already passed.

"Why?" said Bale. "They were *soldiers*, just like you!"

"Treason can never be tolerated, in any of its forms, and desertion in wartime is a crime of the worst sort. Orders are to be followed. To the very letter."

"But your general was marching them to their death."

Keln laughed. "Aren't we all marching there?" He stooped and wiped his blade on Stevran's body. "Rise, spooker. Let's find your Lector so I can be done with you."

They found the site by late afternoon. It was a wide clearing in the forest, far from the nearest trail. There was a fallen tree stretched across the tall grass, and beside it a mound of ash. The remnants of a funeral pyre.

Keln took a swig from his wineskin and took a look about. "How is it you know this is the place?"

"I don't," Bale whispered, moving slowly about the pyre. "Not yet, at least, but I should know soon enough. Stand clear. Please."

Bale felt a tingling sensation settle upon him, a disbelieving giddiness. He'd not dared hope he would succeed in finding the Lector's resting place. But now, he believed he had.

He stooped and began seizing handfuls of ash from the

pyre. With each sampling he shut his eyes and mouthed sacred words of divination. *The body must be here.*

He sensed something. A faint echo, a ghostly call. Then, finally, as he seized another handful of the ash it was there. A presence. An answer. He *knew* Lector Erlorn was one of the bodies burned at this place. He placed the handful of ash upon the ground, apart from the pyre, and said a prayer of passage. *Farewell, my friend.*

He then set about gathering kindling, a few armfuls of dry twigs and crumbling leaves. He brought it to the edge of the pyre and stacked it carefully, enough for a reasonable fire. He knelt before it and withdrew from his pack his sleeve of reagents and compounds. Therein he found a vial of powder and sprinkled it over the kindling. Soon it was ablaze, not with natural flame but with a pure, white fire that burned with minimal heat.

"Another fire, spooker?" demanded Keln. "Must we have this discussion again? The enemy stalks this same forest."

"The fire, like faith, illuminates all things," Bale said, remembering when Erlorn had spoken to him those same words.

"It had best be out by nightfall, and this had best be the last of it. Tomorrow we're returning to General Fane, whether you have your answers or not."

Bale pressed his hands toward the fire, pretending not to hear.

Keln grunted and assumed a seat upon the fallen tree, and after a moment began sharpening his sword with a stone. It produced a squealing, scraping sound, but after a time Bale was able to insulate his thoughts.

Bale withdrew a small brazier and a pair of tongs from his sleeve of pouches. He then found another vial in the sleeve, this one filled with a viscous, milky liquid. He emptied several drops into the brazier and then mixed in a few pinches of ash from the pile he'd set nearby. He positioned the brazier over the flame and sank into the ritual of spellcraft, chanting quiet words of power known only to the Sanctum's most skilled casters.

The concoction hissed and popped and spat, and, above all, smoked. It was a thick smoke which poured from the lip of the brazier, but it did not rise. Rather, it gathered about Bale before settling into a haze near the ground around him. He sniffed, noting a pungent odor not unlike soured wine.

In time the mixture in the brazier transformed, congealing from a pasty liquid into something solid. It appeared decidedly fleshy, like a swatch of skin separated from a body. Bale drew a sharp breath. *The spell succeeded.*

He pulled the brazier from the fire and dropped the substance into his hand. He squeezed it and quickened his thoughts, knowing he had but a precious few moments before the substance disintegrated. His bond to the Lector's body was fleeting, and there was little chance he'd be able to cast the spell again.

He stilled himself, finding an inner reserve of calm with which to surround his thoughts. There, he formed an image of the Lector, of Erlorn, as he looked the last time they'd met. He rubbed at the spongy substance in his hand, and soon felt the connection form.

Much as it did with the Spell of Divination, this Spell of Recounting took Bale's conscious mind from the immediacy of his surroundings to somewhere else. But unlike divination, this enchantment took him not to a place, but to a time. A time when the substance in his hand was, indeed, flesh, to a time when its bearer still lived.

His mind focused and his thoughts distilled, and just then he was there, within the Lector, within another time not long ago. He could sense not thoughts, but the flesh contained a memory of physical action. Bale searched first for the sensations at the moment of death. He waited for his own mouth to move, to mimic the Lector's own. But there was nothing. *Was a confession spoken?* The flesh yielded the answer: the Lector's mouth had not formed words upon death.

Bale was stunned. *A Lector without a confession?* He felt doubt creep inside him, but knew he needed to press onward. The fleshy piece was withering and he knew he had but a brief time remaining with this link.

Of the killer there was nothing. It was as though the Lector's life had been taken in a blind instant, a moment of absolute vulnerability and without struggle. Bale shook his head again, frustrated.

He broadened his inquiry, willing the flesh to yield answers from further back in time. The substance withered further, wasting away as more was demanded of it, but soon there came the swaying sensations of riding, the performance of the routine activities of travel. Prayer, too. Sleep. And then more travel, shifting here to there on horseback. Nausea.

There must be more! Bale set his resolve and pressed

ahead, feeling the substance begin to sweat, liquefying and weakening the bond. Time was not in his favor.

He pushed deeper with his mind, seeking other actions, movements betraying both thought and purpose. Not the routines of travel nor the mundane activities of life, but something more. He paused as he discovered something, and for a moment his mouth moved as the Lector's had. Yet, he sensed these were terse commands rather than revelations of purpose. He gesticulated involuntarily, miming the Lector's motions, but these were random gestures.

He pressed onward again and then sensed a moment. He slowed his thoughts, ignoring the increasingly mushy texture of the physical link he held in his hand and sharpening his attention to this particular time. *This is the moment.*

He shifted the substance from his right hand to his left, carefully transferring the liquid remnants as well as the slight, solid remains. He pressed his right hand forward, closer to the cool flame, and waited.

His hand twitched. At first it moved slightly, but then it jerked with more pronounced force. It snarled into an almost painful contortion and began moving. The motions were halting at first, but soon his hand assumed a rhythm. *The motions of writing.*

Bale attuned all his thoughts to his hand as it moved to form unseen symbols. He bent all his concentration upon the delicate gestures, at first unable to decipher meaning. Not only were the symbols being traced in the hand of another, but in an unusual language as well. A drip of fluid bled through the fingers of his left hand. *Quickly, now!*

After a time, he adapted to Erlorn's idiosyncrasies and his mind sifted through the languages he'd studied. He beheld the gestures of his hand as though watching a quill pressed to parchment. He yielded to the motions and could see the words etched upon the air. He had missed much, but the hand was moving still. *Some answers yet remain.*

"*And, thus, Lyan, I summon you. I implore you to honor once more your most sacred vow. I will come to the Sacred Place at Cirak, and together we must return to Rune before the Necrists pull His power from the Godswell. I have sent summonses to the others. The very fate of the world is in jeopardy, and only we can save it.*"

And then the feeling vanished as quickly as it had come. His hand still trembled, but it was no longer from the echo of the Lector's spirit. Bale breathed deeply and sat in thought. *'His?' Yrghul's?*

He drew a shuddering breath and sat for a long moment. *Terrible things are afoot, and my task grows ever more difficult.*

Bale opened his eyes and in time oriented himself to his surroundings. Night had fallen and the camp was illuminated by a half-moon overhead. An owl hooted nearby, and there was the drone of frogs calling to their mates. Bale rubbed his eyes and set about collecting his tools, clumsily at first, but soon feeling returned to his limbs.

He rubbed his aching knees and studied the camp.

Before him the fire had dwindled to a low glow. Beyond, Keln leaned against the fallen tree, his sword across his lap, and by all indications he was deeply asleep.

Bale thought of General Fane's orders, of his insistence that Bale return directly to him and report his findings. He knew Keln would not grant him additional latitude to search for more answers, or to spend any more time at the site than the soldier deemed absolutely necessary. Bale would be yanked away by his collar at dawn and marched to the front before Fane. And when his answers did not satisfy the general, he would be slain.

This cannot happen. Bale rolled his sleeve of reagents, stuffed it in his pack, and rose. He paused, then found the handle of his knife and took a step toward Keln. The soldier slept soundly, his chest rising and falling with deep, regular breaths. His hands had fallen to his sides, away from his sword, and his head was tilted back against the fallen tree, his throat exposed.

As he caressed the weapon's handle Bale thought of riding off with the horses and abandoning Keln at the camp. But he was no horseman and the beasts would never yield to his command. He thought also of fleeing on foot, but knew the Scarlet Swordsman would hunt him and would never relent. The man was a skilled tracker and quite at ease in the wild, whereas Bale was helpless in this rugged land.

The taking of life was against every precept held dear by the Sanctum. They were practitioners of faith, seekers of wisdom, and healers of men. They were not murderers. But, then, how could an action be condemned if no other choice remained? Staying here would mean losing the scant answers he'd secured from the Lector. It would mean delivering his precious information to a man who consorted with Necrists, the Sanctum's most ancient enemy.

Bale thought of the soldiers they'd encountered earlier. He thought of their grief, of their pain in recounting the battle, and of Fane's grim commands. *He means to lose this war, and to sacrifice everything to our enemies. The Lector knew this.*

Bale set his mind to the task and did his best to dispel any trepidation. *I have no choice.* He withdrew the knife, shouldered his pack, and crept toward Keln. He walked as quietly as he could manage, pressing his feet softly upon the grass. Keln did not stir.

He walked alongside the fallen tree, deciding it would be best to be on the opposite side of the trunk in the event something went awry. Keln would have no trouble clearing the old tree, but it would keep Bale out of reach of the soldier's arms and weapon for at least a few dear moments. He moved carefully to the spot just behind Keln, such that the top of the soldier's head was within easy reach. Bale studied him for an instant, noting the man's eyes were shut and his mouth agape. Below his chin was his defenseless throat.

He felt a flutter in his chest and a tremble in his hands, but at the same time felt moved by a greater purpose. He looked at the knife, wondering for the first time whether it was sharp enough to penetrate skin. It was a kitchen knife, and a well-used one at that, but its point seemed deadly enough. He pressed it against his palm and decided that when compelled by enough force the blade would suffice. He leaned forward over the trunk and held the knife with both hands above Keln's throat.

He breathed deeply again, trying to calm his nerves, but soon realized it was of no use. *I am too weak an instrument!* He took a step back. Doubt flooded his head. *How long will it take for Keln to die? Will he still have the strength to hack at me with his sword?* Bale felt as though his knees would buckle, and a whimper escaped his lips.

Then he thought again of General Fane. Of his cruelty, of his mad ambition. *I cannot allow Rune to fall to this man.* He knew he needed to do this quickly or not at all. He knew also he was not a courageous man, but hoped he could act like one for just an instant.

He swallowed hard and lurched forward, plunging the knife downward, his eyes squeezed shut. The knife jolted suddenly, as though it'd struck against something solid, and then his hands were awash with warm liquid. There was a twist and the knife jerked free of his hands.

He opened his eyes to see Keln flailing dumbly about, slapping at the blade protruding from his collar as though it were a bothersome insect. He groaned and with it came a wet, wheezing gurgle. Bale looked on in horror as Keln grabbed the blade's handle and appeared ready to pull it loose. He struggled upward and stood, wobbling and stumbling as he did. Blood was everywhere.

Dead gods! Bale squealed and turned and ran, nearly stumbling as fear drove his feet. He dashed headlong into the forest and did not dare look back. *Sweet Illienne please spare your loyal servant!*

20
BAD BUSINESS

ENCRESS FALLCROW KICKED her black
stallion in the flanks, and at last the beast
clambered up the rocky slope to the hill's crest.
The horse was a magnificent animal, a generous gift from
Old Crook, but it'd grown awfully skittish once they'd
gotten a sniff of the fighting. "Don't worry, boy," she said,
scratching the horse's neck. "None of us is fearless. Some
are just better at pretending."

The heavy forests of southern Rune had given way to
hills and wide, winding fields between them. She figured
the landscape below would otherwise be a quaint scene of
tiny hamlets and herds of sheep and well-tended crops,
but for the fact it was presently overrun by thousands
upon thousands of men, most of them dead, the rest of
them in the last throes of desperate combat. Farmhouses
smoldered, fields were left trampled, and all sorts of folk
lay about with their guts spilled.

The lads' loyalties were easily discerned, as the

soldiers of Rune were outfitted smartly in silver mail and red sashes and the Arranese looked like charming rustics in hides and leathers. Fencress thought the entire notion of uniforms an odd one, reckoning it would be far more difficult to knife a man if your clothes told him you intended to do it.

There is so little room for subtlety in war. How very typical of men.

"Madness!" said Drenj, beside her.

Fencress tugged her cowl overhead. "It's a damned shame what men will do for love of country, eh, Khaldisian?" She smirked. "Money, of course, is a different matter, entirely. But even the very best of these fools may kill five or even ten men, and not see a fraction of the coin we do for killing just one. Now that's just bad business."

"Rune is losing this fight," Paddyn said from ahead of them, his eyes darting about as though trying to count the soldiers left standing. "The Arranese will reach Riverweave within a week, at this rate. What will we do if they win?"

"Does it matter? My guess is whoever wins this war will find value in our... *talents*. There isn't a corner in the world where killing can't be turned to coin. There will always be work for the likes of us, my friends."

Merek maneuvered his horse ahead of them, his green cloak snapping in the wind. His expression was grave, almost scolding in its severity. "It most certainly matters who prevails. There are such things as good and evil in this world."

Fencress suppressed a chuckle. She knew she needed

Merek's help with Karnag, but found the man's self-righteousness to be something of an annoyance. "Truly? Is that what your order teaches? I'm guessing your position is that we, seeing as we are *we* and not *they*, are the good ones? And they," she said, gesturing toward the Arranese army, "are evil precisely because they are *they*."

Merek ran a hand through his greasy hair. "You're right about who is on which side of things, but haven't the faintest notion of the reason why."

"Listen, friend," Fencress said. "When you've done as much dark work as we have, you learn just what an awful lot we all are. Every one of us. I could give two shits about who sits on what throne and what flag rises from Rune's towers. Whoever it is I have to kneel to is always going to be some vicious swindler who climbed into that throne on the backs of the poor, the broken and the dead. Folks like us are wise to stay out of the way."

Merek glared at her, his brow knotted. "I assure you, Fencress, if you ride with me long enough you will learn to think otherwise. There are forces out there," he said, indicating the battlefield below, "powerful forces at work. They have remained hidden for centuries, waging a secret struggle, but now they are ready to move openly. It has not happened yet, but it will happen soon. You'll be reminded why it is you keep that symbol strung around your neck. You'll learn why our forebears built monuments to the goddess Illienne and to the Sentinels, and why those who remain true to the Old Faith are still reluctant to speak the name of Yrghul, the Lord of Nightmares, and still pray he never returns."

Fencress spat and returned her attention to the

battlefield. The Arranese were very clearly prevailing, and judging from the soldiers both standing and dead it seemed they'd entered the battle with far superior numbers. They were skilled horsemen and wielded their long bows and curved blades with ease as they rode. Rune's forces, by contrast, seemed slow-footed and tight, their meticulously organized formations a clumsy hindrance. The Arranese harassed their flanks, carving away at the red-sashed soldiers standing along the edges and smoothly working to separate them into smaller and smaller groups.

"Those soldiers won't last long," said Paddyn, standing in his stirrups. "The field is lost. Why don't they sound the retreat?"

Fencress's horse stamped nervously and she patted its neck. "I don't know much of military tactics, but it would seem a bad gamble to pick a fight with an enemy who outnumbers you three to one."

"Where are the reinforcements?" Paddyn asked. "How could this happen? Rune's armies are the finest in all the world. More soldiers, better training, better weapons. Arranan was always said to be a nation of savage horse thieves."

Merek dismounted his horse and studied the battlefield. His voice was quiet. "This doesn't look like a battle Rune's commanders intended to win. But why? Why sacrifice so many men? A ruse, perhaps?" He clenched his hands into fists and cursed. "I fear for Riverweave."

Fencress sneered. "Just as I said. Evil bastards on both sides of this thing."

Merek shot her a black look but said nothing.

"Now tell me," said Drenj, "how it is you think we'll find Karnag amidst all this chaos?"

Merek returned to his horse and climbed into the saddle, his face sagging. "He will seek violence. It is his nature. If we shadow the Arranese armies long enough, we will find your friend."

"And when we find him?" asked Paddyn, his tone fearful.

Fencress turned to Merek and smiled. "We pray, right?"

They decided to keep at least half a league between them and the Arranese, figuring the space would offer a measure of safety. They held to higher, harder ground, navigating the steep hills lining the plain below. The ground rose and fell with sheer crests and sharp ravines and the horses struggled for footing. Nevertheless, they kept pace with the Arranese army, and were able to behold the massive gathering of soldiers and supply wagons whenever their path brought them across the faces of the hills.

Fencress kept to the rear of the group, figuring it best to keep an eye on Merek. She wasn't the sort to trust another quickly—her time spent playing deadman's dice had taught her lies could be concealed behind the most earnest expressions. Although she suspected Merek intended to help rescue Karnag from whatever plagued him, she knew the man had an agenda of his own. He hadn't disclosed his secrets yet, and didn't seem inclined to do so.

Fencress reached into one of the pouches stitched in the lining of her black cloak and withdrew Merek's bracelet, his *Coda* as he'd called it. It was an odd thing, strangely heavy for its size and crafted from a dull metal which seemed to reflect no light. It was etched with countless angular symbols, some ancient language with which Fencress was entirely unfamiliar. Merek had asked for the thing on several occasions, but Fencress sensed that as long as she kept it from the man she held an advantage.

Her horse stumbled on a patch of gravel and Fencress looked upward, finding Merek's gaze upon her. The fellow's eyes followed the Coda as Fencress tucked it inside her cloak. "You want that thing, eh?" Fencress asked.

Merek slowed his horse and waited for Fencress to pull even with him. "I can be of far more use to you with it."

Fencress studied the man. He was a nasty looking sort, his face full of stubble and his eyes set too deep in his square head. He appeared much the same as the strong-armed brutes who frequented *The Dead Messenger* but for the look in his eyes. There was an intelligence there, a power. *There is a great deal he hasn't told me.*

She tugged her cowl overhead, shading her eyes from the sun. "Time for some answers, friend."

Merek rubbed at his flat nose. Fencress suspected he was recalling the beating he'd taken from Old Crook's lads before they'd first traded questions. "I will tell you what I can," he said in an even tone.

Fencress rested her hand on the pommel of one of her twin swords. *Folk speak more frankly when there's the implication of violence.* "We'll start with simple introductions, Merek. You've told me your name, you've mentioned your 'order.' Now you will tell me details. The important ones, that is."

Merek stared skyward for a few moments. "You know of the Sentinels?"

Fencress regarded him skeptically. She held many doubts about the Old Faith, but what she'd seen in Karnag compelled her to at least play along. "I've heard the stories. Lullabies cooed to babies. The occasional drunken bard singing in a tavern. I've even stumbled upon an old shrine or two. Relics of a time long gone."

"No," Merek said flatly. "Not relics. These forces persist, and they are eternal." He pulled back his sleeve to reveal a mark near the crease of his elbow, a watchtower. "My order is the Variden, which means 'Vigilant' in the old tongue. We are the disciples of the Sentinel Valis, and we serve as watchful guardians of Rune. We honor the oath Valis took when the goddess Illienne descended to oblivion. We serve to protect Rune."

Fencress cocked a brow, suspicious. "Protect from what, exactly? The likes of me?"

"Hardly. We guard against the dark forces, the disciples of the Lord of Nightmares. He is sealed in oblivion, yes, but his followers still do his bidding."

"Ah," Fencress said, trying to conceal her sarcasm. "The secret war you've mentioned. But don't the old tales say the Sentinels were banished?"

Merek nodded. "They were. Some of the Sentinels abide the banishment, but others do not. Those who don't decided the oath they'd sworn to Illienne was more binding than a decree from the High King."

"So what of your Sentinel? Did Valis obey the High King?"

"In a manner of speaking, yes. He gifted his powers to his disciples, and he faded from this realm. That object you keep from me, my Coda, contains a fraction of those powers. Which is why you must return it."

Fencress caught Merek's gaze. "I will not be handing over your magic bauble anytime soon. You must forgive me, friend, but I can't yet trust you enough to surrender any of my advantages."

"I will require it if I am to be of any help to your friend."

"We've not found Karnag yet."

"Perhaps I can use it to help find him, then. And after, it will keep our purpose hidden from him."

Fencress waggled a finger. "When we find him, perhaps I'll let you have your trinket." She leaned back in her saddle as her horse navigated a downward slope. "Now, speaking of Karnag, what has happened to him and why do you think you can help him?"

"The man you killed, the Lector, was a Sentinel as well. The Sentinel Castor."

Fencress nearly laughed aloud but suppressed it. "A Sentinel? One of Rune's seven legendary heroes? The man bled and died just as any other. Ridiculous."

Merek shook his head. "A great part of me hopes my suspicions are unfounded, but the teachings of my order instruct that Castor's spirit is capable of moving to another body upon the death of his own. He is immortal in that way. What I have seen of your friend implies that those ancient powers reside now in him. We must consider the possibility that he has assumed the spirit of a Sentinel."

Fencress would have branded this chap a lunatic had she not seen what Karnag did in Hargrave. She tugged at her cowl. "Then why isn't Karnag all wise and just and merciful? All of those godly things we're told to believe? That bastard is a killer, and the very worst of them all."

"I don't know. My order suggests a Sentinel's spirit is as water, able to assume the shape of the vessel into which it is poured. One of my order's charges has been to monitor the passage of those eternal souls. A thing such as this has never before occurred, and it seems a great balance has been disrupted. I fear all of Rune is in danger."

Fencress didn't know whether to laugh or shudder with fear. At last she settled upon a long, heavy sigh. "Dark work brings dark rewards, they say."

The Arranese marched north without pause for the remainder of the day, through the night and then well into the day after. At last, as evening fell the great army slowed their march to a halt and made camp. Fencress suggested the company do the same after finding a narrow creek winding through the rocky ground. They set about watering the horses and scrubbed themselves free of the dust and barbs they'd collected on their ride.

She found a spot beside the creek and stretched out to stare at the purple sky, letting the cool water wash over her feet. She couldn't recall the last time she'd had a decent bath. She was no stranger to rough going, but if truth be told she sometimes fancied the comforts of a plush inn. "Paddyn," she called, "do we have any wine?"

"No wine, but we still have a good deal of Old Crook's cider."

Fencress smiled. "Do a friend a favor and bring me one of the skins."

Paddyn did as requested, and soon Fencress had swallowed more than a few mouthfuls of the fruity stuff. She splashed her feet in the creek and tried to remember the names for the constellations of stars in the sky. There was the Dragon's Wing, the Three Witches, the Spitted Sow, and in the sky's center rested the Eldest Eye. She recalled stories of them all, mostly from the tawdry dramas in which she'd performed as a younger woman. She recalled an entertaining moment when, just after a performance, she'd caught the troupe's leader servicing the well-fed lass who'd played the role of the Spitted Sow, and how the man had so much trouble pulling his jingles out of the woman's costume. *Or his "spit," as I called his jingles for months afterward.* She laughed aloud.

Just then there was a clamor behind her, a cascade of dirt and rocks. She started upward and whirled about to see Merek scrambling down a hillside toward the creek.

"Dead gods," Fencress grumbled. "Can't a girl enjoy a bath without you barging in? You have no sense of etiquette, friend."

"There's something amiss among the Arranese," Merek said, scanning the area about them. "There," he gestured. "That hill should grant us a better view. Follow me."

Fencress cursed, tugged on her boots and grabbed her swords. "Saddle the horses," she said as Paddyn looked at her with a cocked brow.

Fencress followed Merek through a dark ravine and

then up a steep slope. It was a difficult climb, but in time they managed the top. There, they were granted a panoramic view of the Arranese camp and the scrubby grasslands about them.

The distant camp looked much like a reflection the starlit sky above, with innumerable, flickering fires adorning the dark landscape. Fencress squinted to sharpen her eyes, and after a moment was able to discern among the fires the faint angles of tents and ghost-like shapes of soldiers.

"Do you see it?" Merek whispered.

Fencress was about to confess she did not but then caught her tongue. On the periphery of the camp there was commotion. Her eyes struggled for details as the scene shifted in that maddening way of the deepest shadows of night where movements seem imaginary. But there *was* something.

"They're forming a hunting party," Merek said, leveling a finger toward the army's edge. "Two riders just arrived at the camp, and now they're gathering greater numbers. Look at the torches alighting. The Arranese have decided to hunt something in the dark."

Fencress could see it, although the scene didn't remain in focus for long. *Perhaps a bit too much cider.* The lights were multiplying, and she imagined soldiers setting torches ablaze and making ready to move. "Let's hope they haven't decided to hunt us."

Merek snorted, whether from amusement or derision Fencress could not be certain. "You see they're moving into a formation. A crescent shape, with the outer ends at the lead. That is their way."

"Looks to be about twenty men, by my count."

"Twenty-one," said Merek firmly. "The Arranese always group into units of seven."

Fencress rolled her eyes and figured she would have repeated back the words in a snarky tone had she swilled any more of the cider. The fellow was useful, yes, but lacked any measure of charm. "You just said a group of two riders returned to the camp."

"Which means five men from that group did not return. The party is heading southwest," Merek said. "And quickly."

"Perhaps hunting down stragglers or deserters?"

"That would seem a strange quarry to pursue at night. I can't imagine an army that size would concern itself with a few desperate and very likely wounded soldiers wandering nearby."

"It could be any number of things."

"It could be your friend."

Fencress stood. "Well we should ride, then."

Merek waved a hand dismissively. "We'll never catch them, not while riding at night on this terrain. We should wait until morning, then track where they went."

"On your feet," Fencress said. "We're following them."

The ride proved more difficult than Fencress had anticipated, and her horse staggered repeatedly on the patches of loose stones. After being pitched from the beast she wondered if it'd be best to abandon caution and ride down from the hills and onto the wide plain below. She thought of the odds, and reckoned it was a necessary gamble. "We'll head down," she called to her companions.

"That will be an easier ride," said Paddyn, adjusting the quiver of arrows slung across his back, "but we'll be awfully close to the Arranese."

Fencress shook her head. "An army that size won't care about a few riders wandering near their flank. They'll think we're farmers or shepherds or something." She looked at Merek. "Won't they?"

Merek pulled his green cloak about him and said nothing.

"We'll head down," Fencress said firmly.

The broad face of the hill was a steep slope, replete with crags and gullies and slicks of mud. It was a place better suited for goats than horses, and at many points the horses stopped dead, not daring take another dangerous step downward. When soothing words failed, the company dismounted and tugged the beasts by their reins. At last the horses complied, and they chose a slow, crisscrossing route across the breadth of the hill.

In time the slope eased and flattened, and they descended into the gentle rolls of the fields. It was an eerie landscape, with a low fog blanketing the earth and set with the pale hue of moonlight. It looked as much like the open sea as dry land. There were also the distant sounds of the Arranese army: the shrill rings of steel being sharpened, the low din of discussion, and the echoes of strange songs sung about their fires.

There came then a murmur of voices nearby, and after scanning the fields about them Fencress caught sight of an Arranese patrol atop a rise no more than fifty yards away. She gestured to the others and they stopped and held motionless. After a long, tense moment the patrol dipped behind the far side of the rise. Fencress patted her horse and congratulated herself on her sense of fashion, her steadfast resolve to dress ever in black. *Hard to see at night, and always welcome at funerals.*

They resumed their ride, kicking their horses to a brisk trot. They'd lost sight of the hunting party, but Merek was certain of the direction they'd headed. He suggested they make their way due south in order to have at least some thin chance of finding them. It seemed a fool's errand, Fencress thought, but then so did this entire endeavor.

As they rode Fencress wondered how long she'd last in this task, how long it would be before she abandoned Karnag. There was war all about them, and the kingdom she'd called her home seemed on the brink of disaster. She held a small fortune in her pocket, yet had chosen a path that left her no chance to enjoy it. She was in the middle of nowhere, hoping to find a friend who seemed to have turned into as wicked a demon as any poet had ever described. And when she found him? Merek seemed to know something of these "old powers," as he called them, but there were no sure bets, no guarantees they could help him. *If this were deadman's dice, this wouldn't be a smart play.*

But she thought too of her bond with Karnag. It was never a romantic thing—nothing with men was after what she'd endured as a slave in her youth. No, it was no romance, but it was just as deep. In their work, she and Karnag trusted each other with their lives when death was the most imminent of possibilities, when all the coins were in the table's center. Their bond had endured the darkest of deeds, had withstood the most depraved acts imaginable. And through it all, Karnag never questioned her, never doubted her capability because of her gender. And because Karnag respected her, others had been made to, as well. Because of him, she'd earned as much sway with the criminals of Raven's Roost as any man.

The odds matter not at all when the prize is the life of my friend.

They pressed on for some time, passing through empty field after empty field and encountering no more than the occasional fallen soldier or burned-out farmhouse. Gradually the stars shifted overhead and the moon sank low against the horizon.

"It will be morning soon," said Drenj. "There's a chance I could track the hunting party with some light, but we're sure to be seen by the Arranese."

Fencress's shoulders sagged. "No. We shouldn't risk being seen or hunted down. We'll head back to the high ground and out of sight." She pulled her horse to a stop and turned it about.

Just then a faint cry caught her ear.

Fencress threw back her cowl and pressed a finger to her lips. The company halted. The field about them was featureless but for a low wall of rocks. The ground was obscured by mist and shadow. Fencress could see nothing.

She listened, and in time heard a quiet sob. She urged her stallion toward the knee-high wall and rode beside it, her companions behind her. She squinted, struggling to discern details in the dark. Soon she saw what seemed to be a shape huddled near the wall.

Another agonized cry sounded, frail and pathetic. Fencress had slain enough men to know the sound of the dying, and this was it. Odds were it was a soldier bleeding from battle, shuddering as he pulled his last breaths. *But perhaps the fellow's seen something…*

"Who's there?" Fencress said quietly, urging her horse another few strides forward.

"Please… No…" came an accented voice.

An Arranese warrior. Fencress slipped from her horse and crept ahead, eyes straining for details in the darkness. The man likely posed no threat, but she dropped her hands to the hilts of her twin blades, just in case.

"No… Don't kill me…" the voice said again.

"Easy, friend," Fencress said as she neared the figure slumped against the low wall. "We have no stake in this fight."

The soldier shifted slightly and his face caught some of the dim light of the moon. His sharp, angular features were covered in black blood and his eyes were wide with fear. He looked not at Fencress with his almond-shaped eyes, but straight upward. His mouth trembled and his breathing was quick and shallow.

Fencress stepped forward, close enough to where the soldier was sure to see her. "Friend?"

"Don't kill me… Please…"

"We're usually an awful lot, but we're not going to kill you." She took her hands slowly from her blades. "You have my word, for whatever that's worth." She held out her hands just as she would after winning a round of deadman's dice, turning them over and then upward to show she didn't have something hidden in her sleeves.

The man's eyes didn't move. They remained frozen,

staring blankly at the sky. It was at that point Fencress noticed the fellow was missing both of his arms.

"Dead gods, man," Fencress said. "That's tough luck. That must have been some rough bastard you crossed. Can I give you a hand?" She paused and frowned. "Sorry. Terrible choice of words."

"Please... No..." the soldier said again.

Fencress stood over the man, hands at her hips. Still the fellow's eyes remained fixed on the stars, unblinking and twitching slightly. "Friend?" she asked again.

The Arranese warrior sucked rapid breaths and did not respond.

Fencress frowned and turned to her companions. "This lad's lost to us, and to the world for that matter. We'll leave him be."

"Gravemaker!" the soldier said loudly, his tone frightened and desperate.

Fencress froze. *Gravemaker.* The name of Karnag's sword.

"The Gravemaker killed us all."

"Where?" Fencress demanded, bending low to the soldier. "Where did this happen? How low ago?" She grabbed the soldier's vest. "You must tell me!"

The soldier said nothing, pulling his eyes from Fencress's gaze as though it were painful. Tears pooled in his eyes and his breath became a gurgling wheeze.

Fencress gently let him loose and stood upright. "Lost to us."

There came then a sound. A low, rhythmic sound carried upon the wind.

Fencress listened, searching the fields for the source. She saw nothing, but shivered as she recognized the sound.

Laughter. Karnag's laughter.

A hand pressed against her shoulder and she spun about. Merek stood before her, his expression grim.

"My Coda," he whispered. "You must return it to me now."

Another cry pierced the night. It seemed another of the Arranese had just met his doom and Fencress knew Karnag lurked in the darkness nearby.

"My Coda," Merek urged again. "You have no idea what we're dealing with, Fencress. You have no inkling of the gravity of our peril. It is possible he will slaughter us just as he has the Arranese, for he knows only death."

Drenj moved beside them. "He speaks truth, Fencress. You remember Hargrave. You remember the look in his eyes. If Merek can help us, we must give him the means."

Fencress thought of that image, of Karnag's dead eyes. She pressed her hand against the Coda concealed in her cloak and knew Merek was right. *I have no hope of dealing with Karnag alone.* She looked squarely at Merek. "What do you intend to do?"

"With the Coda I can draw upon the powers of my Sentinel master, Valis, and keep our purpose hidden from him. I will try to speak with the spirit of Castor. It is my hope your friend has not yet gained mastery of the Sentinel's power, which will allow me some advantage."

"It is your *hope*?"

Merek sniffed. "What else do we have?"

"And what then?"

"I may be able to place the Sentinel Castor at rest—to stay him. Then we can deliver your friend to those who can remove the spirit while leaving him unharmed."

"And who would that be? Others like you? Other witches? Forgive me, but I don't trust you, much less those like you who I've never met. Tell me why I'm mistaken."

Merek regarded her with dark, serious eyes. "The Sanctum. They are devoted to the service of Rune, and, above all, the goddess Illienne the Light Eternal. Together, our actions may save Rune from the utter dark of the Lord of Nightmares."

Fencress threw up her hands in exasperation and looked hard at Merek. "I have no taste for this horseshit. What I need to know is whether we can trust you."

"I am a guardian against that darkness. My intentions are pure."

Fencress shook her head. "So you and your ilk will capture this 'spirit,' and then Karnag will be his old, jolly self again. It all sounds so very lovely. Why didn't you try these things at Hargrave?"

"I needed to confirm Castor's presence. That, and I lack the ability to do these things alone. I may be able to still the spirit, but I cannot extract it. Ultimately, we will need the skills of the Sanctum, at their Abbey in Ironmoor."

There came then a howl, a groan, from some distance away and nearer to the hills. It sounded only vaguely human, but Fencress had no doubt as to its source.

She looked to Merek for a moment before withdrawing the heavy bracelet from the pockets of her cloak and flipping it toward the man. "Very well."

Merek snatched the thing from the air and placed it upon his wrist, where it fastened with a resounding click. Just then, it seemed an aura of green-hued light surrounded Merek for an instant and vanished.

"There," Merek said, his tone certain. He breathed deeply and closed his eyes. "Now we find Castor's vessel."

They pressed cautiously toward the hills, studying the land about them as they rode. In the faint light of that time before dawn they accounted for many of the Arranese hunting party, all of them fallen and broken and missing vital bits. Some had lost limbs, others their heads, and all of them their lives. Fencress pulled her cowl tightly about and kept her hands near her swords. Karnag was as quick and clever a killer as there was in all of Rune, and could catch them entirely unawares if such was his desire. *And that was before he became a devil.*

Fencress looked across the dark, rising landscape. "We've found only twenty. Perhaps your count was off?" She grinned slightly.

"No," Merek said, his eyes glinting in the near-darkness. "The Arranese hold sacred the number seven. Their religion honors the number and holds it holy, so their armies use it in all manners, figuring it grants them some sort of blessing." His brow knotted as he searched about. "They wouldn't have sent twenty men—such would have invited disaster in their minds."

Fencress smiled grimly. "As opposed to this?"

Merek's stoic expression did not change. "There is still one remaining."

"Ahead," hissed Paddyn suddenly. "A structure."

They pulled their horses to a stop and peered into the darkness. There did seem to be a squat farmhouse of some sort nestled at the base of the black hill before them, perhaps a few hundred feet away. It was a small building, just taller than a man and perhaps only just longer, uneven on the edges and leaning to the left as though ruined with age. As Fencress inspected it, it seemed there was something moving slowly about it, a shadow among the shadows.

Fencress leaned toward Merek and dropped her voice to a whisper. "So how is it we do this, Merek? Just knock on the door and say a cheery 'hullo'?"

Merek rubbed at his Coda. "If there is another Arranese yet alive, he may be dealing with him. Best if he is distracted with that when we approach. My Coda will keep me masked from him and he will not suspect my intention, but we have little time."

There came then from the direction of the structure a scream. Not the low, sinister howl they'd heard earlier, but a shriek of pure terror.

"I think we've found the Arranese warrior," Fencress said, pinching nervously at the rim of her cowl. "And it doesn't sound as though he's enjoying himself."

The sky above was brightening, shifting from black to a deep purple. Dawn was not far off.

The scream sounded again.

"Go," Merek said, kicking at his horse's flanks. The beast, however, whinnied and reared up and then began pressing backward. "Damned beast!" Merek hissed. "Forward!"

Fencress urged her own mount ahead but found the result was the same. The stallion flailed its head about, refusing to move forward even a step. As she looked about she saw Paddyn and Drenj, too, had moved nowhere. "Off the horses, then!" she said, swinging her leg over and dropping from the horse.

Paddyn and Drenj crept toward her. "What if he doesn't recognize us?" Paddyn said. "What if he's gone mad?"

Drenj moved close. "He'll kill us, Fencress. Every one."

Fencress paused. She knew her companions could be right, but she could not abandon Karnag. *Not so long as there's hope*, she thought, frowning as the notion crossed her mind. Her hand found the shape of the totem about her neck. *Hope.* In deadman's dice she'd call it her gut. Whatever it was, it told her there was still a chance to save her friend. She looked at each of them in the eye. "We'll be fine, boys," she said. "Trust me."

Paddyn nodded, and after a moment Drenj nodded as well. The Khaldisian held out his hands, palms upraised. "You," Drenj said, "have saved my life and I consider you my friend. I do this for you, but then we are square. I have a family, Fencress."

Fencress nodded and took Drenj's hands. "Square, after this. I'll even buy you a drink or three at *The Dead Messenger*."

Suddenly Merek pushed within their circle and grabbed Fencress's shoulder. "Now!" he snapped. "We must move now. If Karnag is done with the Arranese warrior, I will need him to see you. He will recognize you, and perhaps that will steady him and distract him. Come."

They set off, keeping low to the mist-covered earth. They ran swiftly but quietly, making no more sound than a breeze through the tall grass. Merek took the lead, and although Fencress knew she could outrace the fellow she figured it best if her head weren't the one closest to Karnag's sword.

She fixed her eyes on the structure ahead and it seemed there was no longer movement about the place. Whoever or whatever had been rounding it earlier had either slipped inside or behind the building. She didn't know what worried her more: seeing the shape of Karnag in the dark or not being able to see him at all. She felt her insides twist with fear as she thought on this, and pulled her swords from their sheaths.

They closed to within ten or so yards of the structure and Merek halted. Fencress bounded forward another few steps and stopped beside him. "What now?" she whispered.

Merek stood slack-jawed. "Sweet Illienne," he breathed, his eyes fixed upon the building.

Fencress turned again to regard the structure. It seemed a jumble of stones slick with rain, its surface glinting dimly with the coming dawn. She searched the shadows for Karnag's black gaze, but he was nowhere to be found. She stood still for a moment and heard faint sounds of activity coming from within the building. "He's inside."

She began moving sideways, searching the building's exterior for a door or window. There seemed to be no source of light she could discern from the place, but she knew there had to be an entrance into the ruined structure. She took a few more careful steps forward.

Then she realized what Merek had seen. This was no

farmhouse and the wetness was not rain. The sheen upon the thing was blood. Buckets of it. There were no stones forming the structure, but rather heads and hands and hearts and bones. *The parts missing from the Arranese—the members of the hunting party and many, many more.* It was a monument to death itself.

To Karnag.

Fencress tried to steel herself but could not keep from vomiting the bitter remnants of the cider she'd drank earlier. She swept away the dangling spittle with the back of a gloved hand and stood upright. "Dead gods," she hissed. "What have you become, Karnag?"

Her three companions, led by Merek, came to her side. Fencress noticed Drenj had pissed himself, and Paddyn's lips and hands trembled incessantly. Merek was wide-eyed but self-assured.

"Call to him," Merek said, gesturing toward the sickening shrine.

"Are you mad?" Drenj asked.

Merek's eyes swept across them. "This may be our last chance to save him. The longer he possesses the spirit of Castor, the closer his connection to the Sentinel's spirit will become. He will only become more powerful, more..." He stopped and paused. "You must call to him now."

"There is no need to summon me," came a deep voice. "I hear your call before it is given sound."

Fencress knew the voice, and it chilled her to the very core. She squeezed shut her eyes and, for the first time since youth, she prayed. *Sweet Illienne the Light Eternal,*

I call upon your blessing. Set me forever free of the bonds of darkness and the throes of evil.

"Fencress Fallcrow," said Karnag. "Old friend. You are unwise to come to this place, for your time has not yet come. This is a place of death, and death alone."

Fencress slowly opened her eyes. There, before her, was Karnag. He was awash in blood, some of it dried and black but most of it wet and red. He was as broad and strong in shape as ever, but his cheeks were pitted and his thick braids were covered with debris, the gristly remnants of the dead. And then there were the eyes. Cold and unnerving, ever seeming to look upon an unseen point, far away. Fencress felt they looked not at her soul but through it. To the very end. *The eyes of the dead.*

"Why do you come to this place?" Karnag asked, his tone one of strange concern. "Why do you not enjoy our spoils in safety? I instructed you to leave me."

Fencress steadied herself and met Karnag's gaze. *Are you inside this form, Karnag?* She swallowed and forced down the bile rising in her throat. "I…" she said, her voice more nervous than she would have liked, "I have come to save you."

Karnag regarded her with a puzzled expression. "Save? From what? *I* am what is to be feared. *I* am the inevitable. *I* am every man's ending."

Merek had moved to stand to Karnag's side, and he gave a subtle nod.

"Karnag," Fencress said, "we can help you. We can help you become what you once were."

With that, Karnag let out a horrible cry of pain and sank heavily to his knees.

Stunned, Fencress took a step backward, her blades at the ready. She pulled her gaze from Karnag and saw Merek beside the great slayer, his body aglow with a pale green aura. He held his hands outward and he whispered strange words, just as he had when he'd hunched over Drenj's sleeping form many days before.

Karnag cried out again, writhing and wailing at Merek's feet. He pulled at his blood-soaked jerkin and shred it from his body, and clutched desperately at his chest.

"What is he doing?" Paddyn asked. "Are we in danger?"

Fencress nodded dumbly, her eyes affixed to the scene before them.

Karnag whimpered and screamed once more, the sound of it agonizing. His fingers dug at his chest, ripping into the flesh. Thick veins bulged at his neck and tears fell from shuttered eyes.

Above him Merek's arms trembled as though from great effort and his whisper had grown to a low drone of arcane words. His brow dripped with sweat and his eyes twitched.

Again there was the awful sound of Karnag's cry, and Fencress felt a splash of something wet across her face. She looked to her old friend and saw a split in Karnag's side which squelched and squirted with blood.

Damn this all! Fencress gritted her teeth and took a bold step toward Merek. "You're killing him!"

Merek's face shook as he turned to Fencress. "If need be," Merek said, his mouth still forming the chant and his voice sounding closer to Fencress than was possible, "then yes, I will kill him."

"That was not our bargain!"

Merek returned his gaze to Karnag's squirming form. "I serve Illienne the Light Eternal, not you. There is no bargain."

"This is a foul betrayal!" Fencress said. "Boys!" she shouted to Paddyn and Drenj. "This man's life is forfeit! Cut him down!"

Fencress charged and leapt toward Merek, arms coiled and flexed and ready to drive her twin swords though the man's heart. Closer she came, less than a yard from her target...

But instead of a rough impact there was a flash of light.

Then blackness.

Fencress woke with a hard start. She gasped for air and forced her eyes open. There was a blazing light that seared her brain and forced her to squeeze shut her eyes again.

Her head ached as it had never ached before, worse than any hangover or fever or failed bout at fisticuffs. It felt as though a dagger had been jammed in her skull, but as she pressed her hands about she found no wounds, only the smooth leather of her cloak's cowl.

There were voices. Harsh voices speaking with a sharp accent.

She groaned and bit at her lip and forced her lids open to a thin squint. There was, indeed, a brilliant light. But this was that of the midday sun, not the unnatural flash she'd seen when she'd tried to skewer Merek. There, too, were figures, heavy shadows against the blinding sky.

She rolled to a side and saw the still forms of Drenj

and Paddyn lying nearby. There was also Karnag's great pile of gore, but no sign of the highlander or that bastard Merek.

Several of the shadowed figures moved toward her. "What…" she moaned as she tried to press upward, but she collapsed back to the ground from lack of strength.

Hands seized her, yanking her to her feet. Her body was limp and she could offer little resistance. She opened her eyes as wide as her considerable tolerance for pain would allow and saw all about her olive-colored, angular faces, armors of knitted hides and leathers, and an arsenal of exotic weaponry. She sighed with a sputter of spit and surrendered to their grasp.

"Bring her to me," came a thunderous voice which seemed to send tremors through the very earth.

Fencress rolled her head about, searching for the source of the sound. A short distance away, silhouetted against the sun, was a towering man no less than three feet taller than any fellow she'd ever seen. A colossal, sinewy figure wearing a sword Fencress guessed was taller than she was.

Her carriers dragged her closer until the gold disk of the sun was concealed behind the behemoth. Fencress's vision slowly adjusted to the light and she beheld a great head, shaven and traced with strange, geometric tattoos, lines dividing the face into tiny, slanted squares, like the web of a spider. But as she was pulled closer still she saw this was no tattoo, but rather a nasty stitching splitting the man's countenance into dozens of patches of stretched, writhing flesh.

She shuddered and drew a fearful breath. *And so endeth the tale of Fencress Fallcrow, Death's Dancing Mistress.*

The figure reached out a monstrous hand and took hold of Fencress by her skull. She was plucked painfully upward with disturbing ease and wiggled about like a rag doll. Her neck stretched with a crack in the vice-like grip and she frantically reached upward for support among the massive fingers. She pulled herself up with her last bits of strength to keep her neck from snapping.

"You," the giant said, "are not the 'Gravemaker.' You are but an ordinary thing, a pathetic wretch."

"Yet she is unharmed, Spider King," said a smaller man standing near. "She and the other two were the only ones at the site unwounded. Perhaps the three of them did these things together." Fencress noticed the smaller fellow's head was stitched in a fashion similar to that of the giant.

Fencress dangled as the giant studied her as a midwife would a newborn babe. "Yet," the Spider King said, "I no longer feel the presence of my brother, fleeting as it was. What use could these mortals be?"

"They may know something of your brother," said the other.

"They have killed none of my children. They bear no mark of the gods. They can know nothing, none of the real truths, for they are not wrought from the same substance as I," said the giant, dropping Fencress to the ground. "Leave them."

"Your grace?"

"Leave them to die."

21
STARTING OVER

LANNICK SAT BEFORE the fire in the common room of *The Whaler's Widow*, trolling a spoon through a thick stew of smelts and stringy vegetables at least a few days older than fresh. What the stew lacked in freshness, though, it made up in texture: it was easily chewed and thus only mildly bothersome to Lannick's crooked jaw.

A storm raged outside so the creaky inn near the docks was jammed with sailors and deckhands taking shelter from the downpour and warming their bellies with ale. They were a rowdy bunch, full of salty talk, tall tales, and bawdy songs.

"So then," croaked a fat-faced fellow drinking with friends near the fire, "the wench tells me the kid isn't mine at all! So I ask her who the father is, and the whore tells me 'Sam, I don't give two shits who the father is. I just don't want this little bastard getting your ugly looks.'

So then I tell her my name's not Sam, and she tells me 'Maybe not, but you're just as ugly as he is!'"

The group roared with laughter and slammed their mugs together, spilling a fair amount of ale in the process.

Lannick smirked, finding the crowd to be a pleasant distraction from the troubles haunting his head. He'd made the inn his home for two weeks, staying away from his more familiar spots in hopes of distraction and anonymity. He needed a break from his past, a place to clear his head and think things through. *A place for starting over.*

His wounds had mostly healed, with the only reminders of Fane's most recent brutality being a painful click in his jaw, a faint whistle in his bent nose, and a chipped tooth. He'd also sobered up—nearly anyway— and indulged in only a mug or two of ale near bedtime. He'd even taken to working his sword arm and practicing his fighting footwork on the docks at dawn. And most of all, he'd finally conceded Brugan was right. Something *had* changed within him, and he needed to take hold of it or risk losing it forever.

"Captain!" called a man over the din of the crowd.

Lannick instinctively turned on his stool at the word, dropping his spoon in the stew and finding the hilt of his sword.

"Captain!" said the man again. He was a tall man, his head nearly brushing the tavern's rafters. He shouldered through a knot of drinkers and his eyes moved briefly over Lannick. Then he took a seat at the table behind Lannick's, across from another man wearing a wide, tri-cornered hat trimmed with a large yellow feather. He'd been addressing someone else.

Lannick turned back to his stew and took a deep breath. *Captain*. He'd held that title, long ago. So long ago it seemed now another life. But the memories remained.

He remembered the brisk salutes of his men and their resounding answer of "*Captain!*" after he'd shouted his cry for courage in the cold, pre-dawn hours so many years before. He recalled how he'd charged the icy shores of Pryam's Bay, his division of a thousand men at his heels, and how they'd hacked desperately through the enemy soldiers to set fire to the ships of Tallorrath. He remembered how they'd rescued the captives, gutted every one of the invaders, and saved Rune from invasion.

He remembered, too, the stunned, scorched visage of General Fane. "*Captain?*" he'd asked incredulously, his charred face still smoldering and his mouth agape as Lannick dragged him from the wreckage of a burning ship. Lannick had slain a dozen Tallorrathian raiders to reach the captured general, but not before they'd thrown the general's bound form into the heart of the flames.

He also remembered High King Deragol's kind, appreciative smile when he'd held forth a decorated blade and said, simply and firmly, "*Captain*." The crowd gathered in the elegant gardens of the Bastion had cheered as Lannick bowed low to accept the blade signifying him as a Protector. As one of Rune's greatest heroes.

All had cheered. All but one. Fane had not clapped nor bellowed nor whistled. He'd stood there, strangely still, his face a mess of black scabs and blood-soaked bandages. He'd looked at Lannick with empty eyes as though wishing him death, his thin mouth shifting as through trying to taste glories no longer his own.

And lastly Lannick remembered Brugan, regarding him with a frantic gaze and shaking him from a drunken blur with shouts of "*Captain!*" Lannick had slowly revived and was reluctantly withdrawn from the arms of a Khaldisian prostitute to listen. He'd stood stunned and hollow-chested as Brugan told him Fane's Scarlet Swords had broken down the door of his home, where slept his wife and children.

Where he found them slaughtered.

Lannick moved his hand again to the sword, gripping its handle until his knuckles grew white.

Fane, I will hunt you down, and I will wreak ruin upon all that remains of your soul.

The following day Lannick woke early, his head clear and his body filled with a vigor it hadn't possessed in many years. He *was* different, he knew. Or at least he hoped he was. He knew he hadn't bested his demons—not all the way—and thought with dread for an instant of how easy it would be to slide headlong into those old, miserable habits. *But not today.*

He breakfasted on a meal of soft cheese and dark bread in the common room of *The Whaler's Widow*, thanking the pleasant widow herself for hearing his footfalls and insisting he be fed. He cleaned his plate, donned his sword and cloak, and headed out to the nearby docks.

The docks were awash in the hazy glow of the just-rising sun and striped with the thin shadows of the ropes and spars of ships listing gently in the harbor. There were fewer ships than usual, and most of them were either warships or local fishing trawlers. Trade, especially with such faraway places as Khaldisia and Harkane, had seemingly slowed if not stopped altogether. Many of the vessels appeared vacant, with only the occasional ship hosting the vague semblance of a crew.

Lannick walked along a narrow pier, his boots scratching against the weathered wood. He'd always been fond of the scent of sea-brined air and he breathed it deeply. The rising tide lapped against the supports below and a flock of gulls floated lazily overhead.

Before him were only the endless, churning waters of the Sullen Sea. Every wave's crest and every cloud's tuft was set with the golden hue of the rising sun. There seemed to be only tranquil possibility, only peaceful expanse.

He regarded it all with a wry smile. What lay before him was anything but peaceful, and nowhere near tranquil. Things were about to get quite complicated and quite bloody. Nonetheless, this place seemed a suitable location for starting anew, a place for focusing upon the deeds to be done.

When he reached the pier's end he sank to a crouch and drew his sword. It wasn't as evenly weighted a weapon as the one he'd had forged before Pryam's Bay, or as elegant as the decorative sword the High King had presented him thereafter. This sword's handle was wrapped with fraying leather, the cross-guard was bent, and the blade was chipped in places and heavier at the end than in the middle. It had certainly seen better days.

Not unlike me.

He calmed his thoughts and began. He thrust the blade forward, toward the rising sun, his right leg taking a long step for balance and leverage. He thrust again, stepping quickly sideways to the pier's edge, then parried with a step backward, then another thrust, then one more. He moved quickly, his feet feeling lighter than they had in some time. If nothing else, his recent hardships had trimmed his belly, granting him some of the quickness he'd lost in recent years.

Slowly his troubles drifted from his head and he focused only on his movements, determined to make them all swift and crisp. He slipped to his side, dodged and charged forward. He crouched and lurched and struck, again and again, and the planks of the pier hummed from his footfalls and the sword became a blur in his hands.

His brow dripped with sweat and his muscles burned but it bothered him not at all. It felt right. He wasn't as strong or swift as he'd been at Pryam's Bay, but then he wasn't as slow as he'd been a couple of months ago, either. He felt like a dangerous man once more, a man set with a deadly purpose. He thrust his sword again, imagining it sinking into Fane's black heart.

"Hullo, Lannick," came a scratchy, disconcerting voice.

Lannick whirled about, his sword at the ready.

Standing there on the narrow pier, between Lannick and dry land, was Silas, the one-eyed pawnbroker. Behind Silas were two rough-looking sorts, one a giant hulk of a man with an executioner's axe, the other a smaller fellow with a curved dagger clutched in dirty hands.

Silas's face was strangely placid, his cheeks sagging

sadly. Lannick had seen that look before, usually when the pawnbroker had asked him to draw "interest" from a deadbeat debtor. That generally meant a good beating, the gutting of a family pet, or even slicing off a finger or two. Lannick shuddered at the memory of such deeds.

"Lannick, my old friend," Silas said, his voice weak and withering. "Why have you done this?"

Lannick lowered his blade and moved his other hand to his purse. He had a couple of silver crowns he could spare. "I've been... occupied, Silas. I can pay you something now, and I promise you I'm good for the rest."

Silas shook his head. "Imagine my disappointment upon discovering you've been renting a room in such a pricey seaside inn while owing me so much?" He sighed and looked downward. "I talk not just of your rent and the loans I made to you, but also of the many years I've had you in my employ. Think of all the times I helped you when you were down. Why? Why would you withhold my money and hide from me? You know I am not a forgiving man."

Lannick gritted his teeth. He had no time for lectures or threatening talk, especially from the pawnbroker. There were larger matters demanding his attention. "Silas, I've had to deal with other things. Problems—real problems—from my past. I'm sorry for the delay." He dipped his hand into his purse, brushing across the box of his Coda and finding a couple of coins. He thought for an instant of fixing the Coda to his wrist but decided against it. Instead, he grabbed the coins and offered them to Silas. "I can give this to you now as a gesture of good faith, and you can trust I'll pay you the rest when I can."

Silas slapped Lannick's hand and the coins plopped into the sea. "The time for such gestures is long past. You owe me three months of rent, plus another six silver crowns for loans and interest. That's eleven in all. You either pay with coin now, or you pay with flesh. You remember those terms of mine, don't you, Lannick? I never imagined I'd have to deliver them to *you*."

Lannick straightened and squeezed the hilt of his blade. "I have no quarrel with you, Silas, and no desire for violence, but I don't have that kind of coin on hand. I can give you a couple of crowns now but the rest must wait a few weeks."

Silas tilted his head and took several silent steps backward, his expression unreadable. "That will not do, Lannick. You have betrayed me, and in my business I cannot tolerate betrayal. You should know that."

Lannick's face flushed with anger. "I have not betrayed you, Silas, and I have not been hiding from you. I've been dragged through hell and back. You will get your coin when I can pay you. Eleven crowns and more."

Silas's face froze in a disturbing half-smile and he took another few steps backward, pressing between and behind his two companions. "Boys…" he breathed.

The big fellow was the first to move, blundering forward and heaving his huge axe overhead. As he neared Lannick he threw the axe viciously downward with arms the size of tree trunks. Lannick darted back as the axe head smashed into the wooden planks and shattered one to splinters. Lannick was just able to avoid the blow without falling into the water, but his heels had found the end of the pier and he fought to keep his balance.

The axe head caught in the planks for an instant, but not quite long enough for Lannick to take advantage. By the time his footing was firm the big man had pulled the axe free and was twisting it back to swing it sideways. Lannick knew his short sword would never be able to redirect such a weapon—not in these tight quarters—so he made ready to duck or jump. He figured the oaf thought to bring a fight to an end with a single, overwhelming strike, probably guessing he could split Lannick in two at the belly. *I'll throw myself on the planks, and then make it quick.*

The man spun the great axe about his hip with tremendous force, so much so there was no hope he could adjust its path. Lannick dropped face down as the weapon whistled toward him. He then lunged forward on hands and knees once it had moved over him. He drove the tip of his sword right into the man's bits.

The big oaf dropped the axe and stumbled backward, clutching his bleeding crotch and letting loose a pained squeal. He knocked into Silas before tumbling off the pier and into the waters of the Sullen Sea, causing Silas to stagger backward and fall. The oaf splashed wildly about in the sea, and it was obvious he couldn't swim and would very likely drown.

Lannick turned to the smaller ruffian who stood grinning with a wild look in his bloodshot eyes, his hands caressing his dagger like a lover. He seemed to be the sort who enjoyed killing, and Lannick knew that was never a good sort to encounter.

"You don't want to join your friend, do you?" Lannick asked as amiably as he could manage.

The ruffian shrugged and smiled crazily, his dagger at the ready.

Lannick held forth a hand, pleading. "Silas! We can settle this without more bloodshed! This is a dispute over only money, nothing more. Certainly we can resolve this?"

Silas pressed himself to his feet and dusted off his breeches, his face still disquietingly calm. "*Only* money, Lannick? You should know I don't regard it as *only* money. Money is not an end in itself, but rather the one means to obtain *all* other things, whether they be things of comfort, power, or even love. When you take money from me, you are stealing from me all those other things as well."

"I've stolen nothing."

"Borrowing money with no intention of repaying is the very same as stealing." Silas slipped his hand into his coat and produced a cleaver, its wide blade glinting in the morning sunlight. He moved to stand beside the dirty ruffian, leaving no way around them on the narrow pier. "And when you, a man I trusted, a man I helped, took money from me, you betrayed me in the worst possible way."

Lannick scowled. He'd wanted a break from his past, from those nine awful years. He wished there was another way but knew there wasn't. *Sometimes the past can only be washed away by blood.*

Lannick knew better than to wait this time. He danced toward the ruffian, keeping his strides uneven and unpredictable and flipping his sword in his hand so to hold it upside down. The ruffian sank low, the long dagger swaying in his hands and ready to strike.

The ruffian's dark eyes fixated on Lannick's midsection and he panted like a dog. Lannick had seen such eyes before and reckoned the man would worry only about inflicting violence rather than becoming the victim of it.

He saw there his chance.

As Lannick closed the distance the ruffian's eyes widened and he shoved his dagger toward the spaces between Lannick's ribs. Just as Lannick had hoped, the man had failed to guard himself. Before the fellow's arm had fully extended Lannick's sword was already deep inside that soft space between his neck and collarbone. The ruffian's arm jerked and his dagger dropped from twitching hands.

Lannick withdrew the weapon and stepped back to allow the man to flop headfirst into the sea. He lowered his sword and turned to face Silas, knowing the pawnbroker never committed violence himself—always preferring to watch instead.

"You were always quick," said Silas in his discomforting monotone, "even for a drunk."

Lannick shook the slop from his blade with disgust. "Forget this thing, Silas. Leave me be."

Silas adjusted the patch over his missing eye and his shoulders drooped. "No," he said glumly, and threw his cleaver toward Lannick's head.

Lannick dodged the cleaver easily. However, he didn't see the small knife Silas wielded until it was almost too late. The blade had been intended for his gut, but Lannick managed to shift his body just enough that it dug into his hip instead. His flesh burned as the weapon scraped against bone and twisted about.

Lannick wrenched himself free and seized Silas by the throat. "My blade was never meant for you!" he roared.

Silas's mouth fell open as he gasped for air. Lannick reared back and shoved his sword through the maw, his hand nearly ripping through the other side.

Silas collapsed, dead, his head a bloody mess.

Lannick blinked hard and his mouth trembled as the body fell to the planks, twitched for an instant, and then grew still. He looked upon the pawnbroker's corpse for a quiet moment before kicking it from the pier.

He shook the blood and gristle from his skin as though shaking off an awful chill, and suddenly wanted whiskey more than anything. He limped back toward *The Whaler's Widow*, leaving behind him a trail of blood.

Lannick sat naked upon the edge of his bed in the small, sunlit room, a bottle of whiskey in one hand and a bloody rag in the other. The wound—in the fleshy part between his hip and his rump—hurt horribly and had yet to stop bleeding. He soaked the rag again with the whiskey bottle and pressed it against the wound, and then took a hearty pull himself to deaden the pain.

He swallowed and gritted his teeth, as much from the burn of the whiskey as the memory of the morning's events. He regretted the needless violence, regretted that his past had such an awful habit of grabbing at his heels and dragging him back. All he wanted was a break, a clean break from the mistakes of the last nine years. *But then perhaps there is no such thing as clean break. Not from my past, anyway.*

He took another long strip of the cloth he'd borrowed

from the widow and wrapped it around his pelvis, about the bloody rag and then around twice more. He needed to stitch the wound but his hands were still shaking from the fight. He painfully pulled his clothing on and staggered downstairs to the inn's common room.

The place wasn't nearly as raucous as it'd been the night before. A couple of crusty fisherman chatted near the fire and another fellow brooded over a tankard near one of the room's square windows. The widow was mopping the planked floor, softly singing an old sailor's dirge.

Lannick walked gingerly to an empty table in a corner and eased himself into a chair with a wince. The widow looked at him, her plump face brightening with a kind smile. Her eyes drifted toward the rafters, as though lost in thought, then suddenly she dropped the mop, raised a finger and shuffled to the bar. She rummaged about, retrieved something then rushed to Lannick.

"Oh my," she said in a breathless tone, "my old head is as leaky as that damned boat that drowned my husband, Illienne bless him. I nearly forgot. A great big fellow came here last night after you'd retired. Said someone had left a note for you at his place, some unsavory bar I think, and he asked me to give it to you. That, along with another one."

Lannick thanked her and took the two notes, figuring they'd been delivered by Brugan. The first was folded into quarters and closed with a wax seal bearing a familiar mark: a watchtower. *The mark of the Variden*. He shifted uncomfortably in his seat and then opened the note slowly, almost worried something would jump at him from the parchment.

The note was written in a coded text, a secret language of the Variden. At first it was difficult to decipher, but soon Lannick found the old knowledge returning to him and the meaning of the symbols became clear.

"*Lannick,*" the note began. "*I hope this letter finds you well, and that you've found some kind of peace with your demons. I know things have been difficult, but I know also that within you is the courage to overcome them.*

"*I write to you in desperation and I appeal to your virtue. Our colleague Merek has learned the murder of the Sanctum's Lector was arranged by the Necrists. What is worse, the murderer now hosts the spirit of Castor. Merek managed to capture this murderer and is transporting him to Ironmoor, where he hopes the Sanctum can remove the spirit and restore it in one of their number, so that Castor's wisdom and power are preserved. If this cannot be done, then I fear our ability to fight our enemy will be greatly diminished.*

"*Merek has also discovered that Arranan's Spider King is no ordinary warlord. He keeps the company of several Necrist sorcerers and may be a Necrist himself. This Spider King marches against Rune with an army tens of thousands strong, and has decimated its forces at every turn.*

"*I need not tell you what catastrophe these events portend, nor need I describe to you the stakes. Our worst fears are taking form, and Rune could soon plunge into its darkest moment. Our Order's need has never been greater, and we require every last of our number if Rune is to have any hope of surviving the coming storm.*

"*Come back to us, Lannick. I beg you.*"

It was signed simply "*Alisa.*"

Lannick slumped back into his chair, stunned. He

breathed deeply and his head sagged after reading the note once more.

He set it aside and opened the second note, a roll of stained parchment covered in a sloppy scribble. "*Meet at Gregor's Watch on Averday, on the full moon. Nine o'clock. I have our army, Captain.*"

Lannick recognized the clumsy script as Brugan's, and Averday was but two days away. His head sagged even lower.

"Is everything alright?" asked the widow, mopping the floor nearby.

"I'll need another bottle of that whiskey."

"For that cut of yours?"

Lannick had almost forgotten about his wound and he rubbed it absent-mindedly. "Uh, yeah."

Lannick again sat at the edge of his bed, threading the dark string through the needle's eye. His hands had stopped shaking, but he couldn't be certain whether that was from the passage of time or the effects of more than a couple of swigs of whiskey.

The wound near his hip still wept blood but was otherwise clean. Satisfied, he squeezed it closed with one hand and pressed the needle through with the other. It stung a bit, but not nearly as much as it would have without the whiskey. *A shame that's not the only reason I need to drink.*

He pulled the string through then around the wound and then through it again. After a few more punctures with the needle and loops of the string the wound was sealed, held shut by an uneven, black stitch. *Not pretty, but it will do*.

Lannick pressed a cloth to the mouth of the whiskey bottle, wetted it, and then gently wiped away the blood. As he did so he found himself reminded of that awful night, that passage through the shadows and the hideous faces of the Necrist and her Shodafayn abominations. He remembered with terrifying clarity those thick, grisly stitches binding the faces of his family to the skulls of those demons. He remembered how the flesh stretched and wriggled and bunched, straining against the stitching. He guessed they would not have looked like human faces at all, had their features not been so painfully familiar.

He grabbed the whiskey bottle again and took a long drink and then slammed it down upon his bedside table. After wrapping and rewrapping clean cloth strips about his hips he dressed and strapped on his sword and satchel. He grabbed the note from Alisa and stood still for a long moment, looking out his window at the twilit sky and the purple sea beneath it.

He thought of all his troubles, all the hardships he'd endured both by his own hands and by those of others. He thought of his family, of their deaths and their burial. He thought of all those dreadful nights thereafter, of his nights spent sobbing, of his rejection of the Variden, and of his descent into drunken desperation. He thought of his dark deeds for Silas and of Silas's face impaled upon his sword. He thought of his nightmare in the shadowpaths with the perversions of the faces he loved, and of burying his family once again.

Then he thought of General Fane. He thought of the

man leering over him after he'd been beaten and bloodied, and of the smug smile twisted across his grotesque face.

He thought of his dilemma, of the hard choice between honoring old oaths to the Variden or disregarding them in order to exact revenge upon General Fane, of rejoining his order to fight the enemy in the shadows or galloping to the front to take his vengeance.

He thought of all the things before him, all those impossible deeds needing doing.

His shoulders drooped and he made ready to leave the room.

Is this how heroes are born?

22

THE AWFUL PAST

ANDRACHUS BALE PICKED his way through the mountain pass, his hastily made walking staff wobbling precariously with every uneasy step. He averted his eyes from every vista and every cliff's edge, terrified the heights would cause him to swoon with vertigo. His feet ached, his knees creaked, and his back was bent with exhaustion.

"How much farther?" he said, as much accusing as inquiring.

"Dunno," said the wild-haired, spindly-legged woman walking half a dozen paces ahead of him. She smelled terrible, like a cheese several days too old, but she was the only person in the mountainside village he'd found who was willing to guide him to the ruins of the ancient city of Cirak. That was five days prior, and he surmised this was the first word she'd spoken since.

"Well," he said, trying to sound curious rather than

concerned, "how can you be sure *where* it is if you don't know how *far* it is?"

"Dunno that, neither," she said curtly, squinting at him with sea-green eyes. Her face was wrinkled and caked with dirt, and her shoulder-length hair gray in places and red in others. Yet, Bale suspected she was younger than she appeared.

Bale followed her up a narrow gully full of loose gravel, struggling with his footing. "You've been there before, haven't you?"

"I ran away from home a lot, sometimes to there. I've snooped around a few times. Lots of dry dirt and old bones. A dead place. Last time was years ago, and I knew better than to come back."

"Years ago? Do you remember exactly how *many* years ago?"

"Dunno. I forget."

Bale tucked a long strand of his gray hair behind his ear and shook his head. He'd read of Cirak, knew vaguely of its supposed mountaintop location, but the Southwall Mountains were a vast and dangerous place. Without knowing the location precisely it was very likely they would become lost and then die. "But," he asked, "you *do* know where it is, yes?"

The woman stopped abruptly and wheeled about, a bony finger leveled at him. "Dead gods be damned, yes! Everyone knows where it is, so we can avoid the place! If you don't believe me, then good luck finding it yourself!"

Bale threw up his hands. He realized he had no choice but to trust the woman, and having her dislike him probably wasn't a good idea. Not when she could send him plunging to his death with a simple nudge. He smiled weakly.

They continued on for a while in silence, through tight, winding passes and across an old switchback path carved into the side of the cliffs. Bale found himself shutting his eye closest to the path's edge in hopes of ignoring the sheer height. Invariably, though, his gaze would wander to the edge and he'd see a valley thousands of feet below. His stomach lurched and would have emptied had there been anything of substance within it.

"So," he said, trying to distract himself, "what is your name?"

"Lorra," she said gruffly.

He paused and bowed awkwardly, "Lorra, I'm Zandrachus Bale, Acolyte of the Sanctum of Illienne the Light Eternal."

"Good for you, whatever that is."

"You haven't heard of the Sanctum?"

"No."

"We're students of the Old Faith. Guardians of truth and seekers of wisdom." He pulled at his chin and thought for a moment. "Perhaps you've heard of us referred to as 'spookers.'"

"Ah. Loony wizards."

"A common misperception. Our works are derived from the ancient wisdom of the goddess Illienne. They are divine in nature. The works we perform aren't 'magic,' but rather divine methods of seeking truths. We are also well versed in curing ills of the body."

Lorra stopped and looked at him suspiciously. "You can heal the sick?"

"We have methods. Is there something I can help you with, when we reach Cirak? Or perhaps your family? I'm thinking your help has been worth far more than the few silver crowns I've promised to pay you. I could help."

She paused for a moment. "I have a lot of bad memories. Bad feelings from the awful past. My brothers and father." She sniffed and looked skyward. "Rape and some things even worse. Can you help with nightmares?"

Bale regarded her sadly and then looked at his feet. "I'm afraid I can't help with that."

They made camp for the night near a mountain stream, finding kindling for a fire near a few scraggly trees. Lorra turned out to be a capable cook, making a pleasant-smelling stew of onions and leeks she'd brought from her village and herbs she found near the stream. Bale graciously accepted a wooden cup and sat near the fire to eat.

"It's delicious," he slurred through a mouthful before swallowing. "But you may not like me by the time morning comes. Onions tend to make a trumpet of my, well, you know…"

"You're sleeping downwind, then."

"Very well," Bale said, giggling. He'd always found farts to be a source of tremendous amusement, particularly in the solemn, poorly ventilated halls of the Abbey. He wondered briefly about the acoustics of the mountain faces and laughed a bit louder, imagining the echo of a hearty baritone playing across the Southwalls.

Lorra looked at him with something resembling disgust and resumed eating in silence. Bale felt mildly embarrassed and shifted away from the fire, focusing instead upon the night sky. The moon and stars were brilliantly bright, casting a silvery glow upon the mountains. It was a serene, beautiful place, and seemed a whole world away from the Abbey. Bale smiled, amazed he'd made it so far from home.

Lorra stood and retrieved Bale's empty cup. "Why do you travel to Cirak? It's just a jumble of old, ruined things. A place only of death. A frightful place."

"Old and frightful to some, but a most sacred relic to those like me. Cirak was once a great city, a majestic place. It's said to be the site of the first battle between Illienne the Light Eternal and Yrghul the Lord of Nightmares. And it was home to a grand temple to Illienne." He lifted his chin. "Yrghul defeated Illienne there, more than a thousand years ago, and cast the city into ruin. It's said that after the War of Fates a group of architects and masons went to Cirak and built a new temple atop the ruins of the old, and erected glorious statues to honor the Sentinels. It was considered a holy place, at least until the Sentinels were banished." He rubbed his nose. "You've heard of the Sentinels and the War of Fates, haven't you?"

Lorra waved a hand dismissively. "Never."

"Never? Well," Bale said, pulling his hair behind his ears and settling closer to the fire, "eons ago the Elder God made ready to depart this place, and upon doing so He gifted dominion of the world to His six children. To Illienne He granted dominion over Rune and lands nearby. One of her brothers, Yrghul, was given a land far to the south, in a place now known as the Bowl of Fire. For a time Yrghul's kingdom thrived, becoming like a glittering jewel. But then, in a terrible instant, a great ball of flame from the heavens obliterated his realm. Yrghul grew mad with grief over the loss of his people, and he cursed the Elder God for the tragedy. In his rage he sought fell powers in old hells laid bare by the devastation, those dark places left buried by the Elder God when He turned from this world. With those powers he set out to exact a misguided vengeance, a desire to lay waste to all the lands of his siblings. The struggle that followed became known as 'The War of Fates,' and it happened a thousand years ago. It—"

"I didn't say I *wanted* to hear about it."

"But—"

"No," Lorra said firmly, her green eyes narrowing.

"Oh," Bale said, lowering his head, suddenly reminded of how different people were outside the walls of the Abbey. *Most people find comfort in ignorance.*

They sat quietly for a time near the fire. Bale stirred the embers occasionally with his staff, warding away the chill of the mountain air.

"You're an odd one," Lorra said abruptly. "By the looks of you you've traveled far, and you don't seem to be much of a traveler. Couldn't you have picked an easier place to meet this person?"

Bale thought of the Spell of Recounting, of the feel of the wet, withering piece of flesh in one hand and strange movements of his other as his body mimicked the Lector's own. His hand had jerked and swirled as though writing invisible script, until at last Bale's mind had caught their pattern and recognized the words. "*And, thus, Lyan, I summon you,*" were the words. "*I implore you to honor once more your most sacred vow. I will come to the Sacred Place at Cirak, and together we must return to Rune, before He does. I have sent summonses to the others. The very fate of the world is in jeopardy, and only we can save it."*

The 'sacred place' had to be the ancient Temple of Cirak. Bale grimaced, for the words still frightened him as he wondered what, exactly, he would find in the ruins of Cirak. *Perhaps I'll find the awful past, as Lorra called it.* He shivered and pulled his heavy robes about him.

"Well?" Lorra asked impatiently. "Why are you going there?"

Bale glared at the woman. "For someone who doesn't care to hear my answers, you certainly ask me a lot of questions."

Lorra took the cups and her pot to the stream and set about washing them. After doing so she splashed water on her face, removing some of the thick layer of dirt caked upon it. At least in the flickering firelight, she looked far more comely than she had earlier. Her features were hard but still womanly and, if Bale dared think it, attractive.

Bale stared at her for a long moment before heaving a sigh. "It's a long story. Probably not something you want to hear."

"I asked, didn't I?"

"It's about those Sentinels I mentioned earlier."

"You said that stuff was a thousand years ago. You're going to see a dead person? A tomb?"

Bale chuckled. "In a manner of speaking, I am going to something not unlike a tomb. The Old Faith was rejected as blasphemy after the Sentinels were banished, and symbols of them were forbidden by the High King. But as for the Sentinels themselves, they are immortal."

Lorra looked at him quizzically, her brow curling above green eyes.

"That means they cannot die by mortal means."

"I know what it means," Lorra said sharply, splashing Bale with a handful of water. She then fixed him with a penetrating stare. "So the person you're going to meet is a thousand years old?"

Bale looked skyward again and studied the stars. "That's my hope. There was one among them named Lyan the Just. I don't know what became of her after the Sentinels were banished, but it's my hope she has not... faded away. It's my hope she is still at Cirak. Still waiting."

"And why is it you would want to meet this... person?"

Bale pulled his robes closer. "Perhaps she can help me save the world."

At dawn they found themselves again on a path cut into the side of a mountain, this one narrower and more treacherous than the last. A thunderhead rolled atop the nearby sky and the wind whipped at them and howled in their ears. Bale was desperately afraid of tumbling off and crept slowly along with both hands pressed against the rock face.

He stumbled suddenly on a loose stone, tilting backward for an instant before frantically finding his footing and returning his hands to the mountain face. A tear fell from his eye before being blown from his face by the wind. *Sweet Illienne please spare your loyal servant!* He squeezed shut his eyes and continued shuffling along the path while the wind tugged at him. He thought for an instant of Keln, of the Scarlet Swordsman waiting for him in the afterlife, waiting for revenge with sword drawn and eyes ablaze. *I am too weak an instrument!*

"Damn you!" cursed Lorra from ahead of him. "We're no more than a half-day's walk from Cirak, but at your pace it will be another three!"

Bale sniffled and raised his chin, doing his best to present a brave face in spite of his shuttered, weeping eyes. "I am moving as quickly as my spirit will allow! I am no mountain goat such as you!"

He felt a sharp pull on his sleeve and pried open an eye. There was Lorra, framed against the leaden sky with her red and gray hair swirling madly and her green eyes staring fiercely, the sleeve of his robe bunched in her fist. Somehow she seemed every bit as womanly as she had the evening before, in spite of her pursed mouth, deep wrinkles, and altogether angry eyes.

"You will come, spooker," she said. "You will follow me."

Bale clutched futilely at the rock wall before surrendering to her grasp. With eyes squeezed shut he allowed himself to be towed along, keeping one trembling hand pressed against the rough rock. "How do I know you won't just lead me over the edge?" he asked, his voice choked with tears.

"You don't," said Lorra, harshly. "I don't mean to do that just now, but if you keep complaining like a sheep being sheared I just might."

Bale bit his lip and followed blindly.

By late afternoon the wind had eased and the sky had

calmed. The path remained quite precarious—a narrow passage with a five thousand foot drop on one side—and Bale continued to press one hand upon the rock face for fear of falling. His other hand was still tugged along in its sleeve by Lorra, who remained confident of her footing and impatient with Bale's pace.

"Even with your slow shuffle we are finally getting close," she grumbled, gesturing toward the path ahead. "Once more about the mountain and you'll be there." She turned her head to face him. "I deserve more than you promised to pay me, seeing as you've been so slow. I should have been home a day ago."

Bale nodded. "Whatever coin it takes." His eyes wandered to the edge of the path and over it. "I may need you to lead me back down."

Lorra grunted again and tugged him along. "Just so long as we leave the place before dark."

"I can't promise I'll be finished before nightfall. What if I asked you to wait for me?"

"Nighttime is bad in that place. We shouldn't stay there so long."

"I'll pay you triple."

Lorra looked at him grimly for a moment before speaking. "You're lucky I'm so poor. Had half our goats not died of plague last summer perhaps I'd tell you to find your own damned way down."

Bale nodded graciously. "I'll tarry not one moment too long."

After a time Bale found his steps with greater certainty, whether because of Lorra's grip or the proximity of his destination he could not be sure. He even found the courage to wander closer to the path's edge and peer off the mountain's side.

Through drifts of mist he was able to spy the deep chasms, hidden vales and winding passes far, far below. In one valley there seemed to be the ruins of an old fortress. As Bale continued his inspection, though, he realized this was no vestige of an older time, but a fortress recently razed. Walls and battlements lay toppled, and scattered about it were hundreds of tiny dots glinting in the shafts of sunlight filtered through the clouds. He surmised these were the slaughtered soldiers of Rune, a mountain garrison demolished by the Arranese horde mere weeks ago.

His thoughts turned to the war raging a hundred leagues to the north. Since he'd left General Fane's company he'd heard nothing of it save for the frantic descriptions from the soldier Stevran, just before Keln had murdered him. What Stevran had said was anything but promising, and Bale wondered if the Arranese had already burned Riverweave and marched to Ironmoor. He thought of the Abbey, of Gamghast and Borel in particular, and he was sad. *Could it be I am safer here than I was in the Abbey?* He slowed and stared again at the ruins of the fortress below.

"Come along," Lorra said, yanking his sleeve with greater urgency. "There's another storm on the horizon. At these heights we'll need to find shelter before nightfall."

"Yes," Bale said absently, pulling his eyes from the battered remains of the fortress and staring ahead along the path. There was a line of black clouds ahead. "Another storm, you say?"

"There," Lorra said, pointing. "Headed right for us."

"Yes, indeed," Bale said, becoming once again acutely aware of the precarious nature of his journey. "We should hurry."

Cirak.

Bale beheld it as though seeing a dream take shape in reality. He walked with arms outstretched, eyes wide as he gazed upon the once-great city. It was indeed a relic of an older, more magnificent time, a city that even in its present state of decay could not conceal its former splendor.

Towers once a hundred feet tall lay broken across the mountaintop plateau, the ornate carvings of their turrets fractured and crumbling to dust. Massive structures sagged upon snapped and eroded pillars, like once-proud faces drooped by age and rotted teeth. The wide thoroughfares were awash with yellow dust and littered with smashed earthenware and dry, sun-bleached bones.

Bale had read of the place, of course. Every member of the Sanctum had. He'd even seen old maps showing its location, and had dreamed of making a daring journey to the place to study the artifacts of history. He shook his head. *Never would I have thought I'd find myself here for the reasons I am.*

He scanned the landscape of ruins for the legendary Temple of Cirak and became suddenly fearful. He knew next to nothing of the Sentinel he hoped to meet, Lyan the Just. Chances were she had waited for Erlorn for a few days and then had given up hope. *But what if she's still here?* The Sentinels were powerful beings, godlike, immortal. He knew Erlorn to be wise and patient, but his qualities were not necessarily shared by the other Sentinels. Each was an aspect of Illienne but not the whole, and thus did not possess the entirety of her goodness or godliness. Thaydorne the Strong, for instance, was thought of as domineering and lacking mercy, and Sienne the Quick was often described in the old accounts as untrustworthy and manipulating.

How will Lyan deal with a mere mortal, particularly one who comes on behalf of Rune? What if she has changed in these many centuries, grown embittered by nearly a millennium spent in exile?

He was startled by a hand upon his shoulder, but breathed easier when he saw it was Lorra's. She gestured skyward and Bale looked up to see threatening clouds overhead.

"We need shelter," Lorra said. "Soon. This looks to be a rough storm."

"I agree," Bale said, noticing a flash of lightning not too far away. He took another look about and caught sight of a dome flecked with gold, perhaps a thousand feet away. He hesitated. *The Temple of Cirak?* He searched for an alternative, but all the buildings within view had long ago surrendered to the elements, their roofs ripped with gaping holes or missing altogether.

"The gold building," Lorra said, pointing toward the dome. "That's the only place that doesn't look ready to fall apart."

Am I prepared for this? Bale trembled but yielded when Lorra tugged once again at his sleeve and moved ahead. A hot wind blew from behind him and rain began falling in large drops. *It seems I have little choice.*

They moved as quickly as care would allow amidst the wreckage of the ancient city. They scrambled around and over heaps of shattered stone, their boots snapping bones and shards of fired clay. They ran between the shadows of leaning façades that swayed and groaned as the wind gusted. About them the dust swirled in funnels, wandering about the abandoned thoroughfares like the shambling ghosts of the dead.

Thunder cracked. The skies blackened and the rain became a deluge. Lightning flashed, illuminating the dark recesses of the nearby structures. Bale was certain he saw movement within—a pale shape darting back into the shadows. He quickened his pace, pulling even with the sure-footed Lorra.

Bale pulled Lorra close as they jogged, nodding toward the gaping entrance of the building that was now cloaked in darkness. There was no sign of the figure. "This city is abandoned, right?" Bale asked over the hiss of the rain. "You said it was deserted?"

Lorra swiped water from her face. "I said it was a place of death. There are no living things here."

"There's something in that structure there," he said, pointing. "Something pale moving between the shadows. A stray animal, perhaps?"

Lorra paused and gave him a worried look. "Likely not. Even beasts know better than to wander here. Probably a hobbler." She glanced back at the building and then upward at the darkening sky. "We should hurry."

"A hobbler?"

"A hobbler. A gangleman. Someone who's dead but wakes up again to do bad things. Eating babies and such.

They come out in darkness and that's why no one comes here. This place is full of them."

Bale gasped and moved forward as rapidly as his creaky knees would carry him. He gathered Lorra possessed only limited education and was probably prone to rustic superstitions, but her description had an eerie ring to it. He'd read about such things in his explorations of the dusty depths of the Abbey's library. The waking dead, or "*garghuls*" as they were called in the elder tongue, were thought of by most as mere legend. Older manuscripts, though, recited first-hand accounts of encounters with the garghuls during the War of Fates, claiming them to be vile creations of Yrghul. The notion of confronting a Sentinel suddenly seemed more inviting when compared to the alternative.

Lorra abruptly slowed, and as Bale gazed ahead he saw the road was obstructed by a fallen tower, too high to climb in a hurry. They turned down another ruined street. After a short time, though, they found it, too, was clogged by a great barricade of shattered masonry.

Lightning flashed and a thunderclap shook the earth. The rain intensified and the ground beneath them was becoming a thick, sloppy mud. Just then a pained moan sounded in the distance.

"We need to get to your temple!" Lorra demanded. "It's not safe here!"

Bale looked frantically around him. There was nothing but stone. It seemed the way to the temple was blocked.

Another moan echoed amidst the ruins. This time it was answered by others.

"There!" Lorra said, grabbing Bale's hand. "A passage through!"

Bale's eyes followed Lorra's and he saw it: a tight tunnel formed by two wrecked structures leaning against each other. At its far end was a faint light promising access to the other side.

"Go!" Lorra tugged Bale toward the passage. She pulled him across the street, boots squelching in the mud, and ducked into the low tunnel.

It was an uncomfortably cramped corridor, and Bale crouched to follow. It was dry, at least, but they were forced to walk stooped close to the ground, slowing their journey and making for more than a few painful scrapes upon the broken stones lining the passage.

Bale continued to hold Lorra's hand, his head nearly touching her rear as they crept along. In spite of their peril he could not help but admire the woman's firm physique. Her haunches swayed before him and he smiled. At that instant he thought of all the things he'd missed while holed up in the Abbey, and wondered whether he would have been better off with what most regarded as a "normal" life. *A wife, perhaps children… Perhaps happiness…*

Just then there was a pull against his leg. And another. Stiff fingers knotting into his robes and leggings.

Bale yelped, lurching forward and colliding headfirst into Lorra's rump, sending them both to the ground.

"Fool!" Lorra cursed as she scurried to her feet. "You may be the—" She froze and sucked in a quick breath as she looked past Bale.

Horrified, Bale spun from his stomach to his back while kicking his legs. There, before him, was a pale-skinned creature, eyes bulging and dripping pus and yellow teeth snapping about a slithering, black tongue. The creature lunged toward Bale with hooked fingers, snatching greedily at him.

Bale pulled desperately away from the thing, swatting at its hands with his walking stick. His mud-covered feet slipped on the ground as he scrambled away but at last he was able to get to his feet. The garghul limped toward him, its sickly maw and bony hands snapping hungrily.

Bale's mind wheeled, searching for the words. He knew them, of course, those ancient words of divine power, but his fear had rattled him. *I am too weak for this task!*

The garghul staggered forward, its tongue flailing madly about its wide mouth. Its protruding eyes swiveled wildly, looking at both Bale and Lorra from head to toe as though seeking the most succulent meat.

What are the words? Curse my cowardice!

Lorra shrieked and jumped in front on Bale, a rock brandished in her hand. She reared her arm back and struck, bashing the garghul squarely in the face with a sharp crack.

The garghul stumbled back several steps, clutching at its face. With a gurgle it dropped its hands, revealing half of its jawbone detached and dangling and oozing green pus. It pressed its hands to its face once again, convulsed, then ripped the dangling piece clean from its skull to leave in its place its whipping tongue and wheezing throat. It lunged forward once again, seizing Lorra by the shoulders with its pointed fingers.

At last Bale remembered. *Illienne abralide y ganode*

allum! Illienne awaken and give me light! He whispered the words and leveled his gaze at the beast. "No!" he commanded, his voice booming in the narrow corridor. Bale's hands erupted with a white flame, bathing the entire tunnel in blinding, brilliant light.

The garghul faltered back, howling and shrinking from the light.

"Be gone!" Bale said, courage filling him.

"Dead gods," Lorra hissed beside him, "there are more of them!"

Bale looked beyond the squirming garghul and saw at least a dozen of its brethren cowering behind it. "Run," he breathed.

"Run!" Lorra screamed, snatching him by the forearm and yanking him down the passage toward the temple.

Bale's concentration faltered and the light failed. He tumbled forward as fast as he could in the tight corridor, trying to ignore the sounds of chomping maws and shuffling steps and awful moans behind him.

At last they spilled into the waning daylight, into the mud-soaked street. Bale jerked his head about, trying to locate the gold dome of the temple.

There it was. Only a few dozen yards down the wide road was a foreboding façade showing no withering from age, with a gleaming dome defying the stormy skies above. They charged toward it, Bale's clumsy legs nearly knotting themselves as he ran. *Sweet Illienne please spare your loyal servant!*

The moans followed them. Bale chanced a backward glance and saw the garghuls leering from the darkness of the tunnel, seemingly uncertain of whether to venture into the fading light.

After a mad dash through the sucking mud they reached the temple's stairs, ascended them two at a time, and finally reached the temple's massive doors. The entrance consisted of two giant slabs of granite, each at least twelve feet tall. They were carved with hundreds of intricate symbols, and each slab had in its center a great ring of blackened metal.

Bale looked back again. The garghuls were emerging from the tunnel. "Pull!" he shouted, grabbing the black ring before him. Lorra's hands joined his upon the ring. Bale tugged with all his might, his spine snapping and popping with the effort.

Yet, the door did not move.

"Pull!" he demanded again.

"I *am* pulling!" Lorra snapped.

More moans. Closer this time.

Bale dropped his hands from the ring. It was no use. He searched feverishly about the surface of the doors, looking for some hinge or keyhole or trigger but there was nothing. Only carvings in the rock. Letters from languages long dead, languages even he had not encountered in spite of years sequestered in the Abbey's library.

He swept his eyes across the lines of archaic text, and after a moment it struck him that each line was written in a different language. The text changed, from swirling script to angular runes to strange hieroglyphs. He focused on the last, hoping he'd be able to make some sense of it.

The hieroglyphs were a series of pictograms, first a

robed man kneeling, then him with an open mouth and outstretched hands, then a sun shining upon him, then an open portcullis. *That's it. But what words must be spoken to open the door?*

The shuffling steps of the garghuls, or hobblers as Lorra had called them, were dangerously loud. He peered over his shoulder and saw them—more than a dozen—spread across the street and less than fifty feet away.

"Sweet Illienne," he pled, "please allow your servant to enter!"

He waited for a moment but there was nothing.

He studied the symbols again and thought once more of the temple's origins. He remembered the tales of the builders dedicating the place to the Sentinels. *To the Sentinels.* He pressed a finger to his lips. *The words must be spoken to them. Some verse honoring them as our protectors.*

His mind whirled, sifting through all those many, many books he'd read, through countless poems and outlawed prayers. As he thought, one more than any other pressed upon him. It was the very oldest one he knew, a prayer said to have been uttered by the Sentinels themselves, with High King Deranthol about the Godswell, the very place where Illienne and Yrghul descended into oblivion. He could think of no verse more ancient or significant, so he dropped to a knee before the doors, breathed deeply, and spoke:

The Goddess paled from her great divide,
And fell below, her dark twin denied,
And in her place left eight divine,
To serve her stead 'til end of time.

Bale looked hopefully at the doors but nothing happened. He nervously tucked his hair behind his ears and wondered whether the prayer—which included the High King in the numbering of Illienne's partition— would offend the Sentinels. *Some other prayer, perhaps?*

But just then there came a clicking sound, as though a tumbler had shifted. Bale quickly stood and pulled again at the black ring. The door opened with ease.

"Inside!" he exclaimed. Once more he glanced over his shoulder and saw the hideous garghuls stumbling up the steps of the temple, not more than ten feet behind them.

Lorra darted within and then Bale spun inside and tugged the giant door shut. It closed with a harsh clanking sound, like a smith's hammer upon an anvil, and shut out every last ray of light.

About them was nothing but a deep, silent blackness.

23
ENEMIES EVERYWHERE

PREFECT GAMGHAST LOOKED at the massive wall of stone before him and tapped his fingers against his staff impatiently. He was a thousand feet from the Bastion, standing before an iron grate that served as the end point of the castle's sewers. He huffed and rapped for a third time at the grate with the tip of his staff then looked about his dark surroundings for unwanted eyes. He'd grown suspicious of every stare, doubtful of the sincerity of every smile. He'd even found himself keeping odd hours, only leaving the Abbey in the late evening when the streets were less crowded, and then lying awake at night with his eyes fixed to his door. He pulled his robes close. *There are enemies everywhere.*

There came no answer. He tugged at the unruly wisps of his white beard, cleared his throat and rapped again. As he waited for a reply he looked at the sewage seeping from the grate and into a gutter between his feet, a flow of lumpy liquid lit by the nearly full moon above. Gamghast was a practical man who abhorred luxury, but all of this skulking about amidst shadows and filth was a bit much even for him.

He peered through the grate and into the shadows beyond. There was no sign of movement, and the only sound was that of the slopping sewage. It was bad enough having to enter the Bastion through such uncommon means, but having to wait so long near the sewers in the dead of night was even worse.

A few more moments passed, and Gamghast turned and began walking away. *To think, a prefect of the Sanctum treated with such disregard. How times have changed...*

"Prefect," came a deep voice behind him.

Gamghast turned, relieved but exasperated. Tannin, a thick-necked soldierly sort who served as one of the queen's personal guards, stood on the other side of the grate holding a dimmed lantern. Tannin adjusted the veiled, rounded helmet atop his head and motioned Gamghast over.

"These are troubled times," Gamghast said. "You should have been here precisely at nine o'clock, as agreed. It's dangerous for someone to wait here so long after nightfall, considering the state of things."

"Sorry, sir," Tannin said, his big hands fumbling through the pockets of his red jerkin before pulling out a key. "It's been an eventful evening."

"Yes, yes, yes..." Gamghast grumbled, doing little to conceal his frustration.

"Indeed, sir. An argument between a few of Chamberlain Alamis's men and some of the High King's guard. I thought for a moment we'd be drawing arms inside the castle. Thank the dead gods for the queen's level head.

She calmed things before blood was spilled." He turned the key in the lock and pulled the gate open.

"Oh," Gamghast said, his annoyance suddenly forgotten. He stooped inside the open grate and into the tunnel. It was a wide corridor hollowed out of the rock, through which flowed a shallow but steady stream of waste, both human and otherwise. "An argument?"

"And not the only heated words since your last visit. Chamberlain Alamis and his attendants have been rather… *bold* of late. The lack of support from the more powerful nobles like Thane Brandiss hasn't helped things. Indeed, only five of Rune's eight thanes have committed their oath-bound to the war." Tannin looked nervously about. "But I've said too much already. I'm certain the queen will tell you all you need to know." He gestured with his lantern toward the upward incline of the dark tunnel ahead.

Gamghast knew Tannin to be a circumspect fellow who took his duties seriously. Pressing the man likely would be of no use, but this was ominous news. He decided upon a different tack. "And the queen? Has she been in good health, and in good spirits? Other than tonight, of course?"

"She's been keeping to herself whenever possible."

Gamghast gathered his robes in a fist to keep them from dragging through the muck as he walked. "But what of her emotional state? That can be as important as a woman's physical health during a pregnancy. Is there anything I should know as her, ah, physician?"

Tannin was silent for a time before speaking. "It's been difficult for her. I don't know how she could keep from being upset with all that's happened. I've seen her crying. And more than once."

"The queen and I discuss a great many things during my visits," Gamghast said as he braced himself against the tunnel's moist wall and stepped around a pool of sewage. "Are there any topics I should avoid, to keep from upsetting her?"

Tannin eyed him for a moment and Gamghast sensed anger in the man's gaze. "Avoid anything having to do with Chamberlain Alamis," said Tannin, coldly.

"That's an awfully large topic to avoid," Gamghast said, ducking as they ascended into a more constricted part of the tunnel. "Anything more specific?"

Tannin rubbed at his chin for a time and then spat. "Dead gods. The queen trusts you, so I will as well. The war with the Arranese has been a disaster. Nearly all the lands south of Riverweave have been lost. Alamis has decided to seize advantage of the situation, challenging High King Deragol's authority openly. He and those loyal to him mock the High King's madness and talk of the spoils they'll divide upon his death."

"Those *loyal* to Alamis?"

"Aye. The chamberlain's found support among some of the thanes, and some powerful commoners as well. They circle the throne like vultures about the dying."

Gamghast felt his face flush with outrage. "How can this be? The queen is with child! The High King's line remains intact!"

"The queen hasn't made her pregnancy known, and eight miscarriages have left many doubtful, especially our enemies. Many refer to High King Deragol as 'The Last King.' They're convinced he'll die without an heir, and Alamis and his allies believe they're poised to take the throne."

Gamghast quickened his pace and gritted his teeth. "This is blasphemy!"

Tannin frowned as they trudged up the tunnel. "It seems few share your faith, Prefect."

How times have changed, indeed.

"Through there," Tannin said, gesturing with the lantern toward the round door at the tunnel's side.

Gamghast nodded, too winded from the climb to speak. He thrust his walking staff into the muck below and pressed himself along for the last few steps. Tannin pushed ahead and opened the door, and Gamghast gave him a grateful but weary smile as he pulled him through the door.

Beyond the door was a storeroom, full of hammers and saws and pliers and all the other sorts of instruments used to keep the mechanical parts of the Bastion in working order. Within the room also was a washbasin and a clean set of clothes, just as arranged.

Tannin excused himself, indicating to Gamghast he'd wait outside. Gamghast nodded and dipped his hands in the water, glad to find it cool. After letting his hands linger there for a moment before he pressed them to his face and rubbed off the mix of sweat, grime and water with a towel. He noticed his hands shaking.

The garments were the beige robes of a common servant, complete with a hood large enough to conceal one's entire face in shadow. Such hoods were a tradition in the Bastion, intended as a symbol of humility before the throne. *A custom inspired by vanity, but in these times suited to my purpose.* He pulled the hood overhead and exited the room.

The opulence of the Bastion never ceased to astound Gamghast. Countless golden sconces lined the walls, illuminating the place with soft candlelight. Ornate tapestries told of the brave deeds of yesteryear and sculptures memorialized forgotten heroes long dead. Servants darted about in a rush to tend to the evening comforts of the Bastion's more prominent residents and visiting dignitaries, carrying pots of spiced tea and trays laden with pastries. Gamghast shook his head in disgust. *Meanwhile, there is a war afoot.*

"It's much quieter, now," Tannin said, looking about the vast hallway. "Earlier this night these halls were booming with threats and curses."

"Nevertheless," Gamghast said as he looked about, "let's move quickly. If Chamberlain Alamis has grown as brazen as you've described, then my visits must be as brief and discrete as possible."

They navigated the haphazard passages of the Bastion, turning left and then right and then jogging straight ahead. Gamghast kept his head deep in the recesses of his hood, his eyes trained upon Tannin's cuffed, sewage-caked boots. His ears, though, were open to all things, and he listened intently to the hushed chatter of the domestics. They spoke in tense whispers of the earlier discord Tannin had described. *"It was horrifying, I say!" "Chamberlain Alamis is an awful sort, of course, but is he right?" "Should we flee this place?"*

They moved into quieter areas of the vast castle, walking through lonely hallways lined with empty chambers. An occasional voice echoed through the vaulted corridors, but otherwise all seemed still.

Gamghast was just about to pull off his hood when Tannin halted and threw a hand back, pressing Gamghast against a wall.

"Be still and silent," Tannin hissed. "This is dangerous."

Gamghast did as told, doing his best to assume the meek demeanor of a castle underling. He receded against the wall. As he stood he heard the click-clack of many boots approaching. There were loud, boasting voices among them, and it sounded like a group of men inspired by too much drink.

"You, there!" came a sneering voice.

"Dead gods," whispered Tannin.

"You're the lout who dared threaten me! The very fool who told my men that if they drew their steel their heads would be rolling across this floor! Are you so courageous now? Now that you're alone?"

Tannin squared himself to the group of men, and Gamghast saw his hand pressed upon the pommel of his sheathed sword.

"Well?" came the sneering voice again. "Still the hero? Still ready to apprehend us all?"

There was the sound of a few hard steps upon the marble tiles. Gamghast tilted his head slightly, chancing a look from the shadows of his hood. Tannin's challenger had come to within a few yards of them. He was a full head or more shorter than Tannin, with a swollen face and jaundiced eyes. A half dozen men stood behind him, all of them armed and all of them bearing the flushed complexions of drunks. None wore coverings on their heads, in blatant defiance of tradition.

"Sir Edren of Pyrene," Tannin said, his voice quiet but stern. "You stand in the High King's castle, upon sacred ground. You stand in these halls and dishonor the High King and his ancestors. I would remind you the High King still sits upon the throne, and so long as he does Rune is ruled by him and him alone."

Edren laughed nasally, the sound of it grating. "Such courage! Such ignorance! Why doesn't the High King simply command you to cast us from these hallowed halls? Command you to put us all in chains? Order you to banish the chamberlain? But he does not. He does none of these things because he is weak, and weak-minded."

Gamghast noticed Tannin's hand tightening about the hilt of his sword.

"You speak treasonous words," Tannin said.

"Treason? Against whom? Every man of substance has seen how power has shifted. You've heard of General Fane's change of allegiance, haven't you? No? General Thalius Fane himself has allied with Chamberlain Alamis, and he announced it in the cleverest of fashions. You see, the High King recently ordered him removed from his post. General Fane sent back the scroll, wrapped about the severed fingers of the messenger who'd delivered it." He laughed again. "Your High King has no power, not even beneath his own roof."

"The thanes will not stand for such treachery!"

"No? Why don't they come, then? Why doesn't Thane Brandiss ride down from Stormfall, or Thane Meledin sail from Farwatch to save the High King? Or any of the others? Why? Because they are powerless, just like the High King. Just like you."

There came then the ring of many swords being drawn from their scabbards. Tannin drew his own, stepping back into a defensive crouch.

Edren chuckled. "I'll enjoy seeing you skewered like a pig."

"Gentlemen!" called a voice from down the hallway.

Gamghast recognized the sound and it frightened him far more than the weapons wielded nearby. He turned with as much subtlety as his panicked nerves would allow, at the same time pressing back against the wall.

"There's no need for bloodshed," Chamberlain Alamis said, his blue velvet robes whispering as he strode toward them. "Not *just* yet."

Gamghast tipped his head low, allowing the hood to drape over as much of his face as possible. *Might he still recognize me? Dead gods!* He drew his shaking hands upward, pressing them against his chin in hopes of concealing his unruly beard beneath the cuffs of his sleeves.

"Sir Edren," Alamis said, his voice smooth and serene, "we should allow the High King's guard some measure of latitude. He is a simple man, strictly following orders. He is not in a position to grasp the reality of our situation."

Gamghast gnashed his teeth, eyes madly searching his limited view—the floor, mostly—for signs that things were calming. It seemed Tannin had relaxed a bit, as his knees were no longer bent and he no longer balanced on the balls of his feet. Gamghast breathed easier as he watched Tannin return his sword to its scabbard.

"Sir Edren?" Alamis asked expectantly.

"Very well," said Edren, his tone thick with disappointment. "Another time, though. I'll not suffer insult from a mongrel such as this." He sheathed his sword in dramatic fashion.

"Oh," said Alamis, "there will be another time. Most assuredly there will. I've taken careful note of all who've proclaimed their loyalty to the dead traditions of the past, of all who've implied there's treason in speaking aloud the hard truths which must be spoken. The past is waning, and there will be a new history written." He moved again among the men and laughed smugly. "There will be a reckoning, gentlemen, and these halls will be swept clean of their relics."

Edren snorted and expelled a glob of spittle upon the polished marble. "Keep your sword ready, boy. You'll need it soon."

Tannin straightened his spine but said nothing.

Alamis and his followers laughed and marched down the hall. "Skewered like a pig," Edren said over his shoulder.

When they'd moved out of sight Gamghast let out a shuddering breath and lowered his trembling hands. "How can this be?" he said weakly.

Tannin cursed. "Edren is right, in one regard leastways. The High King lacks the strength to take action against Chamberlain Alamis. Even if he were in better health things would be difficult. Many of Rune's soldiers are off to war with the Arranese. Within the Bastion, Alamis has as many arms loyal to him as the High King has guards. The thanes are divided, and some seem to be courting Alamis's favor. They likely think Alamis will help them lay claim to the throne, though it seems Alamis intends to do so himself."

He stamped his boot against the tiles, his face bent with anger. "This news of General Fane is most troubling."

"She's not safe here. Neither is the High King."

"But where could they go? What is a king without a castle?"

"There must be a place," said Gamghast, doing his best to sound more confident than he was.

Tannin eyed him suspiciously. "Alamis will squat on the throne the very moment it's abandoned. High King Deragol cannot leave this place or there will be chaos." He rubbed at his square chin. "The queen, though, could take a holiday, for instance. Such departures are not uncommon. But to where? Her family hails from Riverweave, which may soon be under siege."

Gamghast thought of the Lector, of the Sentinel Castor, and the many centuries he dared to hide in the very shadow of the Bastion. *Could we do such a thing?* He breathed deeply. "There are places not so far away. Places where Queen Reyis could seek shelter until this storm abates."

They found Queen Reyis at the place they'd arranged, a servant's quarters far removed from the more well traveled halls of the Bastion proper. She arose from a simple chair and moved through a clutch of attendants to greet them. As she approached, Gamghast could not help but be warmed by the woman's radiant beauty, the cascade of her flaxen hair and the glow in her cheeks. She was elegant and stately, and Gamghast dropped to creaky knees before her.

"Rise," she said. "There is no need—or time— for formalities."

Gamghast did as asked, struggling upright. He met the queen's gaze, noticing the dark rings surrounding her eyes and the worry woven upon her brow. *Sweet Illienne, why are our most difficult trials set upon us when we are weakest?* He drew back the hood of his robes. "We must speak privately."

Reyis turned to her attendants, several young women and a withered old man. "Please, leave us."

The young women moved swiftly to the door, and the old man—clearly blind—shuffled behind while tapping a long switch before him. Tannin followed but stopped near the door and gave a quick look to Gamghast. "I'll be outside," he said. "Ready."

Reyis's eyes lingered upon the door for a moment after it had closed and then her gaze rejoined Gamghast's. "You appreciate our danger here, Prefect?"

Gamghast tugged at his beard. "Chamberlain Alamis is consumed by his lust for power. He desires only the throne, and has allied himself with many foes. I have already warned you of his dealings with the Necrists. Now it seems he has courted others to his cause, as well."

Reyis's head drooped. "You have no idea how these betrayals have cut my husband. They were childhood friends. Alamis was the son of one of the members of High King Derandale's council, and as boys he and Deragol hunted together, fenced together, traveled together. All of those things young men of privilege do." She sniffled and pressed her fingers to her eyes.

"I never knew."

"When Deragol's episodes began six years ago, after my second miscarriage, Alamis was the most loyal of friends, the most caring. He would sit with me at my husband's side, soothing his brow until the tremors subsided. But the madness worsened and Deragol weakened. After a time, Alamis seemed to view it as an opportunity." She clenched her hands into fists and her expression darkened. "I could see the change in his eyes—how he looked at my husband with disgust and at the throne with envy. He was a friend only so long as friendship served ambition. The moment he sensed an avenue to power, he seized upon it."

"Does he know?"

"Of this?" she asked, pressing a hand to the swell of her belly. "Dead gods, no. I fear the moment Alamis learns of my pregnancy he'll try to terminate it by any means available to him. A drop of poison in my wine, a tumble down the stairs, even a knife in the gut... There is no evil beyond the man's grasp."

Gamghast grabbed Reyis's hand, grimacing as he realized his sudden breach of decorum. He shook his head, determined to proceed. "You cannot stay here. You are not safe, nor is your unborn child. Come with me. Tell whoever matters that you're taking a holiday, that there's trouble with your family in Riverweave. Tell them whatever it takes to get you clear of the dangers lurking in these halls."

She sniffled again and waved a hand dismissively. "I cannot. You must know Deragol is a mere shell of a man. He would not survive without me at his side. Your own Lector tried helping him, and even he could not determine the source of his illness." Her lip trembled and then she looked away. "His time may be nearing its end."

"If I may speak directly, there is far more at stake than your husband's sanity. More at stake than even his life."

Queen Reyis stared at him coldly before speaking. "Alamis would use my absence as an opening. He would seize the throne."

"He may do so anyway, even with you walking these halls." He regarded the queen grimly. "High King Deragol is beyond our grasp, now. It is you who carries the future of Rune."

"No," she said. "I will not abandon him in this state, and I will not hand Alamis yet another advantage. Many who've remained loyal to my husband would waiver if not for my presence here."

"Please, my queen. Time is not in our favor. Chamberlain Alamis is winning new alliances every day. The Arranese are marching and soon may be at Ironmoor's gates. And what is more, your pregnancy will soon be visible to all."

"But that will give people hope."

"Or it will give Alamis all of the motivation he needs to strike. Consider it, at least."

Queen Reyis glared at Gamghast, but soon her eyes softened. "I will consider it, Prefect."

"Don't wait too long. There is great danger here."

Queen Reyis's shook her head. "No. Not just here. Everywhere."

24
OLD SOLDIERS

LANNICK WALKED BRISKLY along the cobblestoned street, pulling his green cloak about his shoulders. It was a dreary night, with rain falling from heavy clouds aglow from the full moon behind them. All about the street were shadows. Black shadows fell from the wooden buildings crowding the street, dropped from every chimney and every lamppost, and sat like thick pitch in the innumerable spaces between the cobbles.

"Stay clear of the deep shadows," Ogrund had told him when he'd left the Variden compound. He thought of his nightmarish journey through the shadowpaths, dragged along by the hideous Shodafayn wearing the faces of his dead children. His hand drifted to his satchel and he found the outline of the box holding his Coda, just next to his whiskey flask. He wondered which of the two he'd need first.

There came from behind him the muffled echo of

footsteps. He glanced over his shoulder to peer back along the dark street and spotted a figure thirty or so feet behind him. In the dark everything seemed comprised of shadows, and he couldn't identify a Necrist at this distance without his Coda. He quickened his pace.

This was one of the oldest parts of Ironmoor, built along the remnants of the city's original wall. It had a haunting feel to it. Between the rows of run-down homes were the ruins of old battlements and the graves of old soldiers. Few homes showed any sign of habitation, with candlelight spilling only rarely from fogged windows.

Nine o'clock tolled from a far-off belfry. After the rings faded Lannick listened for other sounds hidden amidst the drumming rain. There was still the faint sound of footsteps, but when he glanced back he saw the figure was farther behind him. *Probably not a Necrist, and probably not chasing me.* He took a deep breath and exhaled, wondering if he'd ever feel safe without the company of a stiff drink.

A few hundred feet ahead was his destination, Gregor's Watch, a stout tower silhouetted against the ghostly gloom of the sky. The tower was one of the few landmarks in Ironmoor not named for this or that High King. Rather, it was erected in honor of a brave soldier, a commoner, who'd singlehandedly repelled a score of enemy besiegers from a breach in the wall centuries before, saving countless lives. Lannick had always known Brugan to have a flair for the dramatic, and guessed the location of the meeting had been chosen with such inspiration.

As he approached he saw torchlight near the tower.

There were faces, also, flickering within the shadows of hooded cloaks. Six figures stood beside a door at the tower's base, and Lannick reckoned these were others Brugan had summoned to the meeting.

He came closer and the faces resolved out of the darkness. There was an anvil-jawed fellow with eyes set deeply in their sockets. It was Kevlin, a brawny sheepherder who'd wielded a deadly axe at the battle of Pryam's Bay. Beside him was another familiar face, a thin man with a closely-cropped beard flecked with gray. Cudgen Ashworn, the very man who'd placed arrows in the skulls of two Tallorrathian soldiers standing before Lannick on that hellish night.

There were others, too, whose faces he recognized. Valiant fighting men who'd stormed the shores of Pryam's Bay with him, put the invaders to the sword, and helped rescue General Fane. He cursed the memory and the cruelty of fate.

Lannick slowed as he looked them over, wondering what they'd think of their old captain. These were the very men who'd cheered him after the battle, men who'd carried him up Ironmoor's winding streets to the Bastion when they'd arrived home.

But what will they think of me now? It felt as though the last nine years had left a stain visible to any who'd known him before he'd fallen so far. His hand wandered to the flask he kept in his satchel. *Can I do this?*

The door opened and the men filed inside. Lannick caught sight of many more men within the tower—the room seemed filled with old soldiers.

"Lannick!" came a shout from behind him.

Lannick jumped at the sound, his hand moving instinctively to his sword before he saw it was Brugan brandishing a grin that ran from ear to ear.

"You filthy rascal!" Brugan said, his voice hearty and cheerful. He lumbered over to Lannick and grabbed him in a bear hug, squeezing hard and hoisting him upward. "I'm glad you came, lad. I admit I was worried you wouldn't show."

"B-Brugan…" Lannick said, gasping for breath and wincing from the pain of old wounds. He smiled gratefully when Brugan dropped him back to the cobblestones and released him. Brugan continued toward the door but Lannick stopped him short. "I can't. Not just yet."

Brugan placed a hand on his shoulder and gave him a knowing look. "The first steps are always the hardest, Lannick."

Lannick shrugged. "It's a tough task, Brugan. Tough for any man."

Brugan gestured toward the door. "Well now you're about to have a whole company of good soldiers willing to help you."

"But that's just it. I can't bear the thought of letting them down again. What if we aren't up to this task? What if Fane and his Scarlet Swords get the better of us again? I want vengeance, but I'm not sure others should be risking their lives to help me. And what's more, I'm not exactly the same man I was back then."

"Lannick, you have it in you. I know because I've seen it. And you'd only let these men down by *not* trying to set things right. You aren't the only one Fane wronged, and these men are bitter over how they were treated after

Pryam's Bay. What's more, these are men who see Rune falling to pieces and its armies being led to death by the very man who betrayed them. Many of these old soldiers have relatives—sons, even—fighting under General Fane and perhaps dying as a result of that madman's arrogance and incompetence. They've heard of the deserters leaving Fane's Third Column and massing near the Silverflow River." His grip on Lannick's shoulder tightened and his eyes glared intensely. "They just need a little push. They need a leader."

"The nerves are still shaky, Brugan. This will not be an easy thing."

"Nothing worth doing ever is."

The interior of Gregor's Watch was a wide, round room, filled with a few benches, a few tables, and perhaps two dozen rough men who'd seen better days. Pigeons cooed and fluttered in the high rafters overhead, stirred by the clamor below.

Brugan exchanged cheery handshakes with the men nearby while Lannick slipped into a darkened nook in the wall, eager to avoid notice for a bit longer. A few of the men's eyes found him, though, and he felt his cheeks flush the moment they did. The gazes seemed hard and angry, and Lannick knew they blamed him for their troubles after the last war.

"Well, lads!" said Brugan loudly, arms wide as he moved to the room's center. "Here we are. A long overdue reunion of the *real* heroes of Pryam's Bay!"

"You're right, dead gods be damned," said one of them. The rest grumbled their agreement.

Brugan meandered between the tables and benches, hands clasped behind him as he inspected the men just like he'd done when he was Lannick's sergeant, all those years ago. "You've all heard of General Fane's latest blundering effort."

"Bastard," cursed a man.

Brugan nodded in agreement. "You're damned right he's a bastard! And the very worst one at that!" He pointed a finger and swept it across the room. "We were all there together, at Pryam's Bay. We remember our sacrifices on that cursed night. How we lost so many friends and shed so much blood to save Rune and win the war against Tallorrath. And we also remember what happened after that, don't we?"

More grumbling followed, the men's heads bobbing in agreement and their eyes fixed firmly on the big barkeep. Lannick smirked, remembering how he'd always left the speeches to Brugan.

Brugan spat. "When we all thought we'd be gaining promotions and notoriety and all of those good things after that war, he stole them from us! He forced us to retire, with no ceremony or pension or even a damned thank you. When we complained, he threw us in the brig, just like he did to old Cudgen there!" Brugan's voice sank low and his eyes narrowed. "We were forced to abandon the only livelihood we knew—soldiering—and we were cast out like lepers while Fane and his Scarlet Swords claimed glory."

The men shook their heads and hissed.

"And we also remember what happened *before* the battle, don't we?" Brugan continued. "Those hapless, irrational decisions, those hints that Fane wasn't right in the head? Of course we do. We remember how General Fane nearly lost the entire war. We remember how he left us at midday, so prim and pompous on his black steed, telling us to hold our positions while he and his Scarlet Swords delivered 'the master stroke.' How he and his small group of so-called elite fighters would surprise the enemy on those icy shores, set fire to their ships, and drive them from Rune. We remember how he so desired to claim victory alone and keep us from the spoils. We remember how he thought he could do all of that without us. Without *us*! Without the very men whose blood and blades had gotten him that far! We remember that arrogance, and we remember how *we* had to save him from capture!"

The men shouted elatedly, urging Brugan onward.

"Well, lads, now is our chance! Some of you have sons, others brothers or nephews or friends, fighting under Fane's heavy fist right now. And if that's not enough, all of you have heard the whispers in the streets. Those softly spoken worries that Rune—*Rune itself!*—is losing a war against an enemy who is not our match. And why does this happen?" Brugan paused, looking about the room. "Why? Because the wrong man is leading our armies. The wrong man is ordering good men to war. The very bastard who betrayed each and every one of us."

"Dead gods, Brugan," called out a man. It was Cudgen Ashworn, the archer from Pryam's Bay. "What nonsense are you selling here? You want *us* to march? To march south and fight the Arranese? We're well past our prime, and General Fane would likely gut any one of us on sight."

"Cudgen," Brugan said, moving closer to the man, "I have our leader. Our weapon against Fane and his bastards." He gestured boldly toward Lannick. "Captain?"

Lannick cringed. He hadn't anticipated this. Some if not many of the men loathed him. He had no tongue for inspiring speeches, only clever lies. He had no plan, no idea how he could pull off this whole endeavor. It seemed so impossible, so implausible. *I have no right to ask anything of these men.*

"Captain Lannick deVeers?" Cudgen said, his tone something between mockery and utter disbelief. "You're telling me I should follow *him* again, after all the good it did me last time 'round?"

Brugan silenced him and the rest with a stern gaze. After a moment he gestured again. "Captain?"

Lannick took a tentative step forward. Brugan clapped, looking about the room as though urging others to join him. A few did, though most remained still and silent.

Soon the room quieted but for the restless pigeons in the rafters above. Lannick stood there for what felt like far too long a time, saying nothing as his mind reeled to find words. In the faces of the men he found nothing, just skeptical stares and blank gazes. Brugan looked at him with a wide smile, which Lannick swore was wavering. *I cannot craft a speech. What can I say to these men?*

He cleared his throat and took a few more strides forward, trying to look as though he was about to say something thoughtful. He was nervous, though, sensing that palpable shame, that sinking feeling in his guts that these men knew him to be no more than a drunken wretch, a man unworthy of anyone's trust.

He dropped his eyes from theirs, and as he did he caught sight of his sword. He remembered Brugan asking him whether there was any meaning in him wearing a blade once more. *"The sword's for the bastard who's tormented me for nearly a decade,"* he'd said. He placed his hand on the pommel and gripped it hard. There was comfort in the steel.

He watched his knuckles whiten on the hilt and in his mind he saw it. Fane standing over him as he lay bleeding and broken in the brig. Fane preening before him like some perverse peacock, his red surcoat precisely tailored, his boots polished to a keen shine. A sick smile twisting his scarred face into a grotesque knot. Gloating over the horrors he'd wreaked upon Lannick and his family.

Gloating.

Then Lannick realized it.

I have my hatred.

His timidity vanished, and he wore a mask of cold, indomitable hate. He cleared his throat again, this time with ferocity and resonance, and it sounded in his head like the growl of some great, predatory beast.

He could see Fane leering over him and he so desperately wished he were face to face with the man once more. He thought how he'd seize the man by his throat, and curse him with all the curses of the old hells.

Fane, you took from me my family, my pride, and very nearly my life. But I swear to you before my life ends I will take from you even more than that awful sum.

He lifted his head and beheld the men once more, his teeth bared. He ripped his sword from its sheath and held it upward, his heart thundering with its most primal emotions, rage chief among them.

I need not craft a speech. Only a word.

He reared back his head and screamed to the heavens with a force that came from every corner of his being. The pigeons on the rafters fled from that sound, alighting into the night sky through the windows carved high in the tower. It seemed for a long moment the sound of his scream rang through the old stones of Gregor's Watch.

"*Vengeance!*"

25
DEAD GODS

"I DON'T LIKE THIS place, spooker," whispered Lorra as her eyes darted about the shadows. She shivered and tossed the leg of a broken chair into the fire before her.

Bale was loath to admit it, but he agreed with her. He hunched closer to the fire they'd made at the edge of the gloomy interior of the Temple of Cirak, staring out upon the depths of the yawning chamber. In the center of the chamber stood a ring of imposing statues of the seven Sentinels, their metallic surfaces flickering in the firelight. About them were massive, intricately carved pillars stretching far above toward a domed ceiling decorated with a fresco of the War of Fates. Bale guessed it would have been an inspiring place in a gentler age, a place of reverent majesty. But now it had an unsettling quality to it and its darkness weighed heavy on the heart.

He thought again of his decision to come here and wondered at the wisdom of it. He knew little of Lyan the Just, for the ancient texts mentioned her only rarely. She was said to possess Illienne's sense of justice, but Bale surmised that could mean a variety of things. He glanced ahead to her statue, depicting her holding a sword in one hand and a set of scales in the other. *How would this banished Sentinel judge me? With her scales or with her sword?* He sighed heavily and looked upward into the dark. *What am I really here to tell her? That Castor's spirit is lost and Rune is under attack? What would possibly move her to care about such news? This is a mad endeavor.*

Lorra tugged at the sleeve of his robe. "You're sure?" she said quietly. "You're sure we should stay longer? I'm guessing the daylight will soon be gone."

Bale pressed a dangling strand of hair behind his ear. He looked at Lorra, doing his best to wear a consoling smile. "We should be safe. The Old Faith instructs that garghuls—hobblers as you call them—cannot enter holy shrines."

Lorra's eyes dropped to the fire. She was a handsome woman in the flickering light, her features more fine than severe and her wrinkled brow more dignified than dilapidated. "As long as you're sure."

Bale presented his bravest face. *Of course I'm not.* "Of course I am."

"This place feels like a tomb," she said. "No windows and no way to see the sun. It feels... angry, somehow. It stinks of the dead gods."

Bale found it difficult to maintain any pretense of courage and dropped his head. He so desperately wanted to be inspired by the temple, to be moved to valor and purpose, but instead he felt only the weight of old stones and dark shadows. The temple stirred a quiver in his chest, a disturbing fear he could not overcome.

"How long must we stay?" Lorra asked. "We've been here for an entire day or maybe longer, but I have no idea since we can't see the sun or moon or anything else. Whoever you're supposed to meet is not here, probably long gone or eaten by those hobblers. How long will you wait before you give up?"

"I don't know," he said. He felt lost and afraid, certain he would succumb to one of the many perils about him, whether it be something dreadful within the temple, the snapping maw of a garghul, or a tumble off the mountain path. He so wished to be tucked safely within the Abbey, studying an old book in the soft glow of a candle.

After a time he stood on complaining knees and shuffled toward the statues of the Sentinels. He wandered among them, seeking the slightest hint of solace. There was Thaydorne the Strong, broad-shouldered and brave and standing with an upraised sword—*Ealyr Rigellus*, or Heaven's Reaper in the modern tongue. The very blade said to have wounded Yrghul the Lord of Nightmares, the blade that allowed Illienne to drag the foul god into oblivion. There was Valis the Watchful, depicted with his head deep in his hood, keen eyes studying a far horizon. And then Kressan the Kind, bronze hands held to her heart.

He came then to the statue of Castor, progenitor of his order. The very man whose soul had passed to the friend Bale knew as Lector Erlorn. Bale rested a hand upon the statue and looked up to its wide, wise eyes. *Help me, friend, for I know not what to do.*

"Do you hear that?" Lorra hissed.

Bale froze, stilling himself and listening. Although he heard nothing, he knew Lorra's ears to be far sharper than his own and he'd grown to trust her. He listened for a moment longer and heard a scratching sound, something against the temple's stone façade. The sound of it sent an icy rush up his spine.

"You're sure they can't get in?" Lorra whispered.

"Perhaps just insects," he said with a tremor in his voice. "Or rodents. Or something like that. Certainly nothing to trouble two bold adventurers, right?"

The sound was louder this time, seemingly all about them. *What if they did enter, somehow? Are those old beliefs even true? How could we hold off so many?*

"We need to leave here the moment dawn breaks," Lorra urged. "We cannot wait for your friend any longer or those things will find a way inside."

Bale's heart thumped in his chest. He couldn't stomach the thought of dealing again with those things. There had to be an answer in the temple, some consolation for his dangerous journey. His mind whirled. He thought of the legends associated with the temple, of the story that it had been built atop an even older shrine. *Is there something more to this temple?*

The scratching sound came again, louder this time. Bale imagined dozens of garghuls standing at the temple doors, their teeth chattering and gnashing and eager for living flesh. He thought too of the Sentinel Lyan, bitter over her exile and holding no tolerance for mortal beings. *If one or the other is inside this place, that could mean a most horrible ending... I cannot do this!*

It felt suddenly as though the room had been drained of its air and there was none of it left to breathe. He gasped, feeling a shaking in his knees and a sweating in his palms. The room spun dangerously about him. He whimpered and sank to the floor, his fear and futility overwhelming. He curled his arms about his knees and shuddered. *Forgive me, Illienne...*

A loud crash sounded, from somewhere. Outside or inside he could not be sure.

Lorra sprang upward and moved ahead of him and then reached back to press a firm hand upon his shoulder. Her body tensed and her head moved slowly from side to side as though searching the room. After a time her shoulders relaxed and her stance eased. "There's nothing inside here. No breaks in the stone. We may be safe for now, but who knows how long the doors can hold... Is there another way out of here? Another part of this temple?"

Bale bit his thumb and felt a tear slip across his cheek. *The temple is built atop another shrine...* "Perhaps." He arose, cursing his weakness and angrily swiping the tear from his face.

I am too weak an instrument.

"Here!" Bale said, gesturing toward a broad tile with a shaking finger. "There's a symbol in the center of the tile. It's an old glyph meaning 'passage' or 'doorway.' This must be an entrance to whatever sits beneath this place." He inhaled deeply, thinking of the involuntarily motions of his hand when he summoned the Lector's final actions. *The 'Sacred Place,' he called it. Not the Temple of Cirak.*

There's something else, then. Something below. He took a deep breath and tried to slow his rapidly beating heart.

"Well let's go," Lorra said, holding a makeshift torch near the tile. "We'll see what's there and then leave this place."

Bale stepped away from the tile and looked to the statue of Castor. "Dare we go through with this?"

Lorra grabbed his sleeve and spat angrily. "You're asking *me*, now? After offering me a paltry handful of silver crowns and then leading me to what very well may be my grave?"

Bale sniffled and shook his head. "Sorry. The question wasn't meant for you." *Castor, what must I do?*

"Well *who*, then?" she demanded. "Are you asking those hobblers outside?"

Bale pressed his hair behind his ears. "I'm not a courageous man, Lorra." He choked back an unexpected sob and tried to calm himself. "I have no choice but to try to complete this task. I just worry I haven't the heart to do it."

Lorra regarded him with a harsh gaze but after a time her eyes softened. "You know, I have no regrets about leaving my village anymore. I'm relieved, really. I figure it's not too bad a thing if I never herd goats again, and am never again forced to, ah…" She paused and stiffened. "Let's just say I won't be awfully sad if I don't see my father and brothers anymore." Her grip on his sleeve tightened and she looked at him with earnest eyes. "I'll be your courage, Bale, when you need it."

Bale grinned but the expression sank to a frown as he

pondered the pains the woman had endured. *It's troubling that things so fragile as we are given lives so difficult.*

"Let's do this, Bale," she said. "Together."

He looked at her for a moment longer, seeing the strength in her eyes. It struck him not as a strength born of position or knowledge or talent. Rather, Bale guessed it came from having survived so many untold hardships, from having experienced the most awful betrayals. It was the unspoken strength of the beaten but not broken, that certainty within the soul that one had withstood the very worst life had to offer, and yet remained standing.

Perhaps there is some hope, then, after all.

He clenched his jaw, summoning courage, and dropped to a knee. He looked again at the glyph, noticing it was etched with a thread-thin lining of gold that glimmered in the torchlight. It was an ancient symbol in the divine language of spellcraft, the very tongue gifted to the Sentinels by Illienne long ago. He traced the glyph with a finger, silently repeating its sound, '*Ea-appar*,' in his head.

He closed his eyes and whispered the word, dreading the consequences but refusing to abandon his task.

There was at once a great rumbling, the sound of stone grinding against stone. Suddenly, the tile began to recede, dropping into the darkness below. Bale scrambled backward onto the surrounding tiles, his mouth agape.

Slowly the stone shifted, moving to reveal a narrow stairway. The stone sank into the deep darkness, and at last settled to a stop with a reverberating thud.

"I'll grab some wood for torches," Lorra said. "Then let's go."

Beneath the temple was a series of corridors, a maze of blank stones and black shadows. Bale reckoned if it weren't for the gnawing sense of fear in his gut the place would seem not unlike the Abbey in Ironmoor.

They moved slowly through the tight passageways, frequently stopping to study the darkness ahead before creeping forward. The sputtering torchlight played tricks on the eyes, causing the shadows to dance among the breaks in the stone blocks and creating the illusion of movement. Yet, there were no sounds other than those of their footfalls. Bale pressed close to Lorra, allowing her to lead the way.

"It's hard to see down here," she said quietly. "Why don't you make light like you did with those hobblers?"

Bale shook his head. "Those are divine powers. My order frowns upon their use when mortal means are available."

Lorra huffed and continued on, her pace cautious.

They walked for what seemed a good distance—perhaps a thousand yards or more—shuffling through the zigzagging halls of stone. After a time, the masonry gave way to what seemed a naturally formed cave, with a higher ceiling marked with rock formations and a rough floor that grew increasingly slick.

Lorra stopped. "There's a sound coming from ahead."

Bale froze, his apprehensions overpowering his curiosity.

"It's not what we heard earlier," said Lorra, craning her neck. "It's a rushing sound, like wind or water. And the air… Do you smell it?"

Bale leaned timidly forward and inhaled. He *did* smell it. There was a freshness, a smell like springtime rain. He nudged closer to Lorra and sensed moisture condensing on his cheeks. They moved ahead another several steps and he saw a light far ahead. It was a dim light, but a light nonetheless.

The cave suddenly seemed to assume a feel far different from the oppression of the temple above. Bale felt revived, inspired. His heart shifted and seemed lighter, less encumbered by his earlier fear. He was invigorated by his faith, feeling whatever lay ahead was something righteous, something *good*. He placed his hands on Lorra's shoulders and urged her forward. "Let's go!"

Lorra turned and grabbed his sleeve. "Don't be a fool, Bale. I still think there's something dangerous here."

Bale clucked his tongue. "My order is skilled in such things. Our divine gift is wisdom, part of which is judging good from evil. We are illuminators of truth, and I feel whatever is ahead has been touched by Illienne the Light Eternal. We need not fear!"

She looked at him skeptically. "Then you go first."

The cave expanded as they moved forward, widening from a restricting tunnel to a broad passage. The light ahead grew stronger, illuminating the dark as much as Lorra's torch. And the sound became stronger too, growing from a faint hiss to a loud rush. At times it seemed the very stones about them shook from the noise.

Soon the light ahead glowed with such strength the torch was no longer required. Lorra tossed the burning shaft into a puddle gathered near the cave's rounded edge, and the flame died with an angry hiss. The light was cast with a pure hue, which struck Bale as being quite similar to the light he was able to summon with his divine incantations.

He found himself moving with more urgency, spurred by curiosity and wonder. His fear diminished as he pressed forward, and he was filled with a certainty that whatever was ahead was the 'Sacred Place' to which Lector Erlorn had referred. The passage ahead turned and the light emanated intensely from whatever was beyond. Bale's brisk walk turned nearly into a sprint.

"Careful," Lorra said, tugging at Bale's sleeve.

He nodded impatiently, slowing but still walking with swift strides. He'd never known Lector Erlorn was an immortal Sentinel when the man was alive. Now that he was privy to this incredible truth he was filled with awe, a sense he'd been touched by divinity. And here he was, on the cusp of meeting yet another. He thought of all the books he'd read, all those dusty tomes he'd studied. It seemed to him the tales they told and the histories they recited paled when compared to encountering such powers in person.

They neared and rounded the corner, and what was before them was utterly stunning in its splendor. It was a cavern of astonishing breadth, at least a thousand feet across, set aglow with an ambient light that shimmered from the stone in many brilliant hues. Just before them, near the mouth of the cave, thundered the edge of a waterfall. As they crept closer Bale could see the water plunging into a chasm far below. About the sides of the cavern grew lush plants, leafy trees and vibrant flowers. It seemed a paradise.

The Sacred Place.

Bale stood there for a long moment, moved by the majesty of the place. As his eyes wandered he caught sight of a pavilion at the cavern's far end. It was a circular slab of white stone, ringed with seven tall pillars. Bale narrowed his eyes to sharpen his vision, and there seemed to be a solitary figure standing within the circle of pillars. He drew a shuddering breath, for he knew in his very bones this was the immortal Sentinel Lyan the Just awaiting him.

"There," he said.

"I see," said Lorra. "Is that someone there, or just another dusty old statue?"

"I'm sure of it. It's Lyan." He turned to Lorra and held her gaze. "You needn't come. I don't quite know what to expect."

"Nonsense. I've come this far and I'm not going to abandon you now."

Bale smiled. For some reason this woman comforted him and he knew he'd be braver with her at his side. "Very well. But let me handle the talking." He set off toward the pavilion upon a path of whitewashed stone that wound along the cavern's wall.

"You're sure about this, then?"

"Yes," he said. "Well, no. Not entirely. But I must follow through with it. Believe it or not, much depends upon me, and upon the success of my mission. If I succeed, it may be the entire world is saved from a horrible upheaval, a reign of terror and tragedy." *And if I fail...* He bit his lip and trudged forward.

"It *is* pretty. I guess there are worse places to have something bad happen to you."

Bale glanced about, noticing flowers of every shape and shade imaginable. The waterfall produced a heavy mist, giving the place an almost dreamlike quality, and the shifting colors of the light from the cavern walls looked very much like an ever-changing rainbow. *Certainly nothing awful could occur in a place such as this?*

He heaved a sigh and focused on the figure within the pavilion. Lyan was facing them. Bale could make out neither a face nor features, but felt the discomfort of being closely inspected. His heavy robes were draped about him yet he felt naked. He averted his eyes but did not slow his pace.

In time they'd cut the distance in half. Bale raised his head and looked toward the figure and again sensed that penetrating gaze, that unsettling feeling of unwanted eyes upon him. His pace faltered. He thought of all the questions he'd have for a Sentinel in any other circumstance, of all those many curiosities he'd ask to have satisfied. But alas, his purpose here was a grim one, and that troubled him. *What will I say? Will a mortal's desperate plea persuade a Sentinel to save the very people who cast her aside?* He slowed nearly to a stop.

"No," came Lorra's voice as she placed a firm hand upon his arm. "Finish this."

Bale breathed and took a tentative step forward. They were close now, less than a hundred feet from the pavilion. He clasped Lorra's hand with his own and redoubled his pace, determined.

"*Castor, at last,*" came a voice, stoic and commanding.

The sound was not one sensed by Bale's ears but rather his thoughts, words spoken within a hollow of his mind. Bale glanced to Lorra but her face betrayed no hint of disturbance. *I alone hear these words. How must I respond?*

He looked ahead, seeing Lyan upon the pavilion before them. She appeared to be quite tall—taller than was natural for a person—and her skin, most of it left uncovered by a shift of white silk, looked as though it was dusted with gold.

"*You are not Castor.*"

Bale felt his confidence wavering. He could see now the Sentinel's eyes were entirely black and her bald, golden pate bore the image of a set of measuring scales. As they drew closer and ascended the pavilion he realized she was even taller than he'd guessed, perhaps eight feet in height, and her frame, while feminine, was rippled with sinewy muscle. Her features were severe and her expression harsh, and she appeared quite willing to use the gold sword strapped to her exposed thigh.

"I-I am n-not Castor," Bale said, looking down to his feet. His voice shook and uncertainty swelled within him. *I am too weak an instrument!* He clenched his jaw and decided upon the introduction he'd learned by rote. "I am Acolyte Zandrachus Bale of the Ancient Sanctum of Illienne the Light Eternal."

She studied him for an uncomfortably long moment. "One of Castor's pupils. I sense his teachings in you. He is here, yes?"

Bale jerked his head upward. These words had been spoken aloud. "No."

Lyan regarded him with an unsettling look and took

a step forward to loom over him, her gold skin radiant in the cavern's shifting light. "Where, then, is he? I journeyed far to come here, and have waited many days. He dares send a mere pupil in his stead?"

Bale wanted to speak, but his head swirled and he could do naught but stammer.

Lyan leered over him. "I am immortal, pupil, but even my patience can be stretched to an ending. Tell me, where is Castor?"

Bale cleared his throat, stilled himself and stared upward into Lyan's pitch-black eyes. "Dead."

Lyan hissed sharply and leaned away. "Nonsense. Castor is immortal. If he'd left this plane I would have sensed his departure."

Bale held her gaze though it pained him to do so. He cleared his throat again, hoping to subdue the tremor in his voice. "Castor summoned you, but before he could reach this place he was murdered."

"Murdered... His mortal coil may perish, but his spirit *will* find another." She slowly circled him and Lorra, her movements lithe yet threatening. "Nevertheless, it is troubling such action would be taken against one of *us*. And if this thing did occur, I hold no doubt the killing blade was wielded by one of the many ungrateful mongrels of Rune, one of the weak-blooded descendants of those who dared question our *righteousness!*" Her brow knotted, twisting the mark of the measuring scales, and her hand fell to the pommel of her sword. "You desecrate this place with your presence, mortal. Leave me, and when you find him you will send Castor to explain himself."

"No," Bale said, wringing his hands. He looked to

Lorra and she nodded encouragingly. "You must hear me, Lyan. Castor is gone. I visited the place where he died and used the ways he taught me to observe his final moments. As far as my order can tell, his confession was never heard and his spirit never manifested among us after his death. He's lost to us."

Lyan paused and gazed toward some unseen place. "Castor is my brother, but he is a fool. Rather than treasure the gift bestowed upon him by our Mother, he chose a different path, one where only his spirit was eternal. And why did he choose this? To honor an oath to protect the very lords of Rune who'd betrayed him." She walked to one of the white pillars and pressed her golden hand upon it. "Castor's fate is a just punishment for so casually surrendering his true immortality."

Bale pinched at his chin, uncertain of what to say. He knew he was meddling in things far beyond him, delving into thoughts and emotions hardened by many centuries. He could not hope to fathom this Sentinel's mind or soften her heart. Yet, he *had* to do this. He thought of one of Lector Erlorn's old sayings: *'Character is doing what you don't want to do, for reasons you cannot avoid.'*

He breathed deeply before speaking. "Castor has asked you to return to Rune. Though I know not what he discovered, I know he warned Yrghul was returning and that Rune once again required the protection of its greatest heroes. Will you honor your oath, Sentinel?"

Lyan whirled about, anger dancing across her face. "Will *I* honor my oath?" She drew her sword and walked toward him. "You dare pose such a question?" She brought her blade even with Bale's throat. "I no longer bother with soothing the small worries of mortals, nor do I assuage their tiny concerns. You will leave this place, now, and when you find Castor you will send him to me. Your time with me has reached its conclusion. Be gone."

Suddenly Lorra sprang forward. She pressed Bale backward and moved to stand between him and the Sentinel. "No!" she screamed, her entire body trembling from the effort.

Lyan's brow raised and her mouth curled with a hint of bemusement. "And what is this filthy thing?"

Lorra puffed her chest and clenched her fists. "I'm nobody," she growled. "I'm nothing to you. But I'll not let you treat him this way. Do you realize how far he's traveled to see you? The risks he's taken? How hard it's been for him? Do you? No, you don't, because you know *nothing* of courage!"

Lyan's slight smile turned to a vicious snarl and she whipped the sword to Lorra's chest. "You will suffer for this, mortal!"

"Have at it," Lorra said, leaning forward so that the tip of the blade pressed against her sternum. "I don't fear you. But you wouldn't know anything of fear, would you? Of course you wouldn't. You can't die, so you'll never know what true courage is, or true strength. You'll never have to stare down death, or struggle to survive those moments that nearly break you. We have, so you will listen to what Bale needs to say. And if you won't, then to the old hells with you!"

Lyan tensed, but after a moment she lowered her sword and the menace faded from her gold face. "This one has some fire within her. Very well, pupil. I will allow you to speak your words, but only as gratitude for serving my brother Castor. Be brief, and be forewarned that I will not again allow insults to pass unpunished."

Bale placed a hand upon Lorra's shoulder and eased her away from the Sentinel. He smoothed his robes and looked once more into Lyan's black eyes. "Forgive us, Sentinel, for we mean no disrespect. It's just that we have endured much and cannot bear to see our task fail now. I cannot speak as Castor would, and know not the details of the message he hoped to convey. However, I do know Rune is under siege, both from without and within. Arranan and its Spider King wage war against us. What's more, the High King's chamberlain is in league with Necrists, as is the commander of Rune's armies."

Lyan's gold face was an impassive mask, her eyes merciless.

Bale breathed deeply and held her gaze, undeterred. "There are worse things, too, Sentinel. Castor warned Yrghul's power could be pulled from the Godswell, and I can attest his agents are preparing to do just that."

Lyan smiled coldly. "Then perhaps Rune is receiving justice at last. We should never have been cast out, and now Rune and its king will learn the price of arrogance."

"Then you will break your oath? You will allow Rune and its High King to fall to Yrghul's minions?"

Lyan's face darkened. "My oath, pupil, was broken long ago, but not by my choosing. My obligations to Rune and her people were forfeit the day High King Derganfel declared us traitors and cast us into exile. The day his greed and lust for power above all things blinded him to what was right and just. The day he was corrupted

406

by his petty jealousy, his mad lust to command the adulation we enjoyed from Rune's people. We were *gods* among you, mortal, and your forebears chose to defile our names rather than pray for our favor! Now you come to me and pray for my *help*, for my *forgiveness*?"

"But Castor honored his oath still!" Bale pleaded. "Can you deny his wisdom?"

"Castor is wise, but he is weak. Without us at his side he was nothing. Tell me, of what use is wisdom if it is not followed by justice?"

Bale felt the strength of conviction and took a step toward Lyan, coming to within only a few feet of her towering form. "And what, Sentinel, is justice if it is not *preceded* by wisdom? You speak only of revenge, a misguided desire for vengeance upon people buried centuries ago. You talk of your eternal nature, yet your loyalty is long dead. Illienne demanded these things of you, Sentinel!"

Lyan's hands drew forward as though she intended to wrap them about Bale's throat and she held them just before him. "You dare presume tell me what our Mother demanded? We honored Her with our mercy, pupil. We could have ripped your little kingdom apart. We could have torn your paltry castles to the ground and cast your kind to the old hells left by the Elder God. We could have wiped the land clean of your image, but instead we were merciful."

"If you fail to act now you will accomplish those very things. And when we are defeated and Yrghul's full power is wielded by our foes, do you think *they* will grant you mercy?"

Lyan took a step back. "Yrghul is sealed in oblivion. Even if your kingdom falls, such a thing could not come to pass."

"The Necrists believe the High King will die without an heir," Bale replied, recalling the discussion between General Fane and the Necrist in Riverweave, many nights before. "They say when he does, the Godswell will be open to them. They say it is written in the blood of the dead."

"Yrghul speaks to the Necrists through such means, just as Illienne speaks to us through... other ways." She paused. "Yrghul is a deceiver, though, and lies flow from his mouth as often as breath. Only one blessed by our Mother could open the portal to oblivion, and that would be a terrific undertaking. His servants, even if they've gained new power, cannot accomplish such a thing."

Bale's head filled with many worrisome possibilities. *Where is Castor's spirit? Could it have been captured? If the Sentinels carry such anger, is it so unlikely one of their number could betray us all?* "Unless," he ventured, "a Sentinel has been taken. Or turned."

"Never," she said. "Never..."

"Think of your own anger, Lyan. Think again of Castor's murder, and of our inability to find his spirit."

Lyan looked upward for a long moment, searching the cavern's heights as though the answers were written upon the stone. Then, after a deep breath, she returned her black eyes to Bale. "I will consider these things, pupil. While I do so, you will travel to Zyn, in Arranan, and there you will find my sister Kressan. You will return here with her and we will speak further of these things. Do not tarry."

Bale's eyes fell to the white marble floor and his shoulders slumped. He felt at once relieved and encumbered. The weight of his task had grown even heavier. "But how will I find her? Arranan is a hard country, and Zyn is a large and..." he swallowed, "dangerous city."

"Castor taught you his ways and wisdom, yes? Divination? The seeking stones?"

"Uh, why yes," Bale said, his hand finding the sleeve of reagents he carried.

"Let me touch the stone. My essence will allow you to find Kressan, and the others."

Bale did as Lyan asked, all the while wondering how an instrument such as he could possibly complete the task before him. How could he ever survive this?

Sweet Illienne please spare your loyal servant.

26

THE MOST DANGEROUS BEAST

FENCRESS FALLCROW SCRATCHED her horse's neck, knowing the animal was faring little better than she. They'd spent weeks tracking Merek toward Ironmoor and hadn't seen a decent meal or a reasonable stretch of rest, so she worried another gallop right now might be the mare's last. She reckoned the only option she had—other than hoping to stumble upon a group of road-weary travelers with fresher horses—was to bet the long odds. Maybe Merek hadn't yet slaughtered Karnag with the help of the Sanctum at their Abbey.

Maybe.

She thought of the past several weeks. How she'd hauled herself and her companions across a field of the dead and the dying, and how they'd dragged themselves over ragged hillsides, through prickly bogs, and across vast stretches of desolate land. How they'd nearly starved, and how they'd barely escaped a patrol mistaking them for Arranese spies. Fencress ripped away the cap of her flask with her teeth and took a long pull of whiskey she'd stolen from a merchant's wagon. Weaker folk would've died, but she'd not allow such a thing.

She gazed at Karnag's gigantic sword, *Gravemaker* he'd called it, slung along the side of her horse. She'd found it near Karnag's pile of human parts, still wet with blood and crusted with gore. Perhaps her friend would survive long enough to use it once more. *But to what end?* She gulped down the burning whiskey and grimaced.

The road ahead was paved with flagstones and lined with pennants snapping smartly in the warm afternoon breeze. About them rose low hills covered with heather and sedge, and the air had a brackish taint to it. They were close to the sea, and that meant they weren't far from Ironmoor and its Abbey.

"How far, Paddyn?" Fencress asked, looking askance at the young archer. The lad's grubby cheeks were sunken and his torn clothes were wrapped about him like a leper's bandages. She looked at her own threadbare shirt and knew she looked nearly as wretched. *Alas, dapper looks and daring deeds are rarely partnered.*

"Five leagues or less," Paddyn croaked, his voice raspy. "We should arrive shortly after nightfall."

"If we last that long," said Drenj from behind him. "Remind me again, Fencress, what exactly you hope to gain from this deranged venture? Why are we doing this?"

"Because Karnag is my friend," Fencress said, the force of her voice surprising. "Because Karnag is my friend, and because we were betrayed. I'll not rest until my knives have known the red center of Merek's heart, and neither should you. No one wrongs us and lives to boast about it, friend. No one."

"This is madness," huffed Drenj. "You're sounding like *him*, Fencress. We should be somewhere safe. Spending our gold while this war ruins those foolish enough to fight it. Karnag chose his course, but that shouldn't mean we're bound to it."

Fencress tugged at her gloves, tightening them against her hands. "Long ago, in my glorious youth, I was an acrobat with a traveling circus. For a time we had in our company an old Khaldisian animal trainer, Alil, who worked with all manner of beast, from falcons to dogs to horses. We even had a white tiger from Arranan. Every now and again Alil would have too much ale and entertain the audience by goading the animals, tugging their ears or pulling at their tails. In his final show, he thought to tease the tiger, slapping its nose and belching in its face. The tiger endured this for a short while, but then ripped free of its chains and tore Alil's head clean off, showering the screaming crowd with blood."

Drenj sniffed. "Is there some meaning to this charming tale?"

Fencress pulled at the rim of her cowl. "Never provoke the most dangerous beast."

Prefect Gamghast looked at his window, the rain tapping against the bleary glass with only a haze of gray beyond. The sun was no more than a smear in the leaden sky. *Dare we shelter hope in such times?*

"It's been a long while, Prefect," said Merek from

across the table. "A long while indeed since we've found the need to work together. I'd guess it's been nearly a decade since you and I have spoken. I'd say I'm happy to see you, Gamghast, but the fact that we *need* each other again is a most ominous sign."

Gamghast tugged at the white wisps of his beard. "You know nothing of an acolyte from the Abbey? Nothing of Acolyte Bale? I'd dispatched him south to seek answers to the questions posed by Lector Erlorn's death."

Merek shook his head of greasy hair. "Nothing, Prefect, but then I did not make it as far as the site of the murder. It's possible your acolyte is still searching the south, or even journeying homeward. But, then, all battles leave dead soldiers, I'm afraid."

Gamghast sighed. *Sweet Illienne please spare your loyal servant Bale.*

"If it is an answer you seek, Prefect," Merek continued, "I believe we have found it."

Gamghast breathed deeply, hoping Bale remained alive. He shifted his thoughts to the practical, to those problems that could be addressed. "Yes, yes. The highlander. You're certain he did all of these things? You're certain he committed these atrocities?"

Merek rubbed his Coda. "He did. Before I captured him I saw these things with my own eyes. It was wanton violence, a lust for blood the likes of which would be known only to a madman. That's precisely why you must pry the spirit from the flesh and allow it to find a nobler vessel. When it was spoken, your Lector's confession could be heard only by the sadistic man who killed him, and that man has twisted the spirit's power to awful ends. This beast must be relieved of Castor's spirit or we risk one of our greatest protectors becoming one of our gravest foes."

"It's just…" Gamghast paused.

"You hold reservations? Surely you see the same need for this as I?"

Gamghast frowned. "It is said Castor chooses his vessel upon death. There is always a design, always a purpose behind his choice. Some talent possessed by the person whose body he decides to inhabit, some characteristic enabling him to rise to the challenge of the times. What if this beast, as you call him, was best suited to Castor's purpose? We could be thwarting a divine plan at the most critical of moments."

Merek snorted. "He had no choice this time, Prefect. He possessed this murderer because there was no one else in his own company left alive. Castor's soul is imprisoned by this man, and only by setting him free will he be able to help us fight our enemy."

Gamghast was quiet for a moment, listening to the sound of the rain. *If only I knew your will, Castor. But we are merely men, and can do no more than our best.* He pushed away from the table. "We will begin at first light tomorrow. It's said Illienne's power is strongest then, just as the sun breaks the night. Perhaps her wisdom will shine more brightly upon us, then."

"You needn't doubt me, Prefect. My order has gifts as well, and I know this man's deeds have not been those of Castor. We must relieve him of the spirit, but it will not be an easy thing. There are others to assist us, yes?"

"Yes, those who know the truth of the Lector's identity. Prefects Borel and Kreer, and of course the

Dictorian. They're already researching the Rites of Excision. We'll meet you at dawn."

Merek looked at him grimly. "I'll bring my sword." With a sweep of his green cloak he left the room, and the door rattled shut behind him.

Gamghast turned again to the bleak, featureless sky. *Such little light shines upon us in such days.*

Gamghast tiptoed down the narrow stairs, hoping somewhere there were answers. The stairway led to an antechamber, at the far end of which stood an ironbound door fastened with many locks. Beside the door was a desk, where sat Prefect Borel studying a yellowed tome. The rotund prefect looked up as Gamghast approached, his jowls seeming to threaten to pull his face back into the book at any moment.

"He hasn't stirred," said Borel, his voice tremulous. "I haven't gone in there, though. He seems… unsafe."

Gamghast nodded. "Then you believe Merek?"

"This man is likely not a medium Castor would have chosen. Thus, it does seem the spirit was stolen." He tapped the page of his book. "This is a register of every Lector of the Sanctum since our order was founded eight hundred and twenty six years ago. There is not a single hint of misdeed, malice or murder. Every Lector was a model of the peaceful pursuit of wisdom, a subtle and secret rudder for the High King."

"Were their times as dire as those we now face? Could it be Castor never before saw a need to become something more… visceral?"

"That's desperate logic, Gamghast. You know what

kind of man Lector Erlorn was, what kind of soul was Castor. This *thing* Merek has brought us is nothing like that. Think this through. If we do nothing, and assume this was all part of Castor's plan, we risk a war against our most terrible foes without the crucial aid of our Sentinel. And if we take action and remove the spirit from this man, and it turns out we are wrong? Is it not reasonable to assume Castor would find another host? One among our number?"

"Such a thing has never been done, Borel. We know not the consequences of displacing the spirit."

"But you can imagine the consequences if Merek is right, and we fail to take action?"

"Perhaps," Gamghast said, looking toward the ironbound door. "Yet I cannot help but doubt."

Borel closed his book with a thump, sending forth a cascade of dust. "Such is the curse of every mortal."

Gamghast tugged at his beard and made his decision. "Open the door."

Borel raised his brow. "You don't mean to speak with him? To test the spirit yourself? It's unwise for us to be in this man's presence without all the support we can muster. We should wait until morning."

"Open it."

Borel huffed and fumbled with a ring of long keys. The locks scraped and squealed as they turned, sounding as though it'd been ages since they were last used. At last all that remained was a great bar of iron across the door's middle. Borel tapped a crank at the bar's center. "You're certain of this?"

"No one, not even a Variden, will instruct us in the

ways of our master. If we are to intervene it will be by our own choosing, not at the urging of another."

"Very well, but I'll not dare go with you." Borel paused before placing his hands on the crank. He struggled to turn it, but finally it moved with a dull clank and the door creaked open. "May Illienne guide our hands."

Gamghast pressed through the door and entered the Abbey's ancient crypt. It was a vast chamber, its gloom yielding little to the candles lit along its walls and its stagnant air smelling of death. He flinched as the door clanged shut behind him.

He remained still, peering toward the room's sunken center. The breath caught in his throat as his vision adjusted and the scene before him became clear.

There, bound against the brick floor by heavy chains, was the man Merek had captured, the man who carried the spirit of Castor. Karnag Mak Ragg. A highlander. A warrior. A murderer.

Gamghast crept alongside the old stones of the wall, feeling it best to keep his distance. His hand brushed along the wall's many hollows containing the bones of revered members of the Sanctum long dead. There were among them many Lectors, or rather former bodies of Castor. All of the Lectors had been pious figures who'd guided the Sanctum toward a deeper understanding, a deeper wisdom. *All so different from this man.*

The highlander remained motionless, save for the swells of his broad back as he drew breath. He was a massive man, certainly a most dangerous sort even without the spirit of a Sentinel within him, and Gamghast found himself thankful for Merek's insistence he be held in chains.

Gamghast took a step forward. He paused for a moment, fearing any reaction from the highlander but there came none. He took another step and then another, and soon came within mere feet of the assassin. He squeezed shut his eyes. "Castor?" he whispered.

A slow exhale was the only reply. Gamghast opened his eyes to a squint and studied the man. The highlander knelt before him, bowed low to the floor and wrapped in black iron. His skin shimmered in the candlelight, much of it stained a dark red. His tangle of black braids was covered in filth, seemingly bits of bone and gristle. His powerful arms, pressed out against the bricks, were covered with silvered scars from what Gamghast guessed were many terrible wounds.

Can this be Castor's vessel?

"Castor?" he said, just louder than a whisper.

The highlander made a soft sound, a whimper. Gamghast eased back. It seemed to him the man's breathing was deepening, the rises of his back growing.

"Castor? Is this you? Is this the form you've chosen?"

Suddenly the highlander's hands drew into fists, thick veins stretching against the skin. There was a growl and his shoulders flexed and his chains rang.

"Speak!" Gamghast urged. "Tell me, Castor, what must we do?"

The highlander struggled against his chains but after a time settled. There came then from him a murmuring, a slurred burble of sounds. Gamghast leaned forward, trying to make some sense of it.

"*Necrista traellus,*" hissed the highlander, "*a abridalusi Yrghul y ogo alliata. Illienne cradus e Warduren renden e sallem orn argo apocha.*"

Gamghast pressed a hand to his lips and nearly stumbled. *Is this Castor's confession? Dare we displace the spirit?*

The highlander struggled again against the chains. He raised his head and spoke once more. "*Necrista traellus a abridalusi Yrghul y ogo alliata. Illienne cradus e Warduren renden e sallem orn argo apocha.*"

Gamghast's head spun, his thoughts wrestling with the awful meaning of the words. *The Necrists move to summon Yrghul's power and have found a powerful ally. Illienne commands the remaining Sentinels be summoned to honor their oath before all is lost.*

He shuddered, knowing the words had to be Castor's confession, that secret truth sent from Illienne herself. It seemed then the whole of the world suddenly depended upon the desperate decisions of his order. *Our old enemy works to wield the power of the Lord of Nightmares. Dare we chance interfering with what might be Castor's plan?* He rushed forward and placed a hand upon Karnag's sweaty brow.

Karnag eased at Gamghast's touch, his scarred form seeming to accept its chains.

"Castor," Gamghast said, relieved. "It is you, isn't it?"

"It is I," came a throaty utterance from the highlander. "And it is another."

"Who, then? Is this your plan, Castor? Must we destroy this vessel to allow your spirit to pass to one of our order?"

Gamghast waited for many long moments, but there came no reply other than the guttural sounds of the highlander's breathing.

$$\sim\!\!\!\!\sim$$

"An entire gold ingot?" said Drenj, his dark face twisted into all manner of anger. "And our horses, too? Certainly those guards would have taken a lot less to open the city gates for us, even at this time of night. You didn't even bother to haggle."

Fencress was tired and in no mood for questions. She looked at Drenj and her rage boiled over. She ripped one of her blades from its scabbard and lunged at the Khaldisian, pinning him against a shuttered storefront with a hard thud. "This has nothing to do with gold, Drenj. This is about our friend, about saving his life. If you want the damned gold, then take it and go." She yanked the remaining ingots from her cloak and shoved them in Drenj's face. "But you'd best spend them before I find time to hunt you down."

Drenj's expression quickly changed, his eyes pleading. "I-I'm sorry. I didn't mean it that way. These have been hard days, and that's a lot of coin considering our t-troubles. It's like everything we've done and all we've lost have been for nothing."

Fencress gritted her teeth, pressing the blade closer to the Khaldisian's throat and shoving the ingots into his nose. "I'm not done with our task yet. We have many foes before us, Drenj. I shouldn't need to worry about the men standing behind me." She eased the blade closer.

She felt a hand on her shoulder. Paddyn's.

"We're all tired, Fencress," Paddyn said. "He meant nothing by it."

Fencress held Drenj against the storefront for a moment longer but after a deep breath she pulled back. She held the blade toward the man briefly before slamming it into its sheath.

Drenj rubbed at his neck. "I haven't ridden with you for as long, but with all we've done I consider you my friend. I'm in this until the end."

Fencress spat and forged ahead along the cobblestones. "You'd best be. Both of you. Any patience and goodwill I possessed have been spent. They've been stolen from me by hardships and betrayals and this awful mess consuming us. Pray we finish this, so I can convince myself there's something right in this world. Something looking after even the likes of us."

"We're with you," said Paddyn, running to catch even with Fencress.

Drenj joined them also. "Just tell us where to go."

She marched onward, scanning the streets for any swinging placard set aglow by the warm light of a hearth. "We need rest. We'll find an inn, grab a drink and sleep for a short while. Then we'll find Karnag."

Prefect Gamghast awoke to the ringing of the belfries clanging out the morning's sixth hour. He lay still in bed for a time, waiting for the echoes to vanish. This was a day both invigorating and frightening, and for a moment he was uncertain if he carried the conviction to pull himself from his pillow.

Just then a cock crowed, somewhere, and that

innocent, ignorant sound seemed a signal. He huffed, tossed aside his blanket and arose.

He shuffled to the mirror near his wardrobe. There'd long been many wrinkles written across his brow and cheeks, but it seemed to him this morning there were more. And if there weren't more then at least the ones that had been there were more deeply drawn.

Gamghast rinsed his face over a washbasin and rubbed at his tired eyes. He pulled his robes over his shoulders and tried vainly to straighten the many wild wisps of his white beard. He stood near his door and sighed before opening it. At last he trudged into the hallway.

The Abbey's corridors were quiet at this hour. There was only the rumor of sunlight in the infrequent, narrow windows, and only the occasional door showed any flicker of candlelight through its cracks. The corridors wound and twisted, but after a while Gamghast neared his destination. He paused before rounding the last turn.

Merek, Kreer and Prefect Borel were already waiting for him near the stairwell to the crypt. Merek was draped in his cloak of forest green, his deeply set eyes burning like embers and the Coda upon his forearm resting against his sword's pommel. Then there was Borel, nervous as ever, his drooping jowls quivering as though on the verge of weeping and his hands clutching a heavy tome against his chest.

"And the Dictorian?" said Gamghast.

Borel sniffed. "We await his arrival."

"You need wait no longer!" came a booming voice. "I am here, and Illienne shines brightly upon our deeds, my friends!"

Gamghast turned to see Dictorian Theal, the titular head of the Sanctum, striding toward them in robes of brilliant white, a golden sun emblazoned upon his chest. He was a tall, broad-shouldered man, his hair an even mix of gray and the blond of younger years. He swept toward them with a trail of servants in tow, his cleft chin upturned and his eyes aglow.

Gamghast bowed with his hands outstretched but Dictorian Theal brushed past him to seize Merek's hearty shake. "Our old friends, the Variden, the children of Valis!" the Dictorian said, his smile broad and white. "What a pleasure it is to welcome you to our Abbey, yet how troubling it is to know the reason you're under our roof. Thank you, and your dutiful order, for honoring the old oaths. Thank you for returning our Lector's spirit to us."

Merek nodded and released the Dictorian's hand. "We will proceed, then?"

The Dictorian excused his retinue. As they exited his face darkened and he drew close to the Variden. "That body will *not* house a Sentinel. Not for a moment longer. The spirit of Castor should only reside in a devoted vessel, a vessel capable of heeding the call of Illienne. The divine spirit should reside in someone who strives to emulate divinity. One from our number. One such as me."

Gamghast jerked his head upward. "Are we so certain?" he said. "Are we so certain *we* know his plan better than he? Are we so certain we should interfere?"

The Dictorian spun toward Gamghast, his face bearing a sour look. "Ah, Prefect Gamghast." Theal's handsome face shifted from gentle concern to paternal scolding.

"Always so addled by indecision. If only you possessed the faith Illienne demands of us. Perhaps then you could have achieved more, risen to a higher station. Perhaps you would have been capable of displaying greater wisdom at moments such as these…"

Gamghast stood upright and smoothed his robes. "You lay claim to the wisdom of Castor, now?"

Theal took a hard step toward Gamghast. "Remember, Prefect, it is I who leads our order. Our Lector has died, his voice has been silenced. Now it is my hand guiding us. It is my heart expressing Castor's will. You will do as I say, or you will be cast from this place."

Gamghast studied his feet. "Dictorian, you see things unseen," he said flatly. "I am an instrument of your will."

Theal stood stiffly. "Yes you are." He turned from Gamghast and stretched out his hands. "Merek! Let us begin this!"

Fencress skulked across the slate shingles, searching the Abbey's rooftops for a suitable opening. They'd cased the vast structure just before sunrise and had found few windows and fewer doors, and nothing that wouldn't have required a great deal of killing and commotion. She tugged at her cowl, shielding her gaze from the rising sun, and hunkered against the shingles. She studied for a time the many angles, chimneys and kitchen vents of the rooftop. *There has to be a way inside this mess of stones.*

A moment later her ears perked to the sound of a creak followed by a click—a door closing. She signaled to Paddyn and Drenj, motioning toward the direction of the sound. They moved then in unison, Fencress with silent footfalls and the others making only a faint scrape.

After a few dozen feet they came to the edge of a roof, and below them was an enclosed courtyard decorated with flowering bushes and well-groomed trees. She noticed a withered old spooker strolling about in the morning sunlight, eyes firmly affixed to his feet. He wandered along a tiled path before settling on a bench, and then opened a hefty book. Just opposite the courtyard from the bench was the door.

Fencress thought for a moment of slipping down and slitting the fellow's throat, nice and neat. Yet, the notion troubled her. Her hand found the totem strung about her neck, a wooden carving of Illienne's golden sun. *No. There will be enough blood today as it is.*

Just then there sounded a loud crash. A flight of doves scattered skyward from a nearby tree with a great rushing sound. She looked to see a shingle shattered upon a pathway below. Above it, Drenj perched on the lip of the roof with hands upraised as though pleading innocence. Paddyn squatted a few feet away, staring at the courtyard with eyes wide.

"Shit," murmured Fencress.

The spooker had his face upturned now, head rolling to follow the flight of the doves with squinted eyes. The birds wheeled about in a erratic dance, toward the far side of the courtyard, then high above, then back toward their tree. Fencress watched with dread as the spooker's eyes tracked them, closer and closer to where the three assassins crouched on the rooftop.

Fencress turned her head downward toward the slate

shingles, hoping against hope the black leather of her cloak would conceal her. She cursed under her breath and squeezed her totem. *If there is any god above or below who can save us, I call upon you now.*

She heard the flutter of the doves above them. Drenj yelped something in Khaldisian, a word that sounded like some kind of animal call. Suddenly the sound of the wings faded, as it seemed the doves had changed course toward the courtyard's far end.

Fencress chanced a look and saw the spooker still on his bench, continuing to observe the mad flight of the birds.

He didn't see us.

The doves were a radiant white in the morning sun, twisting and turning in an ever-changing shape. They changed course once again, darting from the courtyard's far side, to above the door, then about a tree shading the spooker's bench. The spooker gawked at them still, head tilted backward and mouth agape.

Fencress studied the spooker's exposed throat and released the totem. She eased back on the roof and pulled her blades from their sheaths. She nodded to Paddyn and Drenj—they needed to dispose of the spooker. *Perhaps a killer can't be expected to be anything other than that.*

She was jarred by a sudden squeal from the spooker. The man sat swiping his hands frantically against his face, spitting and sputtering as he did. He stood abruptly and threw his hands to his sides, revealing a face covered in bird shit.

Fencress smiled, doing her best to suppress a laugh.

The spooker grabbed his book and dashed across the

courtyard, threw open the door and disappeared within the Abbey. The door remained open.

Can it be the dead gods answer prayers from even the likes of us?

Dictorian Theal stood just before the shackled form of Karnag Mak Ragg. "We toil on your behalf, beloved Castor!" he said, his voice booming in the crypt. "We do the bidding of Illienne the Light Eternal, and we will set free what this beast of a man has enslaved!"

The Dictorian and the highlander were illuminated by a column of brilliant sunlight channeled though a shaft hollowed into the rock above, a chute containing many mirrors designed to catch the sun's brightest light. Just outside the light's center stood Prefects Borel and Kreer, and beside them, at the Dictorian's shoulder, was green-cloaked Merek. Gamghast, though, stood beyond the glow, uncomfortable in their midst. *This is a terrible risk we take.*

"Prefect Kreer!" Theal demanded. "The text!"

"As you command," said Kreer, pausing to give Gamghast a disdainful look.

Gamghast stiffened. *Alas, too few find righteousness in uncertainty.*

Theal stretched his hands toward the kneeling highlander as he examined the book Kreer held before his eyes. "The Rites of Excision, the sacred incantations for freeing a captive spirit. Recorded by the Sanctum's twenty-third Lector, only two generations ago and very likely in direct anticipation of today's events. When I begin, be ready. This demon before us may refuse to yield the spirit willingly, and he's likely attained some degree of power as a result of his containment of Castor. And Prefects?" Theal said, glancing over his shoulder. "Join your prayers to mine. Repeat every word of the Rite. Summon all the strength within yourselves, and channel your thoughts to me. The spirit of Castor should be guided thus, and find its place within me."

Gamghast edged forward. *We must not interfere with Castor's choice.* He moved his mouth to speak but Theal's eyes found his and he fell silent.

"Remember your *orders*, Prefects." Theal said. "Question not what I know to be the will of Illienne. I have foreseen this." He returned his eyes to the book and began the incantations.

Dictorian Theal's voice rose to a clarion call. It filled every corner of the crypt and was answered by endless echoes from the stones. They were ancient words, divine words. Words said to be the very tongue of the dead gods themselves, words of power used to work the most potent spellcraft. They hummed in Gamghast's ears well after they were spoken, as though once put to breath they were given life.

Borel and Kreer dropped their heads, their lips moving to repeat Theal's words. The voices became a drone, a chanting repetition of words of power, a reverberation serving to enhance the power of the Dictorian's chant.

Gamghast, though, knew the words were lost to him. He had no heart for this. His mouth moved, but he gave no sound. His head fell, not out of pious reverence but out of profound disappointment.

Then there was a rattle. Gamghast jerked his head up

to see Karnag shifting his broad form, listlessly trying to shed his chains. His skin was stained the color of salmon from much old blood, his back and arms were striated with scars. His head was a mess of thick braids covered in filth, and his face was cloaked in shadow.

The chanting continued for long moments and Theal's voice grew more intense, desperate even. Sweat dripped from his brow and his arms shook as though struggling to pull down the heavens to help him. Yet, there was little evidence of any change in Karnag Mak Ragg.

After a time Theal slammed shut the tome and strolled about the shackled highlander. He thumbed the cleft of his chin, seemingly lost in thought.

Merek moved to Theal's side, eyes intent upon the highlander and his sword half-drawn from its scabbard. "Dictorian," hissed Merek, "why do these spells not work?"

"I have others yet to try," said Theal, his voice thick with arrogance. "Out of respect for Castor I began with the most mild, the least damaging incantations. With these next spells we will rend the spirit from the flesh."

"And if those fail?"

Theal shook his head. "There will be no failure. We will cut his head from his shoulders and pour out the spirit in that fashion, if need be."

Karnag shifted suddenly, violently, and the chains rang. Slowly he raised his chin, moving his face upward toward the light. His gray eyes glittered fiercely beneath his heavy brow. He did not speak, but there was danger in that expression, a grim warning against further meddling.

"Your spellcraft augments the chains, yes?" Theal said, glancing at Merek.

Merek nodded. "I channel my thoughts to the bonds, Dictorian. They will hold."

"Good." Theal walked to Karnag and stood before him. He shoved forth his hand and seized the highlander by his black braids, then yanked his face into the light. An awful growl came from Karnag and his neck twisted at an awkward angle. "Release the Sentinel! By Illienne I command you, release him!"

The highlander jerked about and his body trembled. He choked for air and struggled against the chains. His muscles tensed and the chains scraped and groaned. He turned his eyes toward Theal and bared his teeth with abject malice. "I will yield nothing to the likes of you," he said, his voice deep and eerily tranquil, a matter-of-fact pronouncement of a certain doom.

Theal's eyes widened and his jaw slackened but he soon regained his composure. He released the highlander's head and stood tall before him, as though to display a lack of fear, a righteous serenity. "Is this Castor who speaks, or the twisted captor of his most sacred spirit?"

"I am more than either of those things, Dictorian Theal. I am the ender of lives, the conclusion of souls. I am the ultimate wisdom of death."

Theal stumbled back a step and turned about, his back to the highlander. "You see! Do you see, now? This beast is not our Sentinel, not our master!"

Gamghast glanced sideways to Borel but the rotund prefect betrayed no emotion, standing with eyes closed and continuing his chant. *This is terribly wrong. We cannot question Castor's will in choosing this vessel! There must have been a reason!*

Theal turned boldly toward Karnag. "Have you nothing more to say? Tell us why you've enslaved the spirit of Castor to such ill-meaning ends!" He came ever closer, and then reared back a hand and slapped Karnag sharply across the face. "Release him! Release him to *me!*"

The highlander's great arms pressed forward. The chains stretched and shook with tension. He said nothing but regarded Dictorian Theal with dark eyes—a killer's look—and spat thick blood across the floor.

"Very well," Theal said, striding to Kreer's side and studying the open tome once more. "If you will not offer the spirit willingly, then your mind will be ruined and your body turned to rot. You will cough out the spirit with your last breaths." He looked over his shoulder. "Prefects! Join your prayers to mine!"

Fencress dug her blade into the servant's side, not enough to draw blood but certainly enough to command the attention of any man who valued his life. "Alright, Wit," she whispered into the fellow's crusty ear, "that's a good start. You've seen my green-cloaked friend. Have you seen him this morning?"

"Er, umm, uh…" the gangly man said. He seemed to say that a lot. They'd happened upon him moments before, while sneaking amidst the shadows of the countless corridors. He was the only person they'd spied in the Abbey who wasn't draped in the robes of a spooker, so Fencress reckoned he'd prove the least troublesome.

"Remember, friend, I haven't much time, and even

less patience. Was it this morning?" She gave the blade a good twist to make certain its meaning was clear.

"Yes!" Wit said, shaking his hairy head. "Yes it was. Gamghast had me wake him for their meeting."

Fencress gave the servant a good-natured slap on the cheek. "Now that's the spirit, Wit! That's precisely how business gets done, my friend. You give me information such as that, and I let you keep your hide free of unsightly cuts and bruises. Now, where and when was this meeting?"

"Er, umm... I don't remember!"

"Fencress!" hissed Paddyn, gesturing behind them. "Someone's coming!"

She paused and heard shuffling footsteps. "Help us now, Wit, or this blade goes clean through your guts. That would be an awful shame, especially considering our newfound friendship."

"The c-crypt! The end of this hallway, then right, then left! Just down the stairs!"

She nodded and withdrew the blade. "It should go without saying, Wit, that you haven't seen us and that all is right and well on this fine morning. Just as it should be. I'd hate to have to pay you an unfriendly visit so soon after reaching a solid understanding."

Wit winced, rubbed at his side, and gestured down the corridor. "That way. Down the hallway. Go."

Karnag Mak Ragg pressed hard against his chains, almost upright. The bolts anchoring the chains creaked and the bricks about them splintered. The highlander's body was terribly wounded. Fresh blood streamed from countless striations and dripped from his nostrils and eyes. Old scars seemed to bleed anew and his body twitched with waves of obvious pain.

Yet, he stood. It seemed to Gamghast there was an indefatigable purpose driving the man, an indomitable spirit refusing to yield to the Dictorian's demands. *Can this be Castor?*

Dictorian Theal continued his incantations, now chanting an ancient blood rite intended for the most difficult exorcisms, those in which the body was not meant to be spared. Divine light flashed from Theal's hands and his voice soared. Gamghast had seen bodies ripped apart like parchment with such words, yet the highlander remained standing.

"The old curses are futile," Karnag said, his tone unnerving in its calm assuredness. "Dictorian, I will ask you this only once. Abandon this deed. Set me free, mortal, or I spill your brains from your head."

Theal threw his hands down in frustration, shaking his arms. "He refuses to surrender the spirit!" He turned toward Merek, his eyes mad and his lips shaking. "We must kill him!"

I can be silent no longer. Gamghast cleared his throat, loudly and with meaning. "Dictorian! I cannot suffer this! We cannot claim to know Castor's will, nor can we stand in the way of our Sentinel's intent! Surely you see there is a *reason* the incantations do not work!"

Theal leapt toward Gamghast, his mouth drooling and his eyes blinking. He shoved Gamghast with frightful strength, sending him toppling across the crypt's floor.

Gamghast tumbled across the bricks, striking his head, his arthritic knees, his gnarled hands. He came to rest near the crypt's door, and then pain screamed at him from every joint in his old body. His head swooned and his eyes struggled for focus.

"Be thankful!" screamed Theal. "Be thankful I don't order your death, Prefect! Or should I say Acolyte Gamghast? Yes, that has a much better ring to it. Leave us, Acolyte!"

Gamghast coughed and tasted the coppery taint of blood on his tongue. He rolled to his elbows, and with no small degree of concentration brought his vision into focus. Theal had returned to Karnag and had seized the highlander by his black braids.

"Merek!" Theal screamed, pulling Karnag into the column of white light. "Your blade!"

Gamghast tried to shout his protest but his body would not comply. He coughed again and blood sputtered from his lips. He struggled to stand but knew several of his bones were broken. "Theal…" he wheezed. "Do not do this…"

Theal wrenched Karnag's head backward, exposing his throat. "Merek! Strike now!"

Merek yanked his blade from its scabbard with a ringing sound and brought the weapon before Karnag. He adjusted the green cloak about his shoulders and then pressed a hand against his Coda. He pulled a deep breath and nodded to Theal. "It is the will of Illienne."

Gamghast struggled again but his limbs hardly answered him. His spine was wrenched at an awkward angle and didn't seem willing to move. He slumped back against the door, and his head came to rest against the wood.

He heard then a commotion on the door's other side, the sounds of violence. *What is this?* A trusted acolyte had been left to guard the door, but...

"It is her will!" screamed Theal, his voice screeching. "Kill him!"

Gamghast heard the dull sound of a latch being turned on the door's other side and then felt his body forced uncomfortably aside by the door's opening. He gasped, feeling a searing pain lace his form, then watched as three darkly clad figures stepped indifferently over him and into the crypt. Gamghast tried to voice an alarm, but his lungs would only wheeze.

"Kill him!" Theal shrieked again.

Merek brandished his sword and reared back, preparing to strike at Karnag's throat. But just then there came the twang of a bow, followed by a dull *thunk*. Merek stumbled backward, clutching an arrow protruding from his chest. His sword fell from his hands and clattered against the bricks.

"What!" Theal yelled, whirling about.

Karnag roared then, and screamed and shook, and there came a terrible sound like the roll of thunder. Karnag threw his hands skyward and the chains shattered and fell from him. He lunged and caught the Dictorian by his shoulders and pulled him close.

"No!" cried the Dictorian. "Someone help!"

Karnag squeezed the man to his breast and grasped his skull between thick hands. He flexed and crushed the Dictorian's head as though it were a child's bauble, spattering blood and brain matter across the floor. The Dictorian fell to the stones, limp and lifeless.

"I will bathe in the blood of my brother," said Karnag grimly, "and that of many more. The spirit is mine alone to wield." He stepped over the body at his feet and staggered forward.

Gamghast's eyes drifted toward the crypt's far end, where stood a black cloaked figure over Merek. "Remember me?" said a woman in black. "Remember your betrayal? No one, and I mean *no one*, wrongs me or my friend. You should never tangle with the most dangerous beast. That was your undoing."

Merek struggled for a moment with the arrow protruding from his chest as the woman brandished two identical swords. She displayed them only briefly before shoving them into Merek's eyes. The Variden convulsed and then fell still.

"Boys?" the woman said. "Shall we?"

The three intruders turned and followed Karnag from the shaft of sunlight and toward the door.

The woman paused and looked toward the cringing forms of Borel and Kreer. "You spookers will pray for us. Pray we stay safe, and pray we don't come back. Because if we do, we're bringing Karnag with us, and he'll be the death of you. Every last fucking one of you."

27
OLD REGRETS AND BAD MEMORIES

ANNICK WALKED DOWN Temple Street, trudging through the leaden mist of a rainy afternoon. The rain drummed against the hood of his cloak and made slick the street's cobbles, and the air carried the scent of dead fish. Between the rain and the fishy stench it seemed a familiar day in Ironmoor, and Lannick reckoned he wouldn't miss it much.

He saw the shingle of *The Wanton Vicar* ahead and caught a hint of lamb stew in the air. He smiled, guessing Brugan couldn't bear to leave the place without fixing one last meal.

He arrived at the door and found himself just as nervous to turn the knob as he'd been in the many years before. In those times he'd dreaded the turn because it meant sinking deeper into that same rancid hole, that dark place filled only with old regrets and bad memories. Now, his apprehension came not from the familiar but from the unknown. *Can I do these things? Can I have courage again?*

He studied the dimpled brass knob and thought for a moment of turning around, of running away never to return. He thought of booking passage aboard a merchant's ship, of sailing the endless sea under sparkling starlight, of finding a faraway port where he could make a new life for himself. He thought of how starting over seemed in so many ways better than trying to right his mess of a past.

No. Not better. Just easier. He turned the knob, pulled open the door and slipped inside.

It was a good crowd, something Brugan surely enjoyed. A peg-legged fellow played a screeching fiddle at the room's far end, singing a lewd lyric in a hoarse voice. The serving girl danced a jig beside him and a number of folks crowded nearby, laughing and whooping and taking long draws from tall mugs. Farther away were several greedy-eyed fellows hunched over a game of deadman's dice, and a few more desperate sorts slouched hopelessly against the bar.

Lannick's expression wilted when he noticed one man sitting in what had been his usual spot, only months before. He thought of the anguish he'd experienced since then, but knew if it hadn't been for that he'd still be there, drowning in cheap wine and despair.

He heard the squeak of the kitchen door and turned to see Brugan emerge, toweling off his burly arms with a stained rag. The barkeep grinned widely and gave Lannick a nod. "Glad you came, Captain. Come, have a word with me."

Lannick smiled and followed the big man into the

kitchen. The room was filled with a steam rising from a cauldron over the fire and smelled heavily of lamb and rosemary.

"Hungry?" Brugan asked, ladling a scoop of stew into a mug. "Not many fine meals where we're heading, so enjoy it while you can. The lamb cost me a small fortune, but I reckon that's only right. Farewells always take something from you."

Lannick accepted the mug and dug a spoon into it. He'd not eaten well these last few weeks and knew he'd need his strength. He chewed and nodded, reckoning the stew to be one of Brugan's finer efforts. "Thank you," he said around the mouthful.

"One of my favorites. I'll miss it."

"So will your patrons. Are you closing the place?"

"Dead gods, no. I'll need the coin when we come back. My serving girl Lacy will run things. She's an honest sort and a good sight prettier than me, anyhow. I just hope the walls of Ironmoor are still standing by the time this is through."

Lannick took another hearty spoonful. "You think they will be?"

Brugan laughed. "I figured you'd be more worried about us making it back here in the first place!"

"I am, Brugan. Fane is a ruthless sort, and if he catches wind of our efforts he'll march to fight us and leave Riverweave to the Arranese. And if we defeat him on the field? Then we'll have tens of thousands of well-rested Arranese to battle. I'm not sure I like our chances."

Brugan placed a hand on Lannick's shoulder.

"Everything you say is likely true, Lannick. Yet, in spite of all that, I have faith in you."

Lannick sighed. "It's been a long time since anyone's said that. I'll try not to let you down, old friend. It's just… I'm not sure I can…"

"I know." Brugan blinked and waved a hand dismissively. "Now. Get some of that brash humor and bravado back in your head and remember you're still the Scourge of Tallorrath, the Protector of Ironmoor. Or at least you look an awful lot like that fellow." He laughed and moved back to the cauldron to stir the stew.

"About our business, then," Brugan continued. "Kevlin has a farm about thirty leagues southwest of here, near Thane Vandyl's hold of Rellic. He took a few cartloads of old weapons and rusty armor to the place last week, and has arranged for horses for us a league or so outside Ironmoor. We figured it best to keep such things out of the city, just in case the High King's soldiers start sniffing around for more supplies. You and I leave tomorrow morning. Some of the rest have already gone ahead, and the others won't be far behind."

Lannick grinned crookedly. "A bunch of old soldiers mounting one last charge. Let's hope it turns out better than it sounds like it should."

Brugan slapped Lannick's shoulder. "Not just old soldiers, Captain. Old heroes. Now grab a chair in the common room. Let me finish this stew and then I'll fetch us both an ale. The good stuff."

Lannick found a table not too far from the peg-legged fiddler but far enough from the crowd about him. He eased into a chair, the wound from Silas's sword still bothering him.

The fiddler was between songs and took time to crack his knuckles and turn the pegs on his instrument. He plucked at the strings with his thumb and after a few adjustments seemed satisfied with the tuning. He gestured for the small crowd to be seated. "This one's not for clapping or carrying on," he said gruffly.

Lannick didn't much care for the fiddle. Its wail sounded like a cat being flayed, but the fellow's voice was engaging. There was an earnestness to it, an authenticity of having endured true pain.

The sailors brave, on knees they prayed
Chosen first to fight
The sailors brave, their souls they gave
To Illienne the Light

The Siren's Call set sail at dawn
Her brave young sailors strong
The Siren's Call she'd never fall
With the likes o' them along

On churning seas her masts broke free
The storm would take their lives
The Sullen Sea would not be breached
Even faithful men must die

The sailors brave fell to wat'ry grave
In deep, dark depths below
The sailors brave their souls they gave
To dead gods far below

These sailors doomed, by sea consumed
Sailors brave want not this end
The gods I curse with ev'ry verse
And will ne'er pray to them again.

The peg-legged fiddler stood and limped toward the bar, and there came a muted clapping from the crowd. Lannick clapped also, remembering well the tale of *The Siren's Call*. She'd been the first ship sent to scout the seas near Tallorrath after war was declared, ordered to sail amidst a terrible storm a dozen years before.

Brugan joined Lannick at the table, placing between them two tankards capped with foam. "He was on that ship, you know," Brugan said, tilting his mug toward the fiddler. "The only survivor of *The Siren's Call*. The fellow doesn't talk much, but one night he had a bit too much whiskey. Told me he floated on a barrel for weeks after the ship sank, and that sharks gnawed off his leg before he could fight them off." He shook his head. "What a damned foolhardy thing that was. Those boys died for no reason at all."

Lannick eyed his friend suspiciously. "You remember who ordered them to sail into the storm, don't you?"

Brugan grinned. "I knew you'd catch that, Lannick.

Fane was a bastard back then, and is an even worse one, now. I thought it'd be a nice touch, a way to stir those coals inside your belly and get you ready for this."

"I *am* ready," Lannick said, taking a swallow of the ale. He'd always preferred wine or the stronger stuff, which was probably why Brugan had offered him this instead. It had a bitter flavor, but a better aftertaste.

"Oh, I know you *think* you are, but I still see uncertainty in your eyes. Part of you is still afraid you'll let us down, somehow. Afraid you're unworthy of our trust. That same look you'd wear just before you slumped over my bar for days at a time."

"I can't just pretend the last nine years didn't happen, Brugan. The men *don't* trust me anymore, and what's worse is some blame me."

"They hate Fane more than they hate you."

"That's not exactly a comfort, Brugan."

The big man shrugged and sighed. "It'll take a little time, sure, but they'll come around once they see the changes I've noticed in you. Just keep thinking of your dead family."

Lannick eyed Brugan darkly. "Don't speak of them."

"But that's what this is about, Lannick! Nothing you do will ever bring them back. They're gone. Yet, you can honor them instead of letting them drag you into the grave with them. You can honor them by bringing justice to the man who took them from you. Their deaths aren't on your hands. They're on his. Now, you've gotten better at realizing that most of the time, but not *all* of the time." He drained his tankard in a massive gulp and slammed it on the table. "You need to set your mind to this thing, and never allow it to waver. Not for an instant. Not until this is done."

Lannick took a deep breath. *Brugan's right.*

Brugan's look softened. "You can't let the lads down, Lannick. Even if you tried. You've given them hope just by deciding to do it, by agreeing to take a stab at this harebrained quest for redemption. You've inspired them already. And as for you, that old strength is in you, my friend. If there are times you feel it lacking, just remember you have me and many others to lean upon. We can do this, Lannick. We can set right those old wrongs."

Lannick nodded and took another drink, draining his mug. The fiddler had started a new song, this one much livelier than the last.

"Now," Brugan said, "I have the guestroom arranged for you upstairs. Get some sleep. You're going to need the rest."

They arose before dawn and quietly gathered their things and some satchels of food Brugan had assembled. "Just dried meats and hard cheeses," Brugan said. "Nothing fancy, but it'll keep. And who knows what that old sheepherder Kevlin thinks grown men should eat."

Lannick shouldered a satchel and looked out one of the tavern's clouded windows. The cobblestoned streets were wet with rain and the sky was just shifting from black to purple. He pressed his face close to the glass and watched the rain fall. Just then, he thought he spotted a black figure standing across the wide street. The lights in the common room reflected against the glass, though, and he found it difficult to see clearly.

But then he saw it again.

He pulled away from the window. "Blow out the candles and dim the lanterns," he said. "There's something watching us."

"It's early, Lannick. Before the sun comes the shadows play tricks on the eyes. Besides, it'd be a trouble to—"

"Do it!" Lannick hissed.

"As you command, Captain," said Brugan, his voice thick with irritation. Soon, the common room was dimmed to near-darkness and Brugan sniffed impatiently.

Lannick crept toward the window and again found the figure. It was tall, thin, and draped in black robes. Its face was hidden within the depths of a cowl. A chill crept up his spine.

"Probably just some drunk in a stupor," said Brugan from beside another window. "With all the seedy joints on Temple Street, that'd be nothing unusual."

"I don't think so."

"C'mon, Lannick. All those troubles in your head have you seeing things. Now let's… What in the old hells is that?"

Lannick saw it too, the stunted thing ambling along the sidewalk toward the tall figure's side, pausing occasionally to prod and poke at the shadows nearby. A Shodafayn, one of those twisted beings that served as navigators of the shadowpaths. "Brugan, light all the candles again and brighten the lanterns. And keep them *moving*. Don't let the shadows inside this room remain in place for more than an instant. Do you understand?"

Brugan's mouth fell open. "You just had me blow them all out."

"Do you understand!"

The barkeep huffed but set about his task. Within moments he'd brightened the place considerably, and turned in the room's center while swaying two lanterns about. He paused and looked at Lannick, clearly befuddled. "Why am I doing this?"

"To keep us safe while I think." Lannick tapped a finger against his chin and was surprised to notice his other hand was in his purse, wrapped about the cool metal of his Coda. *Dare I enter that world, even for a moment? If I return only to leave again, the Variden will never forgive me.*

"*Lannick my love,*" came a whisper.

He looked out the window and saw the Shodafayn digging at the shadows near the tall figure. Lannick knew the faces they wore, the horrors they intended to wreak upon him. He fingered the Coda and knew he had no choice.

He yanked the Coda free and slammed it upon his wrist. It locked into place with a dull click and for an instant glowed with a greenish hue.

His head was struck by a cascade of images. Not *his* visions, but those of others, of other Variden. Visions from his green-cloaked companions in places far away. Creeping across hills overlooking a vast encampment of Arranese warriors. Stalking a desert city full of soaring towers, trying to stay on the trail of a dozen black-robed figures. Lurking in the shadows of a great underground complex, avoiding the eyes of any who might see. There were many others, as well. They were the collective experience of the ever-watchful Variden, all of them joined by their Codas.

There were warnings, too. Warnings of profound

danger. Fear that the Sentinel Castor was being help captive by a vicious mortal. Fear that the Spider King of Arranan possessed fell power. And a suspicion he and the Necrists were working in concert toward some wicked end.

And there were voices reaching out to him, also. *"Lannick, are you with us at last?"* came Alisa's voice. *"Brother, you have finally found the strength to fight with us!"* said Ogrund. *"Have you dug out of your wretched hole for a moment?"* asked Wil.

And finally there was *purpose*, the divine guidance imposed upon all Variden by the Sentinel Valis. A pressing need to find the enemy, to protect Rune. To wipe the land clean of the agents of Yrghul. To do all this but remain hidden, to keep safe the High King but never allow anyone to know of the order's existence.

It was a great deal to bear, and it was overwhelming. But Lannick remembered the mental exercises he'd learned when he was schooled in the order's ways, so many years before. He bent his mind to a sharp focus, and after a few moments the flood subsided to a trickle.

He adjusted his cloak on his shoulders and drew his sword. "Bring the lanterns near the door."

Brugan stopped his clumsy dance and blinked. "What is it we're doing?"

"I'm going after those things and you're going to help me. When I open the door, throw the lanterns across the street. Right at them. They hate fire. The shadows shift too much for them so the flames will distract them. Then," he grimaced, "stand clear."

Brugan nodded. "Whatever you say, Lannick. So long as you're certain."

Lannick twirled his sword about, first in one direction and then the other. The steel felt good in his hand. It felt right. He would cut down these demons and give his family their final rest. He stepped to the door, inhaled sharply and looked to Brugan. "Ready."

Brugan pulled the lanterns close to his chest. Lannick threw open the door and reared back, making way for Brugan and his lanterns. The big man shouldered past him and heaved the lanterns toward the street's opposite side. The glass shattered, spraying oil and flame across the cobblestones and the abominations.

A horrid shriek came from them, and their bodies jerked spastically about as they tried to shake and slap away the fire. They seemed confused and surprised, their heads turning this way and that.

Lannick raised his sword and lunged across the street. Words formed in his head. Ancient words, divine words. He felt the power of his Coda, the power of purpose, and he fell upon them with a mighty force. A green fire leapt from his blade and he struck with a strength and swiftness unknown to mortal men. He struck at their flailing limbs and the beasts reeled before him.

The Shodafayn dwarf and Necrist witch fell backward, their black robes torn with wounds and smoldering from fire. Lannick stood over them with his sword aglow. "I will bury you now," he said. "Forever."

The Necrist shook aside her cowl to reveal the face of Lannick's dead wife. Though split by a black stitch the face remained hauntingly beautiful. "Lannick, my love," she said in a voice that sounded so much like his wife's.

448

Lannick paused. *How many times did my wife say those words to me?*

The Shodafayn nuzzled against her and it, too, pulled back its hood. The face of Lannick's elder son gazed at him, burbling through a mouth wet with slobber. It whimpered as though pleading for mercy. "Dada!" it cried, its wide eyes staring through stitched skin.

My son.

"My love," said the Necrist, writhing on the ground and caressing her breasts.

My wife.

"No," said Lannick, but his voice lacked conviction. He brandished the blade but had not the heart to strike again. He staggered back, away from them. Away from their faces.

The Necrist seemed to sense his hesitation. She struggled upward and took a step toward him. She held her arms toward him and shadows pooled about her hands. "My love," she said again.

The Shodafayn toddled to her side, mumbling its childlike babble.

"Lannick!" It was Wil's voice, rising from the murmur of thoughts. *"Don't fall victim to your weaknesses! Strike down the enemy!"*

"No," Lannick said, but was unsure whether he'd meant the word for the Variden or the Necrist.

The Necrist took another step forward. The shadows were swirling now, reaching toward him and curling about his form. They were cold, the feel of them causing his small hairs to rise. But there was a strange comfort to them, a suggestion his pain would subside if only he succumbed.

He dropped his arms, staring deep into the Necrist's eyes. They were black, far darker than his wife's had been, but there was something of that same life within them...

"Strike, Lannick! You must!" It was Alisa's voice.

The Necrist came closer still, closing her eyes and opening her mouth, inviting a kiss. Lannick felt the tug of the Shodafayn's small hands upon his legs and he heard its giggling.

"No," Lannick said again. "No." He closed his eyes and knew the terrible path he had to take. He tightened his grip on his sword and he struck, cutting first at the shadows encircling him and then at the enemy.

Again and again he struck. He hacked at them mercilessly, bringing his blade upon their bones with countless, vicious swings.

They fell, gravely wounded, and still he struck. He cleaved at the faces most of all, and tears fell from him as he cut eyes and cheeks and lips.

Soon there was only blood and splintered bone. But hacked he did, hearing the ring of his blade as it found the cobblestones beneath the bodies. He struck until his hand went numb and he could barely grip his blade.

There was a hand upon his shoulder. "Captain," said Brugan, "they're dead."

Lannick stood still for a moment and looked upon the decimated forms before him. His hands trembled and his sword clattered to the ground. He reeled and spilled the sour contents of his stomach on the cobblestones. He swooned but Brugan steadied him.

"It's alright, lad," Brugan said.

Lannick sank to his knees and his whole body shook.

His muscles burned and his arms fell slack. *They're dead. At last they are dead.*

"*Lannick!*" came an unwelcome voice within his head. It was Alisa. "*You're safe! Now, join us! Find me in Arranan where I track the Necrists. Honor your oath!*"

Lannick did not reply but instead looked wearily upon his Coda, the dull iron inlaid with countless lines of strange script. The words formed the spells that empowered his order, the ancient secrets that granted them the strength to fight the old evils of the world. The same spells that chained his mind to the others of the order and confused the purpose in his heart.

"*No,*" Lannick thought, directing his words to the Variden. "*I cannot. Not now. My task is not yet done, and my purpose is not yet yours.*"

"*Your purpose?*" Alisa answered. "*What, some misguided revenge for your family? Think of your selfishness, your hubris! We are facing the very end of the world if we fail! And you? You are consumed with setting right a wrong that can never be undone. Your family is dead. Nothing you can do will make your family live and breathe again. Nothing!*"

"*You are a prideful fool, Lannick!*" screamed Wil. "*Honor your oath!*"

Lannick fumbled about for his sword, grasped it with tingling hands, and guided the point to the thin gap where the Coda latched to his wrist.

"*Lannick!*" screamed many voices in his head. "*You cannot abandon us again! Not at such a moment!*"

He twisted the blade and the Coda snapped open. A burning sensation swept through him as it slipped from his wrist, the pain of departing power. Voices wailed in his head, making his skull feel as though it would split. But soon the pain left him and the voices fell silent.

Lannick sighed heavily, knowing this latest act would not be taken lightly. Any Variden who abandoned the order was regarded as a traitor of the worst kind. And now he'd just done it a second time. He retrieved the Coda and placed it in its box, just beside the flask of whiskey in his purse. He frowned and shook his head.

Brugan's hand fell upon his shoulder. "I'll not ask what happened here for a long time, Captain. But when I do, I want the truth. You owe me that much, at least."

Lannick nodded and pulled himself up. "When you ask, I'll tell you what I can."

"What should we do with the bodies?" He wiped a tear from his eye with a thick thumb. "Unless my eyes are lying, those were your family's faces."

"No," Lannick said, sheathing his sword. "My wife and children rest safely in their graves. The rats and crows will finish what's left of these things."

"Well enough," he said. "Let's get clear of this place. To Rellic and the rest of the lads. We have a war to wage."

Lannick found again the outline of his Coda in his purse. "Perhaps more than one."

28
REMAINS

ZANDRACHUS BALE TUCKED his hair behind his ears and shielded his eyes from the setting sun. Lyan the Just had revealed to them secret passages through the hearts of the mountains, and that meant stumbling through shadows for days. Now, at last, there was sunlight, but his squinted eyes could barely discern the features of the broken landscape from its shadows.

"I don't miss that lady one bit," spat Lorra.

Bale nodded. Lyan's presence had been unsettling and he was glad to be rid of her. But now they were set upon a journey to a most dangerous place. Zyn, Arranan's capital city, would be a place most unwelcoming of an Acolyte of Rune's Sanctum.

Just ahead of them stood the Gray Gates, the ancient towers said to mark the end of Rune and the beginning of the godless lands. They were tall spires of carved stone, perhaps sixty feet in height, etched with weathered images of Illienne and her Seven Sentinels. Beyond the towers lay Arranan.

As they walked between the spires Bale rested a hand upon one, recalling the poem he'd read before leaving the Sanctum. *A Dirge for Erkelon*, it was called.

The beasts besiege with hearts of black
Whilst tears wander a well-worn track
Set by the smiles of long ago.

"If" calls the herald of remorse
Never daring a righteous course
From tower's height he falls to death below.

The poem concerned an old lord of this place who'd allowed Yrghul the Lord of Nightmares to pass between these very structures, so fearful was he of the black god's anger. Once through the gates, Yrghul broke his promise to pass peacefully and laid waste to the lord's fortress and people. Bale shook his head. *Can there be such a thing as courage in the face of such evil?*

It struck Bale that Erkelon had chosen a course he'd thought to be righteous, one that would spare his people. Yet, it had resulted only in death. Bale wondered if his task would meet a similar doom. He wondered if he'd better serve his order by traveling back to Rune, by warning Gamghast and the others that General Fane had bargained with the Necrists for an object of awful power, an Auruch. Or would he do the better thing by completing the Lector's last endeavor?

There were no assurances. Only perils.

He looked across the darkening landscape before him, an empty place of rocks and dust and stunted trees. He lowered his head. He was about to set foot in the land of Rune's enemy, and was so very far from home.

"Let's hurry," said Lorra. "There's a stream bed between those hills there. That'd be a good place to camp for the night."

He followed along, finding the warm ground treacherous in the dimming light. He nearly tripped over something—a boot. He paused, and as he scanned the low hills about him he spied countless bones and burned-out husks encased in blackened armor. In horror he realized these were the soldiers of Rune who'd been the first to confront the invading army of Arranan. He watched as a hot wind whipped about and caused the skull of a nearby corpse to crumble into a whiff of dust.

Is this what remains of heroes?

He shuddered and hurried to catch Lorra. They hastily made camp in the lengthening shadows, the words between them few.

Soon the sun sank beneath the far horizon, and all was cast in darkness.

Prefect Gamghast shifted about on the bench, his body complaining with every move and posture. There came a sharp pain down his leg and he groaned. The sound echoed loudly through the quiet space of the Abbey's dining hall, empty at this late hour save for the three prefects.

"Are you well?" asked Prefect Borel, eyes glossed with tears.

Gamghast rubbed at his aching back with an aching wrist. He'd used the Sanctum's most potent ministrations but was still reminded at every moment of his wounds. He nodded and sighed. "My pain is a trivial thing when weighed against our real concerns. The highlander uttered words to me, words that could only have been Castor's confession. They were words in the elder tongue, words he could not have possibly known otherwise. He said—"

"The confession!" Prefect Kreer croaked. "The highlander recited what might have been Castor's last confession and you decided to withhold this from us? From the Dictorian? What right have you, Gamghast?"

"What matter is it?" Gamghast growled. "What matter that I kept it to myself? The Dictorian was bound to drag Castor's spirit from the highlander. Knowing that the man heard the confession would only have fueled his lust for power."

"And just what did he say?" Kreer said. "What were the words?"

Gamghast massaged his wrist and grimaced. "He spoke of our old enemy. He said the Necrists are trying to summon Yrghul's power back to this world, and have found a potent ally. He said the Sentinels needed to be summoned."

"The Necrists?" Borel whimpered.

Kreer raised his chin and peered down the length of his long nose. "How dare you, Gamghast. Perhaps if you'd remained truly faithful the Dictorian's efforts would have succeeded."

"On this we agree, Kreer. Perhaps if the Dictorian knew of the confession's utterance he'd have been more ruthless in trying to thwart Castor's plan. Perhaps he would have

456

simply beheaded the highlander before trying to pry the spirit from him."

Kreer leveled a bony finger at Gamghast. "And perhaps thereby he would have saved the Sanctum by transferring the spirit to one deserving of it. Perhaps a more appropriate vessel could have wielded the spirit to defeat our enemy. You have doomed us."

Gamghast pressed against the table, ignoring the painful twinge in his back. "You witnessed the same events as I. Castor would not be displaced. Remember one of our most basic tenets: Castor chooses his vessel. I cannot fathom his motives, but there was a reason for the choice. Theal should have known that. Never confuse faith in the divine with the arrogance of men."

Kreer sniffed smugly. "It is you who is the arrogant one, Gamghast. It was you alone who dared question what both Merek and Dictorian Theal knew to be true. It was you alone who doubted the righteousness of their task."

Gamghast slapped his good hand against the table. "And it is I alone who was right!" He had no patience for this talk. Not anymore. He scowled at Kreer. "And now it is you who stands in their stead, you who knows the will of the gods? You're a fool!"

"Gentlemen!" urged Borel, his voice screeching. "We must stand together through these troubles. Argument serves only to divide us."

Kreer glared at the man. "If calling this something other than argument comforts you, then call this an inquisition. I say if there is a doubter among us, he only weakens our ability to counter the enemies warned of in the confession!"

"And," said Gamghast, feeling his blood rush to his

cheeks, "if there is one so blinded by misguided faith, then we are consigned to repeat the Dictorian's mistakes and end up piled in the crypt beside him."

Kreer's purple lips twisted to a sneer. "You do remember the Dictorian's last act before he died, don't you? He stripped you of the title of prefect. I for one think we should abide Theal's wishes."

"Gentlemen!" screeched Borel again.

Gamghast laughed humorlessly. "Those words were born of madness. Dead gods, the entire endeavor was madness!"

Kreer rose to stand. "I will not have you question the Dictorian's righteousness, not in the mere days following his death. Nor will I simply allow us to abandon his efforts. I intend to carry on his task, and retrieve Castor's spirit. Certainly there are those among the Variden who remain committed to this, as well. I will call upon their assistance, and set aright the placement of Castor's spirit."

"You truly intend to continue Theal's march toward certain doom? You will mindlessly seek to possess Castor's spirit for yourself, rather than deal with the forces marshaling against us?" Gamghast grabbed the staff leaning against the table beside him and pulled his creaking body upward to stand. "If this is your course, Kreer, then I would gladly relinquish my post in order to disassociate myself from you!"

Kreer glowered at Gamghast. Moments passed. Kreer's face tremored with anger but he said nothing. Then, without warning, he stormed from the table.

Gamghast watched Kreer trudge toward the double door that led from the chamber, and noticed Wit standing timidly beside it. Kreer moved brusquely past the lanky simpleton and slammed the door shut behind him.

"P-Prefect Gamghast?" called Wit, approaching.

"What is it?" he said, his voice still stained with anger. He breathed deeply and smoothed the wisps of his white beard. "I'm sorry, Wit. What is it you require?"

Wit chewed at the nail of his thumb for a moment before speaking, nerves creasing his brow. "You have a v-visitor."

"It's past ten o'clock," said Gamghast. "Who is it?"

"At least a f-few people. I think one might be that nice smelling lady who came here a while ago. I think."

The queen? Gamghast pressed away from the table and walked as quickly as his painful ankle would allow. "Lead on, Wit."

"Gamghast?" called Borel after him. "You're just going to let Kreer leave? You're going to let him pursue the highlander without us?"

Gamghast huffed. "I'm through standing between that man and what he thinks his prayers tell him. Castor's spirit is the highlander's to wield, and it's not for me to question why. If Kreer wants to die because he insists otherwise, then so be it."

Gamghast spied the Abbey's vestibule ahead and counted no fewer than six cloaked figures, their faces hidden within the shadows of their hoods. He slowed, concerned at the sight of so many strangers at so late an hour. There was a time when the Abbey had opened its doors to all, gladly accepting the sick and the troubled. But such could no longer be the case. He leaned against his staff and sighed.

It seems from now on our doors will ever be guarded by fear and suspicion.

"That's her," mumbled Wit, gesturing ahead. "In the middle. There's a few other nice smelling ladies with her and two rough looking men."

Gamghast squinted, trying to discern details in the flickering light of the corridor. Indeed, one of the figures had a swell in the midsection, a fullness of pregnancy. By Gamghast's count Queen Reyis was nearly six months pregnant, and complications at such a stage were not uncommon. "Get a room ready, Wit. One with a comfortable bed. Then I'll need you to run to the apothecary. Get nightclover, hagsweed, and powdered tinder root. Be quick about it."

Wit nodded and headed back down the hall. Gamghast paused and then continued his limping march forward.

The figure in the center of the vestibule pressed thin hands against its hood, revealing a face of elegant features framed by a cascade of flaxen hair. *Queen Reyis.*

"My queen!" Gamghast called. He rushed into the vestibule and braced his hands against his staff, sinking as close to a kneel as his injured body would allow. "The Sanctum is honored by your presence." He struggled upright and studied the woman, noticing her eyes were red and surrounded by dark rings. Her hands trembled. A tall figure moved close to her.

"Prefect Gamghast," she said, her chin raised but her voice quavering. "You once offered me shelter. Does your offer stand?"

Gamghast shook his head, confused. "Of course, my queen. The Sanctum is ready to assist you by any means available to us." He patted at the mad wisps of his beard. "Something has happened?"

Queen Reyis drew a deep breath and seemed about to speak when she choked back a sob. She waved a hand as though asking for a moment.

The cloaked figures about her moved hurriedly to her sides, whispering comforting words and placing hands upon her. "I-I cannot…" she breathed. She stumbled forward but was caught by her companions.

The tall figure near the queen threw back its hood. It was Tannin, the castle guardsman who'd allowed Gamghast passage through the castle sewers during his last visit to the Bastion. There was a bloody mess where his left eye should have been and his bent nose was caked with dried blood. He came near Gamghast and placed a firm hand upon his shoulder. "Prefect," he said stoically, "the High King is dead. We need your help."

The High King of Rune? Dead and without an heir? Gamghast inhaled sharply and swooned, squeezing his hands against his staff. It was too much, though, and his hands were too old and wrenched by age. He fell, smacking his head upon the floor.

Tannin grabbed him and slapped him and Gamghast's eyes fluttered open to see the thick-necked guardsman's one remaining eye peering at him intensely from a face nearly ruined.

"Get up, old man," Tannin said firmly. "Death is the only rest we can count upon in days such as these."

29

CHANCE

"**T**HESE ARE DEEP wounds," Paddyn said, a tremble in his voice. The rough lad moved his hands hesitantly above Karnag's unconscious form, seemingly unsure what to do. "He's bled like this for days. How is it he still draws breath?"

Fencress Fallcrow said nothing, for she had no decent answers to offer. Karnag lay unresponsive upon the bed before them, as he had for days now. Blood wept from many vicious rents, and shimmered crimson in the frail candlelight. They'd tried everything they could, all to no avail.

"He needs a healer," said Drenj tiredly as he stared out the room's paned window. "It is late in the evening and I can do no more. I fear he'll die before morning if he doesn't have the help of a skilled healer."

Fencress laughed ruefully. "The best healers in Ironmoor are the members of the Sanctum. I don't reckon they'll be keen on doing us a favor after the bloody mess we made of their Abbey."

"What, then?" said Paddyn. "He's sure to bleed out soon. We just stand here and watch him die?"

Fencress shook her head and sighed. She couldn't say 'nothing,' because that sounded like surrender and she couldn't bear the thought of giving in. Karnag meant too much to her and she refused to relinquish her hope he'd survive, her hope he'd become his old self again.

"And where could we go to fetch help?" Paddyn said. "The city guard won't forget what we did. We're trapped in this city, and certain to be found if we stay."

"He's right," said Drenj. "There's no help for Karnag here. We should leave him here and sneak out. The three of us could manage it, Fencress."

"I'll not leave without him," said Fencress firmly.

"So that's it?" Drenj said. "We stay, your friend dies, and the three of us rot in chains or worse."

Fencress held her head high. She needed to make a show of things, lest the boys think she'd gotten soft. *There is always a chance. There has to be.*

"Well?" said Drenj, his voice cracking.

She turned away from Karnag and paced about the spacious room they'd rented at the inn. "Boys, I'm a damned good killer, a light-handed thief, and a performer of some renown. But in my heart I am first among all things a gambler. Chance is by definition a fickle thing, yet it's been my experience that a string of bad dice is inevitably followed by a fortunate roll. It's a strange notion, but you learn to *trust* chance. You trust that somehow, someway, the dice will turn in your favor."

Drenj looked to her with eyes wide. "What?" he spat.

"Faith, you mean," said Paddyn.

Fencress stopped and fingered the small wooden sun she kept strung about her neck. She needed to believe this, these words of hers. "No, I mean chance. We've tried everything we know, done all we can to hedge our bet, so to speak. Now we let the dice roll and hope for a good turn. There is something inside our friend Karnag that we don't understand, and I reckon the odds he'll make it through this aren't so long as we think."

Drenj snorted. "So we *are* going to just stand here and watch him die. Then wait to be captured ourselves."

Fencress paused. She couldn't bear watching Karnag like this, all weak and wheezing and bloody. Nothing would change his condition so long as they idled about this room, and they were risking capture just as the boys had said. They needed a way to escape the city and save her friend.

"We don't just stay here, do we?" said Paddyn, his eyes pleading.

"By no means," Fencress said. "I am not going to just stay here. I am going to venture downstairs to the bar and enjoy a libation or two, and wait for whatever chance has in store."

"Have you gone completely mad?" said Drenj, waving his arms. "It's the busiest time of evening! Don't you think it's a poor idea to lounge idly about the inn's common room when it's certain to be crowded with patrons? We need to keep out of sight! We're wanted criminals, Fencress!"

Fencress glared at him. "We're killers for hire! Of course we're wanted! What is it about that notion that suddenly seems novel to you?" She snatched her black gloves from a table and tugged them on. "I'll be downstairs."

Drenj rushed to grab the door just as Fencress moved through it. "Madness," the Khaldisian muttered, just before slamming it shut.

The common room of *The Wolf at the Window* wasn't crowded, and no eyes lingered on Fencress overlong as she descended the staircase to its center. The innkeeper, a stout fellow with a neatly-trimmed red beard and an easy grin, manned the bar now, and gave Fencress a knowing wink as he pulled a draught of ale from a cask. Fencress nodded in reply, and found an unoccupied table near the rectangular room's crackling hearth.

The inn was certainly comfortable enough, near Ironmoor's elegant merchant district. The chairs were padded, the candlesticks brass rather than iron, and the tapestry decorating the long wall was likely worth more than the going rate for assassinating a minor royal official. A serving girl with a full set of white teeth wandered among oak tables carrying trays of lamb and pheasant to the bejeweled patrons laughing over glasses—*real glasses!*—of red Khaldisian wine.

It was not at all the sort of place Fencress and her companions had grown accustomed to, but they'd been desperate when they'd stumbled upon its door. Karnag had collapsed soon after they'd stormed their way out of the Sanctum's Abbey, and this had been very first inn they could find. Chance had fallen in their favor, though, as the innkeeper had seemed trustworthy enough. When they'd slipped a gold ingot into his hand in exchange for discretion, Fencress felt confident of the deal.

The man approached Fencress now, hoisting a ceramic mug crowned with golden foam. "Good evening, my lady," he said, setting the mug before Fencress and taking a seat across from her. "What a rare pleasure to see you during the evening. May I sit for a moment?"

"Most certainly," answered Fencress. She'd never given the fellow her name, nor would she. "Any man I trust is welcome in my company." She swept the mug from the table and took a long drink, enjoying the crisp, fruity flavor of the ale. She licked the foam from her lips and smiled. "So, friend, have there been any inquiries concerning our stay at your inn?"

The innkeeper picked at an unseen tangle in his short beard and then leaned close. "Hard to say. That is, there's all kind of talk of strange and terrible things afoot in Ironmoor, but for me to say whether any of it concerns you would require me to know the nature of your business here."

Fencress took another draw of ale and studied the fellow's green eyes. She'd learned a great deal from her many games of deadman's dice, and found those skills as life-saving as any swordplay or footwork she'd acquired. There was always the chance of misjudging or getting a bad turn of the dice, of course, but at least she could get a decent read of the odds. This man's eyes were calm and sincere—his help had been purchased with that gold ingot. "The Sanctum," Fencress whispered. "Any word of the Sanctum?"

The innkeeper sank back in his chair. His red brow

arched and his pink cheeks puffed and he exhaled slowly. "You *were* the ones!"

Fencress matched the man's gaze but said nothing for a long moment. She thought of drawing one of her twin blades for emphasis, but figured she'd leave them sheathed since this seemed a respectable inn. "Let's just say I'm the curious sort, friend."

"Well, if you're asking about the trouble there a week back, then yes, there's been talk."

She eased forward and encircled her gloved hands about the tall mug, just as she would a throat. "Continue."

The innkeeper looked to his side and, after seeming to satisfy himself that there were no eavesdroppers among the sparse crowd of merchants, he pulled closer. "These days the Sanctum doesn't hold much sway with the Crown. That said, murder so close to the Bastion is a serious thing, and there've been guardsmen making the rounds, questioning the proprietors of the local inns and taverns. They're offering a reward," he smiled timidly, "but nothing near an entire gold ingot."

Fencress couldn't help but smirk. *No matter what king men kneel before, money is ever their master.* "And what of the gates? Are the guards as discerning about what—or who—goes out, as they are who and what comes in?"

"From what I hear from the traders who come here, the war with Arranan isn't going any better. With news like that folk have been trying to flee the city for days to head north or west. Problem is, the guards have been detaining people, mainly those stout enough to bear arms. The Crown says it would never have any part in conscription, and claims these restrictions on travel merely ensure Ironmoor's citizens remain secure in the event the Arranese advance this far north. But, just as it's always been, our rulers have a knack for telling us the knife at our back is just a gentle guiding hand."

Fencress tugged at her gloves. "And those who don't look like fighters? They're allowed through?"

The innkeeper shrugged. "Why would the Crown want them? Just more folk to feed, and that means something if the Arranese arrive at our gates and provisions become scarce."

Fencress pondered this, thinking over the odds. Karnag looked awful, and she reckoned she and the young lads could make a good show of illness. "Do you have a wagon you could spare? Perhaps blankets?"

"I do," he said slowly. "But such things are worth coin…"

She thought again of drawing her blades. They'd given the man an entire gold ingot, and had parted with another in order to gain entrance to Ironmoor just a week before that. She didn't feel comfortable parting with any more of their fortune.

Just as she was about to offer the innkeeper a subtle threat, she heard it: that old, familiar sound of dice rattling across a table. She turned and spied two fat, silk-clad merchants huddled over a table on the room's opposite side.

She turned back to the innkeep. "Get that wagon and an armful of blankets ready. I'll have the coin for you shortly, friend."

Chance is a thing to be trusted, after all.

Fencress studied the fatter merchant's eyes, dark and heavy

from much Khaldisian wine. Any skilled player knew it was not in the dice but rather the eyes where the game was truly played. This fellow's eyes shifted nervously as Fencress stared.

He's lying.

She tilted her overturned cup a bit, just so she alone could see the dice she'd rolled. Three cubes, streaked and stained like bad teeth, showed two ones and a four on their upward faces. It was an outstanding roll-in-the-hole, with one pip being the best face a die could show. In the center of the table was a single die, a community die that counted toward both players' cups. It, too, was a one, giving Fencress a total of three of them, or "the stocks" as it was known by experienced players of the game.

The merchant had just laid down a wager even fatter than he was, twenty silver crowns sloppily piled just next to his cup. It was a wager that, considering the stakes, spoke of an excellent cup. He was posturing as though he held the stocks or even more: the four ones that comprised "the racks." The last community die had yet to be rolled, and five ones would make "the gallows."

The slightly-less-portly merchant to the fatter man's side had turned his cup upward immediately upon hearing the bet, signaling surrender. His three dice showed nothing of importance: a three, a five and a six—not a single pair and no ones. A matched pair would equal a one, and the lowest pair would win if no player's cup held a one. This fellow didn't have anything but the community die, and hadn't had the nerve to bluff.

Fencress looked again to the fatter merchant, his round head crowned by a stupid, floppy hat complete with a peacock's feather. His jowly face was splotchy and ugly. And the man's thick, wet lips twisted about like two slugs coupling.

"The wager is yours, little girl," the man said, his tongue thick in his mouth. "You going to match, or give up the ghost?"

"Giving up the ghost" meant surrendering what coin Fencress already had on the table, and it too was a term parleyed about by regular players. Such talk suggested this man knew the game, yet this bold a bluff was uncommon among seasoned participants.

Again, Fencress looked to the eyes. Beady, shifty and wine-sodden. Just above them, on the man's tanned brow, sweat was beginning to form. They were liar's eyes. The merchant was lying, and of that she was dead certain.

Chance has to turn in our favor, considering what we've endured. She drew open her purse, counted out thirty silver crowns, and slammed the fistful on the table. "I'm raising you ten silver crowns, fat man."

"Ha!" the merchant said, clumsily counting out ten more crowns from his silk purse. "Then the final roll is to you."

Fencress took the second and final community die from the table's edge, warmed it in her gloved hands, then tossed it across the table with a practiced flick of his wrist. The die bounced off the merchant's pile of coins, spun about, and settled with a three facing upward. A four would have helped her, giving her enough to match the racks, but this was a meaningless toss.

The merchant looked to her and then spilled another

ten crowns into his pile. "A pity. I was hoping to make the gallows. I guess I'll have to settle for the racks."

There came a sound from outside the tavern, a clanging of bells and shouting. The merchant looked to the window briefly, but soon stared smugly at Fencress once more.

"Three pips under that cup, eh?" Fencress said. She snatched another ten silver crowns from her purse and placed them on the table to match the bet. "Fat man, you strike me as a swindler, haggler, and keen-eyed appraiser of goods and quite possibly young boys. But a gambler you are not. You have too many tics, too much bluster, and far too little patience. The silver is mine." She lifted her cup with a dramatic flourish, revealing her roll-in-the-hole of two ones and a four.

The merchant sat quietly for a moment, rubbing bloodshot eyes with thick hands crowded with gold rings. He then peeked under his cup and began to chuckle. He took a deep draw of his wine and his chuckle turned into a belly-shaking laugh. He slapped the table. "The stocks don't best the racks, little girl!" he boasted, and yanked his cup upward. Sure enough, under it were three dice, each showing a single pip on the face.

Liar! Fencress sat slack-jawed. She could always spot a bluff, always sniff out a lie. She looked hard at the man's dice. Were they a touch cleaner, a bit less pocked and stained? *Have I been cheated?*

The merchant threw out his arms and began drawing all the coins toward his side of the table, laughing as he did. "Little girls should know better than to play a man's game."

I've been robbed. Fencress stood from the table and her hands found the hilts of her blades.

Just then the tavern's door was thrown open, smacking against the wall and bringing with it a rush of warm air that threatened the candles' flames. A guardsman staggered through, clad in a chainmail tunic and a red coat bearing Rune's golden dragon.

Fencress looked desperately to the innkeeper at the room's opposite end and froze. *Have we been betrayed? Has the innkeeper turned us in to the Crown?*

The guard looked not to Fencress or the innkeeper. Instead, he lurched to the common room's center and braced himself against a table. His breathing was labored. After a moment, he straightened and prepared to address the room.

Fencress looked about, searching for a place she could hide or escape from the inn. *Betrayed! Chance can't be so poor for so long!*

Then the guard spoke. "Citizens of Rune," he began dramatically, "our High King, the great High King Deragol, who reigned over a land largely at peace for many decades, has passed."

The merchants leaped from the table, their backs to Fencress.

"What!" the fatter one said. "Our contract!" he exclaimed. "It was with the Crown! Does this mean it's no good?"

The other folk in the room displayed similar emotion, though most over the High King's failure to produce an heir. "What will become of us?" one older man kept repeating.

Fencress grinned and eased toward the table. She sank low and pulled as many silver crowns as she could, filling her purse to the point of bursting. She also eyed the merchant's dice, noticing again their paler hue. She snatched them in her palm, and felt they had an odd heft to them. Then she tossed them on the table. All ones, all with the awkward tumble of loaded dice.

If she weren't in such a rush, Fencress reckoned she'd kill the man. She looked to the fat merchant again, studying his face and committing it to memory. *Just in case we ever cross paths again, friend.*

The patrons were crowding about the guardsman, shouting questions and gesturing wildly. Fencress slipped away, sneaking among the room's shadows and staying low. She neared the innkeeper and shoved a handful of silver crowns in his hands. "That wagon best be ready, friend."

"It is," the innkeeper said breathlessly, eyes wide as he looked upon the silver crowns. "Out back. Try the North Gate—it's always the least watched."

Fencress nodded and darted upstairs to summon her friends. She reckoned they'd be able to sneak away in the confusion so long as they didn't tarry. With any luck, there would be an uproar at the gates, and exiting the city would be an easy thing.

Chance, it seems, has finally turned in our favor.

He drifted along a dreamlike horizon, floating upon a division between light and dark. Beneath him was a breathtaking expanse, a great topography stretching to the limits of his comprehension. This was not a physical landscape, though, but one of future events. It was a vast atlas of fate, a foretelling of the destinies of all things.

Karnag beheld this. His thoughts followed the fates of men and women, watching as cruel events took them from prosperity to ruin. He saw women exult in the promise of pregnancy and then shake with anguish as they held stillborn babes. He saw families feud over scraps of food as their harvests withered. He saw proud heroes rise and then be brought to their knees by calamity, and observed great kings shiver and die alone.

He calmed himself and focused upon these many varied endings. People clawing at their skin while withering from plague. Weeping as their entrails bled from dysentery. Fumbling with gnarled hands over skin knotted with lesions, decaying like lepers.

And he saw, too, men perish at the hands of others. He saw generals plot and scheme, planning deception and disarray. He saw vast armies charging across fields wet with blood. He saw blades clash and shields shatter, and saw warriors gnash their teeth as their flesh was ripped asunder. He heard howling cries of victory and the lamentations of defeat, and watched as a once-great kingdom crumbled.

And upon all these events was cast a shadow. The shadow of a great blade, a blade before which men fell like wheat before the scythe.

Karnag knew this blade, for it had a name.

Ealyr Rigellus. Heaven's Reaper.

And Karnag knew, too, its wielder, for it was his kinsman.

It was Thaydorne. Thaydorne the Sentinel, said to bear Illienne's strength.

Brother.

Karnag beheld this god-among-men. Watched as he wreaked tragedy upon Rune and its children. Watched as Thaydorne slaughtered the very people he was oath-bound to protect. Watched as he took vengeance for a millennium-long exile and worked to pry the power of the Lord of Nightmares from oblivion. Watched as a world cowered before horrors unimaginable.

There was no such thing as chance, only a grim march toward an inevitable ending.

This is the fate of all things.

Then Karnag withdrew, and searched for his own place amidst this destiny.

He saw his hands slicked with blood, grasping a sword humming from bones it had broken. He beheld corpses piled before him, soldiers and beasts alike heaped like precious riches before a king. He beheld hundreds of men die at his feet, and others flee his countenance in terror.

He watched as his rage shook this landscape of fate, and changed events already foretold. Those who were dead arose, and those who were living fell to their graves. He watched as he reshaped destiny, and became the slayer men most feared. Watched as he became the storm of destruction that would change the world.

No. The glory of death would not be Thaydorne's to possess.

This fate is mine alone to make.

He withdrew again, this time into his physical body. It had healed now, nearly enough to fulfill his purpose. He opened his mouth and sucked in a warm, salty air. It filled his lungs and fed his limbs. His fingers twitched, seeking weapons.

His eyes snapped open.

I come for you, my brother.

If you enjoyed this book, please consider taking a brief moment to review it on Amazon or Goodreads. Such feedback is invaluable to an author, and is greatly appreciated.

Next in the Sequence:

THE WRATH OF HEROES

A REQUIEM FOR HEROES, BOOK TWO

COMING SOON.